DATE DUE

THOSE THE SUN HAS LOVED

THOSE
THE SUN
HAS LOVED

Rose Jourdain

DOUBLEDAY & COMPANY, INC.
Garden City, New York
1978

ACKNOWLEDGMENTS

There are many persons to whom I owe a debt of gratitude for assistance generously given in the preparation of this book. To some my debt is enormous:

Jeffrey Nunes, for his imaginative, thorough, and dedicated research; Elaine Markson, my agent and my friend; Larry Jordan, Jill Hausrath, and Cynthia van Hazinga, my editors; Frances Beidler, for many things. Mary Daskais, who much more than typed the manuscript. Also, Virginia Munzer and Sallie Wagner, who typed the first draft. Dr. Elliott T. Skinner of Columbia University; Dr. Joseph Harris of Howard University; Dr. Robert Cummings of the University of Miami; Dr. Christopher C. Mojekwal of Lake Forest College; Professors Dennis Brutus and Jan Carew of Northwestern University; Marian Turner and the staff of the Evanston Public Library; Sylvia Lyons Render of the Library of Congress; Cyrill Jenious and Genie Ermoyan of United States Congressional staffs; Von Gordon, Mary Lou Campbell, Joyce Fischer, Robin and John Tucker, Valjeanne Jones, Lorraine Bryant, and Jerry and Hester Mundis for their key contributions. Dr. Sherman Beverly, Isabel Grossner, Jackie Casselberry, Marc Crawford, Carlis Sutton, Karen MacLeod, Dean Perrin, Pat Patterson, and Dick Meyers for their invaluable help; Elizabeth Reed and Randall Pollard, for much about New Bedford; my mother, Emmaline, for all the things that mothers do; my father, Edwin B. Jourdain, Jr., who provided the inspiration; my brother Edwin B. Jourdain III, who provided both the care and the cash; and my brother Spencer C. D. Jourdain, whose criticisms, guidance, enthusiasm, and encouragement were indispensable to this project.

And last, but not least, to all of my friends who believed and to my grandmother's prayers.

Rose L. Jourdain
Evanston, Illinois
January 31, 1978

ISBN: 0-385-13028-7
Library of Congress Catalog Card Number 77–82952
Copyright © 1978 by Rose Jourdain

For my Father and my Mother
For Bud, Spence, and Honey
and especially for Wifit

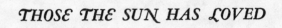

THOSE THE SUN HAS LOVED

Book One

JACQUES

They that go down to the sea in ships, that do business in great waters, These see the works of the Lord. . . . they cry out to the Lord in their trouble . . . He maketh the storm a calm.

PSALMS 107:23–29

CHAPTER ONE

1772

Now he could see the gulls, still specks on the dawn sky, swooping, diving, a welcoming committee from land. The wind had dropped during the night, but now as the sea gave birth to the sun, its warmth was strengthening the wind. The whale ship's sails were full.

Jacques Clavier stood alone on the foredeck, his dark eyes squinting through the shrouds at the sea. What had appeared as a low cloud to the starboard was taking form: great multicolored bluffs rising majestically from the green sea. A quick half smile crossed Jacques's tawny face as he stared at the clay cliffs which he knew from the whalemen's stories must be Gay Head. "Yemangi," he whispered, "goddess of the waterways, accept my thanks."

"Quite a sight, eh, Mr. Clavier?"

Turning, Jacques saw the first mate, Nils Kuykendal, coming up behind him, his pipe, as always, poking from the middle of his blond-whiskered face. His blue watch coat strained to contain his chest which seemed as huge as an iron try-pot and his arms which seemed thick and strong as the oak from which the ship was crafted.

Jacques's eyes followed the first mate's gaze toward the cliffs. "That it is, sir."

Kuykendal's outsized head bobbed vigorously. "Gay Head, they call it. There's the Elizabeth Islands dead ahead. We'll pass through Quick's Hole into Buzzards Bay and on up the Acushnet River to be home 'fore nightfall."

The first mate's voice was unemotional as always, but Jacques sensed excitement matching his own. The *Valiant* had been at sea nearly fourteen months. He himself had been aboard almost a year. It had been what whalemen called a greasy voyage; every stave fitted into a barrel and every cask now full. Fifteen hundred barrels, more than forty-four thousand gallons of whale oil, and most of it sperm.

The rising barometer of Jacques's enthusiasm plunged suddenly. Home. No, he thought, he'd not be home. There was no place to call home now. But his mission here was urgent. And this voyage profitable. The money from even the smallest lay could help set a careful man on his way.

Slowly, almost imperceptibly, Jacques's eyes narrowed and his youthful face was void of all emotion. But, he thought, he must take care. Again he was a stranger in an unknown place. And again alone. He must practice caution, for so much was at stake. Difficult with such need for haste. Suppose it was already too late. Suppose . . . Jacques's full lips tightened. No, he could not afford such thoughts. Not now. Not now. Now he must remember Nsai's words: "Each end is the result of its beginning."

Kuykendal watched the deepening fathoms in Jacques's eyes, saw their quick, fierce undertow and then impenetrable blackness. Resting his pipe on the windlass, Kuykendal searched his pocket and excavated a jackknife and a whale tooth covered with intricate carvings. Stroking his lower lip with the thumb of the hand that held the jackknife, Nils turned the whale tooth slowly in the other.

Jacques followed the first mate's critical analysis of his work. Scrimshawing was a favorite pastime of the crew, but Kuykendal's exquisite engravings of whales, whaleboats, and whalers were by far the best produced aboard the *Valiant*.

Scrimshaw, however, was not the first mate's real interest at the moment. His callused hands were busy from habit, but the tall, fine-looking young man before him occupied Nils Kuykendal's mind.

They had signed on Jacques Clavier in Surinam—that lush, fearsome South American colony which, in 1667, the English had traded to the Dutch for New York. Clavier had declared himself, in the ship's articles, to be twenty years of age and had an ease and self-assurance of men much older, but Kuykendal doubted the lad was yet eighteen. His smooth brown skin did not yet know the razor, and despite his harpoon-quick strength, his control of rope-taut intensity, Kuykendal sensed the boy-soul buried deep by some necessity.

Clavier belonged to that amazing range of colors and types known as the Negro race. Nils had sailed with colored men before—black men, brown men, red men—on the ships that had been his home for most of his thirty-eight years. The sea counted no difference.

However, this Jacques Clavier, who listened intently but said little, whose English, though halting, was proper, who was aloof but not vain, remained a mystery to Nils.

4

The blue eyes in his sun-bronzed face squinted as Nils studied the younger man. Yes, Nils thought, the lad had done well with the whales. An inaudible sigh escaped Nils's lips. In his own grandfather's time, the Wampanoag Indians had hunted the leviathan in small canoes with bows and arrows. Even in his father's time the whales swam nearly to Nantucket's shore. But now the behemoth moved farther, luring its pursuers into the dangers of the deep, into the realms of new gods and those whom they had blessed.

Yes, Nils thought, for certain this Jacques Clavier had the mark; he had been a godsend on this voyage. Now, somehow, he must convince Clavier to sail with him on the next.

"You have been to sea—before this voyage?" Kuykendal felt ill at ease. He was not used to making conversation with the crew. But his need now was crucial.

Clavier's steady eyes met his. "Yes, sir."

"On a whaling vessel?"

"No, sir. Not on a whale ship." Jacques saw question in the first mate's eyes and looked away. He had no time for others' queries. His own business was enough.

But even as Kuykendal puzzled this evasion and sought to reframe his query, eight bells sounded. The new watch came top side banging the mops and pails with which they would begin the inevitable scrubbing of the decks. "By your leave, sir," Jacques said quietly. "I will go to breakfast."

Kuykendal rubbed the whalebone in his hand. Decisions cast in an empty stomach were oft squeezed out with the belly full. "Of course," was Nils's reluctant reply.

A frown twitched on the first mate's weather-furrowed face as he walked toward the companionway, waiting with ill-checked impatience as the seamen ahead dropped their caps on deck to indicate they were below. Damnation. He must talk to Clavier today.

Jacques watched as the first mate disappeared down the hatchway, then, passing the blacksmith and the ship's carpenter already plying their trades, he made his way aft, along the *Valiant*'s lee side, as custom required. Not that he had business in the stern. Men assigned the larboard watch had the forward duty; men on the starboard watch the duty aft. But he knew the areas below deck and the foredeck were now swarming with men, and he sought solitude. After a "good morning" to the helmsman, he found himself alone.

Propping his arms along the rail, Jacques followed the wake of the ship, extending it in his mind across the thousands of miles he had come. On the far horizon of memory, undulating in the vaporous rays of time between reality and illusion, was that place he had once called home . . . the Clavier plantation, already in decay by the time of his birth. All around it lay the jungle, except where the Coppename River twisted its silver way toward the sea . . . the dark and mighty jungle defeating the false bravery of that white-frame, red-roofed mansion in whose lonely, lemon-scented rooms he had wandered as a child. Joy played only in his mother's smile, that quick flash of even teeth against the soft night blackness of her skin, and in her eyes, dark, obelisks filled with love. Leah. His beautiful mother.

His hand in hers, they had wandered over the vast estate after breakfast of cassava under the sun-filtering, green leafy canopy of the coffee bushes, laughing at the red howler monkeys that lived high in the trees along the forest edge of the plantation, moving carefully in the uncultivated areas to avoid anacondas or bushmasters.

Macaws, toucans, and parrots had accompanied their laughter. Orange pheasants, scarlet ibis, pink flamingos, and birds of paradise had marked their path with brilliant color until they came to the stream where the giant lilies grew.

How clear in memory's twisted path, those days. Together, they would swim to a giant lily pad and climb upon it, to enjoy the gentle undulations of the stream, to watch the giant butterflies, to listen to the sweetness of the hummingbird's songs. The air heavy with the scent of honeysuckle and yellow vanilla.

Around her slender neck his mother had worn a medallion. It was an intricately worked wooden carving: a cross inside a star, surrounded by a boat and sail. And then one day: "Tell me again, Mama," he had asked.

Leah had smiled, knowing her son knew the story as well as she. "We are Maroons. Some call us bush Negroes, but our people are D'jukas." She began softly. "We come from many tribes to form one tribe united in the blood of freedom.

"When my grandfather was brought from Africa to these shores, he escaped the white man's shackles. With six other men he leapt from their slave ship. Swimming ashore, they fled to the forests. Moving by night, hiding by day, they came to the upriver country. Many of our people did the same. Deep in the jungle they built small

6

villages. Farming and fishing they lived by the laws of their ancestors and their gods.

"They did not forget their tribesmen who could not escape. On foot, in swift canoes, they came from their jungle homes to free those in bondage, to find women for wives, to seize what they needed. Stalked, hunted, they needed weapons to maintain their freedom. Some became pirates, taking from the sea what the land refused to give. My father, Akime, was their leader. I have told you of his deeds."

The boy's eyes sparkled. "He fought always for freedom for our people," and the boy touched the exquisite workmanship around his mother's neck—"he gave you this."

"Yes, Jacques. He put it around my neck before the men of our village went to sea 'Yemangi will protect you,' he said. And she has.

"The white men used the Carib Indians to hunt our people. They found our small village while most of the men were away." Leah's dark eyes seemed to close, shadowing her thoughts. "The white men are killers; the Caribs . . . cannibals." Her voice was a grating whisper. "Old men, women, children gone. Only eight young women were saved. I was the youngest of them all."

Leah glanced at her son, saw his rapt attention. "The white men corded our hands and our ankles. By flatboat we traveled rivers and streams. Often we saw the black flag of pestilence. Maeka, my mother's sister, sickened. They left her to die.

"Many days we traveled. The whites needed food and water. When the river wound past this plantation, one of them went up to the house. The old one, Madame Clavier, came back to the wharf with him."

"Grandmama?"

"Yes, your grandmother, wearing that thick gold cross above layers of skirts, and it so hot the mosquitoes did not have strength to fly. With her stiff little march, she went to their leader. Her head came barely to his chest. 'And what is your intention with these girls?' she asked.

"Our captor showed her his tobacco-rotted teeth. 'Madame, you know as well as I the legendary curse of Paramaribo is the attraction of its masters to beauties of the darker hue.'

"Her face became the red color of her hair. 'You are vile.' Her voice flew like pebbles in his face. 'Slavery is a necessary evil, but . . .'

7

"'Madame,' he interrupted, 'I ask for food and water, not . . .'

"'That girl,' she said as she came close to me. 'She's but a child.'

"'And a beauty.'

"'No more than ten or eleven. . . . I will not hear of it.'

"He grinned again. 'Madame, you are hardly . . .'

"'I have a pair of gold candlesticks. The only thing of worth I do have left.'

"His eyes slid like a serpent to her hand. 'And that ring on your finger. I'd say it would make a fair price.'

"'Oh,' she gasped, turning pale. 'It is the token of my engagement.'

"The man laughed. 'And are you still engaged? Or is memory worth more than sin?'

"Her lips disappeared. You know how they do. 'It is yours. And food and water. And I will take the girl.'"

"And so you came to live here, Mama?" Jacques had asked softly, not wanting to interrupt her mood.

"Yes. The tall one, your papa, Philippe . . . he was not here then. The Maroons had liberated most of the slaves and there were but six of us—the cook, the housekeeper, and the three men for the fields." Leah leaned back, dangling a slender leg into the stream. "How it rained that summer! The coffee beans rotted in the ground. So hot even the old one wore just one skirt. We sat in her room beneath the statue of her dying Lord, and she taught me the books in French and English, as she now teaches you. It is her delight."

A hummingbird passed above them, then alighted, their neighbor on a nearby lilypad, filling the air with his song. Leah's eyes closed in appreciation of its sweetness as she trailed one hand in the water. "Poor Madame," she began again softly. "How long she has lived to hate this place, to miss the life she loved so as a girl in Paris, before she married Henri Clavier."

She turned to Jacques again with a laugh as soft as the gurgles of the water at the shore. "Can you imagine her arriving here, in the jungle, with her trunks of underskirts and that piano? That great four-sided piano that sits in the drawing room?"

Then Leah's face grew grave again. "The tall one, her son, Philippe, was nine when her husband died. France was once again at war, and no word for her return came from her family. She stayed on the plantation, teaching her son to read French and English, to play the piano, teaching him to hate this life. When he was eighteen, she sent him to Paris. He was to become a great musician, a great composer, to live, she said she told him, 'according to his birth.' "

For a long moment Leah was silent, the only sounds the soft rippling of the stream. When she spoke again her voice had no emotion. "He married and had a child in Paris. Madame has programs of his concerts there. Then came the time she could no longer afford the life he lived . . ."

"And when did he come, Mama? The tall one."

"Your papa."

"I have no father."

She heard anger in his voice and touched his arm. "Oh, yes. And though you have my eyes and mouth you will be tall as he, you know. You are already taller than most your age."

"I have never seen anyone my age." The boy's tone was sullen.

Her eyes shadowed again. "I know, and it is wrong."

He saw her eyes, sensed the changing of her mood and spoke quickly to keep her to her story. "When did he come?"

"Philippe? It was the next year. Or the next. There was fever on the ship that brought him back from France. His wife and child died. He was hollow like the cane when all sweet is gone."

"And drunk."

"Yes, drunk with sorrow. For months he did not leave his room. And when he did, he stunk."

"I do not often see him now." Jacques eyes were fastened to her face.

"I know." She patted his arm absently. "And it is to the best."

"He began coming to Grandmama's room, to listen to you read?"

"Yes. And then you were born."

"Will we ever see them, Mama? Our people? The D'jukas?"

"One day, my little Jacques. When we know where they are."

Jacques remembering now another day. Time, perhaps months, had passed. Again he sat at his mother's side on the lily pad. A soft frown was on her face. "The old one speaks of sending you to Paramaribo to school."

"Is that good, Mama?"

"I think so. The tall one is jealous of my time with you, and you are too much alone. Perhaps in Paramaribo you will learn where our people are."

"And you, Mama . . . ?"

Before she could answer, they had heard a shout from the shore—from his father, Philippe, red hair amuck, frilled shirt open. "Are you here again with that little bastard?"

Pulling off his great boots, he had splashed into the water, swimming like a piranha toward them.

"Quickly, Jacques," Leah whispered, pushing her son before her into the water. Together they had gained the opposite shore before Philippe reached them. Jacques felt the searing grip, heard his father's rum-smelling curse: *Toi, espèce de petit emmerdeur . . .*"

Moving between father and son, Leah raised her lovely head. "The bastard is the father, Philippe, not the child. The child is innocent."

Philippe grinned. "So now you quote my mother to me."

"Come, Jacques," Leah said, taking her son's hand. "We go now to my people."

"Leah!" Philippe yelled. "Leah, no!" But she did not turn, and Jacques stumbled on, dripping, beside her.

In his room Leah ordered Jacques to dress and gather those possessions which he valued most. "Go tell your grandmother goodbye. She loves you and has been good to us."

Jacques had hesitated before the open door beyond which his grandmother lay in her great canopy bed amid lacy pillows. She wailed in protest when he stammered goodbye, her tears falling hot on his face as she held him to her bony bosom.

Then they had heard the horses coming at full gallop, and after a moment the bellow from below: "Leah! Leah! Answer me!"

Yvette Clavier had drawn herself up stiffly. Leaning on Leah and Jacques, she made her feeble way into the hall. Her lacy nightcap defying gravity on the side of her head, she pointed a twig-like finger down the stairs. "Philippe Clavier, you are too old to be a fool."

Philippe had answered with a sweeping bow. "I am a bastard, madame."

"That late development I cannot help."

"But I am about to rectify my wrongs, madame. I am about to end bastardy in my household." Another bow. "I have, see here, brought with me the magistrate who will join me in matrimony, holy or unholy, with Leah, daughter of a Maroon, bush Negro pirate, and legitimate our progeny, so joyously conceived, as the rightful heir to all Clavier misfortunes. I entreat you to join us on this ceremonial occasion, madame, to enter these proceedings in our family Bible, including the birth of our son, Jacques Clavier, who is now the legitimate, et cetera. Now, bride, descend, and, Magistrate . . ." Philippe turned, hiccuping, and gestured to a man waiting near the door. "Magistrate, make haste, as my beloved's people may, as they have before, wipe us out before we are done."

Leah, at the top of the stairs, threw back her head. "No! I am done with you, Philippe Clavier. Move now and let me pass."

Dumbfounded, the magistrate, in deference to the Clavier name, stood rooted to the spot as Philippe swooped Leah into his arms. "Quickly, Magistrate," Philippe commanded, holding his struggling bride, "the magic words that let us bypass hell."

In the weeks following his marriage, Philippe Clavier was obsessed with the subject of his son's education. He wanted the boy sent to Paris. "That city," he told his mother and his wife, "is now quite populated with the progeny of the pleasure of French nobility in the Indies. The daughters are usually left behind, but the sons . . . In Paris, Jacques will find those of his own kind."

Leah pleaded to keep Jacques nearer. "He will be gone for years, and in Paris he knows not a soul."

The boy listened quietly as his father spoke. "Paris is a city of great wonder. The boy will learn and see much. Notre Dame, the church of Sainte Geneviève who saved Paris from the attack of Attila the Hun, the Palace of Justice, where the Romans once stood, the Louvre Palace . . ."

Leah always interrupted this with sobbing, and Yvette Clavier, afraid that she would never see her "beau Jacques" again, added the sharpness of her tongue. Soon Philippe had tired of the problem, and Jacques was sent to Paramaribo, the seaway capital of Surinam, for his education.

At the age of nine, Jacques had been enthralled by that city of broad sandy streets, the big government buildings on the Orange-plein, and the open-air markets under shaddock and tamarind trees which sold treasures he never dreamed existed. He boarded with the Van Hovens, a Dutch shipbuilding family whom the Claviers knew, while studying at the Jesuit school.

But there was so much that was new: people from all over the world, even a troupe of traveling actors from New York, who played with paper crowns and daggers before canvas palaces and painted forests. On streets called Waterkant, Maagdenstraat, and Zwar-tenhovenbrugstraat, he had seen men and women wearing gold,

11

diamonds and silver lace who walked beneath umbrellas held by slaves. Jacques heard the chant from the Beracheve Shalom, synagogue of the Sephardic Jews, and the languages of the street: Dutch, English, French, Portuguese, Hebrew, and Spanish, as well as the indigenous tongue, taki-taki, invented by the bush Negroes.

But from the start Jacques had been most fascinated by the activity in the Van Hoven shipyard, with the barges, which often carried musicians, playing gay music as they passed on the river, and with the brigs and barques bearing flags of lands beyond the sea. After the schoolyard bell had rung to end the day, Jacques would run to the shipyard to watch, to ask questions, to help whenever allowed. Soon after his eleventh birthday, Herr Van Hoven began to pay him for his time.

Each year, Jacques had spent a month at home. But home had changed. His grandmother, haunted by senile reveries, hardly remembered him. His father, even when sober, by and large ignored him. And his mother, uneasy with his rapid growth, the deepening of his voice, and his new experiences in Paramaribo, tried anxiously to keep him close by constant questions about the D'jukas and by her stories which were reminders of their proud and certain destiny as Maroons. And though Jacques felt ashamed that he had no answers to her questions on the whereabouts of their people, his interest in them always diminished when he re-entered the Van Hoven shipyard and heard the sounds of pod auger and maul.

It was just after his thirteenth birthday when Father John, his teacher, had stopped him as he dashed from the schoolyard. "It may be that you should stay here with us awhile, Jacques Clavier," the Jesuit father said firmly. "Maroons, under two who call themselves Captains Boston and Araby, are sweeping through the countryside. Eight plantations were pillaged and burned last night. Eleven the night before." Father John's great jowls shook as he fingered the cross that glittered against the black of his cassock. "Each day they draw closer to the city. Neither the French, Dutch, nor Swiss troops have been able to subdue them. Rumors have it that their spies are everywhere. Panic is gripping the city. I fear it may spread and no Negro will be safe."

"Do you think they will conquer Paramaribo?"

Father John, mistaking Jacques's excitement for fear, touched a consoling hand to his shoulder. "I think not the capital itself. There's talk of attempting a truce, of paying the D'jukas' tribute. I don't know what Boston and Araby will demand. But"—the priest removed his hand—"let me assure you that some time with the studious would not be an adversity to your studies."

"Thank you, Father." Then to the priest's astonishment Jacques had sped from the schoolyard.

Van Hoven had refused him the loan of a boat. "By God, boy," the shipbuilder had exploded. "Don't you know we are at war? And there's fever in the river country again."

Jacques had stowed away on a coffee barge and in two days reached the red-roofed mansion on the Coppename River.

He had found his mother sewing by the oil lamp in her room. She dropped the material and stood, clasping her medallion when she saw him in the doorway. "Jacques"—for the first time he heard fear in her voice—"you should not have come."

"But, Mama," he began, uncertain why her posture forbade his close approach. "The D'jukas . . ." Quickly he recounted what he had learned.

"Then," Leah said, "you must go back to Paramaribo and wait for them."

"And you . . ."

"I cannot come. Your father burns with fever and your grandmother is dying . . ."

"Grandmama?"

Leah heard the sorrow in his voice. "Perhaps you've come in answer to her prayers. Go to her door, Jacques, but no further."

In the glow of the candles beside the crucifix on her wall, Yvette Clavier's eyes were fever bright. Her ashen face smiled wanly when she saw him. "The Lord is with me." She raised a bony hand. "Do not come close. The fever." She fingered her rosary, her mind wandering, then turned toward him again. "Jacques, I have not forgotten you. You were in my heart even when time held you from my mind."

A thin, wistful smile touched her lips. "Oh, Jacques, *mon beau noir fils,* all we have left is in a sack beneath the great tree you loved so as a boy . . ." Her eyes closed, and she seemed to sleep.

"Come, Jacques." His mother touched his shoulder. "You must go now." And in the flickering candlelight he saw the brightness also in her eyes.

"Mama, I cannot leave you!"

"By morning, there will be nothing to leave."

13

Loneliness, fear hollowed through the boy. He felt his fingers trembling, wanted so much to rush into his mother's arms. "But, the doctor . . . ?"

"He is also dead." Leah saw the longing in her son and controlled her emotions with a savage will. "You are a Maroon warrior. You must survive. Hurry back to Paramaribo. Wait there. The Maroons will come. Seek the one they call Akime, my father. Or Afu. He is of my *mbe*, my family. They will give you strength."

Leah's voice faltered. The strength to keep her son from her was fading. Quickly she turned to the basin on the table by her bed and lifted the carving from her neck. Jacques saw her tears as she plunged it into the bowl and washed it fiercely.

Then she turned to him again. Her hand brushed his tears as she slipped the medallion over his head. "Fear nothing, Jacques. Yemangi will keep you safe."

Jacques found Paramaribo in chaos when he returned. The Swiss and Dutch troops had returned to the city and a truce had been declared with the Maroons.

"Imagine," Van Hoven had groaned. "White men paying tribute to blacks."

Nearly a month then passed before Jacques saw the Maroons. Led by their granman, their impressive black bodies clad in brilliant open-sided togas, the proud D'jukas walked with silver-tipped canes toward the capitol to collect their tribute.

For three blocks, moving past abruptly abandoned open-air stalls, Jacques had followed them, then held out his hand to a tall middle-aged man, who looked down at him haughtily.

For an instant Jacques's heart clogged. He steadied his gaze. *"Pardonez moi, je m'appelle Jacques Clavier."*

The black hand swept up. *"Backra schlaff"* snapped contemptuously through the full lips. "Move and let me pass."

The man moved on, Jacques running beside him. "I seek the one they call Akime."

"Akime?" Slowly the Maroon's expression changed. He slowed his pace and looked down at the boy. "What do you know of Akime?"

"He is my mother's father. He is a pirate." Jacques's words rushed from memories of his mother's teachings as he half ran, half walked, keeping pace with the Maroon. "My mother is far from here. She is weak with fever." Tears of desperation clouded Jacques's eyes. "She told me to see Akime. She told me of his deeds."

14

The Maroon nodded, but did now slow his pace. "Of the bravest, he was the most brave."

Jacques's hand searched frantically inside his shirt, finding the medallion his mother had given him. "He gave this to her. It saved her when the others were killed."

The Maroon looked from the carving to Jacques's eager face. Yes, he thought, the eyes were the same. He took the medallion in his hand, probing with his thumb until he found the notches at the edge. Then he looked at Jacques again. "And what do you want, Akime's grandson?"

The tall D'juka listened gravely as Jacques told his story. When Jacques was done, he said, "Akime has been with his ancestors many rains."

"And Afu?"

The Maroon's eyes narrowed, then he nodded. "I will take you to Afu. He will decide if you stay."

They had traveled by canoe, paddling tirelessly through a maze of rivers, streams, and creeks bordered by impregnable jungle, moving ever farther from that which Jacques had been told was civilization.

On the third night as they sat before the fire a drum message was sent. Fani, the D'juka Jacques had first met, squatted by Jacques's side. "We are almost home," he said.

By noon the next day they had reached a village at the head of a terrifying rapids. It was no more than a clearing hacked out of the forest, a foothold for living and growing the essentials of life. Jacques saw the stocky man waiting on the shore. As Jacques climbed from the dugout he held out his hand. "Come, my grandfather's grandson. I am Afu. I will make you welcome."

Clutching his few possessions, Jacques Clavier followed his brawny uncle beneath the silk cotton trees, the home of Mother Earth, into his future.

CHAPTER TWO

"Luck. That's all it is. Just plain luck."

The sound of voices close behind forced Jacques from his reverie. Turning, he saw two of the *Valiant*'s whalemen beside the hurricane house, deep in discussion.

"Arm cut clean off like that and live . . ." The first man, Watson's voice was awed.

"Aye, and no gangrene." Talbert, the third mate's response. "And believe me, I know well the misery of captains' medical ministrations." Talbert's short laugh was harsh with scorn. "Indeed, in truth it's how I made third mate. Two years ago off Nova Scotia the third mate on my ship fell ill of fever. His symptoms matched up with the medicine marked number eleven in the captain's book. The ship had no more of eleven, so the cap'n, frantic to save the man, mixed five and six and gave 'em to the mate, who promptly died."

"Luck." Watson's head bowed slowly with the weight of his conviction. "I tell you, when we put into Paramaribo, I didn't think this ship had the chance of a minnow on a shark's tooth."

Jacques shook his head as he listened. What strange folks these New Englanders were. No child of the D'jukas would have mixed such a potion. By age ten or eleven, they all knew the simple herbs. And so much talk of luck. Man, with the intercession of his gods, made his own luck.

Jacques turned back to the rail. How many things he had learned with the Maroons. With them he had grown to manhood, in the village and traditions that were, the elders told, exact duplications of those of the Boni tribe in Africa. Under the tutelage of Afu, who had been captured twenty years before from his home outside of Akassa on the Bight of the Biafra, Jacques learned the stories by which passed the wisdom of the D'jukas: the long parables of all-wise rabbits, the overall command of loyalty to the tribe. And though Jacques sometimes doubted as the sacred drums summoned the gods —the complex rhythms of the apinti calling the ancestor spirits and the almighty sky god, Nion, while the steady beat of the agida commanded the snake spirits—he had felt the certain conviction of

16

religion as the spirits that ruled the waterways were called for permission to enter their domain. Above all, Jacques learned the awesome powers of Yemangi, goddess of the fresh waters, who loved all that was pure. Yemangi, who had traveled with her people out of Africa, across the great ocean and, on these shores, led them through the streams and rivers away from those who would make her people slave. Yemangi, who had founded their new home in this new land.

At first Jacques was considered *backra schlaff,* one of those who cohabit with whites, a servant, an outsider, and, despite the intervention of Afu, was viewed with suspicion that bordered on hostility. Alone at night he had squatted at the river's edge, following in his mind's eye its twisting trail to the home of his lonely boyhood. Was she still there, his mother? Had she survived? Would he ever see her face again?

In time Aduku, the small lithe first son of Afu's second wife, came to be Jacques's friend. And also Alanya, the daughter of the granman, whose dark skin was soft as the fibers of the silk cotton tree. Alanya was always darting here and there, a flurry of limbs, laughter, and mischievous ideas. But in her laughing eyes, her smile, Jacques found welcome—no, found acceptance, making it no matter that he was forbidden, still the secrets of the tribe.

The years had passed quickly. Jacques learned the taki-taki of the Maroons. With Aduku as his constant companion he assumed the duties of manhood and practiced the rituals of war. Alanya's flurry of movement became grace and her laughter subsided to a smile. The eyes of all the young men were upon her.

Sometimes Jacques and Alanya were alone, but Aduku always found them, seeming more and more to shatter their mood and making Alanya restless to be gone.

In his fourth year with the Maroons, when the moon was but a silver beckoning finger, Jacques had gone to Afu's thatched hut. His hands rubbed his thighs nervously as he stood in the opening waiting for Afu to invite him inside.

"Yes, my grandfather's grandson?" Afu gnawed with satisfaction on the remainders of his dinner, the village delicacy, barbecue.

"Afu." Jacques stretched himself to the fullness of his height. "I would ask you to speak to the granman for me. I would like for Alanya to be my wife."

Jacques saw resistance in his kinsman's eyes. "You have yet to prove yourself, Jacques Clavier. An ornament such as Alanya must

17

be won." Afu lifted a gourd filled with palm wine to his lips. "What have you to offer the daughter of a chief?"

Before the moon was full, Aduku had come to Jacques. "The white men break their word again. There will be war. We go to sea to take what we shall need. My father has spoken to Nsai, the war chief, and has permission for you to join in this adventure." Aduku grinned. "It is a business your grandfather knew quite well."

Alanya's eyes had grown grave when Jacques told her this news. "Oh, Jacques," she said as her slim, dark hand found his. "I will worry so for you."

Laughter had mixed with pride on his tawny face. "Waste not your worries on me, but on those my dagger finds."

"But, Jacques . . ."

His hand clutched hers. "I will prove myself, Alanya. I will show them no one is more brave. Then I will be admitted to the circle of men and you will stand beside me as my wife. And one day, my son . . ."

Laughter flew back into Alanya's eyes and her hands touched her lovely face. "The puma must find its quarry before its young can eat. Yemangi go in you, my Jacques Clavier."

The warriors had departed to the beat of the drums, paddling swift dugout canoes back the way Jacques had come, down the interconnecting rivers, rapids, streams, and creeks that led to the sea.

There, in a clearing, they had met with fourteen other men, Maroons unknown to Jacques or Aduku. Nsai, the bull-built war chief, held council with the other group. The next night they had rowed silently up the Saramacca River, investigating the ships that carelessness had placed at their disposal.

A Dutch frigate was discounted because of its bulk. So, too, a Portuguese brigantine. It was Nsai who spotted the sharp schooner, a long, narrow sloop with the schooner rig. "Probably a smuggler," the war chief had grinned. It was perfect for their purposes.

Jacques remembered how he had feared to breathe as their oars moved noiselessly, bringing their dugouts alongside the ship. Nsai had told Jacques and Aduku to wait, to flee for shore if ordered. Then Nsai's powerful black arm tossed a hooped rope that caught on the ship's davits. From other canoes other ropes went up. Within seconds, the Maroons were on the deck. For several moments all was silent. Then, in their canoe below, Jacques and Aduku heard scuffling and piercing cries.

The Maroons had rowed their bound captives back to shore and returned to what was now their ship. By dawn they were on the ocean.

For nearly five months they had roamed the Caribbean, plaguing shipping in the Guiana basin, running up past Tobago, Trinidad, and Barbados, and down as far as the mouth of the Amazon. Looting cargo ships and stalking slavers, they had returned now and then to the Surinam shore to bury weapons or to rendezvous with Spanish middlemen who paid for the rest of their loot in cash.

Enjoying the life immensely, Jacques learned quickly. His nimble skill and sure sea intuition first won grudging respect, then admiration from the Maroons. Then, in the midst of a raid on a Portuguese pirate ship, Afu was knocked to the deck, the dagger of a swarthy Cape Verdean seaman at his throat. Even before Nsai could move, Jacques leapt on the man, his forearm jerking the Cape Verdean's neck, choking off his breath. As the Cape Verdean's eyes rolled back in his head, Jacques's knife slid through his gut.

Smiling, Nsai had helped Jacques to his feet. "The blood of Akime still flows swift and fierce. You are indeed his grandson and due the honor of his name."

Later, they were plowing the equatorial currents off Guadeloupe when a solitary Dutch ship appeared on the evening horizon. "It's a slaver. I can smell her," Afu had whispered.

"See, the sharks follow her," Nsai added grimly. "Move away and wait until dark. Perhaps we can board her from the silent canoes."

Under full press of sail, the Maroons veered away from their prey, setting a course to circle back across the slaver's path as night fell.

The low tropical clouds of the rain season blocked the moon. The blackness they had hoped for covered the sea.

The Maroon canoes came on amidship, presenting a slim target for the Dutch cannon. Crouching in the stern, Jacques heard Nsai's tense whispered commands. "Silence now. The sound of breathing carries on the water at night. Move her under the bow. We go up the anchor chain." Nsai touched Jacques's arm. "You and Afu stay here for a while. And hold tight to your supper. We'll be sliding in blood before dawn."

"And what if the Africans are killed?" Jacques had ventured.

19

"If they are," Nsai had answered sharply, "then they will die free. And that is as it should be. Man must either be free or dead."

As they neared the Dutch ship, Jacques saw the night watch at the bow, then saw the other Maroons slipping up from the stern, their knives drawn and raised. The screaming began.

It had been nearly half an hour before Jacques and Aduku boarded the Dutch ship. The Maroons' work was cruel and thorough. Men with throats slit and bellies ripped lay across the deck. As Nsai had promised, they fairly slid in blood.

But far more unnatural horrors awaited. As Jacques watched, the door to the hold was opened. Such a racking foulness filled the air as shackled slaves were led out, stumbling, bewildered, emaciated from weeks below deck, that Jacques's stomach had revolted; his supper spouted from his mouth into the sea.

"Quick, a machete," Jacques heard one of the Maroons yell. "There's two corpses chained in with the live ones."

Jacques heard a woman screaming, saw Aduku sag against the ropes. Then he saw the writhing young woman shackled with the other slaves, her belly great with child. Her face contorted with pain. "In the name of all the gods, help her!" Nsai shouted. "Cut her loose."

The woman dropped to the bloodstained deck. Jacques felt Aduku grasp his arm. He turned, saw his friend's face twisting in horror. "ChuKwu," Aduku dared to whisper the name of the Almighty One. "ChuKwu, smile on the child now being born."

Three women surrounded the woman on the deck, calling for hot water, for anything clean. The young woman screamed again, so piercingly that Jacques felt an answering cry rising to his lips. Then, after a moment, the women parted and Jacques saw the small form beside the young woman, who lay still now on the deck. Afu spoke. "They are both dead."

The Maroons had sailed for Surinam then. On shore they made new canoes and headed down the trail of streams and rivers toward their village. Before they gained the final rapids they had heard the drums. "They tell of war," Nsai had said tersely as the oars flashed through the water. "They call the Almighty One to dwell in us."

The village warriors had gathered at the water's edge. Quickly, events and plans were told. A black named Baron had declared war upon the whites. European troops had again been brought to fight. The women and children and new arrivals must go to another tribe some thirty miles downriver. The old women and the children would leave immediately, the young women after gathering the valuables of the tribe. Aduku was assigned to the men guarding the young women. They would rejoin the tribe by dawn.

Jacques had searched frantically in the confusion for Alanya. When he found her, he had led her to the old silk cotton tree where they had spent so many of their youth's free hours.

"I have proven myself now, Alanya." Pride flashed in Jacques's dark eyes. "Nsai will name me Akime, by my grandfather's name. When we have won this war, I will speak to your father . . ."

"I am pleased." Her voice intoned the practiced submission of new womanhood. Then he saw the twinkle of her girlish merriment. "Then you have not forgotten me?"

"Never, Alanya." For a moment Jacques forgot the aloof indifference of the warrior. His voice was a harsh whisper. "I will never forget you."

As the warriors made ready, Kheni, the witch doctor, had prepared for the Krumanti, the ritual fire dance, by building the obia house with twigs. In it he placed the sacrificial doll, rum, and pieces of cloth. The tribe dancers painted their bodies and poured a rum sacrifice to the gods. Then the drums and singing began. Louder and louder the drums and voices exhorted the gods' attention to the ancient pains of man. The graceful dancers moved trance-like onto fiery coals, rubbing themselves with burning sticks, dousing themselves in boiling water, chewing glass and burning wood, slashing themselves with glowing blades, calling the gods to dwell in them.

Even before the women left, the Maroon warriors took to their canoes, rowing downriver to the great clearing.

The next day, against the fiery forge of an orange sun, tribesmen had tested the mettle of their bodies in the rituals of war. And, as the vast indigo night slipped across the earth, Jacques, next to Nsai, had listened as Nsai told again the story of the legendary ZamZam and the other great bush Negro leaders, Captains Boston and Araby, who had won their independence and their freedom.

"We are free," Nsai had said, "because they understood the weapons of freedom. When the white men came with their treaties and their trinkets, Boston sent them fleeing back to Paramaribo. 'We do not need treaties bought with mirrors and combs,' he said. 'We want firearms and gunpowder.'

"Freedom is only a word until we have what we need to maintain it." Nsai's voice had been a soft singsong, foretelling the long saga. Jacques had struggled to stay awake, but sleep surged over him. The jungle was awesomely silent, the soft murmur of the wind-brushed trees the only voice from nature's fastness. Jacques knew the next day would bring devastation and dying. He had heard often enough as a boy what the passage of the Maroons would mean. And the passage of the French, and the Dutch, and the Portuguese. There was little mercy in the minds of men at war. Women and children . . .

Nsai had looked down at Jacques. "So you fall asleep," the war chief laughed softly. "Well, sleep then. Use your weapon as your pillow and the stars as your cover, for we rest on our deeds as we aspire to the skies." Nsai had drawn his dagger, testing the keenness of its blade with his fingers. "And even as we sleep, our ancestors prepare to greet us. Perhaps tomorrow."

In the night, Jacques's sleep had been troubled by whispers coming and going in his semi-consciousness, until one word had roused him to wakefulness: "Alanya." He heard Nsai speak to his brother, Poku, who, with Aduku, had been one of those men charged with taking the women to safety.

Realizing they meant no one to hear, Jacques had inched toward them on his belly. Their voices were low, yet Jacques made out the facts: Alanya and Aduku kidnapped . . . their canoe had sprung a leak . . . they had put ashore to fix it . . . captured by a French planter and his sons with muskets . . . headed for Paramaribo.

Nsai would not tell the granman. There was no time or men for the chase and too little chance to overtake them. Loyalty first to the tribe. He would not risk the lives of many for the few in the canoe. A slow shudder circled through Jacques. Alanya and Aduku woud be lost, perhaps forever.

Crawling back to his pallet, Jacques took the small package that held his belongings, then moved soundlessly into the bush. Minutes later he was in his canoe, paddling with feverish speed downriver toward Paramaribo.

During the night his plan took form, and he set his course for the home of his childhood.

The plantation was deserted. Only the masonry remained of the house. The weeds, grass, and scrub trees grew high. Jacques could no longer tell where the coffee bushes had once provided his shade. Little by little the jungle would reclaim it all.

He had run quickly through what was left of the house, finding little that was recognizable. In the sack buried beneath the great tree he had found a few guilders and the deed to the land. It was all that was left of the Clavier estate.

Jacques had felt one more obligation, but his search did not reveal the graves of his parents. With his dagger, he had fashioned a cross and carved three names on it. "Philippe Clavier, Yvette Clavier, Leah Clavier." Over the last name he etched a replica of his medallion. He mounted the cross in a cleft of rock, knelt and said what he could remember of a Christian prayer. Next dusk he was in Paramaribo.

He had gone straight to the home of Hans Van Hoven. Frau Van Hoven shrieked when she saw the loinclothed, fierce-eyed young Negro approaching her top-opened Dutch door.

Her husband, stumbling to her assistance, had signaled for his musket as he silently slipped the bolt in the bottom of the door and asked, "What do you want, Jacques?"

Quickly, Jacques had made his offer: the deed to the Clavier estate in return for exact information regarding the whereabouts of Alanya and Aduku.

The shipbuilder had been hesitant, reluctant to be involved. For a moment he silently appraised the young defector. But, he thought, the war could not last forever, and land was . . .

"I am prepared to pay their purchase price, Herr Van Hoven." Jacques saw his indecision. "Rest assured, I am alone."

Van Hoven nodded. "I will find out what has happened. Meet me on my wharf in two hours."

Van Hoven had been waiting at the wharf when Jacques arrived. "Your friends are with a planter named Reni Georges. His plantation was destroyed by Maroons. He's now bound for Quebec."

"Bound for . . . ?"

"He booked passage on the *Jeanette*. She sailed on the morning tide."

Jacques's dark eyes shadowed. "When is there another ship?"

"To Quebec?" Van Hoven pursed his lips. "None that I've heard of. The only ship for North America is the *Valiant*, a whaling brig."

"When does she sail?"

"In the morning, but she's not yet captured a single whale."

"You have done what I asked, Herr Van Hoven." Jacques reached beneath his loincloth and brought out the deed. "I thank you."

Van Hoven took the deed and placed it in his pocket. "What will you do now?"

"I will go to North America."

Van Hoven nodded slowly, remembering the Jacques he had known as a boy. "I hear the *Valiant* is taking on crew. Get yourself acceptably attired and I will write a note about you to the captain."

"I would be grateful."

Van Hoven studied the young man before him. "The chances of finding your friends are slim. You will be leaving your home— perhaps forever—for a new and strange land."

Jacques's eyes met his. "I have no home, Herr Van Hoven. And as for the new and strange . . ." He shrugged. "I will appreciate your note to the captain of the *Valiant*."

Van Hoven watched the young man walk away. Perhaps the new land would be kinder to the lad, but from all that he had heard he doubted it. "Jacques Clavier," he called. "God go with you."

A half smile had brushed Jacques's face as he turned, touching his medallion. "I will be safe, Herr Van Hoven. I will be safe."

Now, as the *Valiant* lurched in the choppy waters of Buzzards Bay, Jacques heard the call from the fishing boat off the stern. "Ahoy, the *Valiant!* Welcome home!"

Alanya, Jacques thought. I am coming.

The sun blazed on the clay cliffs of Gay Head: black, red, yellow, brown, all the colors of man. It was, Jacques Clavier thought, a good omen.

In his cabin, Nils Kuykendal slumped dejectedly, feeling his misery vibrating through the four-by-six foot cubicle. He could tell from the motion of the ship that they were almost home; the swells of the Atlantic Ocean had given way to the choppy waters of Buzzards Bay. Soon they would ride the gentler tides of the Acushnet River. This should have been the happiest moment of his life. Only an hour before, the storm clouds which had haunted his horizon for many years had parted. The ship's captain, Able Smith, had told him he had decided not to sail again, and would recommend him, Nils Kuykendal, for the captaincy of this vessel.

Again Nils's blue eyes narrowed. Was the old man sick, as he claimed, or were his fears the same as Nils's own? Kuykendal's broken nails scratched his broad bewhiskered face. Part of him despised this tortuous bout with superstition, but another part, the part most fundamental to his nature, upheld fear as reason.

Was he right in his belief that the *Valiant* had been a doomed ship and that somehow Clavier had saved it from disaster? Or had he exaggerated the series of misadventures that had plagued the *Valiant* before the boy came aboard? For the fiftieth time in as many weeks, Kuykendal now pondered this, moving from event to event, his pipe clenched between his teeth while his knife dug viciously at the whalebone in his hand.

He had not wanted this voyage, had been against it from the start. He had heard the whalemen's talk, on the wharves and in the taverns of Nantucket, of the profaned vessel being built by "off-islanders" at Bedford Village. Over tubs of rope and tankards of beer, rumors had flown that the keel had been laid on a Friday, that the masts had been set on a Friday, and, sacrilege upon sacrilege, that the brig would be completed on a Friday. And then had come the word that the captain of this perfidy would be that gentle Quaker, Able Smith.

Smith had arrived in Nantucket, seeking crewmen for the voyage. But even as the captain spoke, denying with Christian piety the commandments of the deep, Kuykendal had sensed disaster.

However, luck had run at crosscurrent with Nils nigh on four years. Ship after ship on which he had sailed had returned to Nantucket still in ballast, its quarry still unseen. Little by little, wide berth had been given him in the taverns of the island, and sidelong glances accompanied whispers that he had become "a jonah." It was intolerable. He, Nils Kuykendal, a whaleman's whaleman, known the width and breadth of the island for his vision; he, who was able to see farther than any man at sea, had rarely an offer for a cruise. And so, in deep distress, he had listened to the offer of the Quaker, Able Smith.

They had weighed anchor on a Thursday. Less than a mile offshore, the wind had shifted. Unable to make way against the tide, they were forced to haul in.

On Friday, just after dawn, the wind had lifted. To the consternation of the crew, Captain Smith gave the order to hove short. The sails were loosed. The topsails sheeted home. The anchor weighed and catted. The voyage begun.

They had moved slowly down the Acushnet, into Buzzards Bay and out into the Atlantic. Two days passed without incident and Kuykendal had begun to enjoy some feelings of relief. Then, on the third day, Jensen, the boatsteerer assigned to Kuykendal's whaleboat, developed fever which rose rapidly despite the ministrations of Captain Smith. By dawn the man was dead.

Fear crept through the crew. The men bent sluggishly to their tasks, looking furtively at one another as if to ascertain where the hand of death would touch again. They did not wait long. Off Hatteras a gale blew up, the churning sea crashing against the brig until her beams groaned and shuddered in fitful response to the fury of the sea.

"Tumble aft! Jump for thine lives!" the captain bellowed as the men struggled in the rain and wind to secure the rigging. "Let go thy topgallant halyards, fore and aft, clew up, clew up if thee ever want to see home again!"

A wave rose like the hand of God, hovering above the ship as if reluctant to punish the creatures of earth who had ventured into its domain. Then it smashed down, driving across the waist of the ship, breaking the larboard quarter boat from its lashings and sweeping it and Kuykendal's lanceman out to sea. His screams were silenced by the storm, his fate seen only by Kuykendal and Moses Woodson, the giant black cooper who had attempted vainly to snatch him from his doom.

By morning the sea had been calm again. The *Valiant* ran down to

26

the Caribbean under a full press of sail as though attempting to flee disaster. For seven weeks they had cruised those waters, but there was no call from the lookouts on the topgallant crosstrees. They saw no whales.

Off the Jamaica coast they passed a Nantucket ship. Her captain came aboard to tell of excellent fishing off Guiana. The *Valiant* sailed down to South America, but except for a lone finback, too fast to chase, no whales were seen. Around their ship the blue ocean spread, flat, and endless. Few men aboard had ever witnessed such a stretch of bad luck. Muttered complaints became sullen dissension.

"Even the behemoth despises our transgression," said Watson, an old Nantucketer. "Mayhaps we are doomed to cruise in empty waters for eternity."

"Aye," came the response. "'Tis the Kuykendal curse."

Captain Smith, understanding the disposition of his men, had called off the hunt and set sail for Paramaribo, capital of Surinam, where he could sign on a hand or two and ease the tensions that bordered on mutiny.

Jacques Clavier had been one of the new men. It was when they were moving upriver, away from Paramaribo, passing Fort Zeelandia, that Kuykendal first saw him. Clavier had been leaning on his mop with which he was swabbing the deck, talking in halting English with Woodson, the cooper.

"So you never seen a whale?" the giant black was asking.

"Not close on. I know them to be huge."

"Huge, is it? Let me tell you, boy, no animal of land or sea is as large or as strong as the whale. In weight whales can top ninety tons; they go over a hundred feet in length. A whale is larger than a hundred oxen; it outweighs a thousand people and would feed steaks to an army of more than a hundred thousand men."

Woodson nodded, affirming Jacques's astonishment. "It's true what I tell you. I want you to know what you got yourself in for. The head alone weighs thirty tons, the jaws come on for twenty feet, and, though the eye is scarce big as a cow's, the tongue outweighs ten full-grown oxen."

"And they are swift?" Jacques had asked.

"Swift? Is a hurricane swift?" Woodson's broad-featured onyx face twisted in a scowl. "They come a-charging in at thirty knots. With my own eyes I seen one spy a ship the size of ours and shatter it with one blow of its mighty flukes."

27

"And still the hunt goes on?"

"It does. The head of one sperm whale holds five hundred barrels of spermaceti, the richest oil of all. These creatures of the sea is what lights the lamps of the land. But we're pitiful creatures compared to what we hunt."

"Are you ever afraid, Mr. Woodson?"

"Always. But no more than of starving upon land."

"I don't fear the sea, nor its creatures. I never have. I never will."

"You'll learn. Fear is the better part of caution."

A half smile touched Jacques's lips. "Nsai, a man I know, once told me, 'Caution is the better part of wisdom.' But thank you, Mr. Woodson. I will give your words some thought and see which is which when the time comes."

Kuykendal had studied the newcomer. He was different from the sort usually acquired in foreign ports. And so, when the new men were assigned their watches, Kuykendal, as first mate, had first choice and assigned Clavier to his, the larboard watch.

They had come out into the ocean with the evening tide. Clouds rested on the western horizon; a lunar rainbow, like a vast jeweled crown, crested their path. Sunrise was clear. Soon after dawn came the cry from the lookout. "She blows! Thar she blows!"

Running with the men swarming toward the whaleboats, Jacques had felt Woodson's firm hand on his shoulder.

"Take care now, lad."

Jacques saw the grave reflections in the cooper's eyes and smiled. "I told you, Moses Woodson, I do not fear the sea."

"Then," Moses said gruffly, "when the whale is fast, keep yer eye on that land-made line."

Quickly the cedar whaleboats were lowered and away. Clavier bent to the oar near the bow of Kuykendal's boat, while the first mate worked the steering oar in the stern. As the boat cut through the water, a whirlpool of excitement and anxiety tugged at Jacques's gut. These strange white men behind him, did they know their business well?

Their whale was a sperm cow whose suckling young had distracted her usually sharp hearing. "Ready," Kuykendal called.

The boatsteerer rose, harpoon in hand, his left knee wedged in the clumsy cleat. Kuykendal shouted, "Give it 'em!" The harpooner's throw went true. The whale was fast.

The behemoth fought for her life, sounding down into her watery home and rising in red-foamed fury again. The Nantucket sleigh ride began; the whale, a fountain of blood moving at ferocious speed, towing the hapless whaleboat away from her young.

Twelve hundred feet of rope bound whale and men. As the line sped over the snub post, Jacques smelled it burning. The men swayed on the thwarts, straining for an even keel as the whaleboat skidded through the waves.

"Look sharp, Cahill," Jacques heard Kuykendal yell as the man across from him careened from his seat. "Look sharp—the line!"

It was too late. Cahill screamed, choking on his vomit as his bowels emptied in the form-filled boat. He fainted as his arm, amputated by the line, slid between Nils's feet.

Then the hunted became the hunter, turning, charging back upon her predators. The ocean roiled, alive with sharks circling swiftly in the bloody wake. Jacques heard prayers rising from the floundering boat: Catholic prayers and Protestant, prayers to gods unknown, and his own whispered pleadings to the mistress of the deep.

"She's breaching. God, she's breaching, sir!" a man howled as the whale leaped into the air, the vast cavern of her mouth spewing a geyser of blood. Kuykendal threw all his weight on the steering oar, forcing the boat to turn, then seized the lance and tried to stand. But as he moved, a wave spun the boat. Kuykendal fell back, his head striking the oar, his blood spurting out in the rhythm of his heart.

Then Nils saw Clavier stumbling back to take the lance from his hand. He clutched the oar as Clavier stood, feet wide, arm back to hurl the lance. He had but one moment, one mark, one chance.

"Red flag!" the cry. "Red flag!" The throw was true. The whale sounded again, then rose slowly to the triumphant call "Fin out!"

Slowly as memory receded, Nils laid knife and whalebone down. Yes, he needed Clavier. To whom else did he owe, if not this captaincy, his very life? But Clavier was aloof, distant. Perhaps if approached through Woodson . . . ? The cooper had been helping Clavier with his English and the two black men had become friends. Yes, the first mate nodded, he would ask Woodson's intercession in this matter.

For the first time in many days Nils Kuykendal smiled, remembering what had followed the capture of that first whale. He had searched for Clavier and found him fixed in silent communion with the sea. It was, Kuykendal had known then, a good omen.

It was late on an October afternoon in 1772 when Jacques Clavier followed Moses Woodson down the gangway onto the soil of North America. The voyage they had just completed was one of the longest yet from Bedford Village. Nearly all of its residents had turned out to welcome the *Valiant* home. Jacques stared in amazement at the crowd: weeping, shouting wives holding babies up to see their fathers, hucksters hawking rooms and rum, and agents soliciting the weary whalemen for yet another voyage to the ends of the earth.

To Jacques, all was new and strange. Only the sun, a great orange ball lingering beyond the fields and meadows, seemed familiar. Along the sandy beach buttonwood trees provided a brilliant gold canopy for the ways which held the brigs and barks under construction. Shipwrights and caulkers, mast fitters and sailmakers filled the air with their voices and the sounds of their work. And over all hung the smoky, oily stench of boiling blubber from the try-pots on the beach.

To the east, in the green Acushnet River, were islands dark with stands of cedar. To the south, like a broad finger curving from the mainland, was a place Woodson told him was Clark's Point.

"Come on, now," the cooper called, hoisting his sea chest onto his shoulder. "I got a woman and five young 'uns to see. Last time I saw the youngest he was just two weeks old."

Jacques, trying to see it all at once, picked up his carpetbag and stumbled up the beach after Woodson.

A dirt road was the main thoroughfare. Water Street, it was called. Proudly, Woodson pointed out the function of the four dozen or so wooden structures that comprised the village.

"Up there, on King Street, in that fine house, live the Rotches. They're the richest folks in Bedford Village. Cap'n Rotch owned ships in Nantucket 'fore he came here 'bout seven years ago. He built the first ship built in Bedford Village, the *Dartmouth*. Built her for his son, Francis, five years ago. She carried the first load a oil from here to London."

"Where's the port?" Jacques asked, coming abreast of the cooper.

"The port? Why, you seen it." Moses stiffened as though under attack. "Rotch's wharf, Russell's wharf . . ."

Jacques stared at his companion, then looked around him in dismay. Was this, then, the destination of his long months at sea, this clump of buildings in the wilderness? Nowhere did he see a ship on which he could continue to Quebec.

"Why, shucks, all this come about since after you was born," Woodson continued as Jacques walked in silence beside him. "Once all a this was the Wampanoags' land. They hunted and fished and danced their holy dances and worshipped the Great Spirit who provided them with life. The whales swam almost to the shore.

"Wamsutta, son of Massasoit, chief of the Wampanoags, gave rights to this land for thirty yards of cloth, eight moose skins, fifteen axes, hoes and pairs of breeches, eight blankets, a couple of kettles, a clock, eight pairs of stockings and shoes, and one iron pot. Cap'n Miles Standish had rights to a plantation here.

"The whites and Indians held Thanksgiving together. Then when the white men had it all, they didn't have to be thankful any more, at least not with the Indians. The Indians don't have no say in their government. They're not allowed to vote. So the Wampanoags dance the spirit dance and wait on their gods."

Moses saw he had recaptured Jacques's attention and went on. "The first white folks to settle here, leastwise that we know for sure, was the Russells. Everything was forest when they came 'bout twelve years ago. Joe Russell went into the whale fishery. Built himself a try-works on the beach and began to make candles."

Woodson paused, nodding to a tall, vigorous man. "Now, you see that man over yonder? That there's Elnathan Sampson, a blacksmith. He was one of the first ones here. He and John Chaffe, who has a candleworks, used to own equal shares of a slave named Venture. Bought him at public auction in Bristol County. Allowed him to work nights for other folks, only took half his pay. Venture worked every day for them for free and every night for pay for nearly nine years. Two years ago he bought his freedom for twenty-one pounds, six shillings, and fivepence."

"That much?" Jacques stopped short.

"Much?" Astonishment halted Woodson in mid-step. "That's a pittance for a human life. Course now, you don't see too many slaves around here. And when you do, sometimes you don't know they slaves. A lot of them live with they own families. And if the hus-

31

band's free and the wife is slave, he tries to buy her freedom 'fore the young'uns come along. Last count I heard of, about four years ago, they was twenty folks here between the ages of fourteen and forty-five held as slaves here, or what the Quakers call 'servants for life.' We got a lot a Quakers here and they say they don't like the idea of owning human beings. But since, likin' the idea or no, some own them, it makes them feel better to call them servants for life. But the slaves don't feel no better. They slaves, just the same."

Woodson continued his discourse on Quakers and slavery, interrupting himself to point out the cooperage and the long enclosed buildings that held the ropewalks and candleworks. But Jacques no longer listened. His mind was on Alanya and Aduku and how much money it would take to free them.

Abruptly, Woodson stopped before a two-story shingled house. "Well, here we are." A bell tingled as Moses opened the low gate, touching off a wild chorus of "Papa's home," and four running children threatened to knock him from his feet. Woodson, stooping to lower his sea chest, emerged grinning sheepishly from the rings of arms that found whatever hold they could.

"Jacques, this here's my brood. Jo Anne, Beth, Moses, and Peter, say howdy to Mr. Clavier, who'll be staying with us for a time." Jacques smiled down at the suddenly serious brown faces, the girls dipping in grave curtsies, the boys extending hands already familiar with hard work.

Then he saw a woman standing in the door, dark, slim, graceful.

She was part Indian. Part Indian, all woman.

"Come on, Jacques," Moses said, interrupting Jacques's suddenly overpowering thoughts of Alanya, "and say howdy to my wife. Hepsabeth, this here's Jacques Clavier. He came aboard in Surinam."

"Welcome, Jacques." Her voice was soft. "Come on in and make yourself to home."

Jacques stood just inside the door, absorbing the goodness of the place. In the brick fireplace, which took nearly half the wall, a cauldron of beans, pork, and molasses bubbled and steamed. Smells of baking gingerbread that convulsed his hungry stomach came from the oven just inside the fireplace.

Moses's huge arm encircled his wife's waist. "Where's the young'un?"

"A miracle, asleep. Let him be, Moses, least 'til I get the supper on." She smiled almost shyly at her husband. "Why don't you help Jacques take the barrel and water to the room upstairs? You'll both be wanting a bath after a year at sea."

Upstairs, Jacques entered the one large bare-beamed room. It held a sea chest, a pair of ladder-back chairs, and four beds covered with patchwork quilts. "Take either of them beds there," Woodson said, setting down the barrel, which was half the size of a man. "The girls'll sleep in the kitchen. Soap, brush, and towel's in the barrel. Use the brush to clean yourself. That soap'll tear your skin off."

The room was cold, and Jacques moved quickly, taking time only to tuck the leather pouch he wore under his clothes inside his bag.

His fingers were numb after the bath. Wondering that sane mortals would choose to live in such a climate, Jacques hurriedly pulled on the woolen double-flap breeches, shirt, knee stockings, and square-tipped buckle shoes bought on Moses's advice when they had anchored briefly in Barbados. Then, after brushing his still bath-wet sideburns with his finger, he rushed back down to the kitchen.

Supper was ready after much testing and poking amidst constant merry conversation which Jacques could hardly follow. Little Beth brought the wooden plates, mugs, and eating utensils to the table, while Jo Anne brought applesauce and milk from the buttery by the kitchen. Moses hoisted on the huge pot of pork and beans to sit amid the steaming chowders, clam and cod, honey, jams, corn, pies, aged and pungent cheese, and the flat, heavy, delicious johnnycake.

"Stop," Moses said finally, "or that table's gonna break. This is more'n enough to ask the Lord to bless."

The funmaking and laughter stopped for the first time since Jacques and Woodson had entered as Moses approached the head of the table. Around him his family sat with bowed heads.

"Lord, I thank you for reuniting me again with my good family." Moses's grace was a fervent whisper. "I thank you for a good voyage, I thank you for the food, and I thank you for the friendship of Jacques Clavier."

They heard the baby calling. Hepsabeth left the room and came back holding him by the hand. "Now say hello and give a big kiss to your father, Andy," Hepsabeth said, patting the boy's head. "He's been anxious to see you."

Jacques smiled as the handsome child toddled on fat legs toward the table, then gasped as the boy fell into his lap with a squeal of

"Daddy." Woodson's laughter boomed across the table as Jacques picked up the boy and held him against his heart.

The meal was over when no one could eat another morsel, not even eight-year-old Peter, whose capacity so amazed Jacques that Moses laughed, "You gotta kill a lotta whales to feed that boy!"

Moses followed this remark with an emphatic belch, then heaving his bulk from the table, placed a hand on Jacques's shoulder. "I'm meeting Kuykendal at Loudon's Tavern at seven. Come on, let's take a look at the night ways of Bedford Village."

Their breath fogged on the chill air which tightened their nostrils as they walked to the tavern. Water Street was nearly deserted, but the candlelit houses and the call of the lamplighter making his round lent cheer to the frosty night.

"Jacques," Moses began, blowing on his hands, "I got some words that got to get said. Mr. Kuykendal is right anxious to sign you on for his next cruise. Now, there's no rush." Moses glanced at Jacques. "There's plenty of work right here. There's the sea and there's the land. You say you know shipbuilding and I've got friends. But he asked me . . ."

"I have no time for another year at sea."

"Oh?" Moses paused, waiting for Jacques to continue, but his friend did not break his stride.

They walked in silence, curiosity slowing Moses's gait to Jacques's until the younger man asked, "Moses, how far is Quebec?"

"Quebec?" Moses stared at Jacques. "I dunno. Maybe ten, maybe twelve days' sail."

"Do ships sail there from here?"

"Never heard a one," Woodson said thoughtfully. "From Boston and Nova Scotia maybe from time to time. Why? You got business in Quebec?"

"I must go there, and soon."

"Well, unless you want to tell me why, the best advice I can give is to hold fast to every shilling you can. It may be in Boston you can find a ship which you can sign on as crew, but if not, believe me, passage is expensive."

They could hear the din within before Moses pushed open the tavern door. As they moved across the beamed low-ceilinged room, Moses returned the greetings of recent shipmates who now, emptying

34

mugs of ale or sack, began to transform the story of their voyage into legend.

A joyous howl exploded near the back of the room, and a man as huge and black as Woodson surged forward to embrace him. When the backslapping and "I'll be a cod-kissin' catfish" were done, Woodson introduced Jacques to his cousin, Hiram Black. Hiram was a whaleman too. He and Moses had not seen each other for three years.

While Moses and Hiram exchanged news of their families and their lives, Jacques looked around the tavern, or ordinary, as he had heard Moses call it.

Snaggle-toothed seamen sat on benches before the vast fireplace at one end of the room, drinking and playing draughts, moving their pieces slowly, after careful consideration. A game of skittles engaged three pungent-smelling cod fishermen who took time out for loud complaint of the time lost by having to haul their catch in from Nova Scotia. For a few minutes Jacques's eye followed a buxom serving girl. Then he was attracted by four men in tricornered hats smoking long-stemmed clay churchwardens. Vehemently they damned the British with their duties and their taxes and vigorously praised a man named Sam Adams who urged the colonists to think of independence.

"They are talking of war," Jacques said as Moses turned back to him, his cousin gone.

"It moves toward it. All them damned navigation acts," Woodson said angrily, then he shook his head solemnly. "A colored seaman I knew, Crispus Attucks by name, was the first man killed in a skirmish with the British two years ago. Some are calling it the Boston Massacre."

Abruptly, Woodson rose to his feet. "There's Kuykendal now. Stay here. I'll pick up our few shillings for the year's work. He'll be wanting to know your answer. Best to leave all that in stays 'til you catch your breeze."

Jacques crossed to the door to wait for Moses. Two minutes later, they left the tavern together. They walked toward the end of Water Street, where the houses were fewer and of poorer quality. "I'm takin' you to meet a friend," Moses explained. "This lady's name is Charity Long, and she's a widow woman."

"Moses . . ."

"A mighty fine seamstress, I might add," Woodson continued, ignoring the protest in Jacques's interruption. "Does work for all the quality folk in the village. I knew her husband well. Went down on the *Barbara* off the coast of Carolina little over a year ago."

"Moses . . ." Jacques grabbed vainly at Woodson's arm.

"Now, she may be a bit older than yourself, but no matter." A twinkle came into Moses's eye. "The oven can be heated, so long's the coals' alive." Then his great onyx face grew serious. "Look ahere, Jacques. I don't know what things are like where you come from, but I saw you giving that tavern girl the eye. And for colored that's banging on trouble's door. And let me tell you one thing, Jacques Clavier, the lynch rope don't know no difference between a free black neck and slave."

"Moses," Jacques said slowly, finding an opening for a question that had been on his mind. "Were you ever a slave?"

"Me? No, I was born free."

"In your own village?"

Moses paused a moment, then walked slowly on. "No, my daddy freed me."

"Your . . . ?"

"Freed me with his strong black hands." Moses seemed lost in thought a moment, then glanced sideways at Jacques. "Now, this ain't nothing that bears repeating, mind you, but this is how it was. He and my ma and her brother, who is my cousin Hiram's daddy, lived on a plantation in Virginia 'longside the Shenandoah River. My ma was up with me, in a family way, you know, when one day the master beat her. The scars are still on her back." Moses poked out his lower lip in thought, then looked at Jacques again. "My daddy come in from the fields and found her lying tremblin' and whimperin' on the floor. Ol' 'Zekiel, he didn't say a word. No, he just went to work each night past midnight, building him a raft. When it was done, he told my ma, 'We leavin' here tonight.'

"Then he walked up to the big house and on into the master's room. The old white man and his wife was 'sleep. My daddy put his hands round that man's neck and, while his wife thought he was turning in his sleep, delivered him to hell."

Moses turned to make certain no one was behind them. "Then 'Zekiel took the white folks' clothes so the dogs couldn't get the scent. He and Ma and her brother rode that raft 'bout thirty miles upriver, then took to the woods. Outside a Washington they met a free black man who helped them far as Providence. From there they came on to Nantucket. 'Zekiel took the name a Woodson 'cause that's how they had to come, and Ma's brother took the name a Black 'cause that's why they had to come."

"Is that how most of our people get free?" Jacques asked.

"No. Hepsabeth's daddy was a Gay Head Wampanoag. He's a descendant of Massasoit's son, Metacomet, the one known as King Phillip, who damn near ran these white folks clean outta New England. Charity's father was a black French Canadian. Fought with the Indians in the war. He married a woman a Quaker family had set free. There's nearly five thousand free people of color in the colony of Massachusetts and, I hear, more than fifty thousand in all the colonies, and each one got they own story."

Moses cast a quick glance at Jacques. "Speaking of which, you'd best get your free papers . . ."

"Free papers?"

"All free colored have them. Now, I don't carry mine too much 'cause everybody knows me, and round here they hardly ask, but . . ."

"I'll never carry some white man's papers saying that I'm free." Jacques scowled. "What kind of freedom is that?"

"The only kind we got right now."

"Then"—Jacques's eyes met Woodson's—"why are you not fighting?"

Woodson stared at Jacques for a moment, then silently strode through a sagging gate and walked up the narrow porch. "Charity Long," he bellowed as he pounded on the door. "Open up for Moses Woodson and a friend."

The door creaked open. "Moses, what in the name of . . ." Charity began. Then she saw Jacques, behind Woodson, and quickly covered consternation with a curtsy. "I didn't expect you. Come on in. You're welcome."

Charity's small fire gave but little light, and much of the room was cast in shadows. As Charity moved toward the buttery offering cider, Jacques saw her clearly. She was a young woman, honey-colored and slim, her full mouth anxious for laughter.

"Charity," Moses began as he moved a sewing basket and settled into a wicker-backed armchair before the fire, "Jacques here's from Surinam in South America. I was thinkin' you might be good enough to see he meets some folks his own age in Chepachet." Moses turned to Jacques, who sat gingerly in his chair. "That's the part of Dartmouth, the town of which this village is a part, where most of the free colored live."

"I'd be pleased to," Charity whispered, flustered. "Not that there's so much to do. Most of us work sunup to sunup, when we're lucky enough to find work, which, for the colored, isn't always easy. But"—she blushed as she looked at Jacques—"you're welcome, any time. Of course, the law 'bout single folks being alone together . . ."

"Oh fiddlesticks," Moses erupted, seeing Jacques's unease change to astonishment. "That's just some more of white folks' crazy ways. Making laws instead a teachin' common sense. The more fear folks get, the more laws they make . . . and the more laws, the more fear. White folks' laws for white folks and white folks' laws for blacks, and white folks' laws just in case they want to catch you. What you gotta figure is which applies to what." Moses stood. "Now I got you two introduced, and Jacques can find his way here if he pleases. Me, I got a woman I haven't held tight in a year and I'm ready for my good-nights to all but her."

"You'll be coming again soon?" Hope rushed Charity's question as Jacques followed Moses to the door.

"Well," Jacques said, turning to her slowly, "I'll be having little time for pleasure, and I'm not sure I'll be here long." He saw the disappointment in her eyes. "But I'm sure I'll have time to stop by and say howdy, if you like."

Her eyes assured him of her delight at the prospect, though her nod was demure. "Good night, Moses. And do come again, Jacques Clavier."

"Good night." Jacques, backing toward the door after Moses, felt relief as he gained the porch. "Good night, Goodwife Long."

Moses was gone when Jacques awoke the next morning. Hepsabeth smiled from the spinning wheel. "Moses is at the Taber place, seeing about some extra work. You can meet him there soon as you eat breakfast." Jacques ate quickly as the children watched, then he went out to explore Bedford Village.

He spent several hours wandering alone on the wharves, along the beach, in the area called Four Corners. Staid, businesslike Quakers in austere dress moved among the men who sailed their ships: small, quick Portuguese and thick-booted farm boys, beautifully tattooed Africans and dark, fierce Malays, Scandinavians and Englishmen, South Sea Islanders and Wampanoags, and a South American Indian with a shrunken human head bouncing from his belt.

Jacques did not go unrecognized. Several strangers went out of their way to make his acquaintance. The story of the *Valiant*'s change of luck had spread through the village, and several of the crew had linked the black man, Jacques Clavier, with the turn in events. Jacques learned also that he had a further recommendation: he was a friend of Moses Woodson.

Cautiously, he used celebrity and connection to elicit information. No ship, he learned, had ever sailed from Bedford Village to Quebec. Only in New York could he find a scheduled sailing, and with winter coming on he might well have to wait six months. Those who knew enough to reckon figured that one passage was exorbitant —"a rich man's dream"—and that for three passages one could "nigh on buy the ship."

By noon Jacques had wandered to the wooded area known as Clark's Point. A few yards from the beach, in a stand of oak and cedar, he found a small solitary wooden house. Grass grew high around the door, which opened with a touch. Inside were two rooms, home now only to spiders and mice.

The house seemed solid and well built. A question long lurking in Jacques's mind surfaced. When he found Alanya and Aduku, when they were safe, where would they go? He could not go back to Surinam, not to the Maroons, or the Van Hoven shipyard, or to that shell on the Coppename River. No, he was here now, in this cold but open country, on the open sea. He'd best make the most of it, both land and sea.

His eyes went to the window, to the stand of oak and cedar, then moved back to the smooth floor of the cabin. It would be perfect for lofting—for the drafting of a ship.

An hour later he found Moses Woodson standing outside the tavern, enjoying the fellowship of his cronies.

The property, Jacques learned from Woodson as they walked toward his house, belonged to a family which had moved "up the hill." Woodson supposed it was for sale. But before Jacques could continue his questions about the property, he and Moses entered the warm and noisy tumult of the Woodsons' kitchen. The older children had just come in, and Moses turned his attention to the accomplishments of their day.

"They all take lessons with Rev'rend Thomas, who teaches private to the colored." Pride curled the corners of Moses's mouth into a smile. "Sixteen pounds a year it costs me for 'em all."

" 'Tis not a waste of money for the boys," Hepsabeth said quietly, "but for the girls?"

"I tell you, readin' and writin' is the coming thing. We'll live to see a time when half this village, black and white, can write their name." Woodson turned to Jacques. "Peter taught me to write mine last time I was in port. You shoulda seen the look on Cap'n Smith's face when I wrote 'Woodson' 'steada making my mark. My . . ." Moses smiled, recalling the event, then stopped abruptly, remembering that Jacques could not only write but read books, thick books, with ease.

"Well, sit down, Jacques, and have a cup." Moses strolled nonchalantly to the table. "Let's talk about that house."

"I want to buy it."

"Buy it?" Astonishment jerked Moses's head to a sharp right turn. "Boy, you got any idea what houses cost?"

"No."

"That house, and I'm sure the land you spoke about goes with it, must cost close on three hundred pounds."

"Three hundred?" Now Jacques was surprised.

"Things are high now'days, my boy."

Jacques sat down slowly on the bench across from Woodson and, taking the cup of tea offered by Hepsabeth, made a mental accounting of his financial worth. His lay, his share of the voyage, was two hundred pounds, twelve shillings. He had nine Spanish dollars from his bounty from his months of pirateering and one hundred forty gold guilders from his grandmother's legacy.

"The land's no good for farming," Moses warned. "There's a salt marsh on the river side, and much of the rest is cedar swamp, There's a good stand of oak, cedar, and buttonwood. I don't know what you got in mind. You can sell the timber, of course, but cutting it's hard work, and once it's gone . . ." Moses shrugged, then looking directly at Jacques, continued. "The value of the property is it's on the river. And the timber. If it's farming you're interested in, there's better land cheaper up past County Road. But if you're looking to follow the sea . . ."

Jacques met his gaze. "I'm going to build a ship."

Moses sucked in his breath. "Well, I'll be damned," he whispered, staring at Jacques. "And what do you intend to do with this ship? Not whaling?"

"No," Jacques replied slowly. "Not whaling. But from what I've heard, there's money to be made carrying cargo."

"That there is." Moses nodded slowly. "What cargo were you thinking of?"

"Cod, to start. I've heard the cod fishermen complaining about the time they lose hauling their catch from the Cape or Nova Scotia. I was thinking of carrying supplies to them and trading them for cod."

Woodson was silent, appraising the young man before him. In town less than two days and already with an idea for business. Reaching in his pocket, Moses pulled out a plug of tobacco. After a moment of thoughtful chewing, he continued. "Now, I don't want to discourage you none, Jacques, but these here some mighty rough waters. That ship's gonna have to be built tight. Not that they don't do a good job where you come from, but if I was you, I'd get some expert help joining, caulking, and setting those masts. Offer yourself out for work in return for help, if you can't pay. Nothing wrong with that. You'll get a better ship, and the names of experts in the building helps in getting commissions. You know what kind of ship you got in mind?"

"A sloop with a schooner rig."

Woodson let out a slow whistle. "A sharp schooner, eh! I heard a them. Never seen one. They using 'em quite a bit for pirateering."

"I was a pirate on one of them," Jacques said softly.

41

"You was?" Moses's great jaw dropped.

"Yes." Jacques met his eyes. "I'm a Maroon."

"Well, I will be damned." Moses shifted in his seat for a closer look at Jacques. No wonder he came with such big ideas. He was used to men who had, and used, them.

Moses knew about Maroons. Maroons in South Carolina and in Georgia. They were small in numbers but, at that, greater than the odds for their survival. But those were men and women who did not count the odds. Moses had heard that in the islands, Cuba and Jamaica, the Maroon groups were larger, and their chances were better. And in Brazil and Surinam Maroons had fought back until the whites had been forced to sue for peace. So that's what this Jacques Clavier had been about. One thing was sure—Moses's huge head nodded—Jacques Clavier would find spiritual kinsmen in these colonies.

Jacques watched the thoughts crossing Moses's face, hesitating before he spoke again. The man was his friend. Yes, Woodson had proven that. And, Jacques thought, truth was best handled where it was best known.

"It's Maroon business that I am about. Members of my tribe"—Woodson's head shot up at Jacques' use of this word—"were stolen during the war. I believe they are slaves now in Quebec. Two are my friends, a man, Aduku, and a woman, Alanya . . ."

Woodson saw the look on Jacques's face as he pronounced the last name. So that was it, a woman. Aloud he said, "I don't want to be no prophet of doom, Jacques Clavier, but there's things that's best to be considered."

Woodson saw Jacques's frowning question and went on. "There's slavery all around here and in most parts it's hell. You get caught on the high seas by pirates, they'll sell you into slavery sure. A colored man's more protected in a whaling brig or merchant ship, but let me tell you they've been snatched from them too. And if you're thinking about captaining that ship yourself . . ." Woodson's head shook dolefully.

Jacques smiled. "I appreciate that information, Moses. But one thing I've learned so far in life. A man won't accomplish anything who dwells on the 'can'ts,' not on the 'cans.'"

Moses looked at his friend a moment more, then with a hearty slap to Jacques's thigh stood, grinning. "Well, I gotta 'can' that I can do.

I can find out about that land. Just sit tight and I'll be back directly."

Two hours later, for two hundred eight pounds ten shillings, the deed to the ten acres of land was in Jacques's pocket, and he and Moses went off to inspect his property.

It was five miles to the stand of birches that marked the northern edge. There they stopped. Jacques threw his arm around one of the slender trunks, and Moses opened a flask of rum. "To you, Jacques Clavier. May you and your progeny prosper." He closed his eyes, took a swig, then handed the flask to Jacques.

"To thee and thine, Moses Woodson. Health, prosperity and friendship." The liquid did not touch Jacques's lips. "Come on now. I want you to see the place."

Hunger was making harsh demands on Moses's stomach as they walked the bounds of the land, marking trees for the keelson of the ship and others whose natural curves and forks were suitable for its floors and knees. The stillness sang with their footsteps until the shadows deepened. Then Woodson helped a weary but exuberant Jacques carry branches to the cabin for firewood.

"You could have found an easier way to make a living," Moses grunted, dropping the wood before the fireplace. "But then, the Lord tries ambition with hard work. Come on, let's see what Hepsabeth has prepared to hush the howling in our bellies."

"Moses," Jacques said quietly, "I appreciate your hospitality, but I can sleep here now, in front of my fireplace."

"Nonsense, you'll be stiff as a board. Spend the night with us, then pick up supplies in the morning. I can understand your hankering for independence, but it's a fool who sleeps on stone when a friend offers straw. Come on, get a good supper and a good night's sleep. Today makes the difference for tomorrow."

The next day Jacques was up and gone before the Woodsons were awake. Dawn found him in the woods, swinging an ax and sawing.

He took lunch at Loudon's Tavern, then bought quills and ink for the draft of his ship and more tools—adz, pod auger, cant hook—for its building. He carried these home and went back to the woods.

The sun was in the western sky when Woodson joined him. The two men worked all afternoon in silence—the only sounds those of ax and saw against the trees. At dusk they stopped. Walking back toward Jacques's cabin, Moses sniffed the air. "Winter's coming on, and soon." He glanced at Jacques. "Snow'll be two feet deep 'fore long." Moses blew on his fingers. "In a month you'll be looking back on today and swearing this was warm."

Each day Jacques worked furiously from dawn to dusk in the woods and then, when darkness fell, returned to his cabin to the kneeling, crawling work of drawing the essential parts of his ship to scale on the cabin floor. He went to the village only twice, to pay George Glaggon, the shipwright, five pounds ten to come to his cabin and correct his draft for the sloop, and to make arrangements to hire himself out to Sands Wing, Amos Barker, and Soule and Edwards in return for their help with his ship.

Though every muscle in his body begged for rest and his stomach growled for food, though his body stank, he worked on at a ferocious pace—chopping, sawing, drawing his plans, stopping only when his eyes refused his will and closed.

Woodson came almost every day, helping sometimes for hours. They were loading logs onto a wagon to take to the beach when Moses turned to Jacques. "Who'd you get the wagon from?"

"The Russells."

"How much?"

"A load of firewood for two days of the wagon and the beasts."

"Seems fair," the cooper nodded.

They rode in silence to the beach, pulled the logs off, and went back and loaded more.

"Seems to me, oxen about the dumbest animals in the world." Woodson stuck a plug of tobacco in his mouth as they started back to the beach.

"Well, at least they've got the sense to keep a roof over their heads and someone feeding them."

"Naw, they do what they told. They gee or haw and that's their life. More I think about it, the more I realize how right you are, starting your own business. I used to think about having my own cooperage once. But then the children came along . . ."

Moses jiggled the reins and returned his attention to the steam rising from the straining beasts.

Jacques followed the motion of his friend's thick hands. "You know, Moses, I've been thinking too. About how much I owe you."

"You don't owe me nothing, boy."

"I couldn't have even gotten started without you."

44

"You woulda done it," Moses said quietly. "Might have taken a mite more time, but you'da done it."

Jacques turned and faced his companion in the bouncing seat. "Moses," he said, "I want you to be my partner."

Woodson stared at him. "Hey, who do you think I am? Captain Rotch or Mr. Russell? I haven't got a shilling."

"No shillings needed. I was thinking one eighth of the ship."

"An eighth!" Moses's look showed his amazement. "That's much as a captain earns."

"It's fair."

"I dunno." Moses shook his head. "I hate to feel in folk's debt."

"The debt is mine."

Moses turned his head to look at Jacques. Despite all his ways, he was still young, and a stranger. Maybe he could be a help. The cooper thought on this a moment, then his huge head nodded. "Then we're partners. One eighth."

"Done." Jacques grinned, extending his hand to be enveloped in that of Woodson.

Then as Moses's callused hands brushed the reins over the slow-twitching tails of the oxen he turned to Jacques again. "Don't get to grinning too much, Jacques Clavier. Remember, we're still behind the ox's arse."

"That may well be, but at last we're driving them. Just hold on, Moses. In six months time we'll be sailing our own ship."

Woodson looked at Jacques, letting the thought sink in. Then he slapped his thigh, emitting a bellow of joy. "Lord a mercy, colored folk. What you'all coming to next?"

After a moment he turned to Jacques again, a quiet look gentling the strength of his dark features. "Now, Jacques, I don't want to be seeming to give no orders, but take it easy, boy. No need to bust a gut. Even Noah stopped for a rest, and there was a flood acomin'."

"I've seen a flood, Moses," Jacques said evenly. "I've never seen this thing called winter."

CHAPTER SIX

1773

The snow came and the sleet and the bitter cold. The wooden frame of the *Leah-Alanya* rose above the high drifting white, swaying but standing in the mighty northeast winds.

For six months Jacques Clavier bent will and body to her making, sleeping only when exhausted, eating only when faint, buying only the essentials of survival for himself and his ship.

In the first month Moses Woodson had brought his family to help. Jacques had awakened to see men moving in his dawn-shadowed room. He had recognized Woodson, then gasped as he perceived the proportions of the man beside him. He measured a full fathom from his neck to his feet.

Woodson, lighting a candle, turned. "So you're awake at last. No wonder the forest's only half cut with you wasting so much time on your arse."

Jacques's incredulous stare had shifted to Moses, then to the other men now digging through the sacks they had placed on the floor.

"I figured since you made me a partner in your ship. I better see to it the thing gets built. So I brought my father, 'Zekiel Woodson"— Moses nodded toward the giant—"and my cousin Hiram Black, who you know, and his brothers Nathan and Bethuel, who are sawyers, and my brother Joshua. We already had breakfast at my place, so come on grab yourself a spot a tea and let's get going."

"See? Give a nigger a inch and he takes an ell." Ezekiel Woodson's voice rumbled like thunder. "Eat yer breakfast, boy. We kin start without you, if you tell us what to do."

"No. All I need is the tea. In fact, I don't need that." Jacques scrambled to his feet and into his breeches. "Won't take but a minute."

"Don't let Moses tease ye, Jacques," Hiram Black said. "Reason he asked us here was to keep ye from busting a gut working so hard."

"If I got a partnership, I want it honest earned. So I'm putting you all to work to earn it for me." Moses laughed. Then, suddenly serious, "No, Jacques Clavier ain't one to shirk and no question in my mind he can build this boat without no help from us. But the cooper I served my apprentice with is sick, and I'm taking my family to Nantucket for two or three months. It'll make things a lot easier if we lend a hand so he can get some of this done 'fore the earth gets frozen, the snow gets deep, and the cold gets bitter."

"Well, are you gonna talk 'til all that happens, or get going? Jacques's standing there with his coat on." Joshua shook his head in mock disgust with his brother.

Nathan Black looked up from Jacques's drawings for his ship. "These look good. You sure about the scale?"

Jacques nodded.

"You got timber chopped for the keel and the keelson? Me and Bethuel can start on them directly."

"It's ready," Jacques said reluctantly.

"Good. We'll haul it here and cut it by the house. Don't worry." Nathan smiled at the look on Jacques's face. "We done work for Rotch many a time. Both of us worked on the *Dartmouth,* and she's one of the finest ships afloat."

"I wasn't worried," Jacques protested. But he had been relieved to hear about the *Dartmouth.*

Swinging his ax against an ancient oak, Jacques had believed that the happiest day of his life. He had been caught in the close camaraderie of these men, their quips and laughter which rose heartfelt and free above the ringing of their tools. The eldest Woodson moved like a giant of liquid, seeming merely to lift a magic ax to send the trees crashing to the earth. Over and over Jacques had whispered to himself, "Alanya. Alanya, I am coming."

They ate the lunch Hepsabeth had sent in the crude shelter Woodson and Joshua had built on the beach. By nighttime, the ways on which the ship would rest were built and the stocks which would hold it during the building had been hammered into the freezing ground.

That night as they rested before his fire, Jacques had found himself listening with deepening intensity to the words of Ezekiel Woodson.

"This is a strange land you come to, Jacques. And it may be it has a new purpose. This is the land of them what was made humble before they kings and they kinsmens. White folks, red folks, and black folks. All of us, 'cept the Indians, came to this land under duress of hardship. The white folks was either unwanted or starving in they

47

old land, and us, well we wasn't exactly jumping for joy to get here neither. When you look at all the folks God done gathered in this colony, you think maybe He brought us together for some purpose what He have in mind."

Jacques had eased himself closer as Ezekiel Woodson pulled out his churchwarden and began to fill it with tobacco. "See, you gotta understand, it's a strange thing about the Lord. I sailed on merchant ships near 'cross the world and I learnt one thing for sure. God done sent his messengers 'bout everywhere on this earth, cept to them white folks in Europe.

"The China's holy man, which I heard was called Confucius, and the one in India, who I can't recollect, and Mohammed, which I was a Moslem myself when I was a boy, being as how my folks came originally from the eastern Sudan and most all of us was Moslems, anyway them holy men they preached 'bout God to those folks what they thought He wanted to reach. Now, Jesus, who I reflect on now, was concerned for His people, who is the Jews, and folks like them Greeks and Romans, what ruled and lived and traded in them parts where He was—some of which was black."

Ezekiel peered over his long-stemmed pipe at Jacques. "In fact to tell, you know Jesus went to Africa Himself." The old man nodded emphatically and went on. "You know, the white folks' Bible leaves out ten years of Jesus' life. That's 'cause they don't want folks to know what he was doing in them years. See, He belonged, so I was told by folks what know, to this sect of Jews called the Essenes. They was monks and mystics. Didn't have nothing to do with women —just meditated and wrote things down. That's how He learned 'bout this thing white folks call levitation. That's how He could walk on that water.

"Well, anyway, you see, the Essenes came into Egypt and Kush, the same Kush you read of in the Bible. A great black kingdom, Kush was, stretching from the headwaters of the Nile through Egypt clear to Palestine." Ezekiel nodded. "Some say the Essenes went as far as the Kongo kingdom, teaching and learning."

Ezekiel saw Jacques's startled look. "It's true what I tell you. God sent His son to Africa to get and give the wisdom."

The old man packed his tobacco firmly, then leaned back in his seat and lit his pipe. "But now ain't it strange, in all the history God ain't never bothered to send nobody to them English or them Dutch or Portuguese? Could be 'cause He knew they wasn't ready for Him

48

yet. And that's why they so tight-assed about religion and salvation and they interpretations of the Bible."

Ezekiel puffed on his pipe with satisfaction, nodding his approval of the tobacco mixture. After a moment he returned to Jacques again. "The first white man I worked for here—see, they brung me right from the slave fort to Boston and later on I got sold South —this man had a distillery. An' he spent mornings whuppin' niggers, his afternoons countin' his money, and his nights readin' his Bible."

The giant shook his head. "God brought all us here so's He could teach all the peoples. May be His last try and He wanted to make sure all the neighbors He was talkin' 'bout in 'Love thy neighbor' would be neighbors already, you see?"

Jacques's eyes were fastened on the older man as he went on. "That's maybe why we got oppression from England. James Otis and Tom Paine and Sam Adams see it. That's why they speakin' out against slavery. How can you be raisin' hell 'bout natural rights and freedom for yourself and at the same time be keepin' them same things from others? That man's bound to my place who keeps his foot on my back. And while he's watching me to see I don't get no freedom, let me tell you somebody's stealin' his."

Ezekiel Woodson lifted his mug. "This is what they buy men for. Rum! A hundred forty gallons of rum and you buy a man's life. But not his soul, boy. That belongs to God."

The giant had stood then and reached for his coat. "Now this has been a real nice evening, but unless somebody stop that rum, we'll have the strength of babes tomorry."

Standing, Jacques had given his thanks while Moses had beamed at the accomplishments of the day.

"No more'n what we should do," the senior Woodson said. "If a black don't help a black, a black ain't got no help." A gigantic hand dropped on Jacques's shoulder. "Remember, Jacques Clavier, we all here 'cause a some plan. God done moved across the earth to convene some a all his people on these shores. He ain't revealed the purpose. I guess that's up to us."

Jacques had stood in the doorway as his friends left to spend the night at Moses's house. He knew why he was on these shores. He had a ship to build and a voyage to take. And then, with Alanya safe, he would build his family and his own fortune, a fortune that would ensure that what had happened could never happen again. Yes, Jacques thought, Nsai was right. Freedom was only a word until you had what it took to maintain it. And he knew now what that was. The wind was cold, but Jacques had stood there for some time, turning his medallion and staring out toward the sea.

The Woodson family helped for several weeks. Together they had laid the two huge, squared-off timbers that formed the keel, the backbone of the ship. Nathan and Bethuel had scarfed the timbers, slicing their ends at an angle, shaping and notching them to fit tightly as they overlapped to form curves, then bolted them into place.

The angular pieces of the floors were bolted at intervals to the keel. Then a large piece, cut from a curving tree trunk, was fitted to one end of the keel to become the stem, the vertical center of the bow.

A large solid piece of straight wood was fitted at the other end of the keel, to form the stern post, the vertical center of the stern. Then the keelson, a beam parallel to the keel on top of the floors, had been fastened to stem and stern post to straighten the ship and bolted through the floors to the keel.

From then on Jacques worked either alone or with the craftsmen who came in exchange for his labor. While he worked, he nourished himself with daydreams of Alanya and Aduku, wondering if they thought of him and of their times together and imagining their delight when he came. Surely they must know that he would come. Did they wait through anxious, hateful hours? Or did they believe themselves abandoned by all whom they had known?

And what of Nsai and Afu? Were they still at war? And had the granman ever learned what had happened to his laughing daughter?

Oh, Yemangi, he prayed each night, let me finish the ship.

Jacques formed the ship's ribs, the curved sides of her frame, precisely scarfing straight and curved timbers, then fastened them to the floor on both sides of the keel. Then he began the planking.

The planks were solid oak. They had to be steamed to make them flexible. Laboring over the steam boxes in the beach shelter till his body was as damp as the boards, Jacques dragged them one by one through the snow to fasten them to the frame with wooden pegs, or trunnels.

St. Stephen's Eve found him trembling with the flux and near delirious with fever, lurching through the moonlit snow seeking a potion.

No, he could not take care of himself, Charity insisted. With the barest of protest, Jacques found himself beneath the quilts of her wooden bed, drinking bitter, healing tea.

For three days and nights he lay, lost in fever, only faintly cognizant of the scent of lavender spicing the harsh soap smell of Charity's hands as she brought soup or tea and straightened his coverlet.

At night the door closed briefly between them, then reopened to admit the heat from the fireplace to the bedroom and to reveal his nurse attired for slumber, her hair burnished by firelight as she knelt to her pallet on the floor.

By the fourth day Jacques was much better. That evening, sitting before the fire, he watched as she laid out the quilts upon the floor. "I will sleep here tonight, Charity."

Her eyes lifted, quickly, anxiously. "But, Jacques . . ."

"I am well now, thanks to your kindness and your care, and tomorrow . . ."

He saw disappointment, despair in her eyes and, understanding, bent and took her hand. "Then shall we share your bed tonight, Charity?"

Jacques saw her blush but took her lack of denial for consent and drew her to him. Charity caught her breath as she looked into his eyes—dark as the night beyond her door—and repulsing the sin of desire, fled into her bedroom, trembling as she closed the door behind her.

For a moment virtue triumphed. But what triumph in despair? Biting her lip, Charity recalled a saying she had heard often whispered on Nantucket: "Virgins feel the flame, widows the fire." Charity sighed, and this Jacques Clavier would have no need to beg. Tomorrow he could find another woman. And she had been so lonely . . . and it had been so long . . .

Slowly Charity dressed for bed and reopened the door, waiting until Jacques's eyes met hers before she dove beneath the coverlet of her bed. Trembling, she watched Jacques come through the door and cross to where she lay, all but obscured by the quilt. "Aren't you going to close the door?" she asked.

"There's no one here but us, Charity," he said softly.

"The light," she protested.

"The light?"

"I can see you." Her voice wavered. "It isn't right, I mean . . ."

Jacques looked at her a moment, then, closing the door, removed his clothes and lay beside her. She neither moved nor spoke, but he felt

51

her trembling. Whispering her name, he caressed her breasts. "Will you do it all without speaking, Charity?"

Her arms came up. She held him. And he moved into her, riding deep in her silent but tumultuous storm.

From then on Jacques rarely allowed himself to think of Alanya or Aduku, concentrating his fierce energy on the task immediately before him. His few pounds diminished into shillings, and then these filled only the toe of his sock.

The Woodsons were still on Nantucket. He saw Charity only when driven to her by a desperate need for human companionship. Then he went and was never refused, and though sometimes, drifting toward sleep, he thought to ask her why, he never did. And so the winter passed.

March was ending. The first brave green shoots of spring pushed through the thinning snow. The sun was bright in a sky of brilliant blue, and small animals investigated noisily the possibility of spring. All this, however, went unnoticed by Jacques Clavier as he trudged slowly home from Bedford Village. His raw, blistered hands were thrust deep in the pockets of his tattered coat. Dangerous thoughts were in his mind. Dangerous to him and to the men who had refused him.

His stomach growled in hunger, and for an instant his vision blurred. Damn them, he thought, a damnation on them all. Leaning against the slender trunk of a young birch tree, he pulled a withered apple from his pocket, then stared hungrily at a rabbit that scampered across his path. He had not a shilling left.

He had wasted a week of work in a vain attempt to borrow money, money he needed for tools, for rope, for help to finish his ship. He had seen every merchant and mariner in the village, offering his house and land as collateral, dropping his plea from two hundred to ninety pounds. All had refused him, though three master mariners had offered him work and one had offered to buy his unfinished ship for one hundred pounds, an offer Jacques had contemptuously refused.

Today he had tried to sell the house and land outright, but he could find no buyer. Soon now the rains would start, rains that would rot the ship's inner structure. He had to get the ceiling up. His thoughts sped to the safes in the village countinghouses, to the dark streets where rich merchants walked, to his own sheathed knife, quickly drawn. Already this week his hand had flashed to it, signaled by the word "nigger."

It was not morality with which Jacques struggled now, but pragmatism. His color made him conspicuous, and it was known that he was desperate.

Gnawing on his half-rotted apple, Jacques let his weary footsteps move toward home, then suddenly he stopped, seeing his half-finished ship through the trees, and his thoughts grew fierce again. A plan, a plan of last resort, long lurking in the shadows of his mind, came sharply into focus. He hesitated for a moment, then, knowing he had nowhere else, moved toward a new destination: the isolated home of the moneylender, Opius Cree.

It was not so much a hut as a lean-to, built against the cliff at the river's edge. There was no sign of life. As Jacques drew near, his apprehension grew. He had heard of men who had come to this place before him, desperate men who debited ships and land. And he had heard of the foreclosures of Opius Cree. A child pledged by the father, claimed from his screaming mother. A man, once the owner of a forfeit ship, who tried to steal his former property, found floating handless in the Acushnet River.

Jacques stared at the door. Before he could knock, it slid open. Jacques shuddered at the sight of the ancient hunchback being before him. It was not Cree's clothing, a bizarre collection of rags, nor his horrid snaggletoothed smile, nor even his claw-shaped hands that frightened Jacques, but his eyes, his vulture's eyes, predatory and voracious. They said that his grandmother was a witch. She had been burned at Salem.

"So, Mr. Clavier," Cree said. "I have been waiting for you."

Jacques let his breath out slowly. "And I am here, Mr. Cree."

The old man showed the revolting ugliness of his mouth again. "I will not waste yer time. I heard that ye are making inquiries for money. Ninety pounds, I hear, is yer asking. I will loan it to ye—against yer ship and land."

"My ship and land! The land alone is worth three times that."

Cree shrugged his bony shoulders. "Only that interests me. I do not haggle. Take it or leave it. But if ye take it, ye must return it, six weeks hence, this date, or your property is mine."

Jacques felt the quick surge of futile anger. "You are a thief."

Cree emitted the weird, spiraling sound that was his laughter.

"Aye, that I am. And those what come to me know it." His eyes became sharper, more piercing. "Honest men will have no dealings with ye. Bleating Christians with their false mutterings despise ye because ye have the lamb's-wool hair of the Lord they swear to love. So"—Cree shrugged—"there is no one left but me."

Jacques longed to turn his back on the abomination before him, but in hot, flushing reluctance he recognized the truth of Cree's words and knew he had no choice. Damn all white men anyway. The ship, the trip, Alanya and Aduku were his goals. "I will take it."

"Aye, you will take it." Cree held up a bony finger. "Wait here and it will be yours."

Jacques stood uneasily before the lean-to. He ached to crash through the door and seize Cree's ungodly loot. But instinct warned him, every animal has its means of protection. As Cree came out, Jacques saw it, crouching on the threshold, a snarling, menacing beast, more wolf than dog.

Cree carried a quill and a contract drawn on parchment. "Here, sign it before the ink goes dry."

Jacques wrote his name. Cree handed him the pound notes. "Count it if ye like, but be assured it is all there."

Jacques knew it was. He thrust the money in his pocket and turned to go.

"Six weeks." Cree's laughter spiraled behind him. "Six weeks and your ship is mine."

Jacques built the ceiling and began the work inside the vessel, hiring men to help him lift the deck beams which crossed the width of the ship. The stanchions, upright supports from the keelson, were fitted into place. Then the masts were set.

For the next four weeks, Jacques rose before the sun and worked until the moon was hidden in the oak and cedar forests. He began caulking, stuffing the narrow seams with oakum, forcing it, pounding it into every seam, around every trunnel, to keep the ship from leaking.

There were times when the sounds of his labors seemed to echo through the ship, mocking him. His stomach revolted at the sight of the tea and apples, the salted cod and mackerel on which he lived. Each night he stumbled home to scratch another day from the crude calendar he had marked on his wall and to stare with increasing

54

bleakness at the days left to him. Finally, on the pallet on his floor he fell to fitful sleep, haunted by the macabre spectacle of Opius Cree.

One night late in April, scraping the pitch he had spread over the oakum, Jacques felt his hands begin to tremble violently. No force of will could calm his heart's wild dance beneath his ragged jacket. He ran on deck, feeling panic rising, terrified by his inability to control himself. Clinging to the mainmast, he saw visions vaporizing on the beach and jumped from the ship, running headlong down the beach and through the village. He did not realize where he was going or why until he saw her face. "It's done, Charity," he shouted. "It's done."

She lay beside him in the darkness with his seed inside her. She felt sorrow rising and covered her mouth to hush its sounds. Now he would go. He would go from her bed, from her arms, from her life. She closed her eyes against the tears and turned to watch him sleep. Words of love felt but never spoken pushed hard against her lips. She turned her face resolutely toward the ceiling, her pride intact. Tomorrow she would smile and wish him well.

Goodbye, Jacques, she said in her mind, but the words took form and rushed past her long-sealed lips. "Oh, Jacques!" she whispered.

He felt her lips, her arms, her tears. "Charity?"

"Yes, Jacques."

And he moved to her gently, holding her, kissing her, listening to her words of love and answering the only way he could, with the strong rhythmic motions of their joining.

Jacques was in a hurry. He groaned audibly as Woodson, with a shout of "Howdy," veered from his side to speak with the colored family climbing hastily from the wagon on the other side of Water Street. The sky was a savage gray, threatening the onslaught of the second spell of violent weather in a week.

For a minute Jacques paused, waiting for his friend, then shifting his sack, moved on toward Rotch's wharf where his sloop was anchored.

He stopped short when he saw her, sails furled, resting easily on the incoming tide: the *Leah-Alanya*—his ship—flying the pine tree flag of Massachusetts. He smiled, admiring her good lines from this perspective, then hurried onto the wharf.

On board, he dropped his sack and ran up the poop deck. For a moment he stood there, his mind letting the rippling river waters becoming the rushing waves of the Atlantic. How good it would be to sail out, to be emancipated from the earthbound life, from the paltry shenanigans of petty men. Eyes closed, he could see the sea, the elemental, endless, almighty sea, its white-clad arms rising in welcome, in salute of his conquest.

Jacques heard the voices, saw the faces peering from the wharf and went below, running his hand across the ship's graceful curves. Every plank, mast, spar, wooden nut, bolt, every rope and sail had been hand-made and hand-fitted, and she was worthy; worthy of his sacrifice and of the voyage to which her existence was committed.

Suddenly, the frown that had marked Jacques's face crossed it again. Unless the weather lifted, unless he got a commission, unless he got a crew, in six days the ship would be lost; there would be no voyage and Alanya and Aduku would be lost to him forever.

He heard Woodson come on board, his sack thudding as it dropped to the deck.

"Did you see Kuykendal?" Moses asked as Jacques came up the companionway.

"No."

"He's down at Russell's wharf. Going to captain the *Valiant*."

"So you've said a dozen times."

Moses glanced sharply at Jacques. His high cheekbones protruded skeletally, and his rich brown skin now had a grayish tinge. On his return from Nantucket, the cooper had been stunned to see how much work Jacques had accomplished. One look at him had told the cost. The boy had a right to be feisty, but there were other things to be considered. "He wants to see you. He's on his way here now."

Jacques's dark eyes flashed. "For what? You told him we had our own ship."

"He knows that. And I told him you'd be happy to see him."

Jacques glared at Woodson. The big man met the look levelly. The water was too rough now, Moses thought, to give Jacques the helm alone.

Both men knew that the *Valiant* had not been to sea since her maiden voyage. Two days after she had arrived in port her hull had sprung a leak, large enough, some said, for a school of salmon to swim through.

The finest mechanics in the village had worked to repair her hull, recaulk her seams, and overhaul her pumps. The *Valiant* had been pronounced seaworthy by men whose names were respected in every port in the colonies. Now the time had come when Kuykendal could delay no longer. He must be a captain now or be one never. And Moses knew he was anxious to put superstition's account to right.

Jacques was checking the forestay when he heard Moses call out, "Good day, Captain." Turning, he saw Kuykendal coming up the gangplank.

The Nantucketer surveyed the sloop with practiced eye. "She's a fine-looking ship, Mr. Clavier. What is she, forty tons' burthen?"

"Exactly." Jacques's lips were tight as he suppressed a glare at Woodson.

"A cargo sloop, eh?"

"We'll be carrying cod from the Cape and Nova Scotia."

Kuykendal lit his pipe. "Cod's good, but candles're better," he said, suppressing a smile as he saw the flicker of interest in Jacques's eyes. "The sperm-oil candles made in this village are prized across the globe. My brother-in-law has a candleworks. He also has a client in Boston in dire need of a shipment." Kuykendal puffed, satisfied with Jacques's eager expression. "He's looking for a ship . . ."

"My ship's ready now. When would we sail?"

"You could load today and sail tomorrow," Kuykendal glanced at the sky, "if you can get a crew."

"Tomorrow!" Glee flooded Jacques's face.

"If you can get the crew."

"I'll see to it, then." Jacques pumped Kuykendal's hand. "And I thank you, Captain Kuykendal."

Jacques found Loudon's Tavern crowded with seamen. Walking to a table where several men he knew were playing backgammon, Jacques greeted the men by name, then announced, "I have cargo for Boston, and I need a crew." He looked around the table. "I sail with the morning tide."

"Beating up past the Cape in this sea? Not on your life," a sailor called Mason said quickly.

Jacques turned to the man next to him, "What say you, Mr. Clybourne?"

Clybourne scratched his knitted cap as he shook his head. "Too risky, Clavier. Wait a day or two. It may well be the weather'll change."

"I can't wait," Jacques said sharply. "The cargo's for tomorrow."

"Ye built that ship yerself?" a rumbling voice asked from the end of the table.

"I did," Jacques turned to answer Reuben Oates, a freckle-faced tattooed seaman.

"Glaggon, Soule, and Edwards gave a hand in it, too?" Beer frothed from Oates's mouth onto his red whiskers.

"Yes," Jacques answered quickly. "Yes, they did." Oates could be most valuable. An expert seaman, he was well respected throughout the area.

"I hear yer lucky on the sea." Oates looked Jacques over carefully.

"Lucky for every man aboard the *Valiant*." Turning toward the voice, Jacques saw Moses Woodson behind him. "And damn lucky too," the cooper continued, "for any of you who, like myself, is now without a shilling. The winter's been long. I see Mason, a rum man, drinking ginger beer, and Clybourne and myself with holes in both our boots. This trip will be short and the pay quick."

"Hmm." Oates slurped from his mug. "So ye think you'll make it there and back?"

"No question!" Jacques's sudden vehemence gave doubt no chance.

"Then I'll go with ye." Oates nodded as Jacques smiled in relief. "That I will."

"I'll go, Clavier." It was Tim Watson, boatsteerer from the *Valiant*.

"And me." It was a small dark man with quick eyes, a Portuguese named Alvarez.

"Anyone else?" Jacques looked down the table. The other heads shook in negative response.

"You can't sail that sloop to Boston in good weather with four men," Mason said. "That ship'll need at least a dozen men. And in foul weather, too." He looked at Watson. "Remember the *Wand,* left here last week. Sunk time . . ."

"I'll go with you."

Jacques looked toward the strange voice. It belonged to a colored man about his own age, sinewy and sand-colored. He wore splendidly beige knee breeches and a tight-fitting green frock coat. A pearl stickpin shone from his cravat.

"And who may you be?" Woodson asked.

"I'm Anton Key, from Boston." His full lips pressed firmly over his large teeth.

Woodson frowned as he saw the man's unmarked hands. "Have you ever been to sea before?"

"Enough to know the risk involved." Key held himself rigidly, but there was a warm twinkle in his eyes.

"And what were you, a steward? There's not a rope mark on ye." Oates held out his own bruised and callused hands.

"I have desire. I am a willing and apt learner." As Anton Key turned toward Oates, Jacques saw with astonishment the powdered wig under his tricornered hat.

"A nor'easter in spring's no place to learn to sail," Mason said glumly.

Key turned to Jacques. "I'm willing if you'll take me, Captain Clavier."

It was the first time Jacques had been so addressed. His mind swaggered. "Well, you're not afraid, and that's half the battle. I myself knew little on my first voyage. Come to the ship in an hour and let Mr. Woodson see what you know." Jacques looked around the table again but saw no more volunteers. He stood to go.

59

"I'll be there at dawn tomorrow," Oates said. "If there's a change of plans, you'll find me here."

"There'll be no change of plans, Mr. Oates."

Jacques and Moses made the rounds of every boardinghouse and tavern in Bedford Village. They found only one other man, Ben Talbert, also from the crew of the *Valiant,* willing to sail with the *Leah-Alanya.*

Walking back toward Rotch's wharf beside Woodson, Jacques told himself fiercely that he hadn't failed yet. There were still six unscratched marks on his calendar. But was it possible to sail a sloop to Boston with seven men?

Kuykendal met Jacques and Moses on the wharf. "Did you raise a crew?" the barrel-chested man asked.

"Seven men, including Woodson and myself," Jacques said flatly.

Kuykendal nodded. "Make it eight," he said.

All afternoon and evening Jacques and Woodson loaded cargo, aided by Anton Key. On his return home, Jacques scratched another day from his wall calendar. There were five days left to save the ship.

Oates was the first man to board the *Leah-Alanya* the next morning. Jacques's spirits soared as the burly, experienced seaman crossed his deck. Alvarez and Watson followed Oates aboard with Anton Key close behind. Ben Talbert came up the gangplank almost hidden by Kuykendal's breadth.

On sudden impulse, Jacques insisted Kuykendal have both the authority and the accommodations of captain for this trip.

There was no sign of Woodson. Jacques, watching the tide, was about to tell Kuykendal they must weigh anchor when he saw Moses coming down Water Street at a remarkable pace, followed by his cousin Hiram Black.

They wasted no time getting under way. The *Leah-Alanya* moved gracefully down the Acushnet. Despite the gray overcast, Jacques laughed aloud as he stood at the wheel. Every knot he sailed now was taking him closer to Alanya and Aduku.

Buzzards Bay was choppy, and the sloop anchored in a cove off Woods Hole for the night. As soon as they were fast, Kuykendal sent for Jacques, who knocked at the captain's cabin and waited to hear Kuykendal's gruff "Come in, Mr. Clavier."

"You wanted to see me, sir?"

"Yes. Sit down, Cap'n Clavier. After all, this is your ship." With a small amusement Kuykendal saw Jacques's vain attempt to hide his smile.

"We'll be moving into heavy weather tomorrow," Kuykendal said. "I'd like to see Mr. Talbert out to the foremast with—what's his name?—Mr. Key beside. We'll"—Jacques noted Kuykendal's emphasis on "we"—"put Mr. Alvarez to the mainmast. Mr. Oates can take the first watch as lookout, Mr. Woodson will handle the jib sails, Mr. Black the soundings, and you and I can alternate at the helm and on the quarterdeck. We'll cross Nantucket Sound and put in at the harbor. The men have no relief and they'll be exhausted."

"Then we won't arrive in Boston 'til Friday night at the earliest," Jacques said with alarm.

"Very probably Saturday, what with tacking into the wind."

"Captain Kuykendal." Jacques leaned toward the older man. "I must be back in Bedford by sunset Monday."

Kuykendal puffed on his pipe and nodded. "If humanly possible, Mr. Clavier."

Jacques stood, the blackness of his eyes fathoms deep. "Even if not, Captain Kuykendal. Even if not."

They sailed from Woods Hole with the first pale light of dawn. The sky had remained overcast most of the night, and now a mist fell, thick and menacing. Kuykendal sent Reuben Oates to climb the spreaders on the aft mast, to watch for the small rocky islands close to the shore and for the lanterns of any ship that might be passing in the fog.

Jacques took the helm. Kuykendal studied the maps and charts. Hiram Black took repeated soundings of the water's depth until they were well out into the ocean.

" 'Tis not so bad as she looks, Cap'n," Kuykendal said to Jacques as he came up the poop deck to the hurricane house. "I've sailed these waters nigh on a quarter of a century and I know they're treacherous. But knowing's half the battle."

He relit his pipe, puffing until the tobacco burned well. "You know, there was a captain once, sailed out of Nantucket. Swore he could tell exactly where his ship was, anywhere on the globe, by the color and taste of the lead after a sounding. He had a mate, Marden was his name, who determined to fool him. Old Marden took some dirt from his Nantucket garden on a voyage. Some months at sea he mixed his dirt with sea water and took a sounding in one of the ship's barrels." Kuykendal smiled as he puffed. This was one of his favorite tales. "Then Marden took the lead to the skipper, asked him to taste it and give him their bearing.

"Well, the old man did and, by Jove, he started up the companion-way on the run. 'What's wrong?' the mate called. 'Don't stand there, man,' the captain yelled. 'Either this ship's run aground or else Nantucket's sunk.'" Laughing, Kuykendal rubbed his wild mane in hearty appreciation of his anecdote.

A warm feeling for the older man spread through Jacques. "You love the sea, don't you, Captain Kuykendal?"

" 'Tis all I know, Cap'n Clavier. I'm a Nantucketer. 'Tis all I know."

The sky remained overcast all day, but the Atlantic, though gray, was calm. Hard-pressed by Jacques, Kuykendal agreed to sail all night. They made Boston Friday morning and weighed anchor for home that afternoon.

They came out of Boston Harbor on the flood tide, and the ocean, long threatening, turned mean. The deck rang with Kuykendal's brisk commands as the crew sweated in the freezing air to hold the ship to her course.

They slapped from one tack to another, running with topsails strapped against the howling northeast wind. The bowsprit of the *Leah-Alanya* soared and plunged, answering only the command-ments of sea. Rushing below, Jacques gasped in relief as the dull flickering of his tallow dip revealed no seepage below the waterline.

He felt the ship slipping to the starboard, shuddering, groaning like a woman birthing. Stumbling up the companionway, he could see the foremast waving like a storm-blown sapling.

Then he saw fear befuddling the helmsman. As Kuykendal called the order, Jacques leapt to the wheel.

"We're about ten miles off Cohasset," Oates shouted against the gale. "Should we put in?"

Jacques saw consideration cross Kuykendal's face, then heard his own voice shrill above the wind. His hand clutched his medallion. "No, it would be more dangerous. No, we go on."

He saw Kuykendal's quick glance, then the whites of Alvarez's eyes as that man's question—"Is he tetched?"—slashed back at him on the wind.

"Have heart." Kuykendal swayed against the clew lines. "Have heart. He'll pull us through."

For nearly three hours the *Leah-Alanya* rode the storm. Clinging to the wheel, Jacques heard Kuykendal's keen command, watched the wind-whipped men straining to obey. In the wind and water his feeling grew for the whiskered man on the quarterdeck, clutching the dripping pipe between his teeth, who knew their adversary and met its strength with cunning.

Slowly the angry sea found peace. Two by two the men went below to change their clothing. The moon, pale and distant, shed a timid light, and one by one the stars appeared. In the fo'c'sle Oates and Woodson slept in readiness for the next watch. They would be able to sail all night. Kuykendal smiled as he saw Jacques by the windlass. Yes, the sea had been kind to him again.

They dropped anchor off the Vineyard on Sunday and early Monday morning entered Buzzards Bay with a staunch wind at their back. They passed Sconticut Neck as the sun came to meridian. Jacques threw his arm around Woodson's neck and squeezed him in a tight embrace. "We made it!" His shout was jubilant. His dark eyes danced above the hollows in his face. "Oh, Moses, we made it."

CHAPTER EIGHT

1773

With his title to the *Leah-Alanya* free and clear, Jacques put all his energy into planning the rescue of Alanya and Aduku. If possible, he would purchase their freedom, and to this end he hoarded profits from carrying cargo to Boston, Nova Scotia, New York, and Philadelphia.

Jacques and Woodson remained close friends, though more and more Jacques began to spend time with the debonair, fun-loving Anton Key, especially when in Boston, Anton's home. Anton knew Boston's streets and byways well. Orphaned at eight, he had lived with a widowed aunt who had eleven children. At the age of nine he had become a milkman's assistant lifting the heavy milk cans onto the horse-drawn cart. At twelve, to help feed the family, he was stealing from the wharves. Their minister had gotten him the job as a delivery boy for a tailor. After two years he had become that man's apprentice.

With Anton, a passionate follower of Sam Adams, Tom Paine, and James Otis, Jacques became a frequent visitor at the Bunch of Grapes tavern in Boston, a favorite meeting place of the Sons of Liberty. Here the grievances of the colonists against the British were set forth and a philosophy for separation from the mother country hammered out.

Anton Key reveled in the high-sounding phrases of the revolutionary theorists, repeating them with a passion that, Jacques was certain, even their originators rarely felt. Moses Woodson saw in the revolutionary posture a mandate for the end of slavery. Over a year before a group of slaves had petitioned the Massachusetts legislature for their freedom. Though this was not granted, the incongruity of the colonists' position was highlighted.

More and more it seemed apparent that the cause of independence for the colonies was inseparable from the cause of freedom for the slaves. Proponents of the "natural and inalienable rights" theories, on which the rebels' stand was based, found themselves bogged down in intellectual quagmires when attempting to beg the slavery issue. "If we sue for separation because of oppression and are ourselves oppressors, what right have we to ask rectification for the injustices piled upon us?" This was the logic of men such as John Woolman, Anthony Benezet, Sam Adams, Tom Paine, Ben Franklin and the eloquent James Otis, who had affirmed, in his "Rights of the British Colonies," the Negroes' "inalienable right" to freedom. And, above all stood the martyrdom of the Boston seaman Crispus Attucks, a fugitive slave, the first to die in the colonists' struggle against tyranny.

One of the most vocal of the revolutionary-abolitionists was a dark-haired, angular-featured Harvard medical student named Louis Flateau. A month after their meeting Jacques learned that Flateau was from Quebec. From Flateau, Jacques learned that a Monsieur Georges, who had arrived the previous summer from South America, had taken over his brother's tobacco shop on Dog Lane. Cautiously Jacques wondered to Flateau if this Georges owned slaves.

"I have no idea." Louis's clear gray eyes met Jacques's. "Is it of concern to you?"

Jacques knew that he must take the chance. "It is my utmost concern."

Five weeks later, entering the Bunch of Grapes, Jacques saw Flateau motioning him aside. Standing in a corner of the noisy tavern, Flateau whispered to Jacques, "I take this caution because there are spies all about. Reni Georges from Surinam holds slaves on his farm some twelve miles from Quebec."

"My desire for this information rests with you alone?" Jacques's dark eyes were anxious.

"Rest assured it does."

Jacques shook his hand. "You have my gratitude, Louis Flateau."

Quickly Jacques brought Moses and Anton into his new alternative. Anton was enthusiastic, Moses doubtful. "It would be better," the partner cautioned, "To wait, to save enough money . . ."

"No," Jacques interrupted vehemently. "I know where they are. I have a ship, and I have a knife . . ."

Reluctantly Moses capitulated, even to Jacques's demand for a colored crew. "But Oates and Watson . . ." Woodson began his protest.

"There are times, Moses," Jacques said quietly, "that to move, black men must move alone."

The trip was accomplished without incident. They anchored near the isle d'Orléans in the St. Lawrence River two miles from the city to take advantage of the strong five-knot tide. Leaving most of the crew aboard ship, Jacques, Moses, Anton, and Anton's cousin Dawson completed the trip by dory.

It was dark when they landed. They found Georges's shop closed. Walking the city's narrow, winding cobblestone streets around the Place Royale, Jacques asked in long-unused French the whereabouts of Georges's farm. Everywhere he told the same story, that he had a package for Georges from Paramaribo and had to sail on the morning tide. By nine, he had the information he needed.

Jacques hired a carriage, and the frog-eyed Dawson, once a liveryman, took the reins. Jacques had been told that the entrance to Georges's farm was off a narrow road along the high bluff above the river. It was recognizable by its high stone fence and iron gate. Anton and Moses were put down to make their way behind the house.

The carriage moved slowly up the drive, accompanied by the raucous barkings of dogs. Jacques saw a man come to the open doorway of the house, knew instinctively it was Georges. Controlling his flaring anger, he leapt from the carriage. "Monsieur Georges?"

"Oui, mais qu'est-ce que ça peut bien te faire?"

"Je m'appelle Jacques Clavier, du bateau Leah. We have been sent to deliver a package for you from Paramaribo."

"I am expecting nothing from Paramaribo."

"Well, it's marked for you. Will you inspect it and sign for its delivery?"

Georges looked at Jacques suspiciously, then said curtly, "All right. Bring it in."

Jacques nodded to Dawson. Together they carried a box into the house.

"Ben," Georges shouted to someone in the back. "Shut those dogs up." He bent over the package.

"Monsieur," Jacques said softly, "you really should have expected someone from Paramaribo." His knife touched Georges's jugular vein. "You stole Maroons."

Georges straightened slowly, fear in his eyes. "And you propose to steal them back?"

"Not propose, monsieur. Intend. Where are the ones called Alanya and Aduku?"

"You cannot get away with this, Clavier, if indeed that is your name! My sons are here, as well as my servants."

66

"You also have a knife at your throat and a Maroon hand holding it. Now call your sons. And I warn you, there are more of us outside."

Georges read the truth of Jacques's words in his eyes. "Alexandre, Yvon!" His shout was shrill. "Come quickly."

Dawson pulled his pistol. Georges turned an ashen face to Jacques. "You won't kill them?"

"That decision rests with you."

"Papa?" The door opened. Georges's son recoiled as he saw the glint of Jacques's knife.

"Do as he says," Georges whispered.

"Against the wall and don't move," Jacques commanded. The young man stumbled toward the wall.

Jacques heard the quick, light steps of a woman approaching. "Marie, my son Yvon's wife," Georges said, his face twisting with fear.

"Yvon is at the stable, Papa," the young woman said as she came through the door. Then she saw Jacques. "Oh, my God . . ."

"Your scream will silence him forever, madame. Calm yourself and call the servants. Please sit down. It will seem more natural."

Marie looked at her father-in-law. His hands lifted in a gesture of surrender. "They have come for Aduku and Alanya."

"Aduku?" she asked. "The one who . . . ?"

"The one who what?" With one hand Jacques grabbed and pulled him fiercely toward him.

"Nothing," Georges gasped. "He's alive. He tried to escape. He was bitten by the dogs."

Then Jacques heard a new voice, behind him. "Drop that mister. You got the count of three." Turning, Jacques saw a black man with a musket pointed at Dawson's head.

"Ben!" Georges whispered in relief.

"Drop that knife. You got the count a three," the black man said.

"Wait!" Jacques shouted, certain his actions were misunderstood. "I'm here for Alanya and Aduku. They're my friends."

"I don't care what you here for," the man called Ben replied. "At three this nigger dies. One."

"Jacques, for God's sake," Dawson gasped.

"Two." Jacques saw Dawson shudder as the musket touched his skull.

"You blithering black-arsed idiot." The butt of a musket struck Ben's head from behind. As he fell, Jacques saw Moses and Georges's other son, held at gunpoint by Anton Key.

"We got two men bound up in the kitchen, but one got away, so we'd best make haste," Woodson huffed. "I ain't seen your friends, but there's some sheds out back."

Jacques nodded and turned to Dawson. "You and Anton tie these men up, then stand a keen watch at the gate." Jacques glared at Ben, now blinking on the floor. "I wish I had the time to whup your arse." Then he nodded to the woman. "Take me to them."

Marie Georges got up without a word and led Jacques and Moses through the house and out into the starless night. Jacques's heart raced as they walked toward a long shed set back from the other buildings. She paused before the door. "It is not a pretty sight. My father-in-law does not like Maroons. Now I see why." With that she turned and walked away.

"Jacques," Moses began.

"Let her go," Jacques said curtly, staring at the shed with sudden dread.

The wood sighed as Jacques pushed the door open, then he heard a sudden scuttling in the foul, windowless dark. "Alanya," he called. "Aduku?" There was no answer in the quick murmur of voices. He called again, "Alanya. It's Jacques."

"Jacques! Jacques! Jacques!" Over and over again she screamed it as he ran blindly through the shed, tripping over the tangle of bodies and irons. Hands reached up to clutch him as he passed, and the shed reverberated with cries in the suddenly so familiar taki-taki language of the Maroons.

"Alanya!" Jacques called again. Then he felt her fierce embrace.

"Alanya," he whispered, holding her, touching her face, still invisible in the darkness. "Oh, Alanya, you are here."

Jacques saw flashes in the dark. Moses was struggling to light a lantern. "Where's Aduku?" The native tongue came quickly to his lips.

He heard a low, strangled sound and turned into his old friend's powerful embrace. "Aduku?" he asked, and the sound grew stronger.

"It's his throat," Alanya whispered fiercely. "The dogs got him in the throat. He can no longer speak."

68

Jacques gripped her arm. "Let's get out of here."

"We can't move." Her hand led his to her ankle. "We're chained."

The wick caught in Moses's lantern. Jacques saw the iron shackle around her leg. "Oh, Alanya," he moaned, then looked up into her face.

Laughter was gone from her eyes. Her face was marked with sorrow. She saw his look and whispered, "I have changed so, Jacques?"

He could not answer and shifted his gaze to Aduku.

Aduku wore a bloody rag around his throat. The evidence of what had happened was visible at its edges. Rage interlocked with sorrow as Jacques looked around the shed. Two men, eight women, and an infant stared dumbly at him. He could not leave them.

"Come on, Moses," he called. "Let's get them all out of here."

A single shot from Woodson's musket split the coffle's lock. Immediately the Maroons struggled to their feet.

As they stepped outside the shed, they heard their carriage coming. "Make haste, Jacques," Dawson shouted. "The one who escaped went for help. There are horses coming! Many of them."

"Hurry." Jacques grabbed Alanya's arm and signaled the others. "Come with me!"

Jacques saw Aduku and another man running from the shed as he helped the women climb inside the carriage. Not until Woodson pulled him up onto the luggage rack did Jacques see Aduku and the man again. It was the lantern in Aduku's hand that caught Jacques's eye. They were driving a wagon piled with hay, heading pell-mell for the road.

"Aduku," Jacques yelled. "Come back!" But his friend did not turn.

Dawson's whip whistled in the air. The horses strained. They heard the oncoming horses as the heavy-laden carriage sped toward the road. As they careened through the gate, Jacques saw the hay wagon on the road. "Aduku," he screamed, trying to stand, but he was held by the firm hand of Woodson.

Jacques saw Aduku touch the lantern to the hay. It burst into flames. He heard the terrified neighing of the onrushing horses as Aduku drove the fiery wagon into their midst. In screaming, neighing terror, riders and horses plummeted over the cliff. Aduku's body was now a pillar of flame as he stood erect in the burning wagon.

69

"Aduku!" Jacques screamed. "Aduku." But as the scream jerked from Jacques's throat, Aduku arced like a comet to the river below.

Jacques stood at the rail of the *Leah-Alanya* as the ship made her way to the sea. In the frail light of dawn the Maroons came on deck, fed and washed. Alanya was not among them. Jacques went below looking for her and found her sitting alone in his cabin.

"Alanya?"

Her grave eyes met his. "Aduku is dead and I am old. Everything has changed, Jacques."

He went to her and knelt before her. "Yes," he said softly, taking her hands in his. "Things have changed." He touched her thin, sad face with his callused hands. "You are a woman now."

CHAPTER NINE

1773–1775

Aboard the *Leah-Alanya,* Jacques and Alanya became man and wife. Woodson, wondering about the legitimacy of the action, declined to act as captain, and Anton Key performed the ceremony. Jacques felt a measure of peace settle his heart.

The next fourteen months sped quickly by. Behind the house in the woods Alanya planted a garden of vegetables and a smaller one of flowers. In the summer she gathered the wild berries and learned from Hepsabeth to preserve them for the long winters. Her hands were never idle. Her heart was filled with love.

Jacques, too, worked from sunup to sunset. Ashore in Bedford Village he secured commissions and disbursed cargo: much-needed salt from Nova Scotia; sugar, coffee, and chocolate brought by merchant ships to Boston, and, from Philadelphia, Carolina rice and cotton. Then he prepared for the sea again.

Moses Woodson and Anton Key sailed with Jacques. Hepsabeth, who had once complained about the length of whaling voyages, now complained to Alanya that she saw Moses not at all.

In May, the British Parliament banned the sale of tea except by British agents. The Tea Act aroused a storm of protest in the Bay Colony. Although tea was no longer carried in the supply stores of the *Leah-Alanya,* Jacques resisted the efforts of Moses and Anton to recruit his other crewmen to their revolutionary zeal. When they persisted, his temper flared. "I'll have no more talk about this on my ship," he stormed at Anton.

Anton followed Jacques to his cabin. "Look, Captain . . ." he began to argue.

Jacques interrupted him. "Anton, if and when war comes, I will fight for the colonies. Not that I think it'll mean a damn thing in settling the slavery issue. I think Paine and Otis mean what they say, but this country, North and South, runs on slave labor. Slavery won't even be an issue.

"Yes, yes"—Jacques waved an arm at Anton's attempt to speak— "I know men like Jefferson are calling slavery a moral evil—for

71

pragmatic reasons. But ask yourself the crucial question: how many of his own slaves has Jefferson freed? When the war is over, the whites will have both independence and slavery, and there will be a whole new code to justify that." Jacques paused, then said more softly, "My concern is to keep the *Leah-Alanya* on the sea. And we can't do that with discord among the crew."

He saw dissatisfaction cross Anton's face. "Remember your own words, Anton Key. We colored still sit in the back when white folks talk to God. They make us conveniently Yankee or conveniently colored. We are only half free. And no gunpowder I ever heard of knew which half to kill."

Late one mid-December afternoon the *Leah-Alanya* sailed into Boston Harbor, the crew welcoming the sight of the beacon from the highest of the city's three hills. When the cargo was unloaded, Anton and Jacques, as was their custom, walked down Kilby Street to the Bunch of Grapes.

The tavern was crowded and tension was in the air. It was not long in resolution. Just after ten the word came. A band of patriots dressed as Indians had crept onto the ships carrying tea to the British agents . . . one ship, Rotch's *Dartmouth*. The tea now floated in Boston Harbor. Cheers rang through the crowded tavern.

"Then it will be war." Anton grinned, raising a glass of ale.

"It'll be our arse if we're seen celebrating with the Sons of Liberty," Jacques growled. "Remember, it's Rotch's cargo we're carrying. Come on, we sail on the tide."

Time now marched on the beat of history. Throughout Massachusetts, citizens applauded the acts in Boston Harbor. Patriots gave up drinking tea, and even Alanya, influenced by Hepsabeth, vowed to abandon tea drinking until the Tea Act was repealed.

Parliament responded harshly to the colonists' act of piracy. The port of Boston was closed until the price of the tea was paid. Town meetings in Massachusetts were suppressed. Important trials were moved outside New England. Parliament passed the Quartering Act, allowing British governors to requisition buildings to house British troops.

Enraged by these repressions, New Englanders grew more defiant every day. Committees of Safety were formed. Minutemen drilled in fields and village greens. Muskets, powder, and other military supplies were collected and stored quick to hand.

Revere, Prescott, Church, Hancock, and Adams were among thirty men who walked Boston's streets nightly, keeping watch on General Gage and his British troops, meeting at midnight to report on all that they had seen. The church belfry became their signal station, the lighted lantern their signal. Swift horses were ready to ride to the surrounding towns to alert the Minutemen.

In Bedford Village, most people did not want war. The Quakers were against war for religious reasons. Other residents were Tories, and still others feared that war with England would ruin their sea-based enterprises.

Jacques Clavier shared none of these convictions. Quietly he prepared for the business of war, scouting the harbors, inlets, and rivers as Nsai had taught him, locating hiding places for his sloop and interconnecting waterways through which his small ship could move without interception. He kept silent when queried by village merchants about his sympathies, but he listened carefully to the strategies set forth in the Bunch of Grapes.

Spring came late to the colony of Massachusetts, and revolt, already accomplished in the minds of many, followed soon after in their deeds. In mid-April, before the crops were planted, General Gage marched his troops toward Concord to capture rebel supplies. Revere and Dawes sounded the call. The militia gathered on the village green at Lexington. The battle was joined.

The Redcoats left eight dead in Lexington's sunny park and marched on toward Concord. There, at the bridge over a gentle stream, they met the Minutemen, white and black, who fired shots heard around the world. Routed, the Redcoats retreated to Boston chased by a growing force of patriots. The war of rebellion so long in coming had begun.

Anton's friend Lemuel Haynes, who had been one of the black Minutemen at Concord, marched with Premius Black and Epherem Blackman, two more men of color, to join Ethan Allan and his Green Mountain Boys in the capture of Fort Ticonderoga.

On May 10, the second Continental Congress was convened. George Washington, a planter from Virginia, was named commander of the army being formed to besiege the British in Boston.

Later in May, the first naval battle of the Revolution was fought in Buzzards Bay. In June, a desperate battle took place on Boston's Breed's Hill. Jacques was part of the crowd gathered to watch the advance of British soldiers. The rebels were waiting at the ready. Jacques heard the command of the rebel Colonel Prescott, "Don't fire until you see the whites of their eyes." With nails and scraps of iron as often as musket balls in their muskets, the rebels fired on the British. Twice the Redcoats fell back. Then, their muskets empty, the rebels began to retreat.

Major Pitcairn, the British commander, ordered surrender. No voice, no weapon answered. Then one man, Peter Salem, black as midnight, stood forward and blew the major through.

Peter Salem and Salem Poor, two Negroes, were among the men hailed that night in Boston as heroes of "Bunker Hill."

Proudly, Anton kept Jacques informed about other battles in which colored men performed with valor. There were more than a few when, in November, General Washington declared he did not want "any deserter from the ministerial army, nor stroller, Negro, vagabond, or person suspect of being an enemy to the liberty of America, nor any under eighteen years of age, in the Continental Army."

Woodson wept. Anton raged. And Jacques wisely refrained from repeating his predictions.

CHAPTER TEN

1776

Jacques was asleep when he heard the horses coming at full gallop. He leapt to his feet and was pulling on his breeches when he heard the knock and Woodson's voice. "Jacques, open up!"

Wondering why Moses would be on horseback and with whom at this hour, Jacques cautioned Alanya to silence and, crossing the room, slid back the bolt. He found himself face to face with Louis Flateau in the uniform of a Continental Army officer. Behind him were Moses, Anton, and two uniformed men unknown to Jacques.

"Excuse our coming at this hour, Captain Clavier, but we have urgent business." Louis's formality accentuated his words.

"Come in." Jacques moved back, and the men passed through the door.

"There is a British merchantman, the *Winslow,* lying at anchor near Tarpaulin Cove," Flateau said as Jacques bolted the door. "She's carrying muskets and other supplies for the British quartered in Boston. General Washington's men are freezing in Cambridge. There's also a shortage of guns and ammunition. I have here papers to commission your sloop as a privateer. I know the danger of sailing the rivers by dark. But help us get the supplies and, through the admiralty court at Plymouth, we'll arrange for you to keep the *Winslow* as prize."

"I don't need the *Winslow,*" Jacques said sharply, with a swift look at Anton. "I have a ship of my own."

Flateau understood the look. "I impressed Mr. Woodson and Mr. Key to this service. I looked for your ship at the wharf and, not finding it and hearing you were in port, sought out Mr. Key."

"My ship's anchored off Clark's Cove," Jacques growled. "I have no idea which harbor the British will close next."

"We are desperate, Jacques," Louis said softly. "Will you help us?"

"General Washington wants no help from colored people, Louis."

"Washington is a southern planter who can barely read and write. But he is a brave and loyal patriot." Flateau sighed. "It was a stupid

75

mistake to exclude Negroes, especially since they have fought with valor from the very beginning of the conflict."

"He will have to reverse that decision and soon." One of the men Jacques did not know was speaking. "Even now Lord John Dunmore, the British governor of Virginia, is recruiting slaves to fight against the colonists. I've heard from a most reliable source that some slaves of both Washington and Jefferson have run off and are fighting with the enemy." He extended his hand. "I'm Captain Quincy, Captain Clavier, and this is Major Ford."

Quincy studied Jacques as he shook his hand. He'd seen blacks like him before—in the fields of Delaware, in the swamps of Carolina—men proud to the point of arrogance. They might be enslaved in the minds of others but not in their own. They were men who would never be broken and whom, he knew from experience, it was dangerous to try.

"So," Jacques smiled, his teeth white in his tawny face, "Washington wants men he will not have in his army to risk their lives and ships to keep his arse from freezing?"

"Jacques," Anton pleaded.

Jacques heard his friend and shook his head mockingly. "The ways of white men." He turned back to Flateau. "I've seen the *Winslow,* and she's not alone in Buzzards Bay. There's a British man-o'-war nearby."

"Jacques," Anton said softly. "We must do whatever we can to make abolition an integral part of independence." He turned to Flateau. "Louis, you have influence with General Washington. Tell him the colored people stand staunchly on the side of liberty, but what we pay in blood must be for ourselves as well as others."

"This war will not settle the slavery issue, Anton," Jacques said quietly. "You must decide if you are prepared to die for the freedom of those who deny freedom to our race."

"Not quite so, Captain Clavier," Captain Quincy said quickly. "Though there's validity in your position. But the efforts of colored people in this campaign for liberty will not go unnoticed, and though it may take time . . ."

"How much time do you need, Captain Quincy? Another hundred fifty years?" Jacques turned back to Anton and Moses. "The job of free blacks is to become strong. Then . . ."

"No, Jacques," Moses said quietly. "Today's work cannot be postponed until tomorrow."

Jacques saw the steady certainty in Woodson's eyes. He turned so no one could read his thoughts. The risk was great, and Alanya was pregnant now. But if he refused, Louis would surely—even by theft —find another ship. And Moses and Anton would go with him. Without him their chances were small. He alone knew this business. He knew it well.

"It is risky, Jacques." It was Moses, ever loyal when loyalty was crucial. "To sail the river in the dark . . ."

"Risky! It's plain damn foolishness," Jacques said. He stared into the fire, feeling already the pulse of it in his veins. "How many men do you have, Louis?"

"The five of us and four more."

"Have any of the others sailed a sloop before?"

"Two have been seamen on whaling ships."

"I don't know about my crew." Jacques looked at Moses. "Ferguson is a Tory for sure. Miter has more sense than to sail in the dark. Alvarez and Oates . . ."

"We can count on them," Woodson said quickly. "And Captain Kuykendal is in port. He'll come."

"How many are aboard the merchantman?"

"Maybe a dozen or so." The portly Major Ford spoke for the first time. "A ship's boat brought the officers for dinner at Ethan Sharp's, and there are thirty or more of her seamen getting drunk at the Crossed Harpoons."

Jacques looked at Louis. "Get your men and have them at my ship in half an hour. Come quietly. There's no use telling the village what we're about. What time is it now?"

"Nine," Louis said quickly.

Jacques nodded. "Good. The tide will be right. And only a quarter-moon. There's a chance we'll get by with it. Make sure all your men have knives as well as guns. And make sure they know how to use them."

Flateau held out his hand. "Thank you, Jacques."

"Not yet, Louis." Jacques put his hand on Flateau's shoulder. "Not yet. And if we do succeed, tell Washington he fights with the compliments of the colored gentry."

Jacques paced the floor as Alanya made ready to stay with Hepsabeth. She clung to him as he kissed her goodbye, her arms lingering around his neck as he lifted her onto Woodson's horse. "Jacques . . ." Her voice faltered.

He touched his fingers to her lips. "Remember," he said, "we are a fighting people. We are Maroons."

Waiting now for the appointed time, Jacques studied the maps he had made, marking the shoals, sandbars, and coves. Excitement built in him. He smiled, remembering Nsai's long-ago words: "You know, Jacques Clavier, I've never known a man who so much enjoyed being a pirate."

Strapping on his knife and two pistols, Jacques took his rifle down from its place above the hearth. Louis was doing it for the army, Anton for the cause, Moses for the race. Jacques smiled again as he went out into the night. He was doing it for his friends—and because he could do it so damn well.

The moon was a silver canoe skimming on billows of clouds as the *Leah-Alanya,* her flag lowered, her name covered, slid like a phantom down the Acushnet. Her lanterns were dark. The sole light came from the quarterdeck, from the shielded, flickering candle by which Jacques Clavier read his maps.

The men, moving only when commanded, spoke in whispers, casting frequent glances at Clavier and the blackness of the water that surrounded them.

No man aboard had ever before sailed the river or bay at night. The unmarked waters were treacherous, rife with shallow drafts and shoals where a ship could run aground, even in daylight.

The *Leah-Alanya*'s fore and aft topsails were trimmed and strapped. Only the bottom sails, watched by the hawk-eyed Alvarez, were full. Jacques, not trusting the breeze, let the current pull them into the Sound. They moved northeastward, hugging Naushon's southern shore, moving through the fogbanks that drifted across the Sound from Martha's Vineyard. Woodson, on the foredeck, took soundings every sixty seconds, calling them out in a voice that barely reached the quarterdeck. "Six fathoms. We're moving in shallow draft." Then, more urgently, turning toward the quarterdeck. "Four fathoms, Captain."

Jacques looked up the slope of the poop deck toward the wheel. "Come around twenty degrees to port," he said softly.

Jacques sensed the young helmsman's apprehension as the ship swung to the maneuver. He nodded. "Hold her steady on the wind."

78

From his position by the mainmast, Louis Flateau watched Jacques with growing confidence. The captain's voice was calm, obscuring almost his concentrated strength. Slowly it dawned on Louis, who was now fully recognizing the hazards of their undertaking, that Clavier was enjoying it immensely. He was a dashing figure as he stood on his quarterdeck, his hat shoved back on his kinky-curly hair, accentuating his proud handsomeness. Here he was master, a swarthy prince in command of his domain. And as he watched Jacques, calm as the light breeze that bore them toward their destination, Louis felt he could have chanced this night with no one else.

"We're coming on the bay now. Give me a sounding, Mr. Woodson." Jacques looked toward the foredeck.

"Holding at four fathoms, sir."

"Bring her around to starboard ten degrees. We're heading for Sconticut Neck." Jacques saw Flateau watching him and continued his whispered orders. "Make sure your men are ready below, Mr. Flateau. Remind them to make no sound when they come on deck. A pin drop carries on the water at night. And tell Mr. Kuykendal I want to see him immediately."

Jacques looked through the spyglass toward their destination. He could see nothing in the darkness. He heard Woodson's repeated soundings. The depth was still four fathoms, but they were moving into more dangerous waters.

"You sent for me?" It was Kuykendal.

"Yes, Mr. Kuykendal." Jacques handed him the glass. "Take a look and tell me if you can see the *Winslow*."

Kuykendal held the glass against one weather-beaten cheek. "Aye," he breathed. "I see her." He peered through the glass a moment more. "It's the merchant ship. There're two lanterns, for'ard on the bowsprit and on the rigging aft. She's standing in the cove."

"Can you see the man-o'-war?"

Kuykendal lifted the glass again. "There is another ship about an eighth mile beyond, outside the cove. Deeper waters there. I don't make her out clearly, but she's a bigger ship. Could be the man-o'-war."

"Three fathoms." Woodson's voice was anxious.

Jacques checked his map and compass. "We're coming on Egg Island."

"Shoals all about it," Kuykendal said in awe.

Jacques turned toward the helmsman. "Slap her down hard thirty degrees to starboard. Mr. Kuykendal, take the wheel. We'll have to come about."

Kuykendal sprang toward the helmsman's shed as Woodson's voice reached the quarterdeck. "Three fathoms . . . two fathoms."

"Mr. Alvarez." Jacques peered in the darkness toward the man poised below the quarterdeck. "You and Mr. Watson handle the mainmast sails. Put Mr. Key and Mr. Talbert to the jibs fast."

"One fathom, Captain." Woodson's voice was drained.

Jacques heard someone whisper, "We're going to run aground."

Fighting the panic now surging in his gut, Jacques breathed deeply to control his voice. "Keep sounding, Mr. Woodson. Mr. Kuykendal, bring her around on the starboard tack. Mr. Alvarez, we're coming about. Keep a fast hand on those sails."

Ship and sail shuddered as the men worked feverishly in the dark, following the orders from the quarterdeck. Then Woodson called, "Five fathoms. We're through the shoals."

"Mr. Oates," Jacques called softly, "relieve Mr. Kuykendal, I need him for the glass."

Kuykendal, whose prayers had been directed to every god of sky and sea, rubbed his whiskers as he approached Jacques with deference. "You want me to take another look, sir?" he asked.

"Yes. I want to anchor a quarter mile off the lee side of the *Winslow*. Will we be out of sight of both the English ships?"

Kuykendal squinted through the spyglass and nodded. "We're about a half mile away now. Keep her steady on this course." He looked at Jacques. "I'm to go in your dory?"

Jacques nodded. Kuykendal was pleased. "Good. We'll teach John Bull a thing or two."

The dories slid soundlessly through the night-blackened waters toward the lights of the *Winslow*. The men were tense, awaiting what would be, for most, their first confrontation with the British. Jacques, the only man seasoned in these events, felt the tentacles of fear squeezing his belly. Surprise was their only ally.

They passed under the bow of the *Winslow*. Jacques stood up and grabbed the anchor chain. Halfway to the deck he felt Kuykendal starting up behind him. He paused, hands and feet clasping their slippery hold. Then, satisfied they had not been heard, he moved up and swung over the rail. In less than two minutes, six rebels were crouching on the deck.

Two jack-tars were keeping watch on the forward deck. Jacques sent Anton aft to see if a watch was posted there. The waist and stern were deserted. Their pistols drawn, Jacques and Anton crawled toward the two seamen on the anchor watch. Deep in conversation, they had no thoughts of danger and met unconsciousness without a sound.

Leaving Watson to tie them and Kuykendal to keep a sharp eye on the man-o'-war, Jacques led the others below. The forecastle door was ajar. Inside, hammocks swayed with fifteen soundly sleeping men. Anton and Louis kept watch while Jacques and Oates made their way amidship to the officers' quarters.

The first mate was reading, the tassels of his sleeping cap bobbing over his book while his right hand scratched with satisfaction in the rear opening of his long johns. He looked up and blinked with amazement into the muzzle of Oates's musket. "Not a word and no one will get kilt," Oates said.

Jacques found the coxswain asleep. He put his pistol to his temple and woke him. "Do as you're told and you'll live to tell of it."

The rest of the cabins were empty and Jacques and Oates moved the mate and coxswain at gunpoint into the ill-lit, foul-smelling forecastle, where the crew now glared sullenly from their hammocks. Leaving Anton and Louis on guard, Jacques and Oates went back on deck. Moses's men were now moving quickly to the hold, where the provisions were stored. They unloaded two of their dories and dispatched them to the *Leah* with Kuykendal and Oates in charge.

The men worked swiftly and silently. No movement was reported on the man-o'-war as the *Winslow*'s dories were lowered and loaded. It was going well. Jacques was pleased.

"Captain Clavier," Major Ford asked, "about the prisoners."

"We'll leave them, Major."

"We need them for exchange for our men."

"It's too risky. I have no irons on the *Leah-Alanya,* and there are more of them than us. We'll leave them locked in the fo'c'sle. You'll get your provisions. Be satisfied with that."

"Of course, I can't insist, but . . ." The major's cheeks ballooned in flabby petulance.

"No, Major," Jacques said curtly. "You cannot insist."

Heading toward the companionway, Jacques heard a hissing sound. He started down the stairway on the run, then heard a scream. "The powder! The powder's going!" In the faltering light, Jacques saw Captain Quincy running from the hold.

Before Jacques could respond an explosion rocked the ship. Jacques skidded to the bottom of the stairs. Crawling amid tumbling debris and fast-oozing water toward the forecastle, he heard a scream from the men inside.

Louis and Anton stood braced against the door, muskets pointed at their prisoners who scrambled desperately closer, howling in fear.

"In the name of God let us out," the mate screeched. "This ship's going down!"

"Move, you black son of a bitch," a crewman cursed. His knife flashed as he leapt for Anton. Jacques saw the flash of Louis's musket as his own finger touched his trigger. The jack-tar's brains splattered against a swaying hammock.

The British sailors moved back, huddled together like animals. "We'll get you out," Jacques said quickly. "Two by two." He heard the noise behind him and wheeled, his finger ready again on the trigger of his pistol.

"The pump's bust, Cap'n." Tim Watson's soot-stained face was black as Woodson's. "The ship's sinking fast."

"We'll get these men on deck. Stand by to tie their hands as they come up. Have Mr. Woodson dump everything from the last dory and lower another one. Put these men in, face down. Kill them if they make a mistake. Is Captain Quincy on deck?"

"Cap'n Quincy's dead, sir."

The mainmast was a pillar of fire, the catheads aflame. In the spitting, hissing racket, the ship, listing to starboard, sucked in the bay. "Captain Clavier." Major Ford blocked Jacques at the hatchway. "They're dumping the supplies."

"We need room for those seamen."

"We must have those supplies. Those blankets . . ."

"We must take those men!"

The major pulled himself into the posture of command. "Captain . . ."

"Major, this is my command."

The men on deck worked quickly. Wrist-bound, the British were lowered from the white heat of the ship. The first dory was away and the second almost loaded when they heard the shout from the stern. "The man-o'-war has put out boats."

"This ship'll be gone long 'fore they get here." Watson looked at Jacques.

"How many prisoners still below?" Jacques shouted.

"Four, sir," Anton called.

"Get them on deck, fast." Jacques turned to Moses, who had moved beside him. "Go on, Moses. Get in that dory." Then he saw Louis, still beside the mainmast. "Hurry, Louis, get down."

The ship was settling beneath their feet as the last men scuttled down into the dories. Louis, beside Jacques, clung with one hand to the railing to keep from sliding into the sea.

"We can't take another man," Alvarez yelled from the dory. "I'll dump a couple of these jack-tars into the bay."

"No," Jacques shouted. "Pull away."

"What about you and Louis?" Anton, the last man down, tried to stand, almost capsizing the crowded dory.

"We'll make it. Pull away!"

"Jacques, don't be no fool!"

Jacques heard the terror in Woodson's voice. "Pull away, damn it," he shouted. "This damn ship is going down."

The dory moved into the darkness. Jacques turned to Louis. "We'll have to take our chances in the bay."

"You go first, I'll follow."

Jacques's leg was over the rail before he realized Louis had not moved. "Come on, man, for the love of God."

The spray broke on Louis's symbols of command as he pulled an intricately inlaid flintlock pistol and pointed it at his head. "Go on, Jacques, for God's sake. I can't make it."

Stumbling up the tilting deck, Jacques seized Louis's arm. "Get off this goddamn ship. I'll help you in the water."

Louis's eyes were wide with fright and pain. "I can't. My arm's broken."

"Come on!" Jacques shoved him to the rail. Together they swung down into the blackness.

They were a safe distance now from the downdraft of the sinking *Winslow,* but the water was fiercely cold. Louis was a dead weight and Jacques knew they could not make it to the *Leah-Alanya.* For an instant he thought of letting him go. Then he heard him moan, and, damning him, tightened his hold, kicking ever more feebly in the biting blackness.

He no longer felt his arms or legs, and a soft, fluffy darkness pillowed his mind. His stroke was broken, and as he floundered his hand caught on his medallion. Oh, Yemangi . . ." he thought, but he had no strength for prayer. His name seemed to come from a high, distant place, and he closed his eyes. Then strong arms lifted him from the bay.

He was in his billet when he awoke, rum dripping down his chin from the cup Moses forced to his lips. "Am I drowned or drunk?" he choked as relief flooded Woodson's eyes.

"Nothing at all wrong with you 'cept you got a little exercise and now you want to sleep all day."

"What about Louis?"

"Kuykendal fished him out, too. His arm's broke bad, but he's alive." Moses stretched his legs in the crowded quarters. "How Kuykendal found you I don't know. He started back when he heard the explosion and just kept circling. Said he knew you were alive."

"We're under way?" Jacques twisted in the blanket to get up.

"Over two hours. We're nigh on the Atlantic now."

"Oh God, I hope the British don't . . ."

"No reason why they should." Moses grinned as he stood up. "Your friend Anton stole the *Winslow*'s flag. We're sailing under the Union Jack."

CHAPTER ELEVEN

1778

Four years, Alanya thought, as she paused in her doorway, looking out toward Bedford Village. Four times she had watched, as she did now, summer wither and die. She stood for a minute, shading her eyes for a glimpse of her homebound Jacques, then a soft cry called her inside.

At the sight of her baby, Alanya smiled, some of her old gaiety brightening her eyes. She bent over the cradle, reaching into the pocket of her long white apron for a lump of sugar to sweeten the pain of her teething infant. "You are a lucky one, you know, to have a sea captain for a father and sugar to suck, even in times like these."

She heard the whistle of the kettle and turned to pull it from the fire. "Now hush, my little Jacques, and think how good life is."

With Jacques home life was good. But tomorrow he would leave again for France. Alanya sighed as she moved quickly to stir up the fire. How she hated being left alone. And life on the sea was dangerous. The *Leah-Alanya* carried letters of marque and reprisal, but her duties were as a merchant ship. She sailed—often in ballast—to Nantes, a headquarters of patriot activity abroad. There she took on cargo: food, clothing, and weapons desperately needed by the patriots. Though Jacques never spoke of it, Alanya had heard the tales of narrow escapes from British ships and pirates.

But still, she thought, carrying cargo was not so dangerous as privateering, a scheme Jacques had enthusiastically entertained until Moses had threatened to dissolve their partnership. Moses was right in matters such as these. He did, as he often said, know white folks. "There's some things they are not going to let colored do, no matter how much skill we got. They'd swear we were pirates, not privateers," Moses had declared.

But Jacques was interested in money, and the money was in privateering. Alanya had been amazed to learn the men who had gone into it: physicians, solicitors, merchants, even ministers of the Gospel. Men left the navy to join the crews of the privateers that roamed the Atlantic and Caribbean, searching and seizing enemy ships for the rewards granted through the admiralty courts.

Alanya had even seen impecunious seamen selling shares of their prize money before their cruise began. The name of the captain and the ship determined the value of these pre-sold shares, and the name of John Paul Jones raised speculators' bids highest of all. Jones's ship, the *Alfred,* was frequently seen in Buzzards Bay. He himself sometimes came occasionally to Bedford Village. He was a hero to the patriots, despite reports that his adventures had gained him three thousand pounds in eighteen months and that the British were furious with the residents of Bedford for tolerating his presence there.

How despondent Jacques had become when he heard of the money Jones was making! Poor Jacques. Alanya smiled sadly. Being colored was hard on a man with his talents and ideas. Alanya knew that even the end of the war—for which she so fervently prayed— would not keep her husband near. When in Bedford, he was seldom home now, but spent his time overseeing the building of his new ship, a schooner twice the size of the *Leah-Alanya.* Jacques had invested every pound in her. When the new ship was done, he would make enough money to begin to build their new home on the land behind the Keys' homestead.

Charity Key. Alanya grimaced. She was not certain she wanted to live so near Charity. Charity had put on such airs since she'd married Anton Key. She had insisted that poor Anton leave Jacques's crew after the affair on the *Winslow,* saying she was afraid of the sea. Now, after serving two years in the army which had suddenly admitted black soldiers, Anton had a tailoring shop, the trade for which he had apprenticed in Boston.

Not, Alanya thought, dipping water from the barrel and pouring it into the kettle, that tailoring had been a bad choice. His skill and wit had brought Anton quick success. And now he was thinking, "of all things," as Moses said, of opening a Turkish bath.

"Poor Anton, is it?" Jacques had said once. "Poor Anton is getting very rich."

Alanya's lips tightened as she placed the kettle on the swinging crane over the fire. Charity always made her feel so inadequate, especially in front of Jacques. Yesterday she had asked, "Will you come for tea at three on Thursday, Alanya? And bring your needlepoint." Charity knew full well she could not do needlepoint. Alanya frowned at the clock in the corner that Jacques had bought last year. The ticking sound was company, and she liked watching the stick swinging in the glass case, but all those markings . . . ? She must do better. Jacques's face had darkened like a thundercloud when he'd discovered that despite all of Peter Woodson's efforts she could not yet read a word.

Alanya sighed as she picked up her darning needle and reached for one of Jacques's socks. If only they could go back. Back to the good life at home. There she knew the ways, knew how to sweeten life and love.

But they would never go home. Jacques had said so. His eyes forbade her even to mention it again. "You are here, Alanya. The white man has seen to that. The bond with the tribe is broken. We are not even certain where they are. That is why the others of our tribe settled in Boston, as Nsai said, 'A fool makes the worst of the best of things. The wise man makes the best of the worst of things.'"

So then, it would all be his way and she would but obey. He would build the new ship, the new house. And their son would be like him —always thinking of getting more and more. That was how things became if you lived too long around the whites.

Alanya closed her eyes. She yearned to know the life inside Jacques's head. But no one knew. Not even Moses. Had she not overheard him say to Anton, "I'd give a year's profit to know what's really in Jacques's mind. The more you try to search him out, the more he retreats to the center of himself. You've seen the way his eyes seem like to shut you out and turn deep into the fastness of himself."

"Or else he gives you that crazy crooked grin," Anton had responded with a shrug. "Then what's a man to do?"

"Now you take that business with the Masons that the Reverend Prince Hall is trying to form up in Boston," Moses had continued. "That would be the first all-colored organization in this country." Woodson's face had twisted in a scowl. "We've both heard Hall ask Jacques a dozen times to join. But does he—with all his talk of building Negro strength? Gives money, yes, but not himself."

"Jacques will never join another man's organization," Anton had said softly. "He has his own. It's called Jacques Clavier."

Her baby whimpered in his cradle, and Alanya reached to comfort him, touching her dark fingers to the paleness of his face. How the whites stared when she carried him through the village. That frightened her most of all, although she too had been astonished when her child was born with light skin and a mop of reddish hair. But Jacques had only laughed. "Well, Philippe, you old bastard," he'd said. "I've resurrected you from the dead."

With the darned sock in her lap, Alanya's hands fell idle. She did not want to move to the village, not even for the company of the Woodsons and the Keys. For though she knew she could never tell Jacques, she was terrified of whites with their uncolored skin, monkey backsides, hair, and mouths. The first whites she had ever seen had been Georges and his sons, creeping through the bushes, and she had screamed in terror. Experience had proved her first reaction right. She had learned well their talent to inflict misery.

"What? Are you dreaming of me again?"

She looked up to see Jacques smiling from the doorway. "How did you know?" she asked as she stood, feeling the now familiar surge of happiness.

"I didn't. I was hoping."

"And for what else were you hoping?" She smiled, her dark eyes sparkling.

He winked and crossed the room to bend over his sleeping son. "A lazy sort, he is. He should be helping set the masts or lending a hand with the caulking. What does he intend, to sleep his life away?"

"And when he cries you ask does he never sleep. You are never satisfied, Jacques Clavier."

"Then help me to that end," he said, seizing her by the waist. "It will be a long voyage before I see your face again."

" 'Tis not my face that interests you, you charlatan."

"At this moment you are right. The face is a vision to remember when one has nothing there to touch. The child is asleep. The time is short, so why do we delay?"

"That question wants no answer," she laughed, snuggling into his arms.

He smiled and kissed the top of her head. "Oh, Alanya, I love you."

They heard the first call of the birds. It was time to go. Jacques got up quietly, and she called his name softly in the dark. There were just minutes left to them and he spent them on his litany of advice. Then he kissed her and his son goodbye and headed toward the village.

As soon as Jacques had gone, Alanya dressed quickly, pulling on her blue cloak, and wrapped her baby securely in his blanket. She would go, as usual, to the cove to watch his ship move downriver to the sea. Soon it would be dawn, and she knew the tide was right. He would waste no time getting under way.

The dark woods were full of shadows and somehow the noises seemed different from before. But in her haste to wave goodbye Alanya pushed anxiety aside. She was almost to the cove when she heard the footsteps close behind. Frightened, she turned in the semi-darkness and saw a white face moving toward her through the trees.

A man's voice called, "Halt, who goes there?" as she whirled, leaping like a frightened deer for the cover of the trees. For an instant Alanya felt blinding, exploding pain and then, her baby at her breast, fell soundlessly to the ground.

When the *Leah-Alanya* reached Clark's Cove, Jacques peered over the rail for a last look at his wife and son. He saw no one and smiled. She had taken his advice and gone directly to the Woodsons'. Leaving Oates in charge of the quarterdeck, he went below.

Almost half an hour downriver Oates saw smoke spiraling above the treetops from the direction of the village. "Mr. Alvarez," he yelled, "fetch the captain!"

From the stern the men stared in confused disbelief at the widening black cloud. The words "The British!" echoed down the deck.

"Shall we try to put about?" a pale-faced Oates asked Jacques as he came on deck. "I haven't seen a British ship, but . . ."

"The tide's too strong. It'll take too long," Jacques replied, fighting his own panic. "Put down the dories. Load the men with families. Have them take muskets, powder, knives, anything they can find. The rest will stay with the ship until they receive word from me."

Within minutes, four dories raced through the water. Men cursed and wept aloud as they saw the flames leap in the blue sky. Again, Jacques looked for Alanya as they passed Clark's Cove. Woodson's face was rigid. By the bend in the river they could smell the village burning. "My God," Oates shrieked. "Look, the wharf's burning."

"Jesus help us," a man moaned as they saw the flaming ships. Clutching his oars, Jacques watched in horror as his own unfinished ship split apart, spitting fiery sparks onto the river water.

The wooden buildings of Water Street were in flames. Woodson was by Jacques's side as they quickly made the dory fast and ran stumbling up the hill. In the chaos they were separated, and Jacques ran on alone, dodging the tumbling, scorching debris, screaming Alanya's name, scanning grimy, tortured faces for someone he knew.

An old man dragged a pail of water toward a burning house. Jacques grabbed his arm. "Where are the others?"

"In the woods. The fields. Dead." The old man's arm shook, spilling the water. "Many are dead."

Jacques found the Woodson house in ashes. An old woman, their neighbor, swept her porch, laughing hysterically. "I asked them not to burn me and they didn't."

"Get out of there," Jacques shouted. "Fire will catch from the others."

"No, it won't." She smiled. "God will save me."

He ran up the hill, into the woods, still calling her name. He saw an old man in a rocking chair, rocking and smiling toothlessly as he watched a woman counting and recounting her nine children.

"Alanya," Jacques screamed. "In the name of God, answer me!"

Jacques's eyes were wild, his face streaked with soot and tears, when Peter Woodson found him. Grabbing Peter's arm, he begged, "Have you seen Alanya?"

"No, Uncle Jacques. We got out as the Redcoats came up Water Street. She wasn't with us."

Then she had not yet reached the village. Turning, Jacques ran back toward his house with Peter behind.

He found the fire still burning in the fireplace, Alanya's cooking pots swinging on the crane. So she had not left the house to go to the village.

Slowly Jacques and Peter traced Alanya's path to the cove. The woods were silent. The wind, the waves, even the birds and squirrels were hushed. Jacques saw the dark blue of her cloak and her hand, outstretched as if to break her fall. The musket ball had passed through both her and the child. Peter moved silently away as Jacques knelt beside them.

It was growing dark when Moses found Jacques, still holding his dead wife and child. "I have brought a wagon for them, Jacques."

Then Moses knelt and took the sobbing man in his arms.

CHAPTER TWELVE

1782

For four years Jacques Clavier did not set foot in Bedford Village. He sailed up and down the coast and back and forth to France, bringing supplies, dodging the British when he could, turning and fighting only when necessary.

He lingered in no port and, when anchored at a Bedford wharf, stayed only long enough to load or unload cargo. Steadfastly he refused all attempts to persuade him to join in any more excursions against the British. For despite Louis's loud and public protests, the efforts of black men had been omitted in the reports which had circulated after the events aboard the *Winslow* and to Jacques's disgust the whole business was known as "the Flateau affair."

Moses, who had sailed with Jacques the year after Alanya's death, now rarely made a voyage. Instead, he carried on their business in the town. He came to the wharf each time the *Leah-Alanya* docked, often bringing Hepsabeth and the children. Anton Key also came, pleading passionately for Jacques to join them at least for a meal. But no one, not even little Andy Woodson, for whom Jacques had a special fondness, could persuade Jacques to come ashore.

Indeed he seemed to hear little of their news, hearkening only to Moses's reports of their business. "He's remote and solitary," Moses said, "plunging back and forth across the seas with no home port in mind."

"Money and that ship, that's all he thinks of now," Hepsabeth answered sorrowfully. "Sometimes I fear he has left us forever."

"He'll be back," Moses replied. "But not until he finds a reason."

Months and then years passed. Jacques offered no substance to Moses's prediction. In the spring of the fourth year, Peter Woodson joined the crew of the *Leah-Alanya*. Slowly Jacques began to know again the anxious joy of caring.

The *Leah-Alanya* ran the British barricade that spring and put into Charleston for a cargo of rice. Peter helped with the loading. Then, while waiting for the tide, Peter left the ship, with first mate, Reuben

Oates, giving him permission to see the city. When an hour had passed, Oates became alarmed and went below to inform the captain.

Charleston, the wealthiest city in the South, was teeming with the commotion of commerce. Oates followed a stone-faced Jacques down Cumberland Street past the brick-and-oyster-shell-cemented Powder Magazine as they searched places they thought might appeal to young Woodson.

Oates's heart raced as he kept pace with Jacques's quick steps down the tree-shaded brick and cobblestone streets. In the nine years Reuben Oates had sailed with Jacques Clavier his respect had grown for this Negro who had been his captain. Oates clenched his teeth as he reprimanded himself again and again for forgetting that the land-made laws of man were not the same as God's who ruled the seas.

They passed the Exchange Building, the shops and open-air markets, the wrought-iron gateways to elegant homes, then paused for a new direction before St. Michael's Church. Finally, on Chalmers Street, they came to the big slave market. "Let's double back the way we came," Jacques began. "Perhaps he . . ."

Oates's freckled hand touched Jacques's arm. "There he is."

"Why the hell would he come here?" Jacques swore, moving quickly through the throng that attended the sale of human beings.

"Wait," Peter whispered as Jacques yanked his arm. "I want to see it. I want to remember it forever."

Jacques turned his back to the block. The sight revolted him. But the faces in the crowd were no better. Which, he wondered, were the degraded—those who stood nearly naked on the block or those who lurked below? "The lions and the jackals," he muttered to Peter.

Among the slaves in dock was a youth about eighteen, just Peter's age. Jacques saw the auctioneer roughly inspect his arms, his legs, his teeth, his groin, calling out the soundness of each. Impassively the youth looked out beyond the crowd.

"Why?" Peter asked, staring in horrified awe at the slave block. "Why does he stand there and I stand here?"

"Because your grandpa killed the bastard and hauled arse outta there," Jacques said sharply. "For the reasons that the English aren't still slaves to the Romans. Fate is capricious, and reason's just her willful toy."

"And fate decides who is slave and who is free?"

Jacques looked at Peter, then put his arm around his friend's son's

92

shoulder. "Nsai, a man I knew when I was your age, told me, 'Freedom is only a word until you have what you need to maintain it.'"

"And what is that, Uncle Jacques?"

"Money," Jacques replied. "Money."

As they spoke, they heard the rising murmurs of the crowd. Jacques turned and saw her—standing alone, covered only from her waist to her thighs. She was black as the velvet-petaled gloxinia and she was beautiful. A creature made for the gods to love. Jacques blinked as he stared at her. Was his mind playing tricks? Images from years long gone floated past his eyes! Proud and defiant . . . we shall now go to my people. Skin soft as the fibers of the silk cotton trees that were the home of Mother Earth . . .

"See here this Ibo girl, just seventeen years of age, smart, quick . . ." The auctioneer began his litany of praise of the merchandise he sold. The first bid was two hundred pounds.

"Two hundred twenty pounds." The bidder, near Jacques, raised his cane. His eyes drooped as he drawled with loose-lipped lasciviousness.

Jacques's eyes grew fierce. He was stirred as he hadn't been in years. Whatever, they must not have her. Not his mother, and Alanya, and . . . He seized Oates's arm. "Buy her," he ordered. "I don't care about the cost."

Reuben Oates and Peter Woodson stared at Jacques in amazement. Jacques met Oates's gaze directly. "Make the arrangements and pick up the money at the ship. I'll be there."

Oates nodded without speaking and raised his arm to bid. "Come, Peter," Jacques said, and left the marketplace.

Jacques stood in his cabin watching the sand drip down in the hourglass. In furious agony he admitted to himself that even with his money, he had dared not bid for her himself.

"Captain!" Oates knocked.

"Come in." Jacques moved toward the door as it opened. He caught his breath as she came into his cabin. She was dressed in yellow and smelled of lavender. Oates met Jacques's eyes. "It is better this way," he said, and closed the door.

Jacques stared at the young woman. She was even more lovely in the lantern light. She blushed, her question coming softly, "You masta me?"

93

How quickly those words were taught.

"I am your friend," he answered.

"Fren?"

He nodded. "Friend."

She looked about the cabin. "You masta ship?"

"I am master of this ship. I and my men are free."

A look of wonder crossed her face. "I free, fren?"

He smiled. "You are free."

Her hand flew to her cheeks and her eyes danced. "Oh, fren," she whispered.

He watched her for a moment, then asked softly, "What is your name?"

"Noni."

"Noni? What does it mean?"

Her eyes met his. "Gift of God."

CHAPTER THIRTEEN

1787

"Here ya are, Mrs. Clavier." The shopkeeper bit the string and handed the paper-wrapped package to Noni across the cluttered counter. "One copy of *Pilgrim's Progress,* one of *Milk for Babes,* two of *Robinson Crusoe* and *Gulliver's Travels,* and two histories of *Little Goody Two-shoes.* Shall I put 'em to yer husband's account?"

"Please," Noni answered with a smile. "And I'll take eight of those hard candies." Jacques wouldn't mind this small extravagance, she thought, as the shopkeeper's hand reached into the candy jar. He wouldn't mind at all. This was her last day with the children. It was, as Hepsabeth insisted, already too apparent that she was soon to have a child of her own.

Outside in the sultry air Noni's steps were quick and light as she headed down the dust-blown road toward the churchyard. She could see the children playing by the fence. How she would miss them. And who would teach them while she was gone?

Shifting the books, Noni slowed her steps, enjoying the sudden sharp breeze on her face. There was but a tinge of salt air, the salt air she knew so well.

The first three years of her marriage, in fact, had been spent at sea, sailing everywhere with Jacques. They had made trips to Boston, New York, Nova Scotia, and even two harsh winter voyages to Europe.

She remembered sitting in his cabin month after month, listening to the sound of his footsteps on the deck and the call of his command. And as she waited, she had worked, knowing he would ask, "Ah, Noni, have you been busy? Now tell me what you've learned."

And she would show him, to his pride, how her scratchings had become the alphabet, how well she understood his patient pointing finger: "The . . . man . . . can . . . run."

They had stayed with the Woodsons during their rare times in Bedford Village. It was there that Noni had overheard Jacques confess his anxiety to Hepsabeth and heard that good woman's sharp reply. "How can she come to bed with child? First she must have a bed . . . in her own home. There's no need for me to say you're al-

95

ways welcome here. But, Jacques, the sea is no place for a woman. Stay here awhile. Build a new house. Build the new ships you've been talking of so long. Give Noni a home and she will give you a child."

It had been past midnight when Jacques had come to her that night. She had called his name, and he sat beside her in the lamplight. "I've been thinking," he had said softly. "Peter is ready to captain my ship. It's time for us to return to the land and build."

The next day he had bought the land in Bedford Village and brought the stone to it. She had stood beside him as he knelt and carved on it: "Fr. my 1st house, pu'cd from J. Rotch by me Oct. '73; ds'td by British Oct. '78; set here by my hand May 14, 1784. J. Clavier."

He had taken her hand when the cornerstone was in place. "No matter where I sail, Noni, whether I chart my course by the North Star or the Southern Cross, I will know that you and my children are here and it is here that the winds of my soul will blow." Then, hand over hand, they had taken the shovel and begun to turn the earth.

The eager calls of the children interrupted Noni's reminiscence. She felt a moment of sadness as she stepped through the gate, looking down into the small, dark faces of the American-born children of Ibos and Dahomeans, of Fanins and Benis, of Mandingoes and Boni, of Senegalese and Yorubas, of Ashanti and . . . "Come," she said softly. "Sit by me under the tree and I will share with you a new thing I have learned."

The pain seized her suddenly, violently, as she sat among the children. Her dark, slender fingers clenched into fists, and her oval eyes dropped to the oblong protrusion of her stomach. It was time.

When the first pain subsided, Noni did not move. She closed her eyes and carefully thanked the Gods—both of them: speaking first through the spirits to him no mortal dared address, Chineke, the great god of her father's fathers, and then giving thanks to the Father of the new Lord, Jesus Christ—that this *ngozi*, this blessing, had come at last.

"Miz Clavier?" The child's voice was close and cautious. "Miz Clavier, is you all right?"

Noni saw fright and awe in the child's face.

"Yes." She tried to smile. "I'm all right. See, I've brought you a

96

gift. As she opened the package and handed each child a book and a piece of candy, Noni felt a quickening pain in her back. "Carl." She turned to the oldest. "Go quickly for Reverend Thomas. Ask him to hurry here with the wagon. The rest of you must go home now. I'll sit here a spell."

Carl sped away and, as the other children moved with lingering glances toward the gate, Noni leaned her head against the tree and closed her eyes. She did not fear childbirth, or death. These were ordained by the Power, and the Power could be called to dwell in her. The Power was beneficent and the Will, even when contrary to wish, had reason. The Power felt, heard, saw, knew, and moved those of the faith surely, though sometimes slowly, along the road to victory.

The pain came again and passed. Noni's mind wandered back to long-ago moments: completing the foo-foo for the evening meal in the home of her father, Omeluiwe, the ironworker, walking out from the shade of the mangrove trees to swim a cooling moment in the Niger River, seeing the men with white faces approaching by canoe. Turning to swim with strong strokes for the shore . . . her feet touching the sand . . . smelling the suppers cooking in the homes of Aboh . . . And then, the ropes, the chains, the foul and stinking ship, the sailors' ugly faces with open sores and toothless mouths.

She remembered surviving that man-made hell, far worse than any devil could contrive. Chineke, the great god, speaking through her *chi,* whispering in her ear to wait when two dark mothers with their babes in arms leapt from hell into the mouths of sharks.

Doubting. Yes, then she had doubted the Power, lying sideways on the rack of that rolling ship, no room to turn, no air to breathe . . . fearing . . . hoping . . . any moment the sagging rack above would drop its packed bodies to smother out her life.

She had doubted, too, in that rank slave pen in Charleston, hearing there that in a land called Cuba one thousand of her Ibo kinsmen had taken the route of death back home. "A thousand bodies," the old man in the pen beside her had whispered, "swaying above the rich green earth." And Noni had wondered if Chineke of the Aboh and Olodumare of the Ekoi had powers in this awful land, or were they now replaced with one called Jesus Christ?

A small smile touched Noni's lips as she remembered the cabin of another ship: the *Leah-Alanya* and its fierce captain, so beautiful, she had feared he was yet another god. How she loved him, her *dim,* her roaming, restless, ambitious husband. Oh, the ideas that sprouted from his mind. A fleet of whale ships he would own, and sire *umu*, sons, for the quarterdecks of them all. How rich, how strong, the dreams of Jacques Clavier.

Dozing, Noni heard the wagon approaching, saw the ancient, dusky Reverend Thomas whipping his plow horses to haste. Noni stood, and the reverend's leathery, strong arm helped her onto the prickling hay.

In her kitchen, Hepsabeth Woodson pulled a gingerbread from her oven. She nodded approvingly as the center sprang back to her touch, then reached for her shawl. Noni Clavier was heavy on her mind. Miss Jane, the midwife, had warned her time was soon.

At her gate Hepsabeth hesitated as she saw Reverend Thomas's wagon rumbling up the street. "Miz Woodson," the reverend waved his arm. "Miz Woodson, wait."

Instinct sent Hepsabeth running the half block to the cooperage Moses had opened a year before. "Andy," she called as her son appeared in the doorway. "Andy, hurry for Miss Jane." Panting from exertion and excitement, Hepsabeth ran back to the wagon and with Reverend Thomas helped Noni inside.

Miss Jane, a withered black lady of remarkable reputation, arrived full of self-importance and skill. Hepsabeth sprang to do her bidding. From the guest room she could hear Noni's sharp cries coming quickly. Then as Jacques burst through the door, they heard the child's first cry.

"What's taking so long?" Jacques growled at Hepsabeth as he approached and then retreated from the bedroom door.

"Everything is fine." Hepsabeth smiled. "Everything is fine."

Miss Jane opened the bedroom door in the posture of pronouncement. "It's a girl," she said.

Cautiously, Jacques tiptoed into the room. "A girl," Noni whispered as Jacques bent and kissed her forehead. Her eyes followed him as he lifted the baby beside her in his arms. Then, for the first time, Noni heard her husband laugh. "Jacqueline," he said, smiling into the steady newborn eyes. "Jacqueline Clavier."

CHAPTER FOURTEEN

1789

Moses Woodson stood by his sea bag as the sloop slid to the Bedford wharf. With a start he recognized the dark, high-cheekboned young man waving from the dock. My God, he thought, I've been gone barely five months and Andy's grown another foot. And not but seventeen. Another year and he'll be bigger'n both me and 'Zekiel put together.

Moses bent to lift his sea bag, but the quick pain in his back warned him not to try. Confound, he thought, I can't be that old yet. But the pain had been with him all summer. He'd been surprised how long it had taken him to repair his father's house.

"Whatever took you so long, Dad?" Andy bounded up the gangplank. "Mother's been expecting you more than a month." Andy wrapped an arm, solid as a mainmast, around his father, then swung the sea bag easily to his shoulder. "Look over there—Uncle Jacques's new ship." Andy followed his father down the gangplank. "And wait 'till you see his house . . ."

"It's finished, then?"

"And not a finer home in Bedford Village. We're eating there tonight. In the dinin' room."

Moses suppressed a groan. He should have known Jacques would overdo it. He'd told him a hundred times that white folks, even the best of them, hated to see a nigger really get ahead. That sloop and those two brigs was enough to swing their eyeballs. Moses shook his head. He'd have a hell of a time getting commissions now. So what, he'd warned Jacques, if he was the best. White folks were known to settle for second best when the first best was black.

"And then"—Andy, oblivious of his father's inattention, continued his enthusiastic report on Jacques's house—"after the carpenters were done, he and Uncle Anton and I built this secret room . . ."

"Secret room!" Moses halted in mid-step, staring at his son.

"Under the staircase, where Noni—or anyone—can hide if anything should happen . . ."

"What's to happen?" Moses sighed in resignation, then as they approached the open door of Loudon's Tavern, his footsteps quick-

99

ened. "Come in a minute, Andy, and let me have a cup. Despite his teak chests and mahogany whatnots, I'll bet Jacques Clavier won't have a spot of rum."

Andy took a seat by the tavern's door and watched his father moving slowly toward the back of the room. He frowned, puckering his lower lip between his forefinger and thumb. Maybe the old man wasn't well. Andy's frown deepened. Maybe he would have to stay on at the cooperage. Damn, his fist struck the table. He hated this stupid village and Uncle Jacques had promised him a trip to sea.

Looking through the open tavern door, Andy saw Anton Key crossing the dusty street. His powdered wig was a walking advertisement of one of his enterprises as he headed, walking stick in hand, to another, his Turkish bath. The colored folks over in Chepachet called the three of them—Anton, Moses, and Jacques— "the silk-stocking niggers." Anton was "the darky dandy," his father "Clavier's emissary to the white folks, 'cause ol' Jacques's too damn arrogant to sweeten white folks' cup of tea." But, Andy noted, they didn't talk about "ol' Jacques" too much. Not even when he'd started wearing those frilled French shirts that had set the Quaker population quaking. No, Jacques Clavier was almost a god to colored folks. More than two hundred black men sailed on his ships.

Moses was his usual congenial self when they left the tavern. "So Jacques's house is all done?" he asked.

"Yes, Dad." Andy could smell the rum on his father's breath. "How was everything on Nantucket?"

"The hurricane pretty much destroyed 'Zekiel's house, but he's fine, and Nantucket never changes." Moses launched into a report of people and events that lasted until they turned onto Arnold Street.

There it stood—Jacques Clavier's new house—a ten-room, white clapboard structure standing foursquare against the wind. Two brick chimneys rose like sentinels at either end, a captain's walk surrounded the third floor. There were perhaps two dozen houses like it in Bedford Village, some far more elegant. But Moses sensed its individuality, Jacques's stamp on it. It stood secluded, behind tall spreading elms, like Jacques aloof, and, somehow, impregnable. It was more than a house, Moses thought as he approached the huge white-painted front door. It was a statement: the Claviers were here to stay.

The Woodsons and the Claviers sat together at dinner that night in the new mahogany-furnished dining room and drank wine from silver goblets which Jacques had brought from France. "Lord a mercy, Jacques," Moses exclaimed in muted admiration. "I hope none a our clients ever see all this or we'll never haul cargo again."

Jacques was in a rare expansive mood, and as he showed his old friend over every inch of the house, Moses mellowed. His massive head nodded in slow considered admiration of the Swiss grandfather clocks, the tables and cabinets from England, the French chairs, the Persian rugs, the four-sided engraved rosewood piano. And when Jacques took out the cut-glass decanter of rum he'd bought for his friend's return, Moses broadened into conversation. Looking around the parlor, he commented, "Look like to me you bought every doodad they got for sale in Europe.

"Went by to see Nils Kuykendal while I was on Nantucket," Moses continued as he and Jacques sat before the fireplace. Behind them on the mantel were models of Jacques's ships. "He's real bad off. Lung fever. Doubt he'll ever sail again. And all them young'uns. Five of 'em." Moses fished in his pocket for a plug of tobacco. "The oldest boy's tryin' to support 'em, but he just made first mate on one a Russell's small cargo ships. Hardly enough to feed that many mouths."

"That boy's a real good seaman," Jacques commented, lighting a cigar. "He was with us four trips. In fact, he made second mate aboard the *Freedom.*"

"He knows the sea, all right, but it'll be a dozen years 'fore he makes captain. And by then . . ." Moses looked around the elegant parlor for a spittoon.

"I have a brig under construction now." Jacques stood and took a model off the mantel. "This is it. Do you think he could handle it?"

"As cap'n?" Moses examined the intricately made wooden model. "Don't see why not."

"Then next week, Moses, we'll go to Nantucket. Young Kuykendal will captain this ship."

Nantucket Island was wrapped in fog as Jacques followed Moses up the sandy road to Kuykendal's house. Nils's face was the color of his sheets, but his head bobbed with delight when his oar-thin wife announced his visitors. Moses eased his bulk into a creaking chair by the bedside table which held Kuykendal's current etchings. Jacques sat on the sea chest at the foot of the bed. "Moses told me you'd been ailing."

"Aye, but I'll be better come the spring." A wracking cough seized Kuykendal, and Jacques could see blood on his handkerchief.

"You need a warmer place, Nils. The Indies. You could find work down there."

"Aye, and who's to feed these mouths and what's to get me there?" Struggling to sit erect, Kuykendal coughed again.

Jacques opened the parcel on his lap and handed Kuykendal the model. "This ship will be ready this month's end. I want your son, Carl, to be her captain."

Kuykendal nodded slowly as he cradled the model in his gnarled hands. Then he looked at Jacques a long moment and, reaching among his whalebones on the table, he found his sharpest knife. With great care the old sea captain carved into the model's hull: "No Clavier ship will sail in time of stress without a Kuykendal."

CHAPTER FIFTEEN

1796

"I'll bet this is the proudest moment of Jacques's life," Andy Woodson said as the slim, serious girl followed her father up the gangplank.

"Well, Jacqueline's the spitting image of him, that's for sure." Moses huddled in his coat as the wind washed the water high against the wharf.

"And she'll be as tall as he is, too." Charity Key, between her husband, Anton, and their eleven-year-old, Timothy, tightened her lips in disapproval. "What is she now, nine, and already to his shoulder."

"Well, it won't matter if she's a hundred feet tall." Anton gave his wife a look of disgust. "How many nine-year-old girls you heard of have a ship named for them?"

"Where's Noni and Hepsabeth?" Charity asked, arching an eyebrow as she turned to Moses. "I thought surely they would come for such an event as the christening of the *Jacqueline*."

"Noni expects to deliver any minute, and Hepsabeth thought it best to stay with her." Moses's tone was icy. He had years ago wearied of Charity's comments on the Claviers.

"Well," Charity said airily, "I do hope this one's a boy, so he can cease raising Jacqueline as though she's to become a man. Poor Jacques," Charity's arm surrounded her son's shoulders, "what a terrible, terrible disappointment it must be for him not to have a son."

"There goes the flag. The captain is aboard." Timothy bolted from his mother's embrace, his sand-colored face sparkling in excitement as the wind caught the red-and-green flag with the black star and cross, the emblem of Jacques Clavier's ships.

All eyes followed Jacques and Jacqueline as they walked past the smiling, watchful crew and up the quarterdeck. The girl looked at her father. With a smile, he nodded. From the shore they heard Jacqueline's voice, calm and steady, as she gave the orders to get the brig under way.

"How far are they going, Andy?" Timothy asked, moving to the wharf's edge for a better look. "To the lighthouse?"

"No, just far enough to get her really baptized." Andy Woodson's high-cheekboned face showed clearly his Indian blood as he squinted, following the ship's progress. "We're to be under way tomorrow, so we'll have to load today."

"The *Jacqueline*," Timothy whispered as the sails billowed on the river.

Anton heard the awe in his son's voice and saw admiration in his eyes. He smiled as the boy's gaze moved from the ship to the fawn-brown girl with the long braid who stood beside her father on the quarterdeck. "Yes," Anton said softly, putting his arm around his son's shoulders, "she's a beauty."

Anton knew his son's affection for Jacques Clavier's daughter. When Jacqueline was five and Timothy seven, he and Jacques had hired a tutor for their children. The two had spent all their days together. Except when Jacques was in port. Then Jacques took over his daughter's education. Hand in hand they visited sailmakers and ship's carpenters, Jacqueline's small head nodding in agreement as her father explained cargoes and commissions. Anton hoped the new child would be a boy. Jacques so wanted a son. But if it were not to be, Jacqueline Clavier would soon do her father proud.

How, as the group moved down the wharf toward Water Street, Anton frowned, remembering that every bank in Bedford Village had denied Jacques a loan to build a bigger ship, a barque with which he could compete in the fast-growing, lucrative whale fishery. "That," he had heard one of his customers mutter as he tried on a wig, "was more than any damn nigger needs." Still, Anton nodded in grim satisfaction, ol' Jacques wasn't hurting. Five ships were enough for any man.

On board the *Jacqueline,* Jacques explained the new chronometer to his daughter, then went on to discuss cargo, which would be oil.

"Papa," Jacqueline's dark eyes pleaded. "Please can we go as far as the lighthouse?"

"No, Jacqueline." Jacques put his arm around his daughter tightly. "Your mother may be needing us quite soon."

"I haven't been to Gay Head since last summer, and the lighthouse is my favorite place . . . climbing the bluffs and then inside, the dark, curving stairs . . ."

"Jacqueline." Jacques's face sobered. "You have a duty to your mother. She needs you and you must be there. Remember what I've told you, the strength is in the *mbe,* the family. And when the new child is born, you must help take care of him."

"Are the Woodsons in our family, too?"

"Yes, in a way they are."

"It's lucky Hepsabeth's father is a Gay Head Wampanoag," Jacqueline said, looking over the railing at the water. "Without him, Mother says, the Indian council would never have given you permission to build the lighthouse there."

"That's true." Jacques leaned by his daughter's side. "And it was badly needed." He smiled. "I love the lighthouse, too." Jacques straightened and took his daughter's arm. "So, now give the order to turn about and let's go home."

"He's coming up the river," Moses yelled as he ran into the Clavier kitchen. "I saw his flag from the captain's walk." Moses was puffing heavily. His great body was a burden in old age.

Hepsabeth clutched the hem of her apron to her breast. "Oh, God, I hope he gets here soon."

"Well, Anton's gone to the wharf. He'll bring him soon as . . ."

"Oh, Moses, it's so unfair." Hepsabeth burst into tears. "They both so wanted a son."

"Well, the child's not dead yet."

"But nearly. Born with jaundice. Oh, Moses . . ."

"Hush, Hessy." Moses's huge hand caressed his wife's head. "Now we got to be strong for them."

They turned, hearing the footsteps of Miss Jane. The midwife's face was drawn as she appeared at the kitchen door. "How's Noni?" Hepsabeth whispered.

"Asleep. I gave her a potion."

"And the baby?"

"I doubt he'll live the hour."

They heard the carriage, then Jacques coming on the run. He grabbed the doorframe for support when he saw their faces.

"Jacques . . ." Hepsabeth began.

"Noni?" Jacques's eyes were wild. "What's wrong?"

"She's fine," Moses said, too quickly.

"And the child?"

"He's still alive." Hepsabeth moved to touch Jacques's arm. "It's jaundice."

"A son?" Jacques's voice cracked. Then he wheeled and faced Miss Jane.

"There's nothing more I can do," the midwife said softly.

"Jacques." Moses's voice trembled. "There's nothing anyone can do but pray."

"Jaundice?" The dark pools of Jacques's eyes sucked the secrets of the kitchen. Hepsabeth grabbed his arm, but he shook her roughly. "Jaundice? Jaundice, did you say?"

Lunging across the kitchen, Jacques grabbed Woodson's arm. "Moses, where's your liquor? I know you have some."

Moses pulled his flask from his jacket pocket.

"Jacques!" Hepsabeth's voice was shrill with terror. "Jacques, where're you going . . . ?"

"To save my son. To burn the evil from him." Jacques ran from the room. "He will live! And his children, and their children." His shout came down the hallway. "The Claviers will live! We have come a long, hard way, and we will live!"

Book Two

THE CHANGING
OF THE WATCH

Brethren arise, arise! Strike for your lives and liberties. Now is the day and the hour . . . Let every slave throughout the land do this and the days of slavery are numbered. You can not be more oppressed than you have been; you can not suffer greater cruelties than you already have. Rather die free men than live to be slaves. Remember that you are four million. Let your motto be: Resistance! Resistance! Resistance!

—REVEREND HENRY HIGHLAND GARNET
Buffalo, N.Y., August, 1843

CHAPTER ONE

1807

The knocking came at midnight—swiftly, insistently, and, receiving no response, grew bolder. Upstairs in the master bedroom, Jacques stirred uneasily in his sleep.

Outside the front door, Timothy Key cursed the soundness of the house and stepped back a pace to stare at the shuttered windows. He picked up a stone to break the window by the lock then turned and banged on the door again instead. Did he see a flicker of light from Jacqueline's room? "Uncle Jacques," he hissed. "In the name of God, wake up."

In her room Jacqueline turned up the lamp and slipped quickly into a robe. Her quick dark eyes were anxious, and a frown creased the smooth fawn-brownness of her face. Still buttoning her robe, she hurried from her room, then at the head of the stairs she stopped, hearing the door of her parents' room open. Her father moved quickly down the hall.

"No ship of ours is due in port?" she asked softly, voicing the least of their mutual fears that this might be news of a ship run aground or sunk off the Cape or Nantucket Sound. Jacques shook his head. No ship was due. Then it had to do with one of the Woodsons or the Keys—or Alex. Jacqueline's glance at her father as they moved together down the stairs told that his anxiety matched her own.

Jacques's first thought was for his son, Alexander. Twelve now and small for his age, Alexander had inherited both his mother's size and her serious disposition. Noni had kept him close, much too close, fussing over him as though he were still in crispins. The boy's ear was to his mother, to the African diaspora, to Noni's stories of the greatness of the African past. Alexander spent his free hours with her, or reading, or playing the piano, seldom playing with boys his age.

For that reason Jacques had overridden Noni's protests and allowed Alexander to go with Timothy Key to visit Anton, who had opened a new shop in Boston last year. His decision was not made without apprehension. In Boston, as in most places, things were going badly for free people of color. The flood of whites fleeing

Europe had created a crisis in employment. Immigrants, most of them used to nothing where they came from, swore in steerage-learned English that "da damn niggas is what keep da wages down." In Boston, blacks and whites had fought pitched battles for bread and butter. Negroes needed passes to be on the street after nine at night. Last year, whites had celebrated the Fourth of July by attacking the colored citizenry. Talk of recolonizing free Negroes, voluntarily or involuntarily, in Africa, Central or South America, was spreading. Bad times were getting worse.

The new miracles of machine power, the forces of water and steam harnessed to man's will, the growing urban centers in England and America, the entire giant mushroom of commerce and industry, all were growing on the frail stalk of Negro slavery.

In March, President Jefferson had signed a bill banning the slave trade. It had given impetus to slave smuggling. The price of men was soaring. The fugitive slave law made it a criminal offense to harbor a runaway or to prevent his arrest. Free Negroes were being snatched into slavery.

Three black men, Toussaint L'Ouverture, Henri Christophe, and Jean Jacques Dessalines, had led a band of Haitian slaves to victory over the armies of Napoleon and Spain, exploding the nerve endings of the South. The pulse of their blood had pounded in an American slave named Gabriel. Gabriel Prosser and his army of slaves, more than a thousand strong, had advanced against Richmond.

But the single greatest menace to the slave system, both North and South, was the free Negro. He was the possible made incarnate, and to him and through him came blacks who dared all odds to be free. Many white men said, "As long as there's a free Negro, slavery is not safe." Free Negroes answered, "As long as there is slavery, the nation is not safe." It was still a paper war of petitions and publications, but it was a war.

All this Jacques had known as he kissed his son goodbye a week ago. For he had also known no one could be sheltered from his times.

Now, hurrying to face his midnight caller, Jacques whispered to himself that he had done the right thing. Alexander could not live all his life on New Bedford's tree-shaded streets and familiar wharves. Nor could he spend his life reading of the lives of men long turned to dust. What was here, in this world, had to be faced.

Jacques crossed the parlor in long strides, then felt his heart jump to his throat as he recognized the tall, slender shape of Timothy Key through the glass pane next to the door.

Timothy was covered with mud, his face, hands, clothes filthy. But it was his eyes that frightened Jacques. Bleary with exhaustion, they signaled terrible news.

"Uncle Jacques," Timothy began, still standing in the doorway. Then his voice faltered. His eyes dropped to the floor. His words trembled through his lips—half cry, half whisper. "Slave catchers have taken Alex."

Jacqueline's face was frozen in horror. She seemed to stagger as the scream—"Oh my God"—jerked from her throat. For an instant her eyes searched her father's—a supplication for his denial, his refutal of this truth. He held out his arms and she threw hers around him, clinging to him as the sobs heaved through her.

Jacques's face was gray, but Timothy felt the fierce undertow of his eyes. His own seemed drawn into it. "My cousin was with him. They were coming through the Common." Timothy spoke slowly, trying to control himself, as Jacques moved back and he came into the hall. "They grabbed Alex, just grabbed him. They said he was a fugitive."

"You have come tonight from Boston?"

Timothy nodded.

"All right." Jacques's voice was strained. "Come in and sit down and tell us, slowly, everything that has happened."

Timothy sat on the edge of a chair in the parlor. His boots made a muddy patch on the Persian rug. "They shoved Alex on a cart with two other men. My cousin tried to follow, but they went too fast. He ran to get Papa. Papa was at a meeting at the Joy Street Baptist Church."

Timothy ran his tongue over his lips. His gaze jumped from Jacques to Jacqueline, now pacing the floor, then was caught by the older man's steady stare. "The slave catchers took Alex to Leverett Street jail. Within the hour they went before the magistrate. He ruled for the slave catch . . ." Abruptly, Timothy caught his breath.

"Nooo. No. No." Jacques and Jacqueline whirled as the anguished sound, part cry, part scream, arched through the room.

"Noni!" Jacques started toward her.

"Oh, Jacques." She held out her arms to him. "Not my son. Not my son. Oh my God, Jacques, they cannot do this again."

Timothy's soft brown eyes went to Jacqueline. She stood so alone

111

now. He ached to touch, to hold and comfort her. No, that was impossible now. Next month she would become Andy Woodson's wife. What an insane, stupid mistake. Timothy knew that she loved him. Her eyes had admitted it, if her lips had not. And God, how he loved her.

Timothy felt his hands shaking. From exhaustion? From this night? Or from these past two months? Damn his mother.

It was she who had driven his father away with her constant harping about the Claviers. Working him desperate years in her vanity's need to match, to outdo every Clavier possession. If his father still lived with them, if he had not fled to Boston, none of this would have happened and Alex would be safe. Alex would be safe and he, not Andy Woodson, would be Jacqueline's bridegroom.

But no, she with her constant caustic comments. She with her spiteful tongue. She had screamed like a banshee when he told her his plans to marry Jacqueline. "Never! Never will a Clavier live in my house."

"We're planning to travel, Mother," he had stammered his bewildered reply. "Then, when we come back, I can build a house of my own."

"And desert me," she had sobbed, "for Jacques Clavier's daughter."

Later, calmer, she had sat down beside him. "Timothy," she had taken his hand. "You don't understand about that family. They'll never let you be a man. To them, they are the light *and* the way. And Jacques is Jesus, and Jacqueline is the Pope."

Jacques had seemed to sense what had happened. With an odd, sad look he had taken Timothy aside. "Tim, I understand your affection for my daughter. And indeed hers for you. But you have a duty to your mother. She cannot be left alone. And Jacqueline cannot live with her. She would make her life intolerable. And that, Timothy," —Timothy had trembled before Jacques's stare—"that I will not have."

It was less than a week later, Timothy frowned remembering, that Jacques had announced Jacqueline's engagement to Andy. A man old enough to be her father. A man who would spend his life sailing her father's ships. To Andy, who was even then at sea.

Only his mother, Hepsabeth, and Moses were smiling as Jacqueline, her face the same mask as her father's, stood by his side as he pronounced her fate. She had looked, as Hiram Black's wife had whispered, "like one condemned to death."

Now, as Jacques held Noni, Timothy's eyes found Jacqueline's, but she seemed not to see him now. Once again she wore the Clavier mask—cold, untouchable, no anger—no time for that. Just listening, weighing the facts, moving toward immutable decision. Timothy saw Jacques's eyes on him again and went on, feeling relief surging abruptly through him. He had only to relate the facts. The Claviers would do the rest.

"Papa went to Prince Hall. Within the hour the colored Masons were in the street. They were the ones who found out what had happened to Alex, that he was aboard a ship, the *Goddess*. Papa and Reverend Hall tried to talk with both the magistrate and the ship's captain, but to no avail. Alexander had no free papers."

No expression crossed Jacques's face. Timothy moved to ease his position on the chair. "It was then Papa went to your friend Dr. Flateau."

Jacques nodded. Anton had done right. Prince Hall was the organizer, the agitator, the petitioner, the builder of black solidarity who had founded black Freemasonry—African Lodge Number One—in Boston two decades ago. He was the logical first choice. Louis Flateau, whose brother was a United States senator, was the logical second.

"Dr. Flateau was at dinner but appeared the instant he heard about Alex. Within minutes we were on our way to the governor. The doctor demanded and got a writ for Alex's release." Timothy paused, fumbling in his jacket for an envelope, then handed it to Jacques.

"We rushed back down to State Street to Long Wharf, but the *Goddess* had already sailed with five supposed fugitives. Flateau questioned the harbor master, and he told us her next port of call was Philadelphia. It was dark and no ships sailing, Papa sent me for your decision. Dr. Flateau gave me the loan of his fastest horse and papers saying I carried urgent business for the senator. Three times tonight I've changed horses at posthouses on the way."

Timothy reached into his pocket again. "Dr. Flateau also gave me this." Jacques saw the intricately inlaid flintlock pistol in Timothy's hand. "He said to use it to stifle any soul who stood in freedom's way."

Jacques took the gun. For the briefest part of a second he stared at it. Then his eyes met Timothy's again. "Philadelphia, you say?"

Timothy knew the decision had been made.

Jacques turned to his daughter. "Jacqueline, hitch the horse to the phaeton. Go first to Peter Woodson. Tell him what has happened and that we sail in half an hour.

"Tell him to have the men bring guns. Tell him also that Paul Cuffee's ship, the *Traveler,* is in port. He'll know what to do." A sigh escaped Jacques's lips. "I'll use the *Jacqueline,* she's the fastest ship I have. And tell Peter to ask any of my old men he can find . . ."

Noni clung to the arm of her mahogany chair. The wood was the color of her hand. Her dark oval eyes were dry. She could neither weep nor pray. Had her own mother felt the same? Did she feel it, even now? Or had she died from pain, pain on which tears dared not intrude and bade weeping only to whisper to the soul. Noni looked at the young man who had ridden all night to bring her this sorrow. "Come, Timmy, let me fix you something to eat."

"No, please . . ."

"Come, it will give me something to do."

Lanterns were ablaze on the *Jacqueline* when Jacques came up the gangplank, followed by Timothy carrying their guns. Peter Woodson, nearing forty, met him on deck. "We have twenty men, sir."

Tears sprang to Jacques's eyes as Nils Kuykendal, almost seventy, stepped forward with his gun. "I am here again, Captain," the emaciated old man nodded. "No Clavier ship sails in time of stress without a Kuykendal."

Jacques touched his arm, then walked up the quarterdeck. Slowly, the ship slipped into the river deep. High atop the mainsail the red-and-green flag, the star and cross emblem fluttered on the cold night breeze. Jacques saw Noni and Jacqueline on the wharf with their arms about each other. He raised his hand in silent farewell.

On the western horizon the land was vanishing and, to the east, the sea gave birth to the sun. The *Jacqueline* ran smoothly with the wind, sails full on her southward course. Jacques's eyes stung from lack of sleep, but his mind and body were strong. This ship was his country. This quarterdeck his throne.

His first thought was to intercept the *Goddess* at the mouth of the bay, to storm her and recapture his son. It was the way most natural

114

to his being. But to fire on the vessel might endanger those below. No, caution. This time, caution. Alexander must not be hurt. This time he would seek the aid of others first. He would appeal to the laws of the land. But if they were futile . . .

Slowly another plan took form. A plan not based on open war, but on the work of those who fought inside; the mind warriors, the guerrilla fighters. Yes, Jacques thought, he would try it their way first. . . .

On his arrival in Philadelphia, Jacques planned to make immediate contact with James Forten, Richard Allen, and Absalom Jones, the three most powerful Negroes in the nation's largest city.

Forten, a Revolutionary War veteran and arch-enemy of the colonization movement, was a sail manufacturer of considerable wealth. Absalom Jones, an Episcopal priest, had been the first Negro minister ordained in America. With Richard Allen he had organized Philadelphia's Free African Society, a nonsectarian religious organization which functioned also as a mutual-aid society. Then, not a dozen years ago, after Negroes had been pulled from their knees while at prayer at St. George's, the Reverend Jones had founded the Free African Church of St. Thomas, which was Episcopalian, and Reverend Richard Allen had founded a new denomination, the African Methodist Episcopal Church, now thousands strong.

On these three men, Jacques's first alternative rested. Together, they would present the writ of the governor of Massachusetts for the release of Alexander and question whether the other Negroes aboard the *Goddess* were not also misidentified. If their petition were denied, if the men were not released, then Alexander and the others would be recaptured on the open sea.

Alexander! Jacques bit his lip, remembering an incident just a month ago. As he did from time to time, his son had been talking to the Reverend Ian Morris, the white minister who lived next door to Peter Woodson. "Maybe I would like to be a minister," the boy had said. "I have no real love for the sea."

"The church needs strong young men," Reverend Morris had encouraged.

Jacques had interrupted this conversation. "Reverend Morris, I mean no disrespect. But no son of mine is going to . . ."

"Excuse me, Captain Clavier . . ." the reverend had said quickly, "but who are we to tell who is called . . . ?"

"The bellow we hear from heaven is not necessarily a call from your Lord for more men to putter around His house. God Himself knows He has enough ministers to right all the evils of this globe. What He needs is men who . . ."

"You are an interpreter of the will of God, Captain?"

"Insofar as it applies to my son, Reverend, better I than you!"

The hold of the ship was dark. Alexander sat quite still, trying to imagine what his father would do in such a situation. It was difficult to think at all in the painful position to which his shackles forced him. The man chained across from him wept, as he had since they had come on board. "Oh, God, what will happen to my family?"

Alex felt the man next to him stir uneasily. "All that moanin' ain't gon' help."

"Ain't nothin' in the world gonna help," another man whispered in the dark. "They got us. They got us and we dead."

"Not yet," the man next to Alex said. "Not yet."

"Better if we were."

"I ran away before . . ." the man next to Alexander whispered.

"You *are* a fugitive?" the man across from Alexander cried, straining at his chains. "You the one what got me in this mess. You goddamn niggers running away is what's got these slave catchers . . ." They could hear unstifled sobs.

"And how did you get free?" the man next to Alexander asked.

"I was born free," the one across yelled hysterically. "I was born free. My father won his freedom fighting in the Revolution."

"Yea," the man next to Alex said. "Well, I got free in my own revolution."

For an instant all was still, then the man across whimpered. "Things was a whole lot better 'fore you niggers started comin'."

"I got as much right here as anybody." Anger tensed the man next to Alexander.

"You know they gon' catch you. You know they gon' send someone after you. And then innocent folk like me . . ."

"We are all guilty," Alexander said softly. "We are all guilty of the great American crime. We are black."

Silence gripped the hold, the darkness tense with fear. Alexander longed to speak, to hold off the foreboding stillness with his tongue. But the silence was too deep and Alex gave himself to fantasy: his father on the deck, commanding his release, the captain trembling

116

before his awful presence, his mother, weeping, "Oh, my Chinue," knowing the horrors awaiting him, unless . . . his sister for once silent, for once unsure . . .

All of his life Alex had heard of the heritage of his name. "Alexander," his father had told him, "was a great warrior, a conqueror . . ." And lately he had told him of a great modern-day Alexander, a black Alexander, Alexandre Dumas, a general in Napoleon's army. Alexander Clavier blinked in the darkness of the hold. How often, in crimson daydreams, he had imagined himself the avenging savior of his race.

Without warning, the door of the hold opened. Two crewmen came in, silhouetted by light from the passage, carrying bowls of food. Alexander realized he was hungry, but as his spoon touched the mixture, its stench revolted him.

"Shit!" the man next to him shouted. "Who can eat this shit?"

"Niggers. And it's all you get!"

"Then I'll starve and see what good you get of that." The man flung the bowl onto the floor.

The sailor grinned mirthlessly, "Wait 'til the cap'n hears a that!"

The door slammed as the sailor went out. In the darkness came a whisper. "You was a fool. Chained up to that wall—you was a fool."

They waited in silence, Alexander feeling fear creep along his spine. Then footsteps came, heavy in the passage. When the door opened, Alexander saw the cat-o'-nine-tails in the captain's hand.

The sailor held the oil lamp high, pointing out the man who had disdained his dinner. "All right"—the cat flicked as the captain spoke—"lick it up."

"No." In the smoky light, Alexander saw the veins stand hard along the man's dark temple.

"Throw him in it." The captain stepped back, making small circles with the whip as a second, then a third sailor shoved the man, still bound by ball and chain, sending him sprawling on his belly.

"Lick it up." The cat cut deep into the man's back. Alexander trembled as blood gushed over torn flesh and fabric, then gasped as the whip descended again and again.

The man braced himself on his forearms, holding his face above the dark mixture on the floor, writhing, but not screaming, as the whip shredded his back.

There was a looseness in Alexander's bowels, his mouth was full

117

of bile. Then an all-muting flame swept through him. When the whip rose again, he grabbed it in his outstretched hand.

"What? Another one?" The captain grinned maliciously as his foot ground into Alexander's groin. Vomiting, Jacques Clavier's son fell back against the wall.

The captain's venom returned to the man on the floor. "Shove his head in it," he bellowed. The sailor obliged with his boot. The black face jerked up, covered with brown. "Shit eaters," the black man screamed.

The whip slashed relentlessly. Blood covered the man's back and lay in small pools on the floor. Again and again the sailor stomped his boot on the black man's head, forcing his face into the food, thickened now with blood. None of the other prisoners could look, but Alex watched, transfixed in horror.

And then the man's dark head came up no longer, and his dark body ceased to writhe. A sailor jerked his head back and looked toward the captain. "The nigger's dead," he said.

"He was a free one anyway." The captain shrugged. He looked around the hold. "Free today and dead tomorrow. The rest of you remember that." He saw the look on Alex's face and flicked his whip at him. "Remember that."

Alex's lips did not move, but an answer rang out clearly in his mind. I will remember. I'll never forget. And I'll spend my life, my whole life, fighting slavery. I'll fight you. I'll fight you till I die!

The Philadelphia trio gathered at Forten's home quickly. All of them knew Jacques Clavier. He had often given passage to men attending their meetings, and more than once fugitives had fled to freedom aboard his ships. And though he had never joined their organized efforts, they respected his solitary work and his generosity in times of crisis.

Nor was the irony of this situation lost upon these influential men, sitting in this splendid home, guests of a man who was employer to both white and black. And as Jacques began to speak, the Reverends Jones and Allen especially prayed for a swift resolution of this matter, not only for the sake of their brethren aboard the *Goddess,* but out of fear for the revenge of Jacques Clavier. Clavier's tactics were well known to them. If things did not go well in these next few hours, the whites of Philadelphia who screamed "black devils" would certainly see one in the flesh.

118

"If," Forten asked, "things should not go as we plan . . . ?"

"If that should happen," Jacques responded harshly, "I have two alternatives. First to rescue my son on the open sea and, if that should fail, to blow the *Goddess* straight to hell."

"But," Forten's voice was anguished, "your son . . ."

". . . would die." Jacques nodded. "And, as Nsai, a man I knew once said, 'That is as it should be. A man must either be free or be dead.'"

Reverend Jones assumed control, asking Jacques to return to his ship and await the *Goddess,* obtaining his promise that he would do nothing until he heard from them.

The Philadelphians worked feverishly. Petitions flashed through the Negro sections, and by late afternoon they had collected signatures from more than three hundred voters. With the writ from the governor of Massachusetts, these were taken to the duly appointed authorities. While Jacques fumed, threatening to turn his ship around and intercept the *Goddess* at the entrance to the harbor, the matter was accomplished.

The moment the *Goddess* set anchor, the slave catchers were apprehended and the prisoners released. But even as Jacques held out his arms to his son he knew how small and weak were the confines of his protection. And looking into young Alexander Clavier's face, Forten, Jones, and Allen knew another man had been molded for their cause.

119

CHAPTER TWO

1817

Noni Clavier moved quickly, gracefully down the sun-dappled brick walk. The book-filled basket on her arm swung easily with her movement. She was pleased with her day's work. Nearing the Woodson house, she saw a bent figure in the garden. "Good afternoon, Hepsabeth," she called.

"Noni." Hepsabeth got stiffly to her feet, her hand rubbing at the persistent aching in her side as she walked toward the fence. "The missionary club meeting over? Did they vote out money for your school?" Her hand flicked white hair from her forehead. "Lord, it's hot. Come in and take a cup of tea and tell me all what happened."

"Not today, Hepsabeth. This is Jacques's last night at home and I want to get home before Alex does. He's leaving tomorrow also, to give an abolition speech in Concord. I've managed to save enough from the house money so he won't have to ask his fare of Jacqueline. And Lord knows, I want to tell him before he does."

Hepsabeth nodded in immediate sympathy. She knew well the argument that request would evoke. Jacqueline's chronic complaint was that Alexander's spending on abolitionist causes was sending the Claviers to the poorhouse. And poor Noni was always trying to be the peacemaker . . . trying above all to keep Jacques from hearing the arguments that were pulling his children apart . . .

Noni patted her cheek with her handkerchief. "How's Moses?"

"His back's paining him bad. He's back on the cane." Hepsabeth sighed with a private thought, then looked at Noni again. "Jacqueline says things are going real fine at the cooperage. The apprentice she put on last week is working out real nice. Even Moses says the place is doing better than ever." Hepsabeth smiled, "Moses swears Jacqueline can add a column a figures faster'n a man can pour a cask a oil." She nodded with conviction. "She's sure got a head for business. Running both Jacques's business and Moses's . . . Lord knows what we'd done without that child with our girls married and gone and Peter and Andy always at sea."

"Well, she enjoys it, and that's a blessing," Noni said, suppressing her quick sequential thought that Jacqueline, now thirty, was hardly a child. "Give Moses my love." Noni squeezed Hepsabeth's hand. "I'll stop in tomorrow and tell you everything."

The basket seemed heavier as Noni continued down the walk, thinking of Alexander and Jacqueline. It seemed that as your children grew, their problems grew. But even as children, Jacqueline and Alexander had differed greatly—Jacqueline obsessed with her father's stories of adventure and great fortune, and Alexander, Noni smiled, her Chinue she had called him, her God's own blessing, thinking only of his books, and his piano.

Noni smiled suddenly as she remembered the Sunday-afternoon gatherings of years gone by: Alexander playing, and beautifully too, Bach and Beethoven; Jacqueline's stern, emotionless renditions of Shakespeare's sonnets and Byron's odes; Timothy Key's hilarious imitations of his father's customers; and Andy, on those rare times when he was in port, Andy clapping . . . Noni's lips tightened to suppress a laugh . . . always at the wrong times. Such fun-filled times they had been. But all of that had been before . . .

Noni's pace slowed as memories of the awful days following Alexander's capture invaded her mind. How silent he had become, how alone. Resisting school, abandoning the piano, ignoring the entreaties of his family, the invitations of his few friends, living behind the closed door of his room. Writing versed damnations of slavery: long, violent poems that had sent her into consultation with Dr. Makery for a potent to relieve his mind.

Even Jacqueline's long-postponed marriage to Andy, whom Alexander adored, had brought no hint of happiness to his face. At the small ceremony in the parlor he had stood among the Claviers, the Keys, and the Woodsons, as silently, if not as despairing, as Timothy.

Noni frowned, remembering those six months when Alex had filled his desk, his closet, with his poems. Then, under the gentle pressure of Jim Stanley, the Negro tutor Jacques had brought from Boston, he had discovered the Bill of Rights, the Magna Carta, an English version of the Declaration of the Rights of Man. With the appetite of the famished he had struggled with the writings of Montesquieu, Rousseau, Diderot, Helvetius, and Voltaire. Late into the night his bedside candle burned. His eyes had grown weak. He had suffered headaches. Spectacles were prescribed.

121

It was in May, the scent of lilacs floating through Alexander's open window as she coaxed him, "Oh, Chinue, take just a cup of tea," when Jacques had interceded. "This folderol has continued long enough. Alexander will go with me to France. A lycée there . . ."

"No, Jacques, no," she had begun her plea.

"I am studying here." Alexander's eyes in his thin, dark face had been magnified by his spectacles. "I am learning the means of freedom for our people."

Jacques had put a firm hand on his son's shoulder. "As Nsai, a man I once knew, said, 'Freedom is only a word until you have what you need to maintain it.' Not epithets from the starved heart, Alexander, but plans from the strong mind. We sail next week for Paris."

Noni had packed Alex's trunk while Jacqueline seethed with jealousy. She had overheard her daughter say to Timothy—who still visited with clockwork regularity—"Well, now, they all go sailing off to Paris, to London, to the Moluccas, and leave me to find their commissions, to arrange the overhauling of the ships and pay their bills. One day, Timothy, I'm going to see the world. One day I'll pack my bags and leave without a word. Then perhaps they will appreciate me."

"Jacqueline," Timothy had laughed, "you love things just the way they are. You are both boss and martyr rolled into one. Come on, be honest about it. What would you do if Alexander took over your father's business?"

"Then"—her eyes had met his levelly—"I would come and take over yours."

Noni flushed, remembering the sudden intensity in Tim's eyes. "Oh, Jacqueline, if only that could be true."

Alexander had studied in France for three years. It was late in 1811 when he had returned to New Bedford. Little Jacques, Jacqueline's son, was two. War with England seemed inevitable. But Alexander's mind was full of news that had reached him in Paris—of slave revolts in parishes just a few miles from New Orleans. "It is the day, the hour," he had shouted as he first came in the door. Then later, "I have already written letters to speak to abolition groups in Boston, Concord, and Providence. Mama, I tell you the day of freedom is at hand."

How changed he had been, moving with such sure strides around the parlor, his dark eyes fierce in his still thin walnut-brown face. He wore his hair long, in what he said was the African style; his sideburns joined at his chin in a tuft of beard. The Clavier smile which in Jacques's face, and Jacqueline's, was tinged with arrogance, was firmness on his lips. Handsomeness, Noni remembered thinking, had bypassed her son, bequeathing in its stead a seething majesty.

But the day of freedom had not been at hand. Only a few replies had come from the ever-increasing volume of Alexander's offers to speak, to organize groups for the abolition of slavery. He had spent weeks traveling, speaking to Negro groups in Boston, New Haven, Hartford, Providence, New York, then going down to Philadelphia, where he worked with the abolitionist strategies of James Forten, Richard Allen, and Absalom Jones. Energetic, nervous, he spent his time at home writing broadsides against slavery, organizing meetings and speaking to any group he could, despite Jacqueline's rising protests that all his efforts netted not a dime.

"Do you realize, Alexander," Jacqueline had stormed, "that those confounded southern and western war hawks are pushing us into a war with England? Haven't you heard the British are impressing American seamen? Do you care that we have just lost our largest account, with Papa's friend, that British cotton lord Nathan Blackwell? Yes, our biggest, most lucrative account running his goods to the Spice Islands and returning with silk and spice? It may come to you as a shock, Alex, but you are going to have to work for a living. All the money is in whaling now. . . . And if we have a war . . ."

In late August, the British had captured Washington and burned the Capitol. Alexander had come into the house with the news that he was answering Andrew Jackson's call for colored troops.

"That's a southern war," Jacqueline had exploded. "New England is opposed to it."

"General Jackson . . ."

"That Indian fighter . . ."

". . . has asked specifically for colored volunteers. By doing so he recognizes both the Negroes' military value and our valor . . ."

"He recognizes you as cannon fodder," Jacqueline had retorted.

Over his sister's furious protests that he was needed at home, Alexander joined Old Hickory's troops and, as Jacqueline delighted in pointing out, the pirate crews of Jean Lafitte, at the Battle of New Orleans.

Alexander was wounded in the battle, fought two weeks after the peace treaty had been signed. He returned to New Bedford on crutches and even before these yielded to a cane, he was again writing, organizing, speaking for abolition, fighting the movement again afoot to recolonize free Negroes in Africa and Central and South America. Noni had known it would not be long before her son would again call the highway home.

Down the street Noni saw Timothy Key helping his father, Anton, from their carriage. She noticed the children playing on the street ending their games and hurrying home. It was, she knew, exactly five o'clock. It was whispered that even the watchmaker set his time by the Keys. Ken Fulsome opened his candleworks when they arrived at their wig shop. Mrs. Russell put on her tea when she saw them leave the tailoring shop, and Mrs. Talbert put in her potatoes when they left the Turkish bath. In exactly one hour and forty-five minutes Timothy would arrive at the Clavier door each night, holding his five-year-old daughter, Melissa, by the hand. Noni scratched her head with her free hand. That was the biggest mistake that Jacques had ever made—not letting Jacqueline marry Timothy. She had often wondered what Jacques had told her that long night in the study. Jacques had come out to say their daughter would marry Andy, while Jacqueline had run sobbing to her room. But what had been said during those hours together neither Jacques nor Jacqueline would ever say.

Inside the house, Jacqueline laid down her quill and closed the ledger book. She glanced at the great grandfather clock beside the bookshelves in the corner of the study. Three after five. She had been at this desk nine hours. And there would still be hell to pay tonight when Papa saw that bill. This time, she thought with grim satisfaction, Alexander has gone too far.

From a drawer in the roll-top desk she pulled out a bottle of rose water. She let a few drops spill on her hands, then massaged the liquid into her skin, taking care that it would not touch the rings that adorned her hands.

For a moment she flexed her fingers, admiring her rings: the pearl brought by Papa on her fourteenth birthday; the ruby, his gift when she was sixteen; the sapphire, her eighteenth-birthday present, all diminishing by size and beauty the diamond which symbolized her marriage.

Her marriage with Andy. What marriage with Andy? He had been at sea this time over two years. The last time home he had stayed only six days. Six days in nearly four years. Jacqueline drummed her jeweled fingers on the desk top. Less than a month in eight years. And Mama and Hepsabeth preaching, always preaching, that her friendship with Timothy Key was unseemly. She would have gone mad without Timothy . . . without Timothy at least to talk to. Jacqueline's dark eyes clouded. If only Timothy had stood up to her father. But, Jacqueline's hands dropped listlessly to her lap, Papa had been right. Timothy was too gentle, too dominated by his mother. His own business would always be his first concern.

He wasn't gentle, Jacqueline thought furiously. He was weak. He had refused to stand up, to fight for her. Oh, he had pleaded with her to run away, to run like fugitives, but he would not face her father. Weak, weak, weak. Jacqueline's hands trembled in her lap. Oh God, she thought, then why do I love him so?

It was a sin, she knew. A sin, a terrible sin, for a married woman to love another man. But a sin without sin in it.

For behind the closed door of their bedroom they had years ago discovered and declared themselves incompatible. She had known after the first month of his great bulk crashing down on her, after that first month of his endless, stupid stories of the sea. Ha, she knew as much about the sea as he did.

But, Jacqueline bit her lip, it was a successful marriage. Andy's ship, the *Jacqueline,* made the longest, the most lucrative voyages of all of Papa's ships. Twice every sixteen months he made the long, harsh trips around the Cape of Good Hope to the Spice Islands. There had been profit in her marriage to Andy.

Crossing her legs under her long, full skirt, Jacqueline looked out the window. The sun turned the elm leaves to so many shades of green. So many shades of green. Her life was like that pale, inert leaf, the one closest to the trunk. Jacqueline Clavier Woodson. They would write that on her tombstone. But the inscription would lie. She was Jacqueline Clavier. The final insult of womanhood, to have one's identity removed, wiped out. She was not a Woodson. No, her marriage was a sham, a moneymaking maneuver that had consolidated families and built strength.

If only she had listened to Timothy's pleas and run away and married him. Timothy with his wit and grace. If only she had disobeyed

Papa's decision that she marry Andy. But she could not, and it was much, much too late.

A butterfly perched on the pale leaf by the trunk a moment, then lifted its yellow wings and flew away. Oh, leaf, Jacqueline thought, I am like you. Bound to the trunk, to grow old, to wither and fall decayed into the ground.

She heard Alexander's uneven footsteps in the hallway, then sighed as he limped through the door. He always looked a mess. "You do have clean shirts in your drawer."

"Have you been prying in my room again?"

"Not prying, trying to make you look respectable. My Lord, if Mama or I didn't see to it, you'd go out naked as a jaybird."

She saw his eyes searching the desk. "I got the bill," she said.

"Good. You'll take care of it then. Finley gave me quite a break . . ."

"A break?" It was a cry of pain. "Do you call ninety dollars . . . ?"

"The broadsides were urgent, Jacqueline. The meeting is tonight. He printed them overnight. I've been out all day handing . . ."

"I don't care if he printed them in a second. They shouldn't have been printed at all. Papa will never pay it. Who do you think we are, the Cuffees?"

"I know quite well who . . ."

"Alexander," Jacqueline's voice was tense. "I've told you before, you're putting us in the poorhouse. When people ask, as Mama begs from . . ."

"Oh, Jacqueline . . ."

". . . from door to door, what happened to the Claviers, do you know what I will say?"

"With jewelry a-flashing . . ." he smiled, trying amusement.

"Alexander and abolition! Abolition and Alexander put the Claviers in the poorhouse."

"Jacqueline, for goodness' sake . . ." he snapped, now annoyed.

"When are you going to start to work? When are you going to start putting into the till instead of dipping out?" Jacqueline saw resignation to her tirade in her brother's voice and raised her voice. "Do you know why the Cuffees are the richest colored shipowners? Because they all pull together. Five barques, four brigs. One brother the captain of one ship, one . . ."

"And two years ago Paul Cuffee took thirty-eight Negroes all the

126

way to Africa, to Sierra Leone, at his own expense," Alexander retorted. "And you quibble about . . ."

"I thought you were fighting the recolonizing of Negroes . . ."

"Jacqueline!" It was Jacques's shout from the hall. "What in tarnation is this bill from Finley . . . ?" Jacqueline glanced at Alexander as Jacques came into the study, pushing a hand through his thick mixed gray hair. "Ninety dollars. Ninety damn dollars for what?"

"It's my bill, Papa." Alexander's voice was low but firm. Through the window Jacqueline saw her mother hurrying up the walk.

"We're having a meeting tonight." Alexander walked to his father, "We needed broadsides to rally the people . . ."

"And tomorrow you'll need money to go to Concord, and next week . . ." Jacqueline began.

"Oh, all you are in the study." Jacqueline heard the forced gaiety in her mother's voice as she came to the door. "Dinner won't take a minute. The roast is done. Alexander, can I see you for a minute?"

"No," Jacques thundered. "No, I want to get this straight."

Jacqueline saw her mother's defenseless look as she sank on the settee.

"The ninety dollars . . ." Jacques turned to Alexander.

". . . is for the broadsides and the rental of the hall." Alexander met his father's look. "As you yourself have said so many times, 'Freedom is only a word until you have what you need to maintain it.' And our need now is force, the greatest force of all, the force of a thousand, a million people speaking out against an evil and determined to overthrow it. Wars are expensive, Papa, and we are in a war for freedom."

Jacqueline's eyes were on her father as he studied her brother. Then Jacques dropped the bill on her desk. "Pay it," he said.

The pain welled up and Jacqueline fought back the tears.

Noni stood. "Come, Alexander. Help me put the dinner on the table."

Jacques saw his daughter's face and, crossing to the desk, laid a gentle hand on her shoulder. "You think I was wrong."

Jacqueline fought to control the angry tremble in her voice. "It is your money, Papa."

Jacques raised his daughter's face to meet his eyes. "Alexander is my son." He saw her tears. "But you, Jacqueline, you are my soul."

CHAPTER THREE

1827

"No!" Jacqueline's cry was shrill. The tight high waist of her black dress choked her breathing as she stared up at her son. "No, you can't mean that."

"Mama, it's not the end of the world." The stout, dark brown young man smiled at her. "Melissa and I love each other. We . . ."

"But you're barely nineteen, and what is she—fifteen . . . ?"

"She was sixteen last month."

"Sixteen and about to be a mother. My God, boy, what were you thinking of . . . ?"

"I was thinking that I love her. I love her, Mother, and I am going to marry her."

Jacqueline felt tears rising hot and quick into her eyes. Next month. Next month she and Timothy had planned to announce their own plans to marry. Next month it would be a year since Andy had died. She let the tears fall on her dress, made no attempt to wipe them from her eyes. She had waited so long. And just when her time for happiness had come. But now . . . It would be scandalous—and after the whispers all these years . . .

"Mother, don't cry. Please." Andy's voice was soft, "I've already spoken to Uncle Timothy."

"You told . . . ?" Jacqueline's eyes left her son's face for a horrified glance at the door.

"He'll be over in a minute. Mother." Jacques Woodson took Jacqueline's unresisting hand, "everything will work out fine. Uncle Timothy is giving me a job . . ."

"What about school?" Jacqueline's voice was limp, her shoulders sagged. "What about our plans for you to go to sea next year?"

"I'm going into the tailoring business, Mother, with Uncle . . ."

"The tailoring business?" Jacqueline leaped to her feet as the shriek burst from her. "The tailoring business? When Papa Jacques has built a fleet of ships? My God, boy, have you lost your mind?"

"Mama, I want to stay home with my wife. I don't want our life to be like yours was with my father . . ."

"You don't want?" Jacqueline looked in stunned amazement at her son. "Do you think this was what I or Mama wanted? Is this life

128

to be only what you and Alexander want? No," she trembled with rage, "I won't have it. Marry this girl. Yes, marry her. But damn it, you are going to carry on the Clavier, not the Key, business."

"But, Mama . . ."

"Go, go." Jacqueline waved her hand. "Marry Melissa. But damn it, you are going to sea."

"You would never listen to me." Jacqueline turned from the window to see Timothy in the doorway. "I told you six months was long enough to wear those widow's weeds."

"Oh, Timothy." Jacqueline held out her hands to him. "Oh, Timothy, everything is ruined."

"They will marry." Timothy crossed the room and took her hand. "And then, in a month or two, we . . ."

"Timothy." She removed her hand and faced him squarely. "Did you know Jacques was thinking of joining you in the tailoring business?"

"Yes," he answered, a little bewildered by her question. "He mentioned it. But, Jacqueline . . ."

"I will not hear of it." Her eyes flashed as she began to pace the room. "He's a Clavier—a Woodson . . ."

"But he . . ."

"But he nothing." She whirled to face him. "His grandfather has spent his life building a . . ."

He took her shoulders and drew her to him. "Jacqueline, we were talking about marriage, our children's, our own."

"Timothy, I'm talking about how we will live. How we will survive. A legacy. A business my father and I . . ."

He backed off a pace, staring in disbelief. "Is that all you can think of? My God, woman, why the hell have I been wasting all these years?"

A small sad smile touched her lips. "Timothy, we are no longer children. Indeed, we are no longer young. We have our children, our grandchildren to think of now."

"All right, goddammit. All right, Jacqueline." Timothy's face was flushed. "I leave you with your business and your children and your grandchildren and your grandchildren's children. I leave you with Alex and with Papa Jacques. I leave you with your legacy, with memory instead of happiness . . ."

Jacqueline closed her eyes a moment to hold back the tears. "Then for me, Timothy, memory must be enough."

CHAPTER FOUR

1829

"Papa, Alexander's home." Jacqueline, at the casement window on the landing, called softly up the stairs. Then, looking out the window again, she gasped as she saw the slender figure that had followed her brother from the carriage. "My God, his wife looks white!"

Jacques did not stop as he came down the stairs, and Jacqueline followed him silently. She knew he needed her as never before. How he had changed these past two days since her mother had died.

Jacqueline had expected grief and—because he was that kind of man—even rage. But there was only silent abdication. As she followed his somber shadow, a quiet fear mixed with her sorrow. For she had learned that her god was merely man.

At the foot of the staircase Jacqueline paused as Timothy crossed the foyer and opened the door. Then she saw the grief-stricken face of her brother and the awed face of his bride.

They sat in the second parlor, where the family always gathered. In the front parlor, Noni Clavier lay in her candlelit bier, surrounded by roses. Jacqueline bit her lip as she thought of other times and other faces now forever gone. Anton Key, and Peter Woodson, who had been killed fighting at the Battle of Lake Erie under Admiral Perry. Andrew and Moses and Hepsabeth and Andy. Andy . . .

Jacqueline sighed as her eyes followed Timothy, sand-colored and stalwart, as he moved among the guests. His quiet warmth drew young and old to him. He held their grandchild by the hand. Their grandchild—Jacqueline forced the bitter irony of that thought from her mind and returned Timothy's quiet smile.

Then, as Timothy held out his hand to the tall, stooped, aging man now approaching him, Jacqueline's face grew cold again. Carl Kuykendal. Her lips twisted in annoyance as Alexander and his bride joined Timothy and Carl Kuykendal and his son. Papa had often said she should not feel about the Kuykendals as she did, but still it clawed deep inside her soul. Carl Kuykendal, who with the money he had made sailing Papa's ships had bought land, and with money borrowed from the bank—the very bank that had denied Papa the loan to build a bigger ship—the Kuykendals—the sailing Kuykendals —had opened a shoe factory. Already they had stores in New Bedford, Boston, and Providence, and Carl, Jr., had told her they were thinking of opening another store soon in New York.

White people. How they helped each other get ahead. She glanced at Reuben Oates and his grandson, now standing beside his father. His grandson was finishing law school, and rumor had it young Ben Oates would one day run for Congress. As Jacqueline watched, Ben Oates left Jacques's side and joined the group that now surrounded Timothy. The Keys had always been gracious folk, lively and popular; the Woodsons earthy and loyal, and the Claviers, Jacqueline realized with a sigh, were arrogant, single-minded, and often cold.

Jacqueline's gaze fell now on the new Mrs. Clavier as she stood by Alexander's side, taking in with widened eyes the beauty of the room. Resentment rose in Jacqueline as she stared at the woman who would be the new mistress of this house. Of the Persian carpets and Swiss clocks, and most of all of that which she now touched— the wheel of the *Leah-Alanya* and the captain's chair from the *Jacqueline*. She, who had done nothing except arrive, at this of all times.

Timothy, watching Jacqueline, sensed her hostility toward the new member of the tribe. Thomasina. She was a lovely thing, he thought. A frail blossom clinging to Alexander's hand. She would have a way to go, Timothy knew, for Jacqueline was as strong and all-pervasive as the Holy Ghost.

He saw Thomasina looking at him and smiled. She would need a friend. For unless Alex had changed greatly, there would be little in her life save "the cause." The bridegroom was already deep in discussion with Robert Purvis. Timothy shook his head, pondering the race business. All Purvis need do, with all his money, was arise each morning in his mansion outside Philadelphia to a life of endless delight. The son of an English father and a Jewish Moorish mother, few would suspect his Negro blood. Yet there was no man more militant, more actively, avidly Negro than Robert Purvis. He was a friend of James Forten, with whom he had come from Philadelphia for the funeral, and as Forten now joined Robert and Alex, Timothy knew, without hearing, the subject of discussion.

There was a new movement, a new feeling among people of color that, set apart, they must join together. It had started in the church with a separate church, and colored organizations—most with the

131

almost defiant prefix "African"—were growing in membership and militancy.

Some men, like Paul Cuffee, wealthiest of the Negro shipowners, despairing that America would ever practice her proud boast of freedom, were still backing the plan for recolonization. But most free men of color declared that this country, which they had helped build with their labor and had defended with their blood, must keep her promise of freedom. And many were willing to pay with their lives to see that promise kept.

The Missouri Compromise nine years ago signaled that the nation was not ready to end slavery. The thousands of Negroes prepared to march with Denmark Vesey warned that the Negro would not endure much more. This year, race riots had ripped through Cincinnati. More than a thousand free blacks there had fled to Canada.

Timothy sighed. The struggle would be long and bitter. He wondered if any in this room would see it to fruition.

He saw Thomasina, now alone and uncertain in the center of the room. He went to her and took her hand. "At times they will seem strange to you," he whispered, "but don't worry." He glanced at Jacqueline. "You have married a Clavier."

He saw Thomasina, now alone and uncertain in the center of the known she would not long be content with the sparse information she had received on this new Clavier.

Upstairs, Thomasina sat uneasily on the delicate, velvet-covered chair as her new sister-in-law moved about the room.

"This will be your room. It was mine before I married. Alexander's old room is just one large bookcase. I'll have it done into a study for him next month."

Curiosity had captured Jacqueline. As she checked the closet and dresser to ascertain their cleanliness, she formulated questions that would elicit more than the polite "yes" and "no" answers she had so far received from her brother's bride.

Thomasina, for her part, could not keep her eyes from her elegant sister-in-law. Her dress was silk, black with threads of gold and burgundy. Her shoes were silk. From a delicate gold chain around her neck hung a pearl half the size of her thumbnail. Her earrings were jade. Her hands, constantly in motion, were laden with rings.

"How old are you?" Jacqueline's voice was kind, but Thomasina saw sharp scrutiny in her eyes.

"I am going to be twenty-three next month."

"Much younger than Alexander. You know he's thirty-three?" Jacqueline looked at the pale, solemn face opposite her. Maybe she was pretty in a fragile way. Her hazel eyes were wide-set under beautifully curved brows. Her nose was straight and narrow, her mouth full and sensual. But it was her hair that was unusual. It was flaming red, long and kinky, worn in braids that formed a crown around her head. "The white," as Timothy would say, "was still slipping out the door."

"Alexander told me his age," Thomasina answered, her hands folded primly in her lap. She tried not to stare at the room. Alexander had told her his father was well-to-do, but she had never expected anything like this. The outside of the handsome three-story house only hinted at the richness inside. Thomasina knew there were Negroes who lived like this in Washington. Their homes had been pointed out to her. But she had never been invited inside.

"Do you know the Woodsons in Washington?" Jacqueline continued. "My late husband's cousin, Richard Woodson, is a soap manufacturer there. Of the Bushes? Andrew Bush's contracting firm did the excavation for the new wing of the Capitol."

Thomasina twisted the hem of her sleeve between her fingers. "No"—she met Jacqueline's look—"I know none of those people." Jacqueline's manners would prohibit further probing, but Thomasina sensed that her sister-in-law had other means to inquire as to who she was.

"My grandma and my mother were slaves. They lived in Alexandria. When my mother was six, her father, who was her master, set them free. Set them free on the streets of Alexandria. They lived wherever they could. They slept in barns or church basements. Sometimes they slept by the road. Many days my grandma couldn't find work and they didn't eat. People wouldn't pay free blacks when they could have slaves to work for free. But my grandma said she'd rather starve than be a slave again. When my mother was fifteen, they found this new place, Washington. My mother was pretty. She became the mistress of a white man. He gave her a little house. My mother had two children, my sister and myself. My sister and my grandma died of consumption when I was a baby."

"And your father . . . ?"

"I don't remember much about him. I remember him coming,

133

when it was dark and the drapes were drawn. The big horses bringing his carriage from the White House . . ."

"The White House!" Jacqueline stared at Thomasina.

"Yes," she said simply, "the White House. My father was the President of the United States."

"Thomas . . ." Jacqueline began, her mouth falling open. She looked at the girl's red hair.

"Yes." The girl nodded. "He was my father. When he retired to Monticello, he never came again. And we were very poor. My mother took in laundry. I met your brother at our church when he came to speak on freedom. I was at the meeting." Her eyes met Jacqueline's. "He's a very kind man."

Jacqueline was momentarily silenced by the girl's simplicity. Then reaching across her expanse of skirts she patted Thomasina's hand. "So now you are a Clavier." Her voice had the same intonation that Thomasina had heard in church. Rise, she thought, suppressing an irreverent giggle, and go in peace.

Jacqueline studied her sister-in-law a moment more, then stood. "Well, now, we must go back. There are people waiting and duties to be done."

So that was the Clavier word, Thomasina thought. She had never heard the word "duty" so often as from Alexander. She rose, her investiture accomplished, and followed Jacqueline from the room.

CHAPTER FIVE

1830

Thomasina stood in the door watching the lamplighter making his rounds. She hoped he would pause a moment outside her gate. His would be the first voice she had heard all day. She sighed, feeling as she often did like a distant relative who had come and stayed too long—an inoffensive, somewhat beloved intruder for whom there was no place.

It had been different in the beginning. Then she had loved being Mrs. Clavier, going to nice homes and eating good food. But as the talk of abolition had spread across New England, Alexander had spent less and less time at home. Some nights, hearing him come in after midnight, she had gone downstairs to find him near exhaustion still working, writing some pamphlet or speech for the movement.

For a while she had feared he loved another, until Jacqueline, in a rare moment of intimacy, confided, "Alexander is, in many ways, like my father. For them a wife is a sturdy perennial that needs little care, that blossoms of its own volition. But let it fail to bloom—or wither and die—and the garden of their life becomes a bed of weeds."

But she was so often alone, with Papa Jacques at sea and Alex always gone. Lonely she moved through the house, a ghost in her own time.

Thomasina kept to herself, cleaning and dusting methodically, putting each piece back exactly where it had been the day she first arrived. She felt shy and uncertain without Alexander nearby, she was terrified when books or politics were discussed. Her needlepoint, despite sincere effort, was poor. She had no knowledge of music and gave herself, almost with relief, to housekeeping. Once, with grave misgivings, she had complained of her lonely life to Alexander. Exhausted from a long trip, he had snapped, "My God, Thomasina, you have a library full of books and a piano in the parlor. There's plenty for you to do if you would only try. And thank God you are not married to a whaleman who is gone three years at a stretch."

"But, Alexander," she had dared to protest. "All your time's spent with abolition. Oh, Alexander, don't you see, the white man will never let the Negro . . ."

"As Rousseau said, 'The strongest is never strong enough to be always the master, unless he transforms his strength into right and obedience into duty.' "

Thomasina sighed. She had tried hard to do her duty. But she felt so unincluded. The Claviers never asked her opinion or requested her advice as they sat at her dinner table. And though she tried hard to believe herself the hostess, she always felt as though she were the maid.

She was a bit afraid of Papa Jacques, though his words to her were kind. His presence was everywhere in that house, even when he was worlds away at sea, putting into ports she'd never heard of before she called New Bedford home.

"Thomasina."

Guilt for her discontent ended Thomasina's reverie with a start. "Timothy." She smiled as he came up the walk.

"I was worried about you. Jacqueline said Alex has gone again."

Thomasina stood uncertainly. Jacqueline had flown into a rage when she had told her that Timothy had visited last week.

"Alex should be back from New York tonight. He's down there doing an article for *Freedom's Journal.*"

Timothy nodded. He knew the problems of the *Journal* well. Crewmen from Clavier ships which put into New York had orders to pick up the *Journal* from its office at 5 Varick Street and distributed it to all their ports of call. "Well," he said slowly, "thank God the Negroes in New York had the determination to start their own newspaper to answer those disgusting attacks of the white press on colored citizens—and of course the foresight to ask men of impeccable credentials like Cornish, who was educated at Oberlin, and Russwurm, who's a Bowdoin graduate, to edit it."

"And good men to write for it."

Timothy smiled and squeezed her hand. "That's true." Then a frown crossed his usually carefree face. "God knows we need more papers like the *Journal*. Seems that things just go from bad to worse for colored people. I'm talking in general now, 'cause the few exceptions don't prove any kind of rule. If they can't recolonize us, they're going to try to systematically legislate away the little freedom that we have. In colonial times free Negroes could vote everywhere but in

136

Georgia, South Carolina, and Virginia. Then Louisiana disenfranchised us in 1812, Connecticut in 1814, then Mississippi in 1817 and Missouri in 1821.

"In New Jersey we're franchised in one decade, disenfranchised the next, then franchised again. The Congress of the Confederation twice refused to insert the word 'white' in the Articles of Confederation in setting up the privileges of the free inhabitants of each state. Colored in the Northwest Territory could vote, but as those areas became states, the colored were left without a vote. Ohio has some ridiculous law that colored men with more white blood than black can vote.

"Even the church can't decide which way to go." Timothy shook his head. "Before I was born, back in '84, the Methodists declared slavery 'contrary to the golden rules of God' and gave their members twelve months to liberate their slaves. Virginia and some other southern states decided God's golden rule was not important and forced suspension of the resolution. Then the Baptists came along, declaring slavery 'a violent depredation of the rights of nature and inconsistent with a republican government.' But they backed down too.

Timothy turned and faced Thomasina. "Did you know the Continental Congress passed a resolution not to import slaves after December first of 1775, more than fifty years ago? Then they turned around and struck the guts out of Jefferson's strong statements in the Declaration of Independence, where he accused the King of perpetuating slavery.

"White folks are so damn fickle . . ." Timothy continued angrily, then, seeing the darkening of Thomasina's hazel eyes, patted her hand. "Well, there's no sense in worrying your pretty head about it. The Claviers will survive." He looked away a minute, and Thomasina heard his short harsh laugh. "Yes, Jacqueline will see to that."

His eyes met hers again and he said softly, "You should have children, Thomasina. Then you won't be so much alone."

She bowed her head. How could she explain to him that Alexander embraced her with the fevered passion with which he embraced the race. It was—on those nights she shared with him—enough for an entire race. Those nights when he pumped into her the seeds of love, of hope—smothering her in his need, his desperation, his anger, his frustration. Sucking from her mouth, from her breasts the strength to go on. On and on and on and on as though to stop would mean to die. And, Thomasina's breath caught in recognition —it would mean to die, what else was left for a proud black man. A proud black man whose hopes, whose dreams, whose future might never be, who could live only in the anxious activity of the present. Her words were barely audible as she said, "I've tried, Timothy. I've seen the doctor. He declares that I'm just too tense." Tears pent up for days rolled down her cheeks. "I try to relax, but I feel so useless. Sometimes I wonder why I'm here."

Timothy put his arm around her thin shoulders. "Alex should stay home more. He can't outdo his daddy, and you need him, Thomasina."

Alex came home the next morning. "Thomasina," he shouted as he came into the house. "Where are you? You must read this."

His hand and voice were trembling as he came into the kitchen, where she was baking bread. "It's by David Walker from the Boston Colored Association. He writes for the *Journal* too.

"Listen." Alexander shoved his spectacles against his eyes. "An Appeal to the Colored Citizens of the World." He looked to see that he had her attention, then drew a deep breath and read: "When I reflect that God is just and millions of my wretched brethren would meet death with glory, yea, more, would plunge into the fiery mouths of cannon and be torn into particles as minute as the atoms which compose the elements of the earth in preference to a mean submission to the leash of tyrants, I am with streaming eyes compelled to shrink back into nothingness before my Maker, and exclaim again, Thy will be done, O Lord God Almighty . . ."

Thomasina felt tingles on her arms.

Alexander dropped the paper on the table and smiled triumphantly. "White bigots are reading it with terror and damning it." His voice dropped, became low, tense. "The governors of Virginia, Georgia, and North Carolina have called their legislatures into secret session. They've offered a reward for Walker dead or alive." He seized her hands, squeezing them against his chest. "Oh, Thomasina, times have changed. We will live to see manumission. We will see the end of slavery."

David Walker was found dead, poisoned they said, outside his store. But his black brothers had heard his words and those of other black men: George Moses Horton, Robert A. Young . . . Thomasina woke at midnight to answer the knocks of freedom seekers on their way. Almost half the homes in New Bedford, colored and white, were stations on the underground railroad. The room Jacques Clavier had built beneath the stairs had found its purpose.

But Alexander Clavier was no longer content to talk and write of freedom. Now he ventured South, into the land of Cain. And his plans in these undertakings included Thomasina. Together, she posing as a white missionary with her bonnet snugly on her head to hide her kinky hair, he as her driver, they went into Maryland and Virginia and laid plans with slaves for their escape. Each time she grew more frightened. Each time she begged Alexander: "No more." But he heard only the cries of bondage and was ever anxious to return.

In June, Thomasina accompanied Alexander to a meeting in Philadelphia. She was asleep in the guest room of James Forten's home when she heard Alexander enter. "Thomasina, wake up."

She sat up quickly. He was bending over her, silhouetted against curtains that billowed in the cool night breeze. "Alexander, what's wrong?"

"Get dressed quickly. We must leave immediately for Maryland. A new plan of escape is ready, and I must get word to the slaves on the Peterson plantation."

"But, Alexander . . ."

"Hurry, Thomasina." He started toward the door. "We leave in half an hour."

They had traveled all night and most of the next day in the suffocating carriage. In late afternoon they arrived at the Maryland home of the Reverend Biedler, a white Baptist minister whose house would be the first stop for slaves on their way to freedom.

They ate a hasty supper in his austere dining room. Then the Reverend Biedler stood. "My horses and carriage are ready. Peterson is expecting the woman missionary at seven. The slaves will be assembled." He shook Alexander's hand. "God go with you."

Thomasina's fingers trembled as she tied on her bonnet. Her stomach gnawed in fear as they drove through the summer dusk.

Then she was standing inside the circle of sitting, kneeling slaves. Under the watchful eyes of mounted overseers she preached the doctrine of humility while, behind the carriage, Alexander preached the gospel of escape. It was hot, and Thomasina felt the perspiration

139

flowing from her bonnet. How long, she wondered, would Alex need to explain the way to Reverend Biedler's home?

The overseer cast a suspicious eye at the carriage, and Thomasina caught her breath as he moved his horse in that direction. "Let's sing," she said quickly to the sweet-faced girl who had led the last song. "Sing 'Swing Low, Sweet Chariot.'"

"Swing low, sweet char-i-ot," the girl's full soprano began. From the corner of her eye Thomasina saw the black men behind the carriage move quickly into the bushes. After this song, it would be done.

At first it was just a hazy curl of smoke, ignored by the singers, but in seconds, tongues of fire leapt from the big house toward the sky. The singing stopped. For an instant, but just an instant, the slaves stared in disbelief. Then they rose, to separate callings, running, shouting to save the house, to save their cabins, to save the livestock. For some, the hour of deliverance was at hand.

Into this chaos the white men's horses charged. On one, the overseer raised his gun. On the other, the driver wielded his slashing whip. As Thomasina struggled frantically in the mayhem to her carriage, her bonnet fell off. She heard the driver howl, "My God, she's a nigger too!"

Then his hand shot out and she was caught in the shackle of his grasp. His whip coiled like a snake above her. As a scream jerked from her throat, arms strong as iron yanked her to safety.

Her savior was black and huge. He half lifted, half threw her into the carriage and then leapt in beside her. As Thomasina screamed his name, Alexander leapt to the driver's seat. The carriage moved at tremendous speed, the Tennessee horses, twin black pistons, powered now by fear.

Through the window, Thomasina saw the overseer aim his gun. An old slave woman's hand shot up, grabbing the rifle, sending the shot askew. The rifle crashed against the woman's head. She fell, screaming in agony.

The carriage turned, heading back to the fallen woman. Alexander yelled, "Open the door." Thomasina thought her pounding heart would burst her ribs as the carriage slowed. The door swung open, and the man beside her leaned from the carriage, one massive black arm clutching the seat inside.

For an instant Thomasina closed her eyes. She heard the woman moaning, then as she forced herself to look, a second young black

140

man, clinging to the brasswork outside the carriage door, flung himself inside.

Blood gushed from the wound in the woman's head onto Thomasina's skirt. A whisper came through red bubbles on her lips. "Thank de Lawd, I gwine die free!" Her hand clutched Thomasina's. "I gwine die *free!*"

Their carriage had five bullet holes when they reached Reverend Biedler's barn. When Alexander stepped down from the driver's seat, Thomasina saw the blood coming from his arm. She stood silently as the reverend and two newly freed men quickly carried the old woman's body to a nearby shed. Nor did she speak as the two black men threw their arms around Alexander, then leapt into the waiting wagon.

It was not until they were upstairs in the bedroom of the house that she faced her husband.

"Never, Alexander," Thomasina whispered fiercely. "Never again."

CHAPTER SIX

1831

Washington was sweltering. Thomasina, in the smelly horse-drawn streetcar, kept her handkerchief at her nose. Most of the people about in the heat of the day were Negro slaves, moving deftly to perform the tasks of their masters. But among those dark-skinned beings were men and women who were free. Thomasina wondered which of these helped their brothers' flight to freedom. Had any of them known of Nat Turner's plan? Did they involve their families in the risk? Thomasina rubbed her fingers nervously. Or perhaps their families were braver than she.

Not that she was a coward. No, her head nodded decidedly. No, she was not. It was just that she knew enough of danger not to go poking around for more. If, as Alexander would say, the "duty" was hers, she did it. Maybe quaking with fear, but certainly not shirking what must be done.

Thomasina closed her eyes, remembering that first night, she had been alone in that big house. She had heard the knock, the signal knock. Quickly she had straightened her nightcap and, slipping into her robe, gone down to answer it.

She had seen the three black men crouching by the door. "Quick, put out the candle," one whispered. "The slave catcher's right behind."

She had snuffed it with her hand. "Hurry." She had opened the door wider. "Hurry inside."

They had followed her through the parlor to the secret room beneath the staircase. "Stay quiet." Fear sent quavers through her voice. "You'll be safe. I'll bring you food and water later."

Only a moment had passed before she heard the second knock. Leaning against the staircase, she had feared her legs would not support her to the door.

"Open up. We got a warrant." It was a man's rough voice.

Slowly she had crossed the room, asking God for strength. Her hand shook as she opened the door, saw their sullen faces, smelled their stinking bodies. God spoke through her lips. "What do you mean disturbing a woman this time of night?"

"We lookin' for three escaped bucks. I seen 'em turn on this street."
She saw the pistol hanging at his side.

"I haven't seen . . ."

"We got a right to search your house." The big one showed her a paper.

Thomasina thought that she would faint. Her heart slammed in her chest as she heard the words come from her mouth. "Then," she said, "be quick about it. My husband is not home. I should not want to . . ."

"No need. If they ain't here, we'll be out in five minutes. But if they are"—the man leered—"then . . ."

"Just be quick about it."

She had supported herself against the doorway for the eternity of their search, watching shadows from their flickering lamps move through the parlors and the study. She had heard them banging doors inside the kitchen, heard their tramping feet upstairs above her head. "Dear Jesus," she had whispered, "don't let them find them. Don't let me faint till they are gone."

She heard their footsteps as they came down the staircase, moving directly over the tiny room where the fugitives hid.

"All right," the big one had said. "But don't get no ideas about joining this so-called underground railroad, 'cause we'll be coming back."

An hour passed before she dared go to the room beneath the stairs. Two hours before she let them out to bathe and eat.

Before dawn, she had slipped out of her back door, running to the home of the rope maker, Lundy. By sunup the slaves had been in his wagon on their way to Canada.

The familiar sight of an old red barn jolted Thomasina from the past. She got off the car and, holding her dress up carefully, crossed the dusty road and weed-grown field that led to her mother's house. The paths that had been her childhood playground filled her with sharp dismay. Shanties, no longer able to bear their own paint-peeled decay, sagged into yards of dirt and cackling chickens. Children in varying stages of undress leaned from paper-shuttered windows, leapt from broken steps, or, with whoops, chased between noisy pigs up and down the muddy avenue of despair.

Had it always been like this? Thomasina stared at two young girls who in turn were staring at her dress, seeing in their thin and dirty

143

faces a remembrance of herself. Through these dusty lanes Alexander Clavier had come for her.

Lifting her skirts higher, she hurried on, casting a furtive glance toward the area called Alley Domain. Here the poor, black and white, were integrated in terror in the filthy provinces of thieves and cutthroats.

The street rose sharply to the hill known as Negro Hill. Thomasina stopped before a small frame house, then walked hesitantly through the yard to the door, fearful of what the passage of years might mean. "Mama," she called through sudden tears. "Mama, I'm home."

Although her forty-eighth birthday was near, Ella's smooth brown face was unblemished and unlined. Hardship had visited often and remained in her face, but the girl she had been smiled through her eyes and lent luster to the fading edge of beauty. She followed Thomasina's every movement with delight, though she knew from her daughter's face that she had not come this long way without a reason.

Finally, with supper eaten and tins of lemonade making wet circles on the wood plank table, Ella sensed her daughter's reluctance to explain her visit and brought the matter home.

Interrupting her story now and then to brush away her tears, to defend her husband or herself, Thomasina told of her marriage with Alexander. "I'm always alone," she wept. "When I went with him on the trips to free the slaves, at least I saw him. But then when Russwurm went over to the recolonizing movement, Alexander started his own newspaper, *The Dispatch*. Now he's never home."

Ella listened patiently, nodding from time to time until Thomasina had finished. Then, touching her daughter's hand, she said, "What you need's a chile."

"I know, Mama, and Alexander wants children." She grasped her mother's hand and held it tight. "That's why I've come. Will you help me, Mama?"

Ella frowned. It did not always work, the obah, the witchcraft. But her daughter believed in it. And Ella knew that faith was the most powerful of all medicine.

"The help is in yo'self, in yo' belief." Her full, rich voice smiled and caressed. "But I kin boil a little dis and a little dat, and the chile will come if you do as I say."

144

"Oh, Mama," Thomasina rested her head on her mother's bosom.

For a moment Ella clung to her daughter, her fingers dark against the auburn hair. Then she nodded, her faith rising fiercely. I know de Lord don' deal in no mistakes. Aloud she asked, "You didn't just up and run away?"

"No." Thomasina smiled wanly. "I left a note for Alexander. He'll find it when he gets home from Hartford. Oh, Mama, I had to come and see you. Mama, I have to have a child."

"Well, we'll git all that together in the morning." Ella stood. "Now come on, let me get you settled in the bed, 'cause the firs' order of anythin' is to have body and soul together. In the mornin' we go on from there."

Thomasina, exhausted from her journey, undressed quickly. Ella, lamp in hand, looked down at the slim figure in her bed. "They knows about yo' daddy, don't they?"

"Yes, Mama. They do."

Ella shook her head. "I'd hate to have lived in that ol' man's head. Lawd, how this color thing bounced roun' in that man's brain. How mus' he felt when his only sons was colored. An' them his slaves 'til he say in his will they free when they twenty-one." She patted her daughter's arm. "But it don't matter. We movin' on. I feels it in my blood. It gon' take time, but one day we gon' make ourselves a President of these United States. In the dungeons of despair folks has true visions, and on my soul I seen our star shoot bright against the sky."

Thomasina propped herself on her elbow. "Did you love him, Mama?"

Ella rubbed a weary hand across her brow. "On my soul, I don't remember. It been so many hundred years ago. But I do think love's a sunlight thing. It only that old passion bloom at night. Love's a sharin' thing and the only thing that ol' man and I shared was you." A soft smile touched Ella's face as her eyes met Thomasina's. "But we survived, and you, chile, you brought love to me."

Four days passed. The next three mornings brought letters from Alexander with passionate pleas for Thomasina's return.

Each morning the acrid odor of boiling herbs filled the house. Thomasina went to bed early each night, after drinking the evil-tasting product of her mother's efforts. Noon found her still asleep, but laughter followed wakefulness and with quick steps she followed her mother's tour of tasks. On the morning of the eighth day, Ella woke her daughter early. "Yo' husban' is come."

He stood behind Ella, eyes fixed on Thomasina. He looked weary, and his limp was pronounced as he moved slowly to where Thomasina lay. "I have missed you, Thomasina." He took her hand. "Without you I am empty, and nothing"—a smile intruded on the gentle gravity of his face—"not even abolition . . ."

"Oh, Alexander," she cried. Then she was in his tight embrace.

His arms were still around her when Thomasina heard her mother's voice softly from the door. "Name your first chile for us, for the earth. Name him for all mens. Call him Clay."

CHAPTER SEVEN

1845

Alexander's face was twisted in a scowl as he walked down Front Street to Union Street, then turned up Johnny Cake Hill. His cape billowed behind him. His top hat was slightly askew, and his increasing agitation with the large, handsome man beside him showed plainly on his face.

"I realize, Frederick, that we must have whites involved in abolition. But Negroes cannot be just the soul of abolition, nor even the voice. We must also be the brain."

"But you do agree that we must have whites involved in the movement, Alex?"

"I agree." Alexander stopped and faced his companion. "Yes, I agree." Behind his spectacles, Alex's eyes narrowed. "But in a movement for equality, Negroes must participate as equals. We must not suffer ourselves to be placed in subordinate roles. We must not heed the chastisements of others to wait on their direction. At the convention we arrived at that very question, Frederick. And, as you know, I stood with Henry Garnet when he called for a slave revolt and general strike."

A small smile touched Frederick Douglass's lips. "I know indeed."

Alexander nodded. "As my father says, 'There are times that to move, black men must move alone.'"

Frederick Douglass held his silence, watching Alexander carefully. He knew well the details of the convention of colored men in Buffalo. And though he did not share Alexander Clavier's persuasion for the more radical, Douglass did not want excuse for argument. He knew the family pressures that troubled his friend. And lately Alex had spoken of leaving the movement altogether. Douglass frowned. That would never do. Alexander Clavier's scholarly oratory, replete with references to the great African kingdoms of Mali, Songhay, Ghana, Ethiopia, Egypt, and the Sudan; his discourses on Ahmes, Ramses II, Memnon, Sonni Ali, Taharka, Mohammed Askia, Chaka, a whole hierarchy of African heroes, had made him one of the most popular of the abolitionists among Negroes. His following from Providence to Boston was strong, and his newspaper,

The Dispatch, had a large readership throughout New England. Yes, Douglass thought, Alexander Clavier was a man who must remain at the crest of the movement. He held out his hand. "You will be at the meeting to hear Ralph Waldo Emerson tonight?"

Alexander shook it firmly. "I will be at the meeting tonight. I am not against white involvement, Frederick. What I do object to is their insistence on leadership."

Thoughtfully Alexander watched Douglass walk away. His face had been known in New Bedford less than three years, and already he was a leader in the colored community. Now the fame of Douglass's eloquence was spreading throughout New England. William Lloyd Garrison had offered him a job at four hundred and fifty dollars a year as a lecturer for the Massachusetts Anti-Slavery Society. Unlike himself, Alexander thought, or Charles Remond, the elegant son of a free West Indian who had been the most prominent Negro in the abolitionists' movement, Douglass knew slavery from the slave's point of view. He had made a daring escape dressed as a seaman. How often Douglass had said that he had felt safe only after reaching New Bedford.

Yes, Alexander thought, Frederick knew slavery and spoke of its horrors with brilliance and passion that moved even seasoned men to tears. Not for nothing, Alexander nodded slowly, was Douglass called "the silver-tongued orator." Alexander's steps matched his regret. Yes, it would be Douglass who would be the Negro Messiah.

In front of Seamen's Bethel, Alexander hesitated, nodding absently to a whaleman coming out of the church. The depth of his own dilemma tore his soul. He was still needed in the movement, but not so much as in those years when there had been so few to answer the call. Those years when they had stood almost alone: Forten and Purvis, Walker and Cornish, Russwurm and Allen, Jones and Hall. Theirs had been a different task, that of molding the alien and the despised, those of many tribes and many traditions, Bantu and Songhay, Fula and Fanti, Nubian and Dahomean, into one people.

But now new warriors were on the field. The battle cries of black giants—Frederick Douglass and Charles Remond; the Harvard-trained doctor Martin R. Delany and the author-playwright William Wells Brown; Alexander Crummell, the Episcopal priest; the Reverends Samuel Ringgold Ward and Henry Highland Garnet; the University of Glasgow graduate Dr. John McCume Smith, J. W. C. Penning, a doctor of divinity, and the women—Harriet Tubman,

Sojourner Truth—so many, so many now—were sounding on the ramparts and echoing in the hearts and deeds of Emerson, Whittier, Longfellow, Garrison, and the eloquent Boston patrician Wendell Phillips.

And while the south moved to extend its domain into the West, demonstrations against slavery and slave catchers were sweeping across New England. By passive resistance, forceful resistance, sitting down, standing up, going to jail for abolition, men and women were moving the nation ever closer to confrontation. Alexander had seen it happen, had helped it happen. His lips parted in a tight smile as he remembered the words of the Reverend Henry Highland Garnet: "Resistance! Resistance! Resistance!"

And the words of Wendell Phillips: "Peace if possible, but justice at any cost."

But, Alexander thought as he walked up the steps of the church, he himself must let it go. He had helped dig the first hard ground for freedom's edifice. Now let the master craftsmen do their work. His family needed him.

The church was empty, except for the last pew on the left. It was inhabited, as frequently of late, by a melancholy sailor-writer whose name he'd heard was Melville.

The two men ignored each other's presence. Alexander let his thoughts roam to his family. He and Thomasina now had three children, Clay was twelve, Jason ten, and Isabella seven.

Jacqueline's son Jacques and his wife and their youngest child had died four years ago in a smallpox epidemic in Boston where Jacques had opened a tailoring shop. The oldest boy, who Jacqueline declared had been permanently distempered by the fever, had survived. A year later he had suddenly decided to go West, leaving in Jacqueline's care his small son Isaac and his young consumptive wife. She had died last year, and Jacqueline and her little grandson Isaac lived in the Clavier house now. Those rooms, so long almost empty, now rang with voices.

His father was over ninety now and crippled with arthritis. Confined, he had become cantankerous, amenable only to Jacqueline and to his granddaughter, Isabella.

So many mouths to be fed. So many minds to be formed. And Jacqueline, despite her protests to the contrary, was growing old.

For a long while Alexander stared at the ship's prow that formed

149

the pulpit of the church. Let me remember Papa's words, he thought. "It is the family. The family is strength. It is the family . . ."

"Lord . . ." Alexander clasped his hands as he raised his tear-stained face to the pulpit prow. "No, Lord," his voice came hoarsely. "No, Lord, it is the race."

Jacques Clavier sat on his captain's walk, atop his house, wrapped in a shawl. He hoped Alex would not soon come to take him inside. This was his favorite time of day. His aged weather-beaten face broke into a smile as he looked across the red and gold tops of elm and oak trees to the white sails on the river. Whaleships they were, coming home from across the world. Bending, he peered through the spyglass attached to the railing to check the flags, noting intently how each rode in the water. There was one of Howland's ships . . . another good haul, Jacques thought, as that ship moved slowly upriver toward the harbor. How he would like to ride out once again, round the Horn or round the Cape to put in at Tahiti or Japan.

Below, the noise of the children's play changed suddenly. Jacques peered over the rail. Outside the gate, two young white louts—Jacques thought with a grimace—were calling names and throwing stones into the yard where his granddaughter, Isabella, played with his great-grandson, Isaac Woodson.

"Look at that half-white nigga gal. Wonder what her mama knows."

As Jacques tried to stand, cursing age, arthritis, feebleness, his auburn-haired grandchild moved to action. Picking up a stone, she flung it with deadly accuracy at the head of her closest tormentor. Blood spurted from his face. Howling, the boy took to the street, followed by his friend and a barrage of his own stones.

Jacques smiled in approval. She was a spunky one, that girl, and pretty as a sea gull on the wing.

It was a shame the way people treated her. She hadn't handpicked her looks. But black and white gave her a way to go . . . names, taunts, vulgar insinuations. She was lucky she had such loyal brothers. More than once the doctor had been called for Clay after a fist fight in her name.

Clay. Jacques nodded. He was the kindest child he'd ever seen. And Jason, Alexander's other boy, smart as a whole durn school of dolphins. But Bella, Jacques smiled again as the girl took her

150

cousin's hand and came toward the house, she had a way, that one. Bella . . . she was the joy of his old age.

He saw Alexander coming up the street and thought to tell him of the fracas he had witnessed. But by the time his son came onto the captain's walk, it was forgotten and he was asleep.

Isabella was at the foot of his bed when he awoke. "The whole family went to hear Ralph Waldo Emerson, even Aunt Jacqueline." She rose in a puff of skirts to bring his milk. "I stayed to be with you." Her eyes, which were the color of the sea, sparkled with the idea of fun. "Will you tell me a story? About your voyage to Tahiti, or the ladies in Paris, or . . ."

He patted her hand. "Why don't you read to me tonight?" And, with much more help from her than was needed, Jacques sat upright in bed.

Isabella picked up her book and settled herself on her needlepoint stool, which was always near the side of Jacques's bed. He knew she loved this room with its rich, ornately carved furniture and shelves of curios from around the world. It was, he thought, the most beautiful room in the house, excepting the front parlor, in which she was rarely allowed.

Jacques smiled as Isabella opened her book. They were always the same stories, but her eagerness to share with him gave him pleasure. A true thespian, he thought, as she growled or purred the parts of the animals in the tale. And those eyes. Already she used them like a woman. There would be men, Jacques thought with a nod, who would regret the day they met Isabella Clavier.

The knock came from the front door. Isabella darted to answer it. The old man heard her running footsteps on the staircase, then after a moment, her shrill cry "Papa Jacques! Oh, Papa Jacques, help . . ."

He had lived his whole life on his will, and it did not desert him now. Slowly, and with agonizing pain, Jacques left his bed. Lifting his rifle from its place above the hearth, he came to the head of the stairs.

"We're gonna teach you a lesson 'bout hitting real white folks, nigger bitch." The two louts were stalking Isabella.

She backed away, eyes blazing. "My grandpa will get you."

"Jacques Clavier is a crippled old man." The boy laughed as he grabbed for Isabella.

151

Leaning against the banister, Jacques raised his rifle. His voice came from the quarterdeck, from years ago. "But not too old to send you both to hell."

Horrified, the boys stared for an instant, then broke in pell-mell retreat for the door.

"Bolt the door, Isabella," Jacques ordered. Then the pain exploded in his chest.

Isabella saw him as he fell to the stairs. "Papa Jacques! Papa Jacques!" Upward she soared, a sea gull on the rise.

Jacques's hands went to his chest, to his medallion. Each breath cost agony.

Her small arms were around him, her face bent close to his. She saw him pull at his medallion. "Do you want me to have it, Papa Jacques?" He nodded, watching as his granddaughter slipped the medallion from his neck to her own.

"Good," the old man whispered. "Good." The old eyes smiled. "Yemangi will protect you . . . Yemangi . . ."

Then he saw it, rising out of the sea, moving swiftly for him now, and knew he was too old to outsail it this time. Jacques felt his granddaughter's hand tight in his and smiled. Yes, he thought. I've won enough.

"Papa Jacques," she whispered. "Papa Jacques . . . ?"

But now the distance between them was widening. Jacques could taste the salt spray and he heard the last low shrill of the boatswain's pipe. "Yemangi," he whispered. Then he closed his eyes and let it take him out, out, out, into the endless sea.

152

Book Three

ISABELLA

And if a house be divided against itself, that house cannot stand.
And if a kingdom be divided against itself, that kingdom cannot stand.

Mark 3:25,24

CHAPTER ONE

1858

Ringlets of titian hair whipped her peach-gold face, and her eyes flashed the blue-gray-green of the sea before a storm. Heads on Water Street turned as she cracked her buggy whip above the cantering mare for the climb up Johnny Cake Hill. "Isabella Clavier," one black-bonneted woman muttered in dismay.

"Gal ain't got good sense, drive a horse like that through the middle of town," her companion replied.

But "good sense" was not at issue, and most men felt the sharp reining of their horses or quick steps to the side a small price for the loveliness they had seen.

"Someone's got hell to pay," Congressman Benjamin Oates, on the steps of his law office, muttered to no one in particular.

Oates was right. Isabella was in a fury. Her temper rose again as she thought of Eustace Terry, that ugly poor-white trash, whose father had come in steerage and married the daughter of "ol' Will," the rum-sotted town crier. How smart that straw-haired goat had felt telling her, Isabella Clavier, that colored could not try on hats in that horrid little shop. Well, Isabella's head nodded in grim self-satisfaction, that little twerp must have had a fine time sweeping up the flour from the sack she had punctured with her parasol on her way out.

She saw the row of shops across from Buttonwood Park and slowed the mare to a walk. As she gazed at the elegant female vanities displayed in the windows, an idea germinated and slowly took form.

She gave herself a turn about the park to try it on her nerves. She had never dared try it here, in New Bedford. Her family was too well known. But not, she thought with a defiant nod of her lovely head, not in this part of town. She would just walk in and ask to see a bonnet, and no one would even dream that she was colored.

It caused a state of constant consternation, Isabella thought, passing the well-dressed white children playing in the park—always to be remembering you were "colored." Could you or couldn't you? Would they or wouldn't they? It was enough to keep you in a state of chronic indignation. Or enough to make you vomit.

At home she was a person and, if her brother Clay was around, a princess. When Papa was not at home, she read *Godey's Lady's Book*—the fiction only, never the recipes or patterns—or the novels of George Eliot and Emma Southworth, and lived in their world of fantasy. But Papa made her think about being colored. He thought about it all the time. He talked about it all the time. Well, she for one was sick to death of the problems of her less fortunate brethren. There was too much fun to be had in the world.

But Papa . . . Once, when she was six, she had told her brother Clay that she was going to run away and be a slave so when she got home Papa would make a fuss over her too. He had laughed and called her "nutty as homemade fudge." But she had thought of it for months. When she grew hungry at bedtime, Papa reminded her sternly, "You didn't finish your dinner." But let a fugitive slave knock—at any hour—and pots would be filled and ovens would bang, waking everyone in the house in the haste to get them fed. Aunt Jacqueline declared that every escaped slave in America had passed through that house on Arnold Street.

He would give them anything: food, clothing, money. Had not Aunt Jacqueline often said she hoped none of them ever asked for the house, for if so they would be left without a roof? Was not Aunt Jacqueline always warning Papa they would end up poor as church mice? That pretty soon they would be as ragged as the slaves who sought safety at their door?

Isabella's lips tightened in an ugly line. Well, one thing was certain, she was not going to be poor. Poor people had to work too hard. She had been to Lynn and Lowell and seen the factories there and the girls that worked in them. They worked together, ate together, slept together, bought the necessities of life together, always under the all-seeing eye of the matron, who, concerned for their morality, gave them not an instant for an immoral thought. To work twelve hours a day for two dollars a week in those sunless tombs!

And she had seen the girls who worked in the mills of New Bedford, the huge Wamsutta mills, trudging home to the rows of faceless buildings owned by the mills . . . girls bent and old before their time.

Well, she would not work in the mills. Nor would she live like her mother, working from dawn to dusk. The very day she had come home from school, her mother had pressed for her assistance in

156

scouring the wallpaper with chunks of freshly baked bread. The next day, they had cleaned and sealed the fireplaces for the summer.

And yesterday, they had carried out the carpets and beaten them with wicker carpet beaters until both she and her mother looked like chimney sweeps. Then they had carried in fresh straw for the floor and, in complete exhaustion, relaid the carpets.

Aunt Jacqueline did not do it. No, indeed. Aunt Jacqueline sat at her work desk and ran the business and had Miss Evvie do the hard work.

No, that was unfair. Aunt Jacqueline worked exhausting hours, boasting that though she was "well past sixty," her endeavors supported two families, the Woodsons and the Claviers.

Isabella shook her head. There was something about New England that made its women look on work as an almost religious rite. She had heard that Lucretia Mott, a leader of the women's rights movement, washed the silver and fine china from her dinner parties in a cedar tub while seated at the table with her guests. Lucretia Mott washed and Susan B. Anthony dried.

New Englanders! How they gloried in hard work, austerity, and justice. Three years ago the Supreme Court of Massachusetts had ruled school segregation illegal. Boston and New Bedford had integrated their schools. And of course Papa was already talking of her teaching.

But, Isabella's eyes flashed, she did not want to teach. New England was full of schoolmarms and they made little money.

Holding the reins loosely, Isabella let the horse move at her own pace as a new unsettling thought came to mind. She was getting older. She was now nineteen, and the only beau in sight was that simpleton Percy Johnson. She'd had her eye on Danny Wilson till she heard him whisper at a party that he couldn't stand "high-yella gals." And all of Aunt Jacqueline's schemes to marry her off to one of Paul Cuffee's offspring had come to no avail. And who else was there around New Bedford? She had no intention of marrying a whaleman who would spend his life at sea, returning every two or three years to leave six hundred dollars on the table and another baby in her belly.

Isabella's eyes flashed. Never, she had decided years ago, would she ever accept the role of most women—willing, slavish chattel to some man. No, indeed. A "good" husband was more than a kind master. She would find someone who loved—appreciated—her, who would want her happiness as much as his own.

But, the reins went loose in her hands, the Lord knew her brothers were no help with all their college friends. Despite her letters, despite the boxes she had sent of peanut brittle as well as the knitted caps and gloves she had made, she had never set eyes on a soul Clay knew at Chaney College. And the only man Jason had brought home from Lincoln, "a true scholar," Papa had said, had holes not only in his shoes but in his socks as well. Now Aunt Jacqueline had sent Jason to France to the Sorbonne to study and what chance had she of meeting anyone from there?

Isabella frowned. Of all of Papa's friends there was not a single man her own age with money. No, she was on her own in the husband business. Clay and Jason both laughed when she implored their help. "Bella, a man would starve to death while you fidget before the mirror." And Papa, Papa patting her on the head, saying, "You have plenty of time, Isabella." Or, "You should dedicate yourself to worthwhile causes. You write well, and the movement needs good writers. Who knows, you could be another Louisa May Alcott or Harriet Beecher Stowe."

God! That man could turn even a passing comment into an abolitionist meeting.

As Isabella watched the children rolling their hoops in the park, she wondered if her family was, as Aunt Jacqueline had prophesied, on their way to the poorhouse. Tuition for three was a big expense, but last fall she would have left for Oberlin with nothing but those horrible calicoes with the little white collars had it not been for her aunt.

Aunt Jacqueline would not hear of it. Finding her father, as always, stubborn in his argument, "She's going to study, not to dress," Aunt Jacqueline had bought yards of wool, cotton, and silk and called in her own dressmaker.

Isabella had been the most beautiful girl at Oberlin. For the first time in her life, everyone said so. For the first time she could remember, she heard no taunts about her color. For the first time, no one called her "rabbit" as she concentrated on Aunt Jacqueline's admonition to reduce the width of her smile and, as in the novels she had read, give "but a promise . . ."

And because no one had thought otherwise, Isabella had been accepted eagerly into a world of young, wealthy white ladies "of serious persuasion."

As with most of the colored people she knew, Isabella did not want to be "white." She only wanted what being white allowed. She had attended the Friends' Academy in New Bedford, a school that was largely white. At home, most of her neighbors had been "without the race." And so for the first days of her "whiteness," she did not realize she was "passing."

She was friendly with the other colored girls. However, none of them lived on her floor in the Female Wing at Oberlin or took classes with her, and she saw them rarely.

Her first inkling of her new role came as she heard her roommate, Annette Waverley of the railroad-rich Waverleys of Chicago, listing the colored women in their class. Her first instinct was to correct the situation, but then she had thought it would be amusing to see how long Annette would be fooled.

But Isabella had soon realized that the time to tell the truth with grace had passed. And, to her amazement, the other Negro girls, usually sensitive to such things, did not recognize her as colored. She had become afraid of being found out, of being the one on whom the laugh was turned. Soon she became nervous when any colored girls approached.

Isabella traded Annette's stories of her parents' endless balls and travels for those of the high adventures of her Grandpa Jacques, who had given her the medallion she wore, always, about her neck. And though she did not have the money to have wood hauled for the fireplace in their room or to have her dresses pressed, Isabella soon found that she could keep up with any of them. A theme written for a lagging student could earn a week of devoted service, and Aunt Jacqueline's gifts supplied her other needs. Little by little her role became reality.

At Christmas she had gone as Annette's house guest to Chicago, contravening her father's suggestion that she spend the holidays with abolitionist friends in Cleveland.

They had traveled in the private family car attached to the end of the train, giggling and sipping tea in magnificent velvet seats. As the train sped over the flat land, Isabella had quietly thanked God for Aunt Jacqueline's Christmas gift, a ball gown of pale green tulle with a skirt more than ten yards wide.

They were met at the depot by the Waverley family's brougham. A coal-black footman helped them into the carriage and turned up the gleaming sidelights. The coachman's whip snapped, and matched gray horses pranced through the evening lakeshore traffic toward the Gold Coast.

Isabella, awed by the private car, had been speechless as wrought-iron gates swung open and the carriage crunched up the snow-covered drive to pass beneath the turrets of the Waverleys' "medieval" stone castle.

A glittering glass door flew open, and family of all descriptions rushed out, illuminated by a hundred candles twinkling in a crystal chandelier just inside the foyer.

Inside, Isabella was grateful for the gay confusion of the Waverleys. Her eyes, used to the functional, to the rich, even to the ornate, had never seen such grandeur. A Rembrant, gloomy and austere, faced the happier scenes of Jan van Eyck and Pieter Breughel. Great Persian rugs, twenty times the size of those in her home, crossed oaken floors that gleamed like glass, as background to Regency and Directoire furniture, gilded by the master abenistes of France.

Over and around this splendor swirled hooped taffeta and silk, while Annette's small, paunchy father laughed and joked with the members of his family.

Another man was also present. A younger man, dark, ascetic: Annette's brother, Dirk. His attention was fixed on the tall, graceful redhead as she stood amidst his chattering sisters, beautiful and, a miracle in this household, saying not a word.

He watched her as she followed the butler with her bags up the wide, circling staircase. Her eyes met his as she paused an instant, a small half smile on her lips.

"She is a lovely thing." Dirk felt his father's hand gentle on his shoulder.

"She's beautiful," Dirk whispered.

"Well, get to know her more before you fall," the czar of railroads chuckled. "Despite all of your biology and anatomy courses, you may learn that a butterfly can turn into a wasp."

Christmas was a gala holiday at the Waverleys. Luncheons and teas, dinners and balls whirled Isabella through days and nights of holly and mistletoe and blazing candles that lit the mansions of Chicago's rich.

160

Dirk was more and more at Isabella's side, laughing gently at her quick wit, holding, whenever he could, the kid-softness of her hand. One late morning, after they had waltzed all night in each other's arms, the senior Waverley was waiting when Isabella appeared at her bedroom door. With a courtly arm he escorted her down to lunch.

"Clavier," he began with a smile. "I would say New Orleans, but no southern accent."

"No." Her smile took his breath away. "New Bedford."

"Oh, whaling people."

"No." Her green eyes flashed. "Ship owners."

Annette and Isabella returned to Oberlin. Dirk visited every chance he could, lugging a suitcase heavy with medical books. Giddy with excitement, Annette and Isabella whispered like sisters about "a proposal."

But in midnight moments, Isabella was afraid. She was slowly and reluctantly falling in love with the devoted, sensitive, and shy young man who wanted to be a doctor and happened to be a millionaire. Once, studying together in the pasture beside the Female Wing, she had started to tell him the truth. Even if he lost his fortune, he had a future. They could start a new life together.

But what if his family found out before he finished school? However would they live? Pictures of poverty filled her mind: scenes of poor whites living in filth and destitution in Boston and New York, the white niggers. No, she would not be poor. Not for Dirk. Not for anyone.

Summer drew near, and Dirk drew near the question. Isabella's troubled conscience gave her sleepless nights.

Then one evening as she lay on her bed translating French, she heard Annette enter the room. She saw the letter in Annette's trembling hand, her face pale and stunned. Isabella knew her charade was over. "Well," she snapped, "has the cat taken your mind as well as your tongue?"

Annette's voice wavered. "I just received this letter from my father." Her words came thickly. "He wrote a friend in Boston . . . about you and Dirk. His friend checked your background." Angry tears filled Annette's eyes. "He said the only Claviers in New Bedford are, are . . ." She couldn't use that other word. ". . . colored."

161

Isabella's eyes were the bland gray of fog. "So! Go on."

Annette, expecting denial, caught her breath. "You deceived me." Her voice was a hoarse hissing. "You are an impostor, an intruder, a . . ."

Shrugging, Isabella picked up her book. "For all I know, Annette, you could be deceiving people too."

For an instant Annette's mouth opened in horror. Then, with a choking sound, she ran from the room.

Isabella waited a moment. Then, tears streaming down her face, she got up and closed the door.

Annette had her room changed and told everyone why. The three weeks until the end of school had been agony for Isabella. Taunting smiles and sneers and, worst of all, turned heads and stuck-up noses. The other colored girls twittered when they saw her and gave her the sidelong eye. Though she longed to pack her trunk and leave, Isabella was determined not to give Annette that satisfaction. Vowing furiously between clenched teeth that one day she would fix them, would fix them all, she held her chin high and smiled sweetly at the few who still befriended her.

Rage had changed to guilt when she saw her father waiting for her at the depot in Boston. He had squeezed her in his arms. "Oh, how we missed you, Bella."

And it was this guilt as much as her hope of eluding the tasks her mother constantly imposed that had led Isabella to roam the attic her first weeks home.

The Claviers were not wasteful folk. Everything not given to a good cause had been carefully boxed and set back under the eaves: furniture, clothing, the ships logs and mementos of Papa Jacques, including a now famous "Temple iron," the toggle harpoon invented by their onetime neighbor, a Negro, Lewis Temple. But in her father's box Isabella had found her great surprise: a diary begun during the War of 1812. At first she had flipped through the pages, noting with some interest the detailed descriptions of the valor of colored troops. However, it had been her father's description of his courtship with her mother that had whetted her attention.

For the first few moments she had felt uneasy, peeping into pages now three decades old. But to imagine that such words of passion— better by far than even those of Dinah Murlock or the Brontë sisters

162

—had come from that man of stern self-denial she knew as her father!

Then suddenly one passage had ripped through her romantic reverie. She had sat up, reading and rereading: "Now the great President has retired, leaving nothing but that small house with heavy drapes to cloister the secrets of his nights and bar the treachery of his days.

"A man of noble words and perfidious deeds, who has, with a most remarkable agility, swung the full circle of conviction? Could the author of the most remarkable words in human history, words that fired the minds and dreams of men throughout the world—'We hold these truths to be self-evident, that all men are created equal'— be the same soul, who without a backward glance, deserts his own blood, his own girl child, my fair love, Thomasina . . . ?"

The diary had dropped to Isabella's lap. So that was it. That explained her mother's color and her own. And to think that her grandfather, her mother's father, had been President of the United States! What was it she had once read? "The best blood of the South flows in Negro veins." She had pulled an auburn curl and studied it, then tossed it back. She had heard tales of his other children, slave children by his slave mistress, his hostess, the beautiful quadroon, Sally Hemings. His own sons and daughters, his own flesh and blood, his slaves. What a creature he must have been!

For a long moment Isabella had sat in scowling thought. Damn white people. Damn them to hell and back. Then for the first time in many months Isabella had thought of the medallion around her neck. She had raised it to her lips and kissed it.

She saw the ball bounce into the street and reined her horse in sharply. She had come full circle, back to the shops across from the park. Waiting as a boy retrieved the ball, she looked in the window again. Yes, she thought, the hat in the window of La Couturerie, that soft blue tulle, would be lovely with her traveling dress.

In the park, Clay Clavier looked up from the pad on which he was writing poetry, startled by the familiar figure moving from the surrey to the shop. Colored did not buy in this part of town, and Isabella knew it.

Curiosity, anxiety quickened Clay's steps until, through the shop

163

window, he could see his sister, blue tulle bonnet atop auburn curls, admiring herself in the mirror held by the shopgirl.

For a moment Clay was stunned. Though he knew people who passed for white, some permanently, some for employment only, and though he knew well the suffering of Bella's girlhood, he had never really associated "whiteness" with his sister. Indeed, family and friends had always spoken of the remarkable resemblance of the Clavier children, most especially of the striking likeness between Isabella and himself.

Clay was the darkest of the children of Alexander and Thomasina Clavier. Tall and lean, with black curly hair, he had inherited the compelling Clavier eyes, handsome forehead, and well-boned face. More than once, by both colored and white, Clay Clavier had been called "the most handsome man in New Bedford."

Clay looked from his hands, which were the rich, warm brown of well-rubbed maple, to those of his sister, now adjusting the ribbons of the hat.

At first entranced by his discovery, Clay suddenly thought how horrified Papa would be. Sadness touched him as he watched his sister through the window. They had been so close, he and Bella. He had never thought race had wounded her so much.

Clay did not notice the two ladies as they passed him and entered the shop. He saw the shopkeeper turn in his direction. Then his sister met his eyes, and that slow half smile rested on her lips.

"The nerve of some niggers. The way they look at us," the older lady confided to her overstuffed companion as she tried on a hat.

"They are absolutely bold in these parts," the fat one twittered in response.

"Oh, don't put on so," Isabella snapped as she paid for the hat and watched it disappear in a box. "You love even the idea of it. The very idea that a good-looking man like that would look at a pair of sacks like you."

She glared at Clay as she came out of the shop and passed him without a word. It was starting to rain as she unhitched the horse and climbed into the surrey. She turned to her brother, still by the window, with her own half smile on her lips. Behind him stared three curious pairs of eyes.

"All right, Clay," she said. "So you disapprove." She held out her hand. "But you'll always be my friend, won't you, Clay? No matter what I have to do?"

164

Isabella sat on her bed in chemise and pantalets, listening, in glum contrition, to the sounds of gaiety downstairs. The guests were arriving now, for the only exciting event of the summer, and here she sat, a self-proclaimed exile in her room. But, she thought, touching the hem of her favorite dress, downstairs she would have to face the aloof disgust of her father and the resigned anger of her mother.

Really, it was they who had gone too far. Yesterday she had worked like a slave, sweeping, polishing, bending over that hot oven until she thought her back would break. Even this morning, she had snapped the string beans for an hour, and the instant she had finished washing her hair, her mother had asked her to black and polish the stove. To black and polish, and be a mess, with all these famous people coming for dinner. They could be so . . . so . . .

Well, she had not done it, had told her mother she would not do it. "No," she had answered her mother's pleas for help. "I'd rather not see them at all than see them with messy hair and filthy nails."

Flopping over on her stomach, Isabella buried her head in her pillow. Everything, everyone was trying to make her life hell.

Yesterday Papa had bought her ticket for the train trip back to school. And two days from now the men would be picking up her trunk. She would have to decide on something soon.

The sudden sound of laughter interrupted her thoughts. Crossing to the door, Isabella opened it a crack. In the downstairs hall she recognized the spare frame of Ralph Waldo Emerson. He had spoken at many abolitionist meetings in New Bedford and had been a guest before at dinner. The man beside Mr. Emerson she recognized as Bronson Alcott and the young woman beside him, talking with Frederick Douglass and Dr. Martin Delany, must be Mr. Alcott's daughter, Louisa May.

She opened the door an inch or two wider and caught a glimpse of her brother Clay, deep in conversation with his idols, Henry Wadsworth Longfellow and David Thoreau. Near him her father was in passionate discussion with his heroine, Sojourner Truth. And going into the parlor now was William Lloyd Garrison, the famous editor of *The Liberator,* with the black man who had arrived the day before, H. Ford Douglass, the orator from Illinois. The meeting of the Bristol Anti-Slavery Society at Liberty Hall tonight would be quite a success. What a coup it would be to tell how she played hostess to this gathering when she got back to school . . .

Slowly, Isabella closed the door, turned, and faced the open half-packed trunk beside her bed. She was not going back. All summer she had known it. As she packed her clothes she had known it. They would be waiting for her like vultures on a tree.

Slumping on her bed, Isabella stared at the trunk. How could she tell Papa she was not returning? He would demand to know what had happened. And he would find out! Her hand rumpled her hair. Everything was horrible. Incredibly, unbearably horrible.

She would not stay in New Bedford. That she would not do. She would not help endlessly clean the house. She would not teach and she would not work in the mills. If only she had never mentioned this stupid town to Mr. Waverley.

She picked up the age-yellowed envelope on top of her clothes in the trunk and opened it to reread the message for the tenth time that day. "My dear Isabella—Perhaps by your twentieth birthday you will not need this at all. But, it is my joy that I can give it to you. Use it well, for it did not come easily. Use it for something that will bring you happiness." The envelope contained another item, and now Isabella pulled it out. It was a check for five hundred dollars, dated the day of her birth, and signed Jacques Clavier. Last week, on her birthday, it had been hand-delivered from the bank.

The arrival of a new carriage interrupted her thoughts. Running to the window, Isabella pulled back the curtains to see which new presence she would be denied. A squeal of joy rose to her lips as the trim elegant figure of her brother Jason got out of the carriage. Banging on the window in frustration of raising it, Isabella saw a second figure, tall and blond, follow her brother up the walk.

Her state of undress mandated modesty. Racing to the bed, she scooped up her corset and struggled to bind herself inside. It was an awesome task—first the front hooks, then the lacing down the back, and excitement lent ignorance to her hands. It took a full three minutes to accomplish, then she stepped into her crinolines and began the job of fastening them.

It was easier to rig a ship, she thought, pulling her petticoat over her head. Boned at the waist and padded from the knees down, it was but a prelude to a third petticoat of starched flounces. Panting, Isabella bent to tie her grosgrain slippers.

Her dress was floating over her head when she heard the knock at her door and Jason's voice, "I say, Bella, wake up! The work's all done. It's time for fun."

Rushing across the room, almost tripping on her skirts, she threw open the door and tumbled into his arms.

Jason had not seen his sister in nearly two years. He held her at arm's length, adjusting to the change. *"Je dis"*—his eyes belied the gruffness of his voice—"those years before the mirror have served you well, after all, *ma belle soeur*."

"However did you get home so soon?" She drew him into the room and closed the door, his scrutiny making her conscious of her incomplete toilette. "We didn't expect you until next week."

"We came on my friend's ship, the *Lucretia*. She quite puts the *Friendship* to shame."

"That white fellow with you?" Isabella stood before her mirror now, her brush in her hand.

"Yes, Ethan Barclay, a classmate of mine at the Sorbonne. His father is the largest shipbuilder in New England."

"Oh?"

Jason recognized coquetry and laughed. "Save those looks for a chap you can have. But come on, tie a ribbon in your hair and I'll take you down to meet him."

But Jason quickly learned that there was more to his sister's toilette than a simple tying of a ribbon. Leaving her to fret her curls into place, he went back to the guests.

It was a full half hour before Isabella appeared. Every head turned as she came down the stairs in a swirl of green Lyon silk.

"Mon Dieu, Mama," Jason whispered, pausing behind that frail figure, a tray for the buffet in his hands. "She looks like an angel."

"Pretty is as pretty does," Thomasina snapped. "And it's high time she learned she's not the only bee buzzing on this tree." She saw the smile spreading on her son's lips and stopped. Perhaps she had said too much. She never knew with certainty what Jason and Isabella were thinking. Only Clay did she really know. Dear, honest . . . But Jason and Isabella? So smart in all their airs. But what could be expected? Thomasina grimaced. Alexander had allowed Jacqueline to raise them.

Now, as that creature, rings a-flashing, appeared before them, Thomasina murmured greetings and hastened to the parlor. Balancing his tray in one hand, Jason kissed his aunt's soft hand and cheeks. "Aunt Jacqueline. You do look marvelous." It was spontaneous, true.

"And you fit as a fiddle." Eyes eager, anxious. "Tell me, how was school . . . and Paris?"

In a voice low as with a fellow conspirator, Jason spoke the cogent words, French phrases, Greek analogies.

Jacqueline smiled, appreciated. The verbiage was amorphous, but its meaning clear—the Clavier ascendancy—her money, her life well spent. "Oh, Jason!" The proudest applause, the supreme approbation: "Papa Jacques would be so proud of you."

Ethan Barclay stood near the parlor door, staring as Isabella approached, moving gracefully, with smiles, little curtsies, and gracious handshakes, ever closer to where he stood.

She lingered a moment with a colored man dressed in the latest mode—dark frock coat and tight-fitting checkered pants—Dr. John Rock, an abolitionist from Boston. Ethan held his breath, hoping she would not be long delayed.

But then she turned to him, drawing him into the deep whirlpool of her eyes. "I'm Isabella. And you must be Ethan, Jason's friend?"

He moved at her side among the clusters of people, hearing, not hearing, the discussions of the guests. Garrison's new position: that the South should secede so the Fugitive Slave Law would have no effect in the separate northern country; talk of the impetus of the women's movement, talk of the stupendous impact Frederick Douglass had made spreading abolitionist fervor in England.

Then they were in the garden, and they spoke of themselves. He is a fine man, she thought. He thought her the most beautiful creature in the world.

In the rose arbor he murmured, "I would not have dreamed Jason would know a girl like you."

She knew then he did not know. Even here, in her own home, she had been mistaken.

She drew back as Ethan took her hand. "I wish I could take you to Paris and have Ingres paint your portrait," he whispered. "Then I would hang it in the Louvre so that the world could see your beauty. But only I would know the original of the masterpiece."

Inside the house, dinner was over, the guests preparing to leave for the meeting. Jason turned from discussion with his boyhood friend,

168

Alexander Kuykendal. "Have you seen Ethan?" he asked his brother.

The same thought had been in Clay's mind. Knowing his brother's explosive disposition, he did not mention that another person had also been missing for some time. "He's around. I'll get him for you."

Clay's steps were slow as he moved down the garden path until he saw them, his sister and his brother's friend. When he spoke, he chose his words with care. "Say, Barclay, Jason's looking for you. What in the world has my sister been talking about all this time?"

For an instant Ethan stared at Isabella, doubting. Then his hand loosed its hold of hers. Rosettes blotched his face as he stepped back, stammering. "Your . . . I didn't know."

Anger fought with tears for Isabella. They were all the same. She turned her head as Ethan backed—with profuse, profound apology —away.

Clay watched him go, then gently turned his sister's face to his. "It's a dangerous game you play, Bella."

She lifted her skirts, starting to move away, then turned and touched his arm. "I am a woman, Clay. I can have only what a man will give me. And I want a great, great deal." She tiptoed and kissed his cheek. "Watch, Clay. One day I will have it." Then her eyes, hard and green, met his. "And one day I will bring it all, all of their wealth and power back to us."

Sorrow welled in Clay as he watched his sister run toward the house. He did not doubt, an instant, that she would try to make her words come true.

Isabella stood at the rail of the steamboat watching the waterfront of Philadelphia come slowly through the fog. Her hands trembled inside her muff. Her journey was half over now. Philadelphia would be her last chance to change her mind and take the train to school.

Two days ago when she had kissed her parents goodbye in Boston and boarded the train for Ohio, she had not been certain she would get off in Framingham and there take the train to New York. But in that short time, scattered thoughts had fused into decision.

She could not go back to school and face their taunts or cold indifference. Nor could she stay home and face Papa and Jason's cold disdain. Her alternatives were clear, if few. She could not sew. She could not teach. She had no brain for business like Aunt Jacqueline. What else could a woman do?

She had known the answer as the train puffed slowly from the Boston depot, as she saw the last flutter of her mother's hand. There was one thing she could do. One thing that required neither skill nor brains. She could be white.

And with her looks, with the social graces learned from her family, she would get the richest man around.

In the past two months, since her secret probing of her father's diary, Isabella's imagination had clothed her grandmother in the fabric of romantic intrigue. She imagined her as one of the beautiful New Orleans quadroons, the *placées* she had heard and read of, women kept in splendor by wealthy white men who were husbands in all but title. Ofttimes the darlings of white fathers (who dared not admit this progeny to their own society), many were educated by tutors, or abroad, and played music and entertained in quarters as elegant as any seen by a Bourbon bride. And despite the diary's warning—"leaving nothing but this small house"—in Isabella's imagination her grandmother had become a fading rose in a crystal vase.

Not that she would settle for less than marriage. No, indeed! She would establish herself in elegant quarters. Papa Jacques's check would see to that. But her grandmother would know the rich men,

170

the available men, and, as in the French novels she had read, the ins and outs of their affairs.

With this in mind, Isabella had gotten off the train in Framingham and boarded the Boston and Worcester Railroad for New York. It cost five dollars and took nine and a half hours, but by the time she checked into the Brevoort Hotel in New York her plan was set.

The management of the Brevoort had registered her reluctantly. A woman traveling alone and with no reservations was a rarity in their establishment. Only the richness of her dress and her obvious breeding had saved Isabella from embarrassment. To make certain no other such impediment should arise, Isabella's first stop the next morning was the telegraph office. There, for fifty cents, she sent a telegram to the Willard Hotel in Washington stating that Miss Isabella Clay of Concord, arriving on the evening train next day, requested accommodations until met by relatives.

Then, after a wistful look in Tiffany's, across from the City Hall, Isabella hailed a carriage. "Grand and Chrystie." She smiled as she gave the driver the address of Lord and Taylor. She had been to that Greek palace before with Aunt Jacqueline. Two hours later she emerged triumphant with two elegant town dresses and, the greatest prize of all, a gown by Charles Frederick Worth, favorite designer of the Empress Eugénie.

But by midafternoon, back in her hotel room, Isabella had begun to have misgivings. She had never seen her mother's mother. Ella had declined all invitations for a visit. Suppose . . . No, it was too late for such thoughts now. And to chase them from her mind she had left the hotel and taken a carriage up Fifth Avenue to see the new Central Park. She had read about the park in *Godey's*. It had been begun the year before by the famed park designers Frederick Law Olmsted and Calvert Vaux.

She had gone to bed early and caught the steamboat to South Amboy at six this morning, in order to catch the train to Camden that connected with this steamboat to Philadelphia. Now she would be able to take the express train from Philadelphia to Baltimore, change trains there, and be in Washington by seven tonight. Yes, Isabella thought, she would do it. There would be no turning back.

A strong wind blew across the bay. The fog lifted and Philadelphia came clearly into view. To the amazement of the two fashionable young gentlemen who had been covertly admiring her, the red-haired

171

girl threw her head back and laughed. It was, as Papa Jacques used to say, a good omen.

Ella peeked at the two pig's feet in one pot, and sighed as she lifted another cover to check the rice. There was hardly enough to fill one belly, much less two. Things were rough and gettin' rougher. It had been months since she'd had a full day's work. Not that there was much work, for the colored at least. Not any more. The immigrants took to washtubs and flatirons like they'd been birthed in laundry tubs. And now, with Ben out of a regular job . . .

Carefully, Ella wiped the bare table and set two places. Things had been better when Ben had a regular job as a coachman. Especially when he worked for the Wingates.

Ella's mouth watered, remembering the delicacies Ben had brought home from the Wingate mansion. But an Irishman had that job now, and Ben worked only part time driving a livery carriage. They'd almost starved to death last summer when Congress was out. But Jesus had saved them, with money from her daughter.

Wiping her hands on her apron, Ella went into the parlor to sit down. It was a shame when folks got up in years and all the pennies in their cookie jars were spent. Ella said, as she did each evening at this time, a silent prayer for their deliverance.

She heard the carriage and looked up with curiosity. It was too early for Ben and all the folks she knew used foot power not horse power. Ella caught her breath as the girl got out. The only time rich white folks visited colored was when someone was dead, or dying, to pay their last and only respects. Or, as Ben would say, "to see da nigger all da way down in da ground." Now, for what was this fancy-lookin' white gal coming to her door?

Isabella hesitated as she stepped through the gate. This was not at all what she'd imagined. The place had needed paint for near a decade, the drapes split wide enough to air the house. The small, carefully tended flower beds on either side of the door could not dispel despair nor the time-eroded goat tied to the bottomless wicker chair persuade prosperity. At the depot, the liveryman's head shot up when she gave this address.

"You mean Swamp Poodle?" he'd exclaimed.

"I don't know what you call it," she'd replied haughtily, "but that is the address to which I am going." "No offense, ma'am." The

172

apology thickened the Irish brogue. "I just didn't think you knowed. You don't often see quality folks headin' there."

For an instant Isabella wanted to leave, but curiosity moved her to the door. The knocker was dusty, and she blew on it before touching it with her gloves. The knocker was still in her hand when the door opened. Isabella caught her breath as she stared at the woman inside.

Her gray hair was tied up in a red-checked kerchief. She was wearing a dress that had never been made for her. Isabella's voice trembled as she asked, "Are you . . . Ella?"

Ella, angered by her scrutiny, snapped, "I is. An' what kin I do fo' you?"

Slowly Isabella extended her gloved hand. "I'm Isabella Clavier . . . your . . . grandchild."

The old woman stared in confusion, trying to grasp the fact that this elegant, exquisite young lady—with all that glory on her head—was indeed her Thomasina's child. Her eyes widened and narrowed as she studied the blue tulle bonnet with its velvet ribbons, the full puffed sleeves that accentuated the narrow waist of the fine multi-buttoned blue muslin traveling dress.

Isabella, flattered by the impression she was making, was gracious. "Remember those horrible towels I made for you each Christmas?"

Ella nodded, recovering her senses. Her frowning face allowed the small beginning of a smile. "You the one what made them crazy stitchings?" The door opened wider. "Come in, chile, and make yourself to home."

Isabella settled herself gingerly on the threadbare sofa, staring at the stuffing working its way loose from the room's only chair. A rusting pot on the buckling floor caught the leakage from the roof. Ella patted her apron nervously. "You done come from New Bedford today?"

"Yes." Isabella smiled carefully. "It was a long trip."

Ella remembered the few tea leaves she had been saving in the bottom of a jar. "You mus' be thirsty. Kin I make you a cup of tea?"

Isabella accepted gratefully, and Ella went toward the kitchen. At the door she turned, with a small wistful smile. "Does they still call you Bella?"

Recognition caught Isabella's breath. With quick steps she crossed the room and took strong, rough hands in her own. "Yes, Grandma. Yes, they do."

She followed her grandmother into the kitchen, and to answer the old woman's deluge of questions, relayed a picture of her family in New Bedford. Isabella had determined, seeing the destitution of her grandmother's condition, not to mention her own plans. But she quickly grew fond of the lonely, quick-witted, warm old woman who, like herself, she was discovering, had a great zeal for adventure. And so, when Ella finally asked, "An' now tell me, what you doin' in Washin'ton?" Isabella hesitated only a moment before replying, "I've come to find a husband. A rich husband."

Ella had learned enough about Isabella Clavier in the hour or so that had passed not to be shocked by anything she said. She merely nodded and asked, "I s'pose by that you means a rich white husban'?"

Isabella shrugged. "The richest ones are white, aren't they?"

Ella nodded vigorously. "Dat they is and Lord knows dat's de way they intends to keep it." Her sharp eyes studied her granddaughter intently. She had spent enough time in the households of the well-to-do to know the difference between wealth and quality and, she thought to herself, none of them women got nothin' on this chile. Then the sobering thought crossed her mind. Except that they was white.

Ella's lips tightened. Now she didn't hold with deceit. And white men could sure bring on the misery. But white folks set the rules. It would serve them right to have their trick cards played right back on them.

Isabella watched the thoughts crossing her grandmother's face. She knew she would need help from someone who knew, who understood the ways. "Will you help me, Grandmama?"

Ella scowled in concentration, her lower lip protruding. It wasn't to be taken lightly. Lord a mercy on that child if they found out. But then, there was more than one cook or maid on Negro Hill who had a sister or brother or cousin they said "ma'am" or "sir" to. Leastwise when white folks were about.

White folks . . . they'd had enough colored women for free—for free and even profit. If a white man lay with a colored woman, and she was a slave, all their young'uns were slaves. And even if the colored gal was free, there still was no respect. Seemed like half of them raggedy high-yella young'uns in the "Alley Domain" had pappies on Capitol Hill.

174

The race business was rough. There were white women who came to court to divorce their man because of some slave wench he couldn't stay away from and then there were white women who owned plantations and married some black man. And the craziest thing she'd ever heard was from a nigger that had run away from a plantation owned by niggers.

Ella shook her head, remembering days when she'd known that old man. Lord a mercy, how they'd been talking about that Burr and Hamilton duel startin' a way back when Burr callt Hamilton a nigger. Everybody knew that uppity high-yella, Hamilton's mama, was mulatto from the Islands. She'd always wondered were there naps under that wig. But, then, he had the wig . . .

Ella looked at Isabella again. It was a shame and a disgrace what she was planning. But the shame was not to the colored. No, in-deedy. The shame was to the whites. They were the reason why colored men had nothing for their women—and then when the white man came for her, he gave her even less. He'd leave, just walk away from their own young'uns. Yes, Ella thought, it was time colored women got some of the good things. It was time they stopped work-ing dawn to dusk. It was time they were sitting in the big house. Ella's lips pressed in a firm line. "How you gonna meet this man?"

Isabella shook her head. "I don't know yet. I have reservations at the Willard . . ."

"Da Willard!" Ella exclaimed. "That's da place to be. All the big mens be down there at night." A sudden thought struck Ella and she looked at Isabella sharply. "Your folks know where you at?"

"No," Isabella replied, her eyes on her grandmother's face.

"Well, you write and tell them yo' plan, and I'll do what I kin to keep you from gettin' kilt."

By the time the stout gray-bearded Ben arrived it had been worked out. Ben shook his head when he heard the idea. But he soon came to Ella's recognition that, with them or without, Isabella was deter-mined.

And so, by ten that night Isabella and her small entourage were bumping through the broad stream of mud called Pennsylvania Ave-nue toward Fourteenth Street and the Willard Hotel.

The Willard was indeed the meeting place of the notables of the city. As Isabella came through the lobby with Ella a respectful two

175

feet behind, pronouncements, predictions, and politics were momentarily forgotten.

When the bellboy returned from taking her bags to her parlor, he was pressed by questions from the elite of Washington's bachelor corps. He told what he had overheard: that Miss Isabella Clay had been living in a place called Concord with an aunt who'd died. She was here awaiting the arrival of relatives she'd never seen—the only family she had left upon this earth.

Isabella went to bed almost immediately, exhausted from her trip, but her conscience allowed her little sleep. Several times during the night she crossed the dark living room of her parlor to Ella's room. There in the shadowed doorway, listening to her grandmother's soft breathing, her courage returned, only to leak slowly away before she reached her bed.

The next morning she had deep hollows beneath her eyes and remained in her rooms all day. After supper, Ben arrived with the carriage to take her for a breath of air, across Long Bridge into the Virginia countryside.

It was Ben who had been busy that day. As he chomped on portions of their dinner, secreted out of the hotel by Ella, he relayed the names of the wealthy and the well-connected young men accustomed to spending evenings at the Willard. Ben's research, done at the basic level of kitchen and carriage house, was thorough. By the time they drove back toward Washington, Isabella had a mental picture of each of these men or, as Ben had put it, she "knowed exactly how de ankle bone connected to de foot bone."

Bouquets, candies, and the calling cards of several young men were in her parlor when Isabella returned. Anxiously she compared these cards with the names given her by Ben. Two matched. John T. Kenmore and Carleton Dulane.

The next day Isabella and Ella left the hotel early. Strolling through the spacious grounds of the Smithsonian Building, they could see the twenty-foot shaft that was to become the Washington monument. The Capitol was completely encircled with scaffolding, a dangling crane above its uncompleted dome.

They walked for nearly an hour. Isabella felt loneliness encircle her as thoughts of what Papa would say if he were here came into her mind. "Just think, Bella, a Negro surveyor named Benjamin Banneker helped plan the streets of the nation's capital. He also made the first clock in America. Papa Jacques used to get his almanac every year for years." She felt the sudden moistness in her eyes. Papa. Her hand rushed to her eyes. Damn! She had to figure out a proper introduction to either Kenmore or Dulane.

The sun was hot, and each passing carriage raised choking dust. Before the iron gates of the White House, Isabella stopped and, to Ella's horror, thumbed her nose at the bronze bust of Jefferson guarding the front door.

"How?" she asked Ella for the twelfth time.

"Pray," Ella answered fervently. "Pray like Daniel in de lion's den, or Jonah in de whale."

"Ha," Isabella retorted, tossing her auburn curls. "What worry did they have compared to two colored women in the Willard?"

They were on their way back to the hotel when Isabella panicked. "Oh, my God," she whispered, grabbing her grandmother's arm. "There's Mr. Downing, Papa's friend."

George T. Downing, in dark frock coat and striped pants, was indeed moving straight toward them. His attention was distracted by his companion, a younger man. He had not seen them yet, but in a minute . . .

Isabella looked about her frantically. Through what door could she escape? A block away she saw the wooden Indian of a tobacconist, and still farther the green jar of an apothecary.

She yanked her hat with its long floating feathers low over her eyes. Then, as she started across the street, a splintery wooden wagon splattered her dress with mud. She raised her head as it stopped beside her. The hunchbacked driver jumped down, reaching for his wares. In a surprisingly loud voice he cried, "Here 'tis. The latest installment of Dickens's *Household Words*. Just landed from England . . . Charles Dickens . . ."

As George Downing passed the little group, he saw only the hunchback frowning as the old lady dug in the purse and the quivering hands of a young woman whose face was hidden by a magazine.

"How many folks you know down here?" Ella asked her granddaughter sharply as, the danger past, they walked quickly toward the Willard.

"Nobody else. Nobody. I completely forgot about Mr. Downing."

"Well, he ain't nobody to forget." Ella's eyes met Isabella's. "He owns the House Restaurant and lots of them folks you wanting to know knows him."

Isabella frowned. How had she forgotten George T. Downing? Had she forgotten anyone else? The Washington Woodsons would never recognize her. She hadn't seen them since she was a little girl. The Bushes, the only other Washington couple who had been to New Bedford, were both dead and she had never met their children. She had known but one girl at Oberlin from Washington, and she would be at school now. . . . No, Isabella told herself firmly, if she stayed away from the wharves, where she had no intention of going, anyway, there was almost no chance of seeing anyone she knew.

But "almost" lingered in her mind. One thing was certain, she could not stroll about town. Inside carriages, inside the fashionable homes, she would be safe. But on the streets was danger.

She remained in her rooms that night, unnerved both by Ella's— "Maybe you bes' think about this here thing again"—and by the fact that she had nowhere, nowhere else to go.

She prowled the parlor till long after the call came from the street: "Twelve o'clock and all is well." She was too tense even to read.

She slept till noon the next day and took lunch in her room.

"There's just no way," she told Ella, who came in at three from "checking" on her house. "There's just no way for me to meet one of those men properly. I've written notes to three or four thanking them for flowers or candy, but how can I go to dinner with a man I don't even know?"

"If it's meant to be, it's meant to be." Ella gave a look of disapproval at the mess Isabella had created with her tea dishes, magazines and books. Her eyes narrowed as she picked out the book titles: *Retribution, The Curse of the Clifton, The Hidden Hand*. What kind of ideas had that Southworth woman writer put in that child's head? As she picked up the dishes, Ella said grumpily, "The Lord didn't intend you for no poor man, that's for sure."

That night Isabella decided again not to go for her ride. Ella went down with Ben's dinner to tell him of the change in plans.

She walked slowly through the lobby, careful not to spill the gravy sloshing in the bowl beneath her cloak. "Is she ill?" several of the young men queried. They met short reply until one young man gently touched her arm. His voice was soft. "Excuse me, Auntie. Please tell Miss Clay that if I can be of service . . ."

His face was open, eager like a child's. His mouth was full and

178

soft. Ella smiled. "She tired, dat's all. An' lonely, waitin' for her folks."

Lingering not even a minute with Ben, Ella went back into the hotel and just happened upon the colored porter emptying the spittoons. "Dat's a mighty nice young man, over there."

"Him?" The porter's thumb jerked in the proper direction, and Ella nodded. "Why, that's Carleton Dulane." It was a pronouncement. "They don't come no finer. They owns Four Winds. Why, the Dulanes 'bout the richest folks in the state of Sous' Carolina." The porter looked at Ella shrewdly. "Seem like he done taken quite a tumble fo' yo' young miss."

Smiling, Ella re-entered the parlor to find Isabella lying on the couch, reading. She frowned as she saw the new title. *The Missing Bride.* "What kind of crazy stuff is that?"

Isabella looked up. "You came right back?"

"I seen that one callt Carleton Dulane."

Isabella sat upright. "What does he look like?"

Annoyance twisted Ella's lips. "Good enough for the purpose what you got in mind."

Isabella ignored her snappish tone. "What about the other one, John T. Kenmore?"

"I saw him yestitty." Ella shook her head. "Eyes like steel. Naw, he too cagey. You try for dis one. He young and easy handled."

By the next afternoon Isabella's bill had reached one hundred dollars. Her nerves were on edge when she came down into the lobby. The crowd was larger, noisier than usual. Above the commotion Isabella heard the words that, since childhood, had signaled distressed. "Went down." "Not twelve miles out." "No sign of survivors."

Instinct, training forced Isabella through the crowd, touching strange shoulders, asking again and again, "Which ship?"

No one yet knew the ship's name. Isabella, a New Bedford woman, waited in agony. Her brother Jason was reading for the bar. He would not be on his way back to France for nearly a month, but Clay . . . Biting her lip in apprehension, Isabella looked from face to face for any sign of news.

Carleton Dulane saw her from across the room and knew this was his moment. Face set, he moved through the crowd to comfort her. For most of his twenty-two years Carleton had been, as he had too often heard himself called, his father's puppet. At Four Winds, his father's plantation outside Charleston, he had never made a decision.

179

Inclined toward West Point, he had gone to Princeton, his father's choice, and there had taken that man's choice of study. And although the young Dulane would have preferred a career in electoral politics, his elder already had his congressman and his senator. The father decreed the son's career would be to oversee his advocates and to lobby for the interests of the Tidewater planters.

But now, his grandfather's will had made him rich and recently he had begun to resent the insinuations of his peers that he had no mind of his own. So now, spurred on in part by competition with men he knew considered him simply a dilettante, his father's pawn, Carleton pushed urgently through the crowd to be the first to reach the beautiful Miss Clay.

Isabella was watching him cross the room when the word came. The ship was the *Constance,* an old Fairhaven ship, one of the last built by George Glaggon, who had corrected the draft of the *Leah-Alanya* and become famous for building the *Constitution.* For years, there had been talk that she should be scuttled. Such a proud ship, Isabella thought sadly, to have met such an ignoble end.

Then she saw the slender, dark-haired young man beside her. He was exactly the same height as she, his clear hazel eyes were eager in his suntanned boyish face. At once, she knew the *Constance*'s last signal had been her own survival.

"Miss Clay." His bow was precise, military. "I'm Carleton Dulane, at your service." His voice lowered appropriately. "You knew people on that ship?"

"My relatives," she whispered, and reached for Ella's arm.

In Ella's life there had been no need to invent the theatrical. But now, cued by Isabella's hand, she put on a virtuoso performance. "Oh, my baby." Her arm surrounded her granddaughter. "My po' baby. Lef' widdout a soul in this whole wide world."

"Let me help." Carleton moved quickly to assist.

"Leave her a minute." Ella raised a plaintive face. "Leave her a minute wid the Lord."

How Ben got there, Isabella was not sure, but he came into Isabella's parlor with consternation on his face. "What all them folks doing outside a this here door?"

"Ben, quickly go down to the Custom House and get the passenger list of that ship." Isabella, voice low, linked her arm in his. "We can't

180

see anyone until you get back. If anyone should ask, all you know is, my relatives were on that ship."

Ben blinked, nodded, and sped to do her bidding.

People are drawn to tragedy as to the edge of a low-walled cliff. In protected fascination, they experience vicariously the unthinkable horror. During the hour that followed, Ella did centurion duty at the door, delaying those who would peek and express condolences. Each encounter brought her back to Isabella with a message from some noteworthy person, most staying at the hotel, who wished to extend a word of sympathy. Pacing the bedroom in mist-green silk, Isabella snapped, "I wish to God he'd hurry, before they all get tired of it."

Ben did hurry. A couple from Oregon, whose family would not hear of the tragedy for days, was selected as Isabella's relatives from the list of those on the doomed ship. Ella admitted the first of their guests, the wife of a senator from Alabama.

The news that she was receiving swept the lobby. The young men hastened to her parlor. The management sent food and drinks. The guests talked in low tones. With Carleton Dulane hovering at her side, Isabella almost forgot it was not a celebration. Standing with him at the window, overlooking Washington, she had to squelch a victorious smile.

Carleton was awed that she had chosen him. His face glowed as he saw envy in his companions' eyes. And so when Isabella began, haltingly, to speak of her return to Concord, he quickly pressed reasons why she should remain. Hesitatingly, she agreed to stay a day or two, to gather her wits, to rest for the long, long trip home. By the time Ella ushered the last guest from the parlor, insisting on "Miss Clay's" need to rest, Isabella had capitulated to Carleton's pleas to dine with him the next evening.

Isabella "Clay" remained in Washington five days. On the sixth day, at exactly ten-thirty, she walked alone to the altar of the elegant New York Avenue Presbyterian Church, known as "the church of the Presidents."

From under a veil fastened to her hair by a crown of daisies, she saw her bridegroom waiting before the minister. His face wore a smile, but his fingers spread nervously against his morning coat.

In a pew on one side of the aisle, Isabella saw Ella's face, beneath a small silk bonnet, drawn and anxious. Beside her, Ben's face twisted in a scowl.

On the other side of the aisle sat eight of Carleton's friends, their faces still expressing shock at this event, of which they had learned just the night before.

The man of God began the prayers. He raised his face and asked, "Who giveth this woman to be married to this man?"

Behind them, Carleton's friend, a young congressman from Virginia, stood. "I do," he said, and sat down.

The minister placed Isabella's hand in Carleton's. His hand squeezed hers. She bowed her head to hide her triumphant smile.

Their guests toasted the bride and groom with champagne aboard the clipper ship *Flying Cloud*. At noon, Isabella Dulane and her husband sailed for a honeymoon in Paris.

"Clay?" Jason called as he hurried into the dusty, cluttered offices of his father's newspaper. On the floor beside the door were stacked copies of the *Dispatch*. "Clay, where are you?"

"Over here." Clay looked up from the papers he was bundling near the potbellied iron stove. "Close the door. It's cold as hell outside." Clay held out a copy of the *Dispatch* as his brother crossed the room. "Look, Dad ran your analysis of the Dred Scott case on the front page. Judge Tilison said he'd never seen a more brilliant critique of the arguments of both Daniel Webster for Scott or Jefferson Davis against."

"Clay, listen." Jason tucked the newspaper under his arm without looking at it. "I just learned the slave catchers are planning to grab Dixon, the fugitive who's to go before the magistrate in an hour."

"Carl Kuykendal heard whispers about it at his factory." Clay stood, pulling his thick sweater down around his hips. "He and Dad are in the back right now planning a way for the abolitionists to grab him first." Clay picked up one of the bundles. "Give me a hand with these. They have to be on the ship to Philadelphia in half an hour and . . . Oh, my Lord." Clay's voice dropped as, looking through the sooty window, he saw the figure approaching. "Here comes Aunt Jacqueline."

Jason and Clay exchanged quick looks as the old lady sailed into the shop, her jade pendant earrings swinging beneath the gray braid encircling her head. Her hands were settled deep in her beaver muff. Without a greeting, she turned to Jason. "Where is your father?"

"In his office, Aunt Jacqueline. With Carl Kuykendal." Clay interrupted before his brother could speak. "If it's about that paper bill, Dad's been so concerned about Bella . . ."

"Don't make excuses for your father, Clay Clavier," Jacqueline snapped. "He was behind in bills before Isabella was conceived." She paused, then in a softer voice: "You've heard nothing more?"

"More?" Jason turned toward his aunt, brushing an imaginary speck from his topcoat sleeve. "Pray tell, what more is there left to hear? We are consigned to the locked room. The dark—ah, that word—forgotten past. 'My dear family,' our princess pens from Paris, 'please understand . . .'"

"No, Aunt Jacqueline," Clay interrupted. "The answer is no, we've heard no more."

For a moment no one spoke. Three figures, quite still, each with private thoughts of what that letter meant. Isabella was gone. She had married well, should not be sought. Isabella was gone . . .

Jacqueline was the first to speak. "Well, God knows she had reason enough to leave, poor thing. Your father . . ."

"Poor thing!" Jason exploded, then bowed in mock exasperation. "I will pay the paper bill, Aunt Jacqueline."

"The paper bill? If only that were the end of it." Resignation muted Jacqueline's voice. "Your father's bills are like a hydra. I cut off one and two more spring out to take its place. Abolitionist." Her rings flashed as her hands caught the beaver collar of her black woolen cape.

"Be patient, Aunt Jacqueline," Clay said softly. "Jason and I will make it up to you."

"You couldn't." Jacqueline's voice quavered with indignation. "Not in fifty years. Your father has squandered a fortune . . ."

"I would hardly say squandered . . ." Clay's smile was gentle.

"Call it what you will. All I know is that I have worked night and day for forty years to keep this family solvent, while your father piddles away every dime. The underground railroad, is it? That house is as well known as Boston Station. That time last fall when I went down to check the preserves—why, my Lord, that room under the stairs looked like a slave ship in middle passage." The gray head shook sadly. "All of Papa Jacques's work. I just thank God I had the foresight to remove the oriental rugs from the second parlor."

Jason listened to his aunt with growing anger; his wide nostrils flaring, his hazel eyes narrowing in his bronze high-cheekboned face. He turned away, studying the velvet buttons at the wrist of his Parisian coat. He'd heard enough for five lifetimes about the defaulting of his father. His father was a fool to allow Aunt Jacqueline to demean him so scurrilously. How could he care for the crass accounting of coin when at hand was the great issue of the ages—freedom! Who gave a damn how many salmon were shipped to Philadelphia!

Clay's thoughts concerning his aunt's tirade were gentle. For he knew that despite all her rantings, she had never denied her brother a dime. His mind was still on Isabella, remembering a time when, as children, they had raced home through the woods. Isabella had cheated, had taken a shortcut. Her dress torn and filthy, she had arrived first. As he and Jason came into the yard, they could hear the sounds of a spanking. Then she had come out, her dirt-covered face clean only where the tears had run.

"Oh, Bella," he had whispered. She had stuck out her tongue and flounced her torn skirt. "Don't look so smart, Clay Clavier. I won. Didn't I?"

The door to the back room opened. Over the top of his steel-rimmed spectacles, Alexander saw his sister. "Jacqueline! Did you bring the carriage?"

"No." Jacqueline moved toward her brother. "I walked. Alexander, I must speak with you this instant."

"Not now." Alexander's thin, lined face was firm. "I'm too busy." He turned to his youngest son. "Jason, hurry and get the carriage. Carl and I have concocted a scheme to get Dixon out of jail." A thin smile touched Alexander's lips. "Remember Shadrack in Boston? Have the carriage behind the jail in"—Alexander pulled his gold watch from his ink-stained vest—"exactly ten minutes."

"Right." Jason's eyes danced as he ran from the office.

"Clay"—Alexander looked up at his older son—"make certain those newspapers make that ship. I want the Dred Scott decision to be the focus of that convention in Philadelphia."

"Alexander . . ." Jacqueline began again.

"Later." Alexander patted her arm absently. "Later, Jacqueline. Carl and I are going to get Dixon out of that jail."

"You mean . . . ?" Jacqueline gasped as she seized the rolltop desk for support.

"We'll have at least three dozen men there. Old Jackson won't put up much fuss then." Alexander turned. "Carl, are you ready?"

Carl Kuykendal, tall and stooped, his blond hair now thick with gray, appeared in the door. "I'm ready."

"Alexander, please . . ." Jacqueline reached for her brother's hand. For a moment he gripped it tightly, then before Jacqueline could say another word, Alexander Clavier went out the door.

Paris was created for Isabella Dulane. It had been waiting two thousand years for her arrival—its broad boulevards for her promenade, its cathedrals for her meditation, its flower shops for her delight, and its famed restaurants, gathering places for the princely and the prosperous to admire her beauty.

Carleton swaggered as he heard the questions of the curious. Who was he, the bridegroom of this beauty? "A great planter?" "A senator?" "A scholar of international note?" "Carleton Dulane his name is." "From Charleston, in America, I hear."

On their wedding night Carleton had asked Isabella about the medallion she wore about her neck. She told him it was a good-luck charm given to her by her grandfather. Admiring the craftsmanship, but thinking wood too coarse for his bride, Carleton took the medallion to Cartier's to have it copied in diamonds and emeralds.

He could not do enough for Isabella. On and about the Place Vendôme, he searched Cartier's, Boucher's and Van Cleef's for jewelry to please her. Exquisite *doubles*, modeling latest fashions of the finest couturiers of Paris, paraded until weary while he and Isabella selected a wardrobe that would be the sensation of Washington. From the town houses of impoverished nobility came silver and china, the souvenirs of the rich. At her feet must the treasury of Paris lie.

Passers-by smiled as the Dulanes left their elegant rooms in the Païva Hotel to stroll in the Tuileries Gardens, to visit the Church of Sainte Clotilde to hear the organist, César Auguste Franck, and the Madeleine to hear Camille Saint-Saëns. Heads of the powerful turned as they arrived for the première of Offenbach's *Orpheus in the Underworld*. At the Opéra, their box was adjacent to Rossini's, who was attending a performance of his *Le Comte Ory* and two evenings later they left the Païva in a thunderstorm, running from their carriage into the Théâtre l'Odéon to see Gounod conduct his work.

It was all that Isabella had dreamed life could be. Her breath caught in wonder as she listened to the great musicians, as she admired the splendid buildings and works of genius enshrined in the museums. Her eyes sparkled as Carleton lavished her with clothing, jewelry, and furs.

But it was while visiting the Louvre that Isabella made her sole request. They were in the Grand Gallery, where, Isabella commented to Carleton, Henry IV had once brought in trees and rocks to hunt foxes for the amusement of his son, when they came to the work of Jean Auguste Dominique Ingres. Isabella turned to her husband. "How I would love for him to paint my portrait. Just think, Carleton, I would live forever."

Next day Carleton sought out the famous painter. Ingres at first protested; he was now seventy-eight, he had too much work. He was completing a difficult work, "The Turkish Bath," his masterpiece. No, he could not take another commission.

"At least see her," Dulane begged. "You will agree, she is the most beautiful woman on earth."

Ingres smiled. He had heard this from a hundred young men. But at last he yielded to Carleton's passion and agreed to *"jeter un coup d'oeil"* at Isabella Dulane.

Ingres saw her first from across the room. The light caught her hair, set off the exquisite bone structure of her face. The old master caught his breath. She was a perfection of chiaroscuro. Then she turned, and he saw the fire of her eyes.

"Ah, oui, monsieur," Ingres whispered, crossing the room. *"Elle est exactement comme vous l'avez décrite."* Isabella sat by the window as his wrinkled hands cupped her chin, turning her face slowly. Then he stepped back. "Be here at six in the morning."

The Dulanes canceled their dinner plans. Isabella was asleep before the lamplighter made his rounds. Carleton spent the sixth night of his honeymoon drinking in the Café de la Paix, staring sullenly down the Champs-Elysées at Napoleon's Arc de Triomphe.

For seven weeks Isabella retired immediately after supper and arose each morning before dawn. In a gown designed for her by Charles Frederick Worth, her jeweled medallion at her throat, she arrived at Ingres's studio promptly at six. There, watching the sun come over the rooftops of Paris to dance a moment on the Seine, she felt a serenity she had never known. She spoke of her river and the great whaleships that sailed from it to the far corners of the world. She told of her *grandpère* Jacques Clavier and the original of the necklace which she wore. "Ah, then," the master said, "your name was Clavier."

"Oui, Isabella Clavier."

Alone, Carleton prowled the streets and museums of Paris. He spent hours in the Bibliothéque Nationale, reading with fascination the strategies of François Etienne Kellermann, Napoleon's great cavalry commander, making intricate diagrams of Kellermann's great victory at Marengo. Evenings he appeared at Procope to drink pastis and find whatever companionship he could. The attention he'd attracted with Isabella on his arm was gone now, and alone and lonely he found fault with all that was Parisian.

Above all, the Gallic arrangement with their niggers galled him. Africans fraternized with whites in the cafés and cabarets of Montmartre. One of their blood sat in the government. Incredulously Carleton learned that a man he heard the French speak of so often, Alexander Pushkin, the father of Russian literature, was a nigger. His black great-grandfather, Hannibal, had been a general in the army of Peter the Great. And in the Moulin Rouge he saw another nigger general's son, Alexandre Dumas—oh, God, was it true that a nigger was the author of his boyhood's favorite book, *The Three Musketeers?*—in the company of Flaubert, Baudelaire, and George Sand. A nigger at the center of the most creative minds in France?

With fury Carleton learned that the fat old Negro's home—Monte Cristo—was virtually a castle. With a pang—was it of jealousy?—he heard of the parties the old man gave. One, held many years before at carnival time, was still spoken of with special glee. Dumas had been a guest at parties given by King Louis Philippe and the Duc d'Orléans and had determined to outdo them both. He had enlisted the aid of some of the most celebrated artists in France: Delacroix, Nanteuil, Decamps, the Boulanger cousins, all friends of Dumas, to do paintings on his walls for this occasion. Chevet, the most famous caterer in Paris, had prepared the buffet. Two orchestras, they said, had played in flower-decked rooms while a thousand bottles of champagne, Burgundy, and Bordeaux waited on ice to cool the throats of guests worthy of a coronation. Lafayette himself, and Rossini in disguise as Figaro, at a nigger's party! And his damn son, another writer, now married to a princess. It was appalling, it was disgraceful. It was dangerous.

Carleton tried to enlist his wife's sympathy for his disgust at these outrages, but she turned from him in their bed. "Carleton, there is so much for you to learn. Please now, let me sleep."

"But you are always either asleep or gone."

"Ssh." Her finger reached to touch his lips. "Soon the painting will be done."

Carleton went to Ingres's studio only once. The painter would not admit him. He stood on the street, calling Isabella's name until she opened the window and leaned out. The wind whipped her hair into a fiery halo around her head. "Come down, Isabella," he pleaded. "Paris is empty without you."

"Go away, Carleton," she laughed. "I am becoming immortal."

He left then and went to Procope, to drink absinthe and drown rampaging importance. *"Bonjour, monsieur."* Carleton saw the Frenchman approaching through green liquid fog. *"Votre jolie femme a-t-elle déjà Paris comme amant?"*

Carleton saw disdain twist the Frenchman's smile. His chair crashed to the floor as he leapt to his feet.

"Monsieur." The Frenchman backed away as heads around them turned. *"Monsieur . . ."*

Carleton flung the contents of his glass in the Frenchman's face. *"Merde, bâtard,"* the Frenchman swore as with one hand he dashed the liquid from his eyes while the other seized the wine bottle from the table.

Someone yelled for the maître d' and as he came on the run, Carleton's fist exploded in the Frenchman's gut.

Dazed, the Frenchman brought the bottle hard on Carleton's shoulder, then doubled over as Carleton threw his second blow.

Around him Carleton heard the sound of crystal smashing, of silver crashing, of chairs falling to the floor as with angry, harsh words, the fashionable, bejeweled guests scurried to call for the *agent de police*. Carleton heard, he saw it all, peripherally, as in the beveled edge of a mirror. But he was in the center of that mirror. A young Mars, beloved by a Venus.

Quickly, Carleton walked back to the Païva. Inside their bedroom, Isabella slept. He stood over her, impervious to her silent seduction. "Isabella, wake up and dress. We're having dinner."

"Oh . . ." Murmurs from far away. "Tomorrow, Monsieur Ingres . . ."

"Tomorrow you will tell Monsieur Ingres I have no more time to waste while you pose. Tell him we leave for home in three days."

"Three days." She sat upright, then saw his eyes and averted her own. Had not Papa Jacques often said, "The wise captain knows when the tide runs too strong and it's best to drop anchor and wait."

Ingres, as was his custom, had made innumerable sketches before selecting the one from which to paint. Now, with the portrait nearly completed, he no longer needed Isabella. "But," the old master warned, "it will be a week."

Isabella and Carleton came to see it for the first time together. It was in the afternoon. A sheet hung over the canvas.

"It is a masterpiece," the painter said wistfully. "It should hang in the Louvre."

He pulled the sheet. The passage of the north light caught the whirlpool of her eyes. Her lips were parted in her half smile and it seemed, in just a moment, she would speak. "Oh, my God," Carleton whispered.

"It's so, so sensual." Isabella clasped her hands to her mouth. Then with a squeal of joy she threw her arms around the master.

"You are a goddess, Madame Dulane," Ingres said with a bow. "My humble craft only builds your shrine."

The painting was crated and taken aboard their ship at le Havre. They were standing at the rail, watching the ropes that bound them to France slide over the davits, when Isabella saw a familiar figure disembarking from another ship.

"Jason." Her arm waved frantically. "Jason." For a moment Jason turned, his eyes searching the ship as it slid slowly from the wharf.

Carleton pressed against her, his eyes searching the crowd on shore. "Whoever are you waving to?"

Slowly Isabella turned her eyes from the figure now walking on French soil and faced her husband. "Jason," she said as a great wave of loneliness swept over her. "Jason Clavier."

The rains of November were falling when the Dulanes returned to Washington. Carleton found a telegram from his father waiting. His hands trembled as he read the terse message: "Get yourself to Four Winds immediately."

There was no greeting, no signature, but Carleton knew not only who had sent it but the temper with which it had been dispatched.

One thing was certain, he thought as he walked through the Willard, he would not take Isabella with him. He knew too well the tantrums to which anger could persuade his father, and he would not give that ogre the pleasure of performing before his bride.

Carleton's steps were slow as he walked down the carpeted hallway. How could he explain to Isabella? His boyish features twisted in a scowl. His wife had made it plain in Paris that she shared the Gallic sense of equality. She had rushed up to that old, fat Dumas and told him that she loved him—loved him!—and she had told the *fils*—in his presence—that *The Lady of the Camellias* was her favorite play.

Nor was that the end of it. On the ship, returning from Paris, when he had spoken of his home in Charleston, she had said she would not abide slave labor in her home.

Carleton groaned aloud. Jesus, what a scene that would be when she met Joe Dulane.

But it could not happen yet. Not yet. He needed time.

Isabella was unpacking, dressed in only a low-necked silk negligee, when he entered their room. Unconsciously, he wet his lips as he saw the soft skin of her shoulders.

She turned, sensing his presence. "Carleton, all these things will never fit in these closets or this dresser."

"I will see about a house as soon as I get back."

"Back?"

He crushed the telegram in his hand. Why did she hold her mouth like that, in that taunting way?

"Back from where?"

"I have to go to Richmond tomorrow." Her eyes looked through him. "Business for my father. It will take only a day or so. You should get in touch with your maid, Ella. You've given her enough time with her friends. Tell her she's to stay here with you while I'm gone."

Isabella lifted a velvet jacket from her suitcase. "You haven't told me yet what you'll pay her. In Concord . . ."

"I know well enough about Concord," Carleton snapped, then caught himself as Isabella slowly turned her head. "I think it's ridiculous to pay niggers," he muttered, "when my father . . ."

Isabella laid the velvet jacket on the bed and faced her husband. The top buttons of her negligee were undone, and he could see the cleavage of her breasts. "I thought we had all that arranged." Her eyes were flat and cold. "Ella and Ben . . ."

A curl dropped from its pin and made a soft circle on her neck. Her parted mouth was moist. For seven weeks in Paris she had denied him the pleasure of her body. For two weeks on the ship home she had declared she was sick.

He moved toward her. His hand touched the sash of her robe.

"Ella and Ben?" Her hand held his tightly.

For just an instant he hated himself for his weakness. "Ella and Ben," he groaned, and drew her down onto the bed.

Carleton left the next morning before Isabella was awake and took the train to Charleston. His first mood was defiant. He had sent his father a telegram moments after his wedding telling of his plans. He had left things in good order. Three months was little to ask. Hell, he really didn't need Joe Dulane. His grandfather had seen to that. Damn it, he was grown, and there was more to life than being Joe Dulane's son.

But what? That question made Carleton's stomach queasy. What else was he besides a lovely lady's husband and Joseph Dulane's son? One day, of course, he would be master of Four Winds, ruler of those vast lands, owner of the finest stables in the state, perhaps with a career in Congress. But all of that depended on his father and his own acquiescence to that man's pervasive will.

This succession of thought mitigated boldness. Carleton pulled out his flask for the courage bottled there.

Tight and disheveled when he got off the train in Charleston,

Carleton cursed himself as he saw the grin on Ike's face—Ike, his brown-skinned double, his nigger look-alike. Ike had been sent with the carriage to take him the forty miles to the plantation.

Ike held the horses to a funeral gait. Carleton could almost hear his father: "Ike, pick up Mista Carleton at the depot and bring him home, but in no hurry. Just let him bounce along and stew in his own juice."

Well, he'd not give that nigger the pleasure of asking for haste so he could answer, "Mista Carleton, *Masta* Doolane say . . ."

Carleton felt no special animosity toward Ike, no more than to the other four or five niggers around the place that bore his father's likeness. But Ike was not the regular coachman. Ike was the overseer— the goddamn nigger overseer.

Carleton was sober by the time he reached the white-columned Greek Revival magnificence known as Four Winds. His mother, a thin, worried, once-pretty woman, hastened from the veranda to greet him with a peck. "Oh, Carleton, your father . . ."

"Mista Carleton," Philip, the rotund black butler's voice rolled from the doorway, "yo' daddy is waitin' . . ."

Carleton patted his mother's arm with a smile, but his eyes were bleak as he followed the butler into the house. "I know my way," he snapped as Philip showed him across the marble, statue-embellished foyer toward the library.

He was in that room, halfway to his father's desk, before Joe Dulane looked up. "Close the door," he snapped.

It took all of Carleton's will not to rush, to hold his pace, to turn with grace and slowly close the door. He had not released the knob when he heard, "Have you lost yo' goddamn mind?"

Carleton clutched hard to wavering self-respect. "To what are you referring, sir? I told you I got married . . ."

"I know that." Joseph Dulane jerked open the lid of a silver humidor and pulled out a large cigar. "Hell, everybody in Washin'ton knows that." He stuck the cigar in his mouth and with a *ptuck* sound sent its end neatly into the copper spittoon by his desk. "That's the first damn thing Ben Clifford tol' me when I got his ass down here."

Carleton waited, hoping the congressman might have mentioned the beauty of his bride, but the elder Dulane rushed on. "Do you

193

know what's happenin'? The hell them folks out West been raising while you been layin' on your ass in Paris, France?"

Carleton opened his mouth, but his father stood, hammering his cigar into the space between them. "Do you know this country's goin' straight to hell? Do you know Oregon got admitted as a free state and there is a real war goin' on in Kansas? You know how much real estate we got out there? Do you care what will happen to the South if they get another damn free state? Is yo' brain still in yo' head or has it fell down to yo' cock?"

Carleton knew well the cause of his father's alarm. There were two issues crucial to the survival of their way of life—the perpetuation of slavery and the doctrine of states' rights. And both of these were dependent on the South's maintaining its balance of power in the legislature. The presidency they already controlled. Buchanan's body was northern, from Pennsylvania, but his mind (such as it was, Carleton thought) was southern.

But this did not concern Carleton at this moment. He was still standing, had received no invitation to be seated. His father was ignoring his marriage, making no mention of his bride, and talking to him as though he were Ike—or some other goddamn nigger.

Carleton leaned across the broad mahogany desk and flipped open the humidor. Lifting a cigar to his lips, he bit off the end, resisting the temptation to spit it into the spittoon for fear he might miss. "Well," he said, sitting in the Hepplewhite chair at the edge of the desk and crossing his legs. "What the hell do you want me to do about it?"

Joseph Dulane stared at the young man across from him, a thin, graceful figure in a fawn-colored jacket, the frills of his shirt showing above slender work-ignorant hands, at hazel eyes suddenly cold. His thin lips were compressed—in anger? Goddamn, Joe Dulane thought. At last. What did they say her name was, that redhead he'd married? The little heifer'd sunk in her hooks and found a backbone.

But compliments were foreign to Joe Dulane. "You ain't never been that dumb. Go on, take a bath an' git yo' mind in order. Me, I'm twice yo' age. I run this whole plantation, got one gal in the wenchin' shed and another wid a watermelon ripe to drop, and I don't look like you. Damn, a woman git a holt a you and you pussy-whipped and look like hell."

Carleton lit his cigar and leaned back in the chair. To his father there were three kinds of women: ladies, niggers, and trash. "Court

194

de ladies, fuck de niggers, and ignore de trash. Lavish de white and ravish de black." He had heard it a thousand times since puberty.

Until this moment his father's boasting of his sexual prowess had threatened Carleton. Now, suddenly, it revolted him. For the first time in his life he admitted to himself that he hated the healthy, balding bastard behind the desk.

"And when you git back to Washin'ton, you remember why you there." Joe Dulane smashed his cigar in the Dresden ashtray. "You eat 'cause a niggers. You sleep 'cause a niggers. You got this house 'cause a niggers. Everythin' you got, you got 'cause a nigga slavery, and if they end that, you ain't got shit. Now go on take a bath. Yo' mama is waitin' for you."

Carleton put his cigar on top of his father's. "So is my wife." He pulled his watch from his pocket and looked at it. "If you'll send for Ike, I can make the evening train to Washington."

"And if I don't send for Ike?" Joseph Dulane's voice had lost its former gruffness, but Carleton did not notice.

"Then," Carleton said, standing, "goddammit, I'll walk."

His father watched until Carleton opened the door. His throat contracted. "Ike," he bellowed.

Carleton turned with a short bow. "Thank you, Father."

"Jesus!" Joe Dulane said softly as his son went out and closed the door. "That's one woman I sho' do wanna meet."

195

The Dulanes leased a twelve-room house in Alexandria. Isabella hung the portrait by Ingres in the front parlor, over a magnificent fireplace of Italian marble, but she had little time to enjoy it now. Afternoon, evening, and night Ben drove her two matched horses across the Potomac to teas on the White House piazza, to state dinners, grand balls, and late informal suppers given by those who sought and wielded power. Isabella Dulane was the new crown princess of "Mr. Buchanan's court," the lady the *Evening Star* called "the most beautiful, the most intoxicating, in the nation's capital."

Under blazing chandeliers, above the swish of magnificent gowns, against the beat of waltzes played by forty-piece orchestras, soft voices drawled of secession and even war. But the music was too gay, the time too sweet, and life too beautiful in the halls of marble to heed the lightning flashing on the plains.

Only rarely did Isabella give in to the insistence of a friend to sit awhile in the ladies' gallery at the Capitol. There the reality of war came closer. There the divisions of the nation were clear. The South determined to extend its domain into the West, to maintain its balance of power, to protect the institution of slavery and the doctrine of states' rights. The West anxious to have no competition with slave labor. The North determined to keep the Union intact. New England determined to abolish slavery.

There, in the gallery, Isabella heard what Carleton and his colleagues would not, as they exulted in the fiery oratory of Pryor and Barksdale, Rust and Davis. She heard the conviction of Thaddeus Stevens and Charles Sumner that no man could put himself above the truth. Together they thrust open the long-locked door of Justice, and though others denied, hesitated, equivocated, compromised—the door was open and other men looked inside.

There were times when Isabella lost her temper, hearing Carleton and his friends go on about their "niggers." "Such flagrant displays of your own ignorance," she would storm. But they understood that she was from Concord, the intellectual, impractical Athens of America, and not at all used to dealing with the realities of Rome.

And always, Isabella had another serious concern. Any child she

196

bore might be distinctly colored. She had discussed the matter with Ella.

"Never kin tell." Ella's gray head shook with the weight of wisdom. "But one thing's sho'. Black blood's stronger'n white. That's what drive them white folks crazy. An' lotta folks, first time they know they colored is when they pop up wid somethin' look like it don' belong to them. Now you jump up with a young'un look like you' Daddy . . ."

"What can I do?" the granddaughter asked.

"Well, I kin give you a little somethin'. But lemme tell you, it don' always work. There's nights you best to say, 'Ah's tired, honey,' and git right on to sleep."

But sleep was not always possible and Isabella worried each month until her menses came.

Ella ran the house, needing not to lift a finger, and only rarely her voice, to keep cook, maids, gardener, and her beloved Ben in line.

There were two slaves in the household: Lura, the housekeeper, who had once lived at Four Winds, and Silas, Carleton's body slave, given to him by his father on what had been, ironically, the twenty-first birthday of both men. Silas was tall, dark, and slim, with close-cropped hair, unrevealing eyes, and a way of appearing the instant before being called. He was pleasant enough and efficient in his tasks, but aloof. Isabella often wondered what he did when he was not in view.

That Christmas Carleton decided that he and Isabella would go with their retinue, not to Four Winds, but to his home in Charleston: a white-columned, stucco mansion with a magnificent free-flying staircase of Honduran mahogany and marble inlaid floors. Designed by Robert Mills, who had designed the Washington Monument, the house had been willed to Carleton by his grandfather. But it was the stables, the six magnificent Tennessee horses, that were Carleton's real delight.

"My grandfather was the first really civilized Dulane," Carleton told Isabella one afternoon as they rode in the countryside. "His father, Three-Finger Joe, the first of my ancestors in this country, arrived in Georgia after leaving two of his fingers in England as punishment for stealing.

"Old Joe Dulane served the first three years of his indenture, then crossed the Savannah River to South Carolina on a raft and began to cut out a rice patch for himself.

197

"In three years he was owning slaves; within nine he had brought four thousand acres under his domain. When he was forty, Joe took to wife the gangling spinster daughter of a genteel Baptist minister who lived with him a year and bore a son and died. Old Joe's son, my grandfather, was raised by his mother's family in Charleston while Joe Dulane, satisfied he had an heir, spent his nights populating his plantation in the cabins of the slaves.

"My grandfather went to Yale Law School and married a belle of Philadelphia society. Both my grandmother and grandfather hated plantation life. My grandfather wanted to practice law. When my father was born, Old Joe built the house in Charleston in return for my grandparents' promise that their son, Joe, would spend summers on the plantation.

"My father, the young Joe Dulane, idolized Old Joe. My mother says he mimicked him in swagger, tough talk, and indomitable will. And I admit he had the old man's farsightedness. When he was barely twenty, he began to entrench himself into the political superstructure of South Carolina. By the time I was born he had added three thousand acres to the plantation my grandfather named Four Winds. They tell me that before my father's thirtieth birthday he was one of the most powerful men in South Carolina and one of the richest."

Joseph Dulane had his grandfather's long view of history. He did not need a commanding son. He needed a commanding grandson and was anxious to meet the woman who would bear him that heir.

He was furious, therefore, when he learned that his son and his bride were spending the holidays in Charleston. He knew the reason and arranged an occasion his son could not ignore, a ball commemorating the twenty-fifth anniversary of his marriage, an event that promised to be one of the largest ever in a state famous for social spectaculars.

Isabella was terrified. Although she had now seen hundreds of slaves in Washington and in Charleston, she had somehow managed to pretend that these butlers, blacksmiths, maids, gardeners, carpenters, and masons were not slaves, but folks who went their way with duties done. It was incredible to think that Carleton *owned* Silas, could *sell* Silas, and that Silas would have to go. The absurdity defied belief.

But the runaways who had come to her father's door had told of

198

the horrors of the great plantations, plantations such as Four Winds, to which she now was going.

Reluctantly she packed her trunk, determined to see no more than she was forced to, praying she could ban her father from her mind.

They were met at the depot by a gleaming carriage. Carleton sat silently beside a pale Isabella until the carriage turned off the road to move between matched pines up the wide, pink gravel path that led to the Greek Revival temple of the Dulanes. The last rays of the sun caught the alabaster columns, Doric and regal. "Oh, Carleton," Isabella breathed.

"Four Winds," he murmured, and looked out of his window again.

Carleton's mother stood on the veranda with her receiving line of slaves. Isabella saw the dark faces watching her as she stepped from the carriage. She knew their thoughts: What kind of woman was now arriving? Was she kind or cruel, this young lady who would one day be their mistress? Slowly, and with deliberate care, Isabella shook their hands as she was introduced, stunning her mother-in-law and bringing consternation to her husband's face.

Joseph Dulane was not there to welcome them. Nor did he appear until they were in the parlor. Isabella was standing at the window, leafing through a first edition of Shelley, a gift from Carleton's mother, when she heard the bellow. "Car-ul-ton. You home, boy?"

Isabella saw Carleton's sudden flush and then his mother rushed to the door. "He and his lovely bride are in the parlor, Joe."

Her hands trembled as she remembered Carleton's stories, and she kept her eyes fixed on the book during Joe Dulane's boisterous entrance. "Where is she? Where's the blushin' bride, boy? Or is she still blushin'?"

Isabella turned, her eyes blazing. Then she saw Joe Dulane's Adam's apple slide.

"Jee-sus," Joe Dulane whispered, and with a bow hastened across the room, his hand outstretched. "It is my honah, Isabella Dulane. Welcome to Four Winds and know that it is your home fo'ever."

His eyes were blue and narrow. She met his gaze levelly. So, she thought, this paragon of power is only a man. She kept her eyes on his and let her father-in-law make the conversation, answering his questions about Paris and Washington in a low and gracious voice. But tension knotted her stomach. Just as she thought his scrutiny would make her scream, Joe Dulane turned to his son.

"You done got somethin', boy. Goddamn if you ain't got somethin'. And since I didn't give nothin' for your wedding, you know that prize stallion you . . ."

"Wind Song?" Isabella saw the eager, boyish look on Carleton's face.

"Yep." Joe Dulane grinned. "That shore's one fine mount. Go on, try him while I show Isabella Four Winds."

While Carleton rushed to the stables, Joseph Dulane, holding Isabella's arm, showed her the twenty-five-room mansion, now a beehive of party preparations. He swaggered by her side as they walked from the stables to the animal pens, the blacksmith and carpenter sheds. But Isabella saw the covert looks of the slaves, and her sense of unease grew. With relief, she agreed to Joe Dulane's suggestion that they go on horseback to see the rest.

From a windblown knoll Isabella saw the black bodies toiling in the fields, then Joe Dulane turned his horse. "Now I'll show you the quarters."

"No." It came out quickly, fiercely. She saw the old man's sharp stare. "Really it has been too pleasant to introduce such misery now."

She saw Dulane's face twist in a scowl, then in a voice gruff with emotion he said, "You know, that's what I hate most about you Northerners. Yo' hypocrisy. You all want to admire the pillow and forget the plucking. Hell, the North benefits jus' as much by slavery as the South. The shipbuilders and sea captains what bring the niggers here, the cotton mills, the manufacturin' what makes you rich, they built on slavery. And not just black, but white and yella slavery. Them Chinese coolies—slave labor. Them immigrants from Europe in yo' factories and mines—slave labor. An' let me tell you, my niggers live a damn sight better than a whole lot of them folks y'all got hoppin' off the boat up in New York."

"But they're free," Isabella said quietly.

"Free?" Dulane boomed. Isabella drew in her reins sharply to keep her horse from shying. "Free to do what? When a man got nothin', he ain't free to do nothin'."

No, she thought, she would not be intimidated by his booming voice and narrowing eyes. "But they aren't bought and sold like cattle."

"I seen a whole lotta white men sell their own souls for a helluva lot less than I pay for a nigger." Dulane laughed harshly.

"But they made that decision." She did not want to continue the conversation, but somehow the words rushed from her mouth. "Even if their alternatives were few, they made the decision. I'm speaking of breaking up families. Separating a mother from her child. Breeding human beings . . ."

"That's a lie," Dulane shouted. "That's a goddamn lie."

He kicked his horse and started away, then, circled back again, his face like the funnel cloud of a tornado. "I'll tell you one thing"—his words pelted like hail—"you ain't never seen my niggers starvin'. When a nigger gets old, or sick, we feed him. He may not be dressed up fine, he may be barefoot, but he ain't cold. He may sleep in a shack, but there's a roof on that shack. When one a yo' miners gets old, he starves to death. One of yo' factory hands gets sick, he freezes to death. In the South we got slavery and damn if we don't intend to keep it. But we honest about it. An' let me tell you, Isabella Dulane, you don't know niggers. They one hell of a lot better off slave than free."

Isabella watched him ride away. Her heart pounded in anger and in fear. Oh God, she whispered, why did I come to Four Winds?

His whip cracked above Wind Song, and Carleton felt the power of the great gray stallion surging through his loins. The trees, the road went by with blinding speed, and a wild exuberant yell burst from his throat. His spurs dug into the stallion's side. Faster, Wind Song, faster.

Half an hour passed before he allowed the horse to break the pace. The scene beside the road was impossible to ignore. Six filthy, ragged white people stood before a gray, unpainted shanty set on stilts above marauding filth.

"Able, what the deuce is wrong?" Carleton cantered toward a sun-reddened man of indeterminate years who prodded a bony donkey laden with dented pots, brooms, and a rocking chair. Behind him a gaunt gray woman nursed a baby from a breast small and hard as a white potato while three scrawny children looked on with empty eyes.

"Mister Doolane, ah'm givin' it up. We goin' West."

"What?" Carleton exclaimed, staring at the bare feet and bare heads that belonged with the blue eyes staring vacantly at him.

"Gonna join a wagon train in Louisville."

"But why? You've been here ten, fifteen years."

"Twenty." The skeletal face twisted in a grimace. "Twenty years, and I don' own one mo' inch a this place than I did the day I came. Twenty years, Mister Doolane. You was jes' a tyke when me and my

201

ol' lady started croppin' for yo' daddy. When we come here, this place was wilderness. Yo' daddy own it. He say, 'Work, clear it, pay me my share, an' someday you own it.' I don't own it, Mr. Doolane. After twenty years I don' own a inch, and even the soil is starting to scream, 'No more!' "

For a moment Carleton studied the green flies now buzzing at the toe of his immaculate boot. "Where're you going?" he asked at last.

"Kansas. Bloody Kansas an' fight like hell to bring it in free soil."

Carleton nodded slowly. Those goddamn land promoters were doing their work well. Able would get a farm out West, one already cleared and worked and lost by a farmer who, like Able now, was forced to move on.

The government wanted the land settled. The promoters ballyhooed it. But Able would never own it. Even as here, he would get ever deeper in debt while serving the further purpose of voting for free soil. Sooner or later the big landowners, the industrialists, the combines would foreclose, and Able would be moving on again.

Carleton nodded. "Good luck, Able." He turned his horse toward the woman. "Goodbye, Mrs. . . . ." He stopped, realizing that after twenty years he did not know their names. He wheeled his stallion and raised his whip. "Good luck."

Dinner was served at seven. When Isabella came into the dining room in a gown of palest blue, Joe Dulane's mood brightened. After several toasts to the bride, he reached over and took Isabella's hand. "I haven't given you yo' wedding present yet. So, I propose to give it to you now. Any slave you want from this plantation."

Isabella's eyes flashed. Her hand slipped from his. Then, as Carleton spoke quickly, thanking his father, she swallowed the words rushing to her lips. Perhaps she had gone too far this afternoon. Perhaps this was a prelude to something else. She bit her lip as she remembered Ella's warning that she'd best "to walk on eggs in the nest of them Dulanes." But as she struggled to control herself, she noticed the serving girl, her lovely dark eyes pleading with silent desperation. Isabella flushed at pathos in eyes so young. Then as her own eyes went to the girl's again, she saw her silent "Please, take me . . ."

"Well, Isabella, what do you want?" Joseph Dulane smiled. "A maid, like that Loretta? A serving gal? A coachman? Now I hope you won't say Clara, 'cause she's the finest cook in the Carolinas, but . . . a promise is a promise. Loretta, or Susie, or . . ."

"Well," Isabella said slowly. "As you know, I don't believe that anyone has the right to own, to give away human beings . . ."

"Then I'll make the choice," Carleton said quickly, seeing anger slide into his father's eyes.

Tears sprang to the serving girl's eyes. The vegetables on the platter shook with the trembling of her hand. "I thought the choice was mine," Isabella said abruptly. "I'll take that girl."

Joe Dulane's hand came to the table like a mountain falling. His eyes blazed at the girl whose own now danced with joy. "No, goddammit!" he roared. "Not Monique. Any goddamn nigger but Monique."

For an awful moment no one moved. Isabella saw the twitch of Mrs. Dulane's mouth and her hand shook as she pushed her silver spoon back and forth through her soup. Carleton was rigid, his face set as in stone. Then Isabella's gaze returned to Monique, now immobilized by fright. Joe Dulane spoke again, his voice soft as magnolia. "Monique, you git back to the kitchen. No, go on to yo' shack." He lifted his crystal wineglass. "Choose another one, Isabella, and, Carleton, pass the butter."

The meal was finished in silence. Isabella murmured she wanted no other slave and when Joe Dulane passed the offer to Carleton, he replied, "Give us whom you will."

Later, at her bedroom window, listening to the low conversation of the Dulanes still gathered on the veranda below, Isabella did not hear her door open or close. When the girl whispered from the shadows, Isabella jumped in fright.

"Mistruss, it's me, Monique. Please, mistruss, kin I talk with you?" Slim, black, lovely, she walked through the stream of moonlight that passed through the window.

"What is it, Monique?"

"Please, mistruss, take me with you. Oh, mistruss"—tears rushed from the girl's eyes—"dat man, Masta Dulane, gon' kill me." Dark, slender fingers wound themselves around each other. "I don' care 'bout myself. I don' care 'bout me at all. It's my baby. What will happen to my li'l boy?" Tears sparkled on sable cheeks as Monique struggled to control her sobbing. "I seen how you act so nice to niggers when you come. I know you got a heart, mistruss." Her hands reached imploringly. "Take us, please."

Isabella felt the shaking in her soul. Her lips parted. She hoped she was smiling. "Why in the world would Mr. Dulane want to kill you? A beautiful girl like you?"

"Oh, dat's why. Dat's why! Oh, you don' know, mistruss. De most horrible thing in the world is to be a slave an' pretty. My mama say it de wors' curse any nigga gal kin have. Den dey don' leave you alone. Den dey come, sometime fo' you even twelve. Dey come into yo' cabin and dey put yo' mama out . . ." Monique's breasts were heaving, her eyes wide as though reporting something happening before her eyes.

"Dat first night he come, Mama scream an' plead wid him, beg him to leave me be. He call Ike to take her out. An' all de time he doin' it, I hear my mama screamin'."

Tears splashed down Monique's face. "De baby born and die. Den he start again. Dis time de baby live." Her dark eyes closed in hopelessness. "He two months old. An' already dat dog back again . . ."

Isabella bit her lip as she paced the floor, then turned and looked again at Monique. "Mrs. Dulane . . ." she began.

The slave girl's lip curled in contempt. "Her. She mo' skeert a him than I is."

They heard the footsteps. Isabella, convinced now this was the House of Usher, grabbed Monique. "My husband," she whispered. "You must leave, Monique. I will think of something. I promise."

She tried to propel Monique toward the door, but the girl was already on the run, moving not to the door but to the gilded floor-length mirror than hung next to the bed. It slid back easily, revealing the staircase behind. Monique hesitated. "They always skeert a slave uprisin's. But a course a slave hadda build the way out."

Then she was gone, the mirror sliding back into place, reflecting only Isabella's frightened image at its still unsteady center. As she reached to steady it, Carleton's querulous image joined her own. The door behind him was still closing. He could not have been there when . . .

"My God"—anger spewed Carleton's words at her—"is that all you ever think of—your goddamn looks?"

His jacket, jerked off and flung, missed the chair. Like a balloon deflating, Carleton sat down to remove his shoes.

He neither spoke nor looked at his wife as he stripped, then, throwing back the bedcovers, lay down, arms beneath his head. For a moment he stared glumly at the ceiling, then turned to Isabella. "Now you see how it is. My daddy and those black wenches . . ."

She wanted to touch, to ease him, but she was caught fearful and immobile in the quicksand of emotions and events.

Carleton misread her fear as arrogance. Despair drew on the armor of cruelty. He grabbed her arm and pulled her roughly down on top of him. "Don't feel so damn superior." His fingers bit into her flesh. "Even a goddess has to pay for her goddamn keep."

She awoke late the next morning. Carleton was already gone. Loretta came to help her with her toilette. "Mista Carleton," she said, had gone hunting with the "masta."

It was an hour before Isabella went down the winding staircase. In the foyer and parlors, roses, gladioli, Cape jasmine, and gardenias brought by the barrel were being arranged by artful black hands.

She was alone when Carleton found her. Eyes anxious, he held out his hand. "Forgive me for last night, Isabella."

"It's this awful place," she whispered.

"Four Winds?"

"And your father. Carleton, I'd like to leave."

"Leave?" He gasped, staring at her. "With guests arriving? Whatever would he say?"

She saw him then, blustering through the gleaming foyer with two men at his side. One was Carleton's age. The other approximated his father's years.

"Ah, Isabella," Joe Dulane called, moving past a marble cherub. Then, jabbing the younger man with his elbow, "Everything I said, eh, Fenton?"

He stood over her, smelling of leather and horses. "Isabella Dulane, may I present Congressman Fenton Laury? An' this"— Isabella noticed the pride in Dulane's voice—"this here gentleman is Cary Sykes, who owns the Towers, the biggest plantation in the state."

Gravely, Isabella extended her hand, then, the social amenities done, she turned to her father-in-law. "May I speak with you a moment?"

"Of course." Dulane grinned, taking her arm and walking a pace apart from the others. "What is it, honey?"

In her gaze, his face was framed by cherubs' wings. "I'd like to leave. Now, if you don't mind."

Once, when she was small, Clay had taken her to a farm. There was a bull there, a huge, old bull which had just been separated from a heifer he was attempting to mate. Insulted pride, rage, and denied pleasure had conspired to make an awesome noise. It was just this sound that erupted now from Joe Dulane. "What the hell?"

"Last night you offered a gift, then took it back."

"I didn't take the offer back. I took Monique back."

"You told me . . ."

"I know what I told you."

His face was turning purple now. For an instant Isabella thought that she should stop. Then remembrance, Monique's face, canceled indecision. "You renege on your gift, I renege on your party." She turned to walk away. "Please send someone for my trunk."

"You little bitch," he hissed, seizing her arm. Then above her head he saw the curious look on Fenton's face and the amused eyebrows of Cary Sykes. "All right," he said, loosening his grip. "You got her."

"And the baby too?"

Color flooded his face again. "That wench been talkin' to you?"

"How could she? You sent her to the quarters. Loretta mentioned that she had a child."

"I tol' you one nigger."

"That was last night."

Joseph Dulane felt Cary Sykes appraising the situation. She had him by the balls. A nigger or two, even a fine fuck like Monique, wasn't worth getting Sykes in on his business. "All right, Isabella Dulane. They're yours."

All talk that evening was of Isabella, of her beauty, her charm, her Paris gown. Joe Dulane beamed as his cronies whispered, "Don't say that boy of yours ain't a chip off the old block. He got himself some woman."

Smiling, Isabella waltzed in her father-in-law's arms. "It is all so lovely, Papa Dulane."

"Course it is," the planter replied. "I don't do nothing half-assed. Now I give you that gal, mind you, and when you get back to Washin'ton, I want you to return the favor. Stop playin' 'round in that bed and tend to business. Next year I wanna see a grandson. I wanna see the man-child that'll one day own Four Winds."

"You know"—she leaned back in his arms, an odd smile on her lips—"I really might do just that."

Joe Dulane did not know why, but her laugh made him uneasy.

CHAPTER EIGHT

1859

"Monique, for goodness' sake, hurry." Isabella fidgeted before her vanity mirror as Monique pinned the last of her curls in place. It would be an hour's drive to Washington.

"There." Monique stepped back, checking her work. "You sho' look pretty."

"I'm late. Is Ben outside?"

"Yes, ma'am." Monique hurried to get Isabella's cloak as her mistress picked up her gloves and gave herself a last appraising glance in the mirror.

Then, as Isabella moved toward the door, she whispered, "Kin I have it?"

"What?" Isabella looked at Monique impatiently.

"Da book."

"It's in my drawer under the chemises."

"Lura catched me readin' a sign the other day." Monique saw the look on Isabella's face but rushed on as she followed her to the door. "She do so want to learn. Please kin I teach her?"

Isabella turned and stared at Monique. She had sworn to keep their lessons secret. And for her to share them with Lura, with Lura who had once lived at Four Winds? Perhaps it had been a mistake to teach Monique to read. Then, involuntarily, Isabella remembered her father's words: "The worst is the attempt to corrupt our minds with ignorance and false learning. No man is slave until he believes himself a slave. The man who pursues knowledge finds freedom."

"Mistruss, please . . ."

"All right," Isabella nodded. "But make certain Mr. Carleton doesn't know. Or Silas."

"Oh no, ma'am. I knows to do it when we is alone."

The devil take Carleton, Isabella thought as she hurried down the stairs, but a frown creased her face. Her husband had been furious when he found her teaching Monique.

"Don't you know teaching niggers is against the law?" he had shouted. "There is nothing more dangerous," he had whispered, "than a nigger who reads."

Isabella's frown deepened. Carleton had changed these past five months. Nervous, high-strung, tense, he moved with alacrity to meeting after meeting, or with an ever-growing group of men sat around a table in their parlor. Over and over she heard the word "mobilization," the word "now." And more and more, she realized, men were listening to Carleton.

His new mood was affecting the entire household. The servants avoided him as much as possible, watching him from behind partially closed doors. And twice now she had overheard Ella and Ben whispering about war.

But, Isabella thought, it would not come to war. Surely the South would recognize that its position was untenable. Surely soon the slaves would be freed. But, her lips tightened as she crossed the foyer, even she avoided Carleton now. Their convictions were too different and he no longer tolerated her outbursts, her tirades—they had grown to be—against slavery. And, he no longer tolerated her excuses when she did not want to share her bed.

Last week he had come into her bedroom in a rage after she had said at a dinner party that slavery was a sin against God. Then advancing toward her like a hurricane he had seized her by her shoulders. "Not another word against slavery, do you hear. To my friends, to me, to anyone. I am no longer interested in your opinions. I only want from you the news that I will have a son to rule Four Winds." His fingers had tightened, bruising her flesh. "And I will have it, Isabella. I will have that news soon."

She had thought to leave then, to take Ella and Ben, to take Monique and her son, Jimmy, to take Lura—all of them—where? To New Bedford and confess to her father, to Jason, to Clay, who her husband was? Isabella took a deep breath. No, soon this would pass. The South would realize . . .

Isabella's hand lingered on the doorknob. She turned and saw Monique, still at the top of the staircase, the book in her hand.

Carleton was in Washington. He would not be home all day. But Silas was here. Cool, impenetrable, he was always here, knowing everything. And she did not know if Silas shared knowledge with Carleton.

Soon, Isabella had decided, she would free Monique and her child. But, as Papa Jacques had said, "freedom is only a word until you have what you need to maintain it." She must make certain that

Monique had what Papa Jacques had called "the weapons of freedom." She would have both herself and her son to support.

"Monique," she called softly up the stairs. "Monique, take care."

It will change, Isabella thought as Ben helped her to the carriage and she told him she was taking tea at the White House. It will change simply because a lie cannot exist forever.

At the precise moment that Isabella was entering her carriage in Alexandria, a man wearing an ill-fitting suit and carpet slippers was mounting a scaffold in Charleston, Virginia. A black cap was put over his head, a noose of a rope slipped around his neck. For a long time everyone waited while three companies of badly drilled infantry moved to position. At the end of the rope, the man stood silent, erect, stoical. Then the sheriff raised the hatchet. As it fell a voice rang out. "So perish all such enemies of Virginia."

At the same moment, as near as he could calculate, William Wadsworth Longfellow was writing in his diary, "This will be a great day in our history, the date of a new revolution quite as much needed as the old. Even now, as I write, they are leading old John Brown to execution in Virginia for attempting to rescue slaves. This is sowing the wind to reap the whirlwind, which soon will come."

Throughout Concord, the pens of the mighty dipped into ink to foretell blood: Henry David Thoreau, Oliver Wendell Holmes, Harriet Ward Beecher, Harriet Beecher Stowe, Ralph Waldo Emerson—and James Russell Lowell:

> Truth forever on the scaffold,
> Wrong forever on the throne—
> Yet that scaffold sways the future,
> And, behind the dim unknown,
> Standeth God within the shadow,
> Keeping watch above his own.

CHAPTER NINE

1860

Gaiety was fleeing Washington. There were no teas in the White House now. The rift between North and South was vivid—the clear hatreds, the irreconcilable points of view. Pale and distraught in the elongating shadow of war, James Buchanan paced the hallways of power murmuring, "Please, God, not in my time."

Relentlessly, Carleton traveled to meetings in Washington, in Columbia, in Charleston, as the South moved to erect a new bastion of power. His stride grew longer, his demeanor more determined. No longer was he merely the messenger from Four Winds. Decisions were poised upon the moment, and history swayed on those decisions. Joe Dulane heard at Four Winds the fait accompli.

Two women—separate and in conflict—now stalked inside Isabella's head. Would the South really go to war to keep slavery? Would they be so foolish as to fight the machinery of the North? It was madness. She had told Carleton so. Angrily he had pulled her to him. "Are you against me then?"

"Not you, Carleton. I'm against what you are for." Her voice rose out of control. "It's crazy. Immoral . . . to go to war to perpetuate evil. I'm not against you, but I am . . ."

He stared at her in astonishment. "Just tell me, Isabella, what the hell difference is there between a man and what he believes?" His eyes grew cold. "Or have you never believed in anything—except yourself?"

She ached for news from home. Seeing on the street a black man with a copy of *The Dispatch,* she forgot the danger and rushed to buy the paper from beneath his arm.

Then, lying across the bed she shared with Carleton Dulane, she wept through the fiery editorials of her brother Jason and the passionate poetry of her brother Clay.

In October, with Washington in an upheaval over the coming elections, Monique discovered her reading the newspaper. "I didn't know you knowed 'bout *The Dispatch,* Miz Isabella."

Isabella jerked upright. "How dare you come in without knocking?"

The glass in Monique's hand shook. Miz Isabella was usually so kind. "Ah'm sorry. Ah thought you was asleep. Ella tol' me to bring this up. I was jes' gonna leave it by yo' bed."

"Give it to me. I'll drink it now." Isabella snatched the glass, trying to restrain her new anger—with Ella. She knew better than to give the herbal drink to Monique, or anyone. Sometimes, lately, her grandmother acted foolishly, then cried if criticized. She would have to speak to Ben. This afternoon she would speak to Ben.

Concerned now with Ella, Isabella did not notice Monique peeking at the paper. Carefully, the girl picked out the words of the editorial:

Oh, brothers, you must cry "death to slavery." Do not lend your support to a man whose only concern is to bar slavery from those territories where white people do not want it, indeed where it is unlikely to seep. Ask yourselves what are the differences between the anti-slavery politics of Abraham Lincoln and those of the old Whig party and Henry Clay, who did no more for our great cause than our declared enemy John C. Calhoun.

Brothers, our support must be to Gerrit Smith, the candidate of the Radical Abolitionists, a man who stands uncompromisingly for the freedom of black men, North and South.

"Interesting, isn't it?"

Monique felt Isabella's eyes, cold and stern, and dropped into a confused curtsy. "Yes, ma'am."

Isabella watched her carefully. "One day, Monique, there may be a war between North and South. It's good to know what both sides say."

"Dat's what Silas say. Who you think gon' win?"

Isabella hid a smile at the earnest simplicity of the girl's question. Then, suddenly curious, she asked, "What did Silas say?"

"He say de North. He say the South think de North won't fight. He say the South think the niggas gonna help de slave owners, and they in a sorry mistake. He say . . ."

"Silas has been saying quite a lot," Isabella interrupted, remembering her admonition to keep their reading secret from her husband's body slave. "Has he said anything about reading?"

"No, ma'am." Monique's denial was emphatic. Then she looked furtively about and whispered, "But Silas kin read." Monique nodded, affirming Isabella's startled look. "Yes, ma'am. I seen him in

Masta Carleton's study looking in dis book. I seen the way his lips was moving. After he lef' I went in to check an' he was saying them words right. You know what Silas say?" Her head went back in a pretty laugh. "He say if niggas was really like them Jews what was in Egypt, an all we had to do was cross dat li'l Red Sea, we'd a been home long ago."

Nearly twenty minutes passed before Isabella mentioned her husband's body slave again. "Monique, what does Silas do all day?"

"Um, um. Shine Masta Carleton's boots, of which he mus' got thirty pair, an' see his clothes in order." Monique shrugged. "I dunno what he do. Lura say maybe he got a woman . . ."

"A woman!" It was the first time Isabella had thought of it. "How in the world could he support her?"

"Maybe he can't. Maybe that's why he so mean."

Isabella looked at Monique a long minute. "All right," she said finally. "Read the next story. And please, Monique, try not to say 'dis' and 'dat.' "

It was more than an hour before Monique left. As soon as she had gone, Isabella stuffed *The Dispatch* into the fireplace.

She was about to touch the candle to it when she saw Clay's poem again. Over and over she read the words: "This is our time, my brothers—oh, rally those whom the sun has loved . . ."

Isabella put down the candle and cut out the poem and placed it in her Bible.

On November 6, Abraham Lincoln was elected the sixteenth President of the United States. In ten states he received not a single vote. In fifteen states no electoral votes. He carried most of the free states.

Said *The Dispatch:*

Abraham Lincoln says he is not an abolitionist. But he has broken, at long last, the haughty, arrogant power of the South. Washington is no longer the capital of Dixie. And Dixie will have to deal with that!

On November 8, the Dulanes' Washington possessions, including the double-crated portrait by Jean Auguste Dominique Ingres, were loaded onto the *Aquia Creek* steamer, and Isabella, Ella, Monique, and her son Jimmy, Lura, Ben, and Silas took the train for Charleston.

On November 10, the senators from South Carolina resigned.

On December 20, South Carolina seceded from the Union.

212

On December 27, South Carolina seized Fort Moultrie, Castle Pinckney, a lighthouse, and a federal schooner.

The President-elect was still in Illinois, reiterating his promise that he had no intention of abolishing slavery, only preventing its extension into the territories. Rumors of plots for his assassination swept the capital.

On December 31, South Carolina captured the United States arsenal, the post office, and the Custom House in Charleston. Isabella and Carleton stood beneath her portrait in their parlor and toasted the New Year with champagne. Then he kissed her cheek and left quickly for a meeting.

CHAPTER TEN

1860–1861

Clay Clavier sat on the rocky seawall beside the wind-whipped Gay Head lighthouse. In his hand was his pencil, on his lap his pad. But Clay's mind was not on poetry now. He frowned as he watched the inexpert handling of the skiff now close to the shore. Damn it, why had Jason never learned to sail? He followed the zigzag motions of the small craft until it reached the shore, then reluctantly put his writing materials into the box beside him. He would have no more time alone. Clay sighed as he stretched his arms above his head. He had been looking forward to this time for six months. And now, after only a day . . .

"Hello, Clay!"

Below him, Clay heard his brother shout as he struggled to secure the skiff. Clay stood up. "I'm up here, Jason."

With a tinge of amusement, he watched Jason climb awkwardly toward him. His brother had spent too much time behind a desk and too much time with their mother's rice puddings.

"Clay"—Jason puffed as he climbed the last few yards—"the state of Virginia has called a peace conference with that damn Crittenden Compromise as a basis for reconciliation."

"Well"—Clay extended his hand to help his brother to the rocky shelf—"Virginia's not anxious for war . . ."

"But the Crittenden Compromise cannot be the basis of any sort of reconciliation." Jason scowled. "It provides for the protection of slavery in the slave states and the District of Columbia, prohibits interference with the interstate slave trade, disenfranchises all free blacks, and calls for their recolonization abroad."

"It's already been proved that recolonization can't work." Clay picked up his box, and started toward the lighthouse. "Even using every ship in this nation, every ship flying the American flag, the black man can never be recolonized. The rape of Africa has produced too many souls."

"We've got to agitate against that compromise." Jason wiped the perspiration from his brow as he followed his brother. "Even some northern states are listening to the senator from Kentucky. Dad wants you to come home immediately."

"Do I have time to get my bag?" Clay asked cryptically.

Jason had returned from France after learning of John Brown's raid at Harpers Ferry and had raised the fervor of abolition in the household from Papa's fanaticism to sheer frenzy. His brother had persuaded even Aunt Jacqueline to hold meetings. And Mama, Clay smiled as they entered the small dark room below the lighthouse's winding stairs, Mama had been persuaded to give a speech to the New Bedford Women's Library Club.

"You're going to have to write, write as even you've never done before," Jason said as they walked toward the narrow beach. "I'm arranging speaking engagements in every church and barroom I can find."

"I thought you were standing for the bar next week."

"Next week, next month, next year. Damn it, Clay, we've got to defeat the Crittenden Compromise."

"The Garrisons were right," Clay said as he expertly adjusted the sail and the skiff moved out into the bay. "The North should let the South secede. That would put an end to it. We could organize even better ways of rescuing the slaves, and the minute they step into a northern state . . ."

"That was a ridiculous notion," Jason said sharply, holding the side of the boat as the small craft rose and fell on the choppy waters of the bay. "If the North allows the South to sedede, there'll still be war. A war for the West. And no part of this nation can survive if we become like Europe, a dozen different feuding sections. No"—Jason shook his head vehemently—"we have but one alternative. This whole ignis fatuus of compromise is but a beguiling illusion." His eyes met his brother's. "There can be no compromise. There must be war."

For the next few weeks, the Claviers worked frantically. Jason traveled by horse, carriage, train, and boat to speak against the compromise before ever-growing crowds of Negroes and whites. Alexander and Clay worked day and night writing and printing bulletins and broadsides, sending them by express riders to towns throughout New England.

On Thursday, February 14, a mass meeting was held at Boston's Joy Street Baptist Church. Colored people from across the state

215

thronged to adopt a manifesto written by George T. Downing, the wealthy colored restaurateur. Excerpts appeared on the front page of *The Dispatch:*

> In this hour of darkness and danger, we appeal to you, fellow citizens, to bear in mind the following facts:
>
> Virginia invites Massachusetts and other states to a convention with a view, as alleged, of settling the present national difficulties. . . . Oh, men of Massachusetts, tell us not that there are two kinds of rights— rights of the rich, which you respect because you must; rights of the poor on which you trample because you dare. . . . Speak out, Massachusetts! You are the acknowledged head of New England. The movers in this injustice will not disregard the voice of New England.

The Massachusetts legislature instructed its commissioners to the Peace Convention to oppose the Crittenden Compromise.

That night, still at his desk, Alexander Clavier died of a heart attack.

Once again men and women named Key and Woodson, Oates and Kuykendal, gathered in the Clavier parlor. Once again the old years were relived.

The minister stood. "I am the resurrection and the light." Behind the flag-draped coffin they started from the house. "Whosoever believeth in Me shall never die . . ."

And far beyond the sobbing of his mother and his aunt, Jason heard it coming: the promise of God and the sound of angry, marching feet.

On Saturday, February 23, Mr. Abraham Lincoln, master of wit, wisdom, and political strategy, arrived in the capital in a drizzling rain. Thousands waited in and about the station to meet his train. But Mr. Lincoln did not get off. The President-elect, in slight disguise, had gotten off before the train reached the station and, accompanied by his law partner, Ward Hill Lamon, and detective, Allan Pinkerton, went directly to his rooms at the Willard Hotel. On March 4, he was inaugurated President of the United States.

Convinced that the tenure of the prairie President threatened the southern "institution," Alabama, Georgia, Louisiana, Florida, Mississippi, and Texas seceded from the Union, and formed a new confederacy with the state of South Carolina.

The majority of Virginians were against secession, but it was felt by the Confederate government, now in session at Montgomery, that if war became a reality, Virginia would throw her lot in with the southern states.

To accomplish that end, on April 12, forces under the command of General Pierre G. T. Beauregard were sent to demand the surrender of the United States fort at the entrance to Charleston's harbor. Senator Roger Pryor was offered the first shot. He refused, and the honor went to an old secessionist, Edmund Ruffin. The shot sped across the water from Stevens Battery and lodged in the wall of the fort, inches away from the head of Abner Doubleday. Major Robert Anderson and his troops refused to evacuate the fort.

Isabella was alseep, and the sound of thunder woke her. "Carleton." She shook her husband's shoulder. "Wake up. Help me close the windows."

Carleton stretched sleepily, then awoke instantly.

"Oh, my God," he whispered, racing to the window with Isabella close behind. Shells burst like stars over the bay, and the rooftops nearby were filled with people.

The chimes of St. Michael's Church sounded half past the hour against the booming of the cannon.

Isabella saw her husband's ashen face. "Carleton, what is it?"

"We have attacked Fort Sumter. Anderson is answering our fire." His eyes met hers and he held her tightly. "We are at war."

CHAPTER ELEVEN

1861–1862

"We're moving North." The braid of Carleton's uniform caught Isabella's hair as his arm surrounded her waist. "It may be some months before I'm home again. But I will write."

Isabella nodded. The edge of his buttons was hard against her cheek.

"You'll be safe here in Charleston." His hand caressed her hair. "Fort Wagner and Fort Sumter are impregnable." He smiled. "Richmond may be the capital of the confederacy, but Charleston is its soul."

She moved from his touch. "I will be fine."

He frowned, seeing her nervousness. "It won't take long to finish off the Yankees, but I'd sure like to do it before they get a head of steam."

Isabella was silent as they moved, side by side, down the winding stairs. Locked thoughts now pounded on her conscience. She glanced at her husband, the avowed enemy of her people, hell-bent on their perpetual enslavement. He saw her looking at him and took her hands in his. "I love you, Isabella." Her lips trembled against his. He held her tightly. "I wish I had another hour. Then I'd make damn certain you'll give me a son."

Her hand went to her throat, caught her wooden medallion. Oh, Carleton, she thought, thank God that you do not.

Watching as he tied his sash and adjusted his saber in its scabbard, she knew he had never been so happy. He had found a purpose and a command.

Family position had elevated him upon enlistment to the rank of cavalry captain. Family pride demanded that rank be well deserved. His men were superbly trained, hard-riding, fierce-fighting young hotbloods, who saw the war as a justification of their breeding.

Outside in the street a young corporal held the reins of Carleton's horse. He kissed her again, then opened the door. "Write me, write me soon, that I will have a son."

Her eyes followed him as the corporal handed him the reins and he mounted his horse. He saw her still in the doorway and lifted his sword in salute. "Come, Wind Song." He wheeled his horse and cantered down the street.

Slowly Isabella closed the door. Thank God, he was gone. If only the North would win the war quickly. If only the South would just free the slaves. How long could she continue this charade? There were times when she woke trembling in the night, wracked with self-loathing, struggling in a net woven not of her deception, but of her deceit.

When Carleton had left to accept his commission in the Confederate cavalry, she had withdrawn into her garden. She worked in no war effort, made no uniforms, rolled no bandages, refused to donate her silver for bullets or to buy Confederate bonds, and in moments of emotion she had confessed to friends that she abhorred slavery and did not believe the South would win.

Over and over again she told herself that she remained in Charleston only to protect Ella, Ben, Monique, Lura, and Silas, that by fall the war would be over and they would be free.

The harvest of east, west, north, and south was blood. And, as the period of enlistment of the Union soldiers began to run out and draft riots accompanied attempts to recruit more men, attention was turned to the potential of the Negro soldier.

There were those who said he would not fight, that he could not fight, but in the grim study of the White House, the man of the hour looked back into history and learned.

On July 22, 1862, Lincoln submitted a draft of an emancipation proclamation to his cabinet but was persuaded by Secretary of War Stanton to wait for a Union victory to issue it.

On September 17, the Union defeated the Confederates at Antietam. Seizing the occasion, Lincoln issued a preliminary proclamation. It stated that on January 1, 1863, he would sign the Emancipation Proclamation. All slaves in the rebellious states would be forever free.

CHAPTER TWELVE

1863

His boots tore huge holes in the new-fallen snow, and he did not turn though he heard his brother call. No, Jason thought, it is too obscene.

He heard Clay's steps coming behind him and increased the pace of his own. To hell with them. He would not go back. He would not speak another speech, sing another song, pray another prayer. No, damn it, he would not.

So what if Lincoln did not sign. He could leave New Bedford in the morning for South Carolina or Kansas or Louisiana. Black regiments there were ready to march. The 1st South Carolina Volunteers, made up of former slaves, stood ready under the command of a Massachusetts man, Colonel Thomas Wentworth Higginson. The 1st Kansas Colored Volunteers were ready under James H. Lane, United States senator and veteran guerrilla chieftain. And in New Orleans, General Ben Butler, another Massachusetts man, had found, to his surprise, two black regiments prepared to march, one under the command of Negroes, each of whom had at least ten thousand dollars in the bank.

They would march, they would fight, wanted or not.

"Jason." Clay had caught up with him. "They're waiting for you. You're next on the program."

"Goddammit!" Jason whirled to face his brother. "To hell with programs. I have nothing else to say. Every offer we have made, for regiments, even for a fire-fighting brigade . . ."

"Jason." Clay touched Jason's arm. "I know . . ."

"You know, hell . . ." Jason jerked his arm from his brother's grasp. "You are as content as they to sit in that church, waiting for word that Lincoln has signed. How long has it been now? Twelve, fourteen hours? Waiting, waiting, goddamn waiting." Jason reached beneath his coat and yanked his watch from his waistcoat pocket. "It is midnight now, dear brother. The first of January has come and gone. Lincoln has not signed the Proclamation. We must ourselves to arms and unwanted and alone begin our battle. We must heed no longer the promises of men who vacillate and barter the timing for freedom. I am no longer interested in what Mr. Lincoln says or does."

"Then call others to your cause. The church is packed. This is no time to sulk and walk away. Come back and spell your plan. Other fires can be lighted from your own."

"I doubt it. They are content to sit and pray."

"Do not deceive yourself. Blood boils in other veins as well as yours."

Jason looked at his brother, at the snow collecting on his brows and his mustache. "I cannot bear to be so impotent. In the name of honor we must do something or we shall all go mad."

"Come back for an hour, Jason. Then I'll join you."

"Clay . . ."

"Here." Clay brought a flask from under his greatcoat. "Have a swig of this. Whiskey is the salve that keeps the too-honed mind from breaking. Here." He held out the flask. "Take some. A cracked stick points a poor direction."

The flask was tilted at Jason's lips when they saw the boy running like one possessed toward the church.

"I wonder . . ." Clay whispered.

"It is." His brother yelled. "By God, it is!"

The whiskey made dark circles in the snow, flowing from the flask to the tracks from which the brothers sped. "What is it?" Their shouts reached the streaking form ahead.

"It's coming," the boy screamed wildly. "It's on the wires now. Lincoln has signed the Proclamation. The black man is free."

They saw him burst inside the church. "It's coming. It's coming," danced back through the falling snow.

"Glory." A single cry. A woman's cry.

Then Jason saw Clay's tears. And he fell into his brother's arms and wept.

Governor John Andrew was authorized to raise a Negro regiment, the 54th Massachusetts. Company C was raised largely in New Bedford. The fifth and sixth names on the enlistment rolls were Clay and Jason Clavier. Number seven was Benjamin Oates, Jr. Number twelve was Alexander Kuykendal.

Isabella sat on the side of her grandmother's bed, stroking her forehead. "It's all right," she whispered. "It's all right." She bit her lip, thinking how fast Ella had failed since they left Alexandria.

The old woman smiled, her eyes bright with fever. "Now you do as I say, you hear me, Thomasina. I'm gonna be jus' fine. You go wid that man. He love you. Go on to the better life."

Isabella patted the work-eroded hand and looked aimlessly about the room. She was thin to the verge of peakedness and there were deep hollows beneath her eyes. Slowly, she pushed herself from the bed, feeling the rush of nausea, forcing it back. Then, wiping the tears now rushing down her sallow cheeks, she whispered, "Oh, dear God, what shall I do?" She looked down at Ella. Her grandmother was asleep.

Isabella stood for a long time in the middle of the room, considering again the possibilities rejected a hundred times before. There was no way out. The war had disrupted train service. Ella, sick and senile, could not make the trip by carriage. Nor could she. She was five months pregnant.

She should have left ten, twelve weeks ago; when she first thought she was pregnant. She should have gone when she first discovered Ella no longer remembered her contraceptive mixtures. But when she had finally realized she was to be a mother, Ella was too sick to move. She should have heeded Ben's advice and left Ella with him, but they needed her. All of them needed her: Ella, Ben, Monique, little Jimmy, Lura, even Silas. Without her they would have been sent to Four Winds. And she had heard that Joe Dulane was selling Negroes further south.

Now, most of her time was spent here, in this room. She had heard the whispering, from Silas, from Lura, even from Monique. "How come she take care a Ella herself?" What a fool she'd been to think a miracle would happen. That somehow she'd be saved. Pacing the floor, she remembered Clay's words, "It's a dangerous game you play, Isabella."

The stationery had been on Ella's dresser nearly two months. She could put it off no longer. Carleton must be told. Not the whole truth —but at least that she was pregnant.

Paper in hand, she sat on the bed again, frowning in concentration, her hand twisting her medallion. The idea came quickly and she bent to write. "Dear Mother and Papa, Clay, Jason, and Aunt Jacqueline . . ."

They were a solemn group, the men of the 54th Massachusetts, as they broke camp in Readville and boarded the train for Boston. They knew what lay ahead of them, this first Negro regiment raised in the North; their triple jeopardy. For not only were they soldiers on their way to the bloodiest conflict in the history of their country, but the world was waiting to see if they would fight. If they would fight in Dixie. Nor was that the worst of it. From the South had come the ominous warning: captured Negro soldiers would not be treated as prisoners of war. They would be sold into slavery or shot.

Clay Clavier looked out of the window at the slim, blond figure of Robert Gould Shaw, commanding officer of the 54th. A Boston Brahmin, educated at Harvard, Shaw had been handpicked by Governor John Andrew for command of the regiment. A veteran of the 2nd Massachusetts, Shaw had distinguished himself at Winchester and Antietam. His parents had been among the first people of wealth to support the abolitionist cause and he was related to such important anti-slavery families as the Lowells and the Barlows.

But Clay knew it had not been easy for Shaw. There had been hostility and ridicule for the Negro regiment and lampooning for its officers. Governor Andrew had publicly countered this prejudice, saying that he was resting his reputation on the 54th.

Shaw had been a strict disciplinarian, drilling his men exhausting hours. Now, as the last man saluted the colonel smartly and stepped onto the cinder-singed platform, Shaw nodded with satisfaction. Yes, he thought, they are as good a regiment as ever marched.

Inside the misty coach, Sergeant Jason Clavier shoved his Enfield rifle on top of his knapsack. "To think they don't even want to pay us the same as white soldiers," he muttered to his brother.

"Well"—Clay smiled wryly—"now we fight for no pay at all."

"No pay or equal pay," Jason said adamantly. "Until they at least pay us as equals, the 54th Massachusetts fights without pay."

Pulling a book from his pack, Jason sat down on the hard seat beside his brother. In front of him, behind him, were row after row of set, dark faces. "I know I've said it a hundred times, Clay, but it still galls me we have not a single Negro officer. This treatment of Negro troops defies all codes of decency . . ."

A thin smile crossed Clay's face. "Does one really talk of decency when one talks of war. Necessity perhaps, but . . ."

"It makes a mockery of what we are about."

Clay glanced at his brother, at the book on his lap—Dante's *Inferno,* the French translation. The hands that held it were scrubbed, the nails well cut, immaculate. Beneath the flawless skin of that haughty face, at the neck of the impeccable uniform, the soft fold of a cravat. Dante . . . the French translation . . . the black body dug the necessaries, marched in the segregated units . . . the body accepted . . . the mind did not.

The civilized man in this uncivilized world. And was Joseph—was Nat, was Cinque, was Vesey—laughing all the way home?

Jason felt Clay's quiet gaze. He closed his book and looked at his brother. "You know, Clay, they may not call us gentlemen, but damn if they won't call us men. And though history may ignore us, it cannot deny that we were there. We'll fight. Damn, if we won't fight. We'll fight them to the gates of hell."

"Through," Clay said softly. "Through the gates of hell."

Ben took Isabella's black-banded arm as they turned from the new grave in the weed-tortured cemetery. Behind them, Lura, Monique, and Silas walked silently. Outside the broken iron fence, Wade Hampton's troops passed, guarding the city from attack.

"Ben." Isabella lifted her veil. "I want a monument for her grave."

Ben nodded, gripping her arm tighter, hearing the low hysteria in her voice. "I'll see to it tomorrow." He paused a moment. "Ain't too much to put on it. Just Ella and the date of her death."

"No." Isabella met his eyes. "It will say—Ella, mother of Thomasina Clavier and beloved grandmother of . . ." The words caught, and Ben's heart resumed its beating. He resisted the urge to turn and ascertain how much distance separated them from those behind. But Isabella's voice was clear. ". . . And beloved by Isabella Dulane."

The two old women stood alone in the throng, listening and looking. Every street, window, and balcony from the depot to Boston Commons was jammed.

"They should be here any minute," Jacqueline whispered.

224

"Yes, any minute," Thomasina agreed.

They heard the marching, the band playing John Brown's song. An old black man took off his cap. Tears streaming down his face, he whispered the words: "Mine eyes have seen the Glory . . ."

It went through the crowd. Other voices joined: ". . . of the Coming of the Lord . . ."

Governor Andrew and George Stevens, who had raised most of the money for the regiment, waited on the reviewing stand. ". . . He is tramping out the vintage where the grapes of wrath are stored . . ."

Handkerchiefs fluttered, men cheered. ". . . He has loosed the fateful lightning . . ."

Robert Gould Shaw, riding at the head of his troops, reined his horse an instant on State Street at the spot where Attucks fell. ". . . His terrible swift sword . . ."

Then line after line of taut black troops marched by. ". . . His truth is marching on . . ."

The fiery old Garrison, standing on the balcony of Phillips House, leaned against the bust of John Brown and wept. John Greenleaf Whittier, the confirmed pacifist, stood on the street and cheered.

To the most tumultuous reception in the history of Boston, the 54th boarded the steamer *De Molay* and sailed for South Carolina.

CHAPTER FOURTEEN

The drapes were drawn against the night. Naked before the mirror, Isabella caressed her swollen roundness. In days, now, her child would be born. She felt a kick and touched the spot. "Quiet down there, you," she laughed.

It was marvelous how nature planned, she thought. Months ago, her thoughts had been only of herself, but as time passed, love for this life within her had grown. Above all else, the child must be protected.

Slipping into her robe, she fumbled beneath her mattress for the letters that had come in the afternoon post, bearing dates almost a month old.

The first was from her mother. She smiled at the childish scrawl and flowery style. In her own letter home, Isabella had written of her pregnancy, of her fear of what would happen if the child were dark. Her mother had responded to this urgency.

My dear Mrs. Dulane,
Words cannot express my joy at hearing from you. Do not despair. Help is *closer* than you know. C and J are where you would expect them to be, knowing who they are and where they are *from*. I am praying for you. With all my love.

T. C.

The second letter was from her aunt.

Dear Isabella,
Don't be a fool. You have a home and people who love you. If you have any problems, both Jason and Clay are attached to the 54th Massachusetts now bivouacked at Hilton Head, which, according to my map, is quite close to you.
We love you and await your arrival.

Love,
Aunt Jacqueline

P. S. The money enclosed is for your fare.

Isabella nodded. Tomorrow she would go to Hilton Head. Tomorrow she would leave this house forever, and her baby would be safe. Far safer born in a Union Army camp than in its father's house. Yes, Isabella thought, that way was best. Jason would know what to do. He always did. And it would be good to be with Clay when her time came.

The vague discomfort which had denied her sleep came again, then passed. She picked up a book, leafed idly through it, then put it down. Everyone was asleep. The quiet of the house disturbed her. She crossed to the window, then, on impulse, decided to sit awhile in the garden. She did not take the lamp but went quietly out the back door to the swing on the shrub-enclosed patio.

Voices coming from the arbor startled her. She stood, then recognized Silas's voice, low, almost a whisper. "This here's a drawin' of Fort Wagner. See all them big guns up there on the ramparts? This ditch here outside the fort is mean, and these real deep places the creeks cut in the sand is treacherous. An' mos' importan', see this wall? It go thirty feet almost straight up."

As Isabella hesitated, she heard the other voice, its New England accent unmistakable. "You think it will be risky?"

"Me, I'd say impossible. Guns from Sumter, Sullivans, and James islands all cover Fort Wagner. Be sure hell to try to take that fort."

Chills circled Isabella's body. Silas—a spy!

They were moving now from the arbor, the white man and the black, moving toward her. Suddenly she froze with fear. To them she was the enemy. Holding the edge of the swing, Isabella slid awkwardly to the cement patio, crouching there as they paused almost above her. Struggling not to breathe, she could feel the baby kick.

"Silas"—the other voice. "It'll be too dangerous for us to go together. I can make it back. Here, here's a pass through our lines."

Silas's hand rested on the shrubs inches from Isabella's shoulder. "No, thanks, Sergeant. If I'd a wanted to go, I'd a been gone long ago. Naw, my whole life's been waiting for this minute. When the Yankees come marching through, I wanna be standing wavin' from that slave block where they sold me from my family when I was nine years old."

They moved on, their voices growing fainter until silence claimed the garden. Still Isabella dared not move.

She was still trembling when she slipped into the house, moving like a shadow to the staircase. She had reached the landing when the pain seized her. She clung to the banister, fearful she would faint. "Oh, Lord," she whispered. "Please, let me get to Hilton Head."

Balancing herself on the railing, the walls, the furniture, she made her way to Ben's room. He answered her knock, his voice thick with sleep. "Who is it?"

"Isabella. Hurry."

Holding his pants up with one hand, Ben opened the door.

"Ben, we must leave now for Hilton Head." Her face was pale and damp.

"You mean . . . ?"

"Right now. The baby's coming." Apprehension knitted Ben's brows, puckered his lip. She grabbed his arm. "Ben, in the name of God . . ."

In her room, Isabella lifted her packed suitcase to the bed and tucked her jewelry case in. Then the second pain forced her to her knees. She made no sound as she clung to the sheet, and when the pain had passed, she moved quickly to get the cash box from the top of the armoire. It was beyond her reach. Pushing, dragging, she moved the upholstered armchair to the chest. The cash box was in her hand when a new pain wracked her body. She clung to the armoire as the scream contracted her throat.

She heard the sound of running feet. Her door flew open and she was in Monique's strong arms.

"Oh, Miz Isabella." The girl helped her from the chair and wiped her face. Then, turning toward the door, Monique yelled, "Silas, Silas, hurry for de doctor."

"I'm all right, Monique," Isabella panted. "Just help me get dressed."

"Get dressed! Where you goin' wid da baby comin'?"

"*Please,* Monique."

Monique's gaze fell on the suitcase, on the spilled cash box on the floor. "Oh, Miz Isabella," she whispered, "you can't go nowhere."

But Isabella was already pulling on her clothes, her hair damp strands about her face, her breath coming in shallow takes.

Monique, hearing Ben's heavy footsteps in the hall, ran to the door. "Ben, quick, git da doctor."

But Isabella was in control again. Walking to the door, she leaned against the sill. "No doctor, Ben."

Ben looked hesitantly from Isabella to Monique.

"I don't want the doctor." Isabella's voice was calm. She turned to Monique. "Will you help me, Monique?"

Past events came together in Monique's mind. The newspapers, her mistress's devotion to Ella, Miz Isabella's strong talk against slavery . . . Her arms went around Isabella, and she held her tightly. "Oh, yes, Miz Isabella. We kin take care a this ourselves."

Isabella's son was born at seven that morning. She waited, weak and anxious as Monique wiped and wrapped the infant and placed him in her arms, then laughed aloud as his brown eyes seemed to look directly into her own.

"You gonna name him Carleton?" Monique asked.

Isabella remembered. She pulled the blanket open.

"You got no cause to worry." Monique nodded, touching the child's head. "It's dem ears that tell da tale. The color on de curve of dat earlobe is da color dey gonna be. A real high yella, I'd say. An' you can tell the hair gon' stay straight 'cause it's coarse and kinda flappy like.

"I'll call da doctor now," Monique went on, ignoring Isabella's stare. "Everything gon' be fine. Just rest, 'cause da one thing in this world don' have no mercy is a hungry young'un."

She named him Jacques Clay Dulane. Propped up by pillows, she wrote one line to Carleton. It told that his son was born.

CHAPTER FIFTEEN

1863–1864

Fingers of lightning clawed the Southern sky as the 54th Massachusetts came through the swamps to board the ferries that would take them to Morris Island. They had been on the march for two days, hardly eating or sleeping since fighting a bloody skirmish with the Confederates on James Island. In a blinding rainstorm they came through the swamps to the ferries that would take them to Morris Island. On one of the ferries moving across the narrow strip of water, four men squatted near the stern, huddled together for protection against the driving rain.

"Fort Wagner'll be hell," Sergeant Jason Clavier said quietly, sheltering his rifle.

"Well"—Lieutenant Alexander Kuykendal, next to Jason, grinned —"this won't be the first time the Claviers, Oateses, and Kuykendals been in hell together."

"I just hope to God we get out like our grandpas did." Benjamin Oates, Jr., hunched beneath his knapsack as he whispered. "Damn, I don't know which I want the most—rest, food, or water. Damn it, listen to those guns."

"Don't think of it." Clay Clavier touched his shoulder. "Just think of the victory and the peace."

The ferries touched the shore of Morris Island. With no rest, no water, the 54th moved up under heavy bombardment to join the other regiments gathered for the attack on Fort Wagner. General Strong, in command at Morris Island, knew it would be a bloody business. The attack would be made by volunteers.

Dusk fell. The 54th Massachusetts stood ready to lead the assault. Colonel Shaw, dressed in a close-fitting jacket and light blue trousers, paced his lines and looked again at the heavy fog moving in from the sea. The body of the scout sent to secure intelligence on the approach to the fort and its defenses had been found floating in the harbor tied to the body of an unknown Negro. Generals Strong and Gilmore had decided not to delay the attack.

Shaw moved to the center of the rows of men and faced his regiment. Quietly, reminding his men that the world was watching, he gave the order to fix bayonets. The officers of the regiment grasped hands, then moved their holsters to the front.

Jason Clavier glanced at his brother. "Clay," he whispered. "Clay, stay close to me."

"Just hold on to mother's letter." Clay's eyes were on the colonel. "We'll take the fort, then we'll go get Bella."

Robert Gould Shaw gave a last look at his men. He raised his sword, and six hundred black men moved into the softly falling night.

The blue line moved at quick time, then at the double quick. The Confederate guns spit out a sheet of flame. The line buckled, then plunged ahead, into the steady fusillade of fire. Jason glanced to see that Clay was still beside him as they moved forward through their reeling, dying men. "My God," a man nearby groaned. "We shore 'nough in hell."

Now the batteries from James, Sullivans, and Sumter began a blinding cross fire. Jason saw the dark face of Sergeant Will Carney, his neighbor in New Bedford, twist in pain, saw the blood spurting from his shoulder. Carney stopped and pushed a handkerchief over his wound and, shifting his rifle, moved forward toward the fort.

Clay's heart pounded. His eyes fixed on the parapet. "Oh, God," he whispered. "Let me stand up there. If only for an instant, let me stand up there."

Their lines were decimated now, but they were still moving up, through the grape and canister and bodies of their dead. Fifty feet from the fort, they were cut off from all support, the other regiments pinned down by Confederate fire.

"Jason! Jason, in the name of God." Jason turned, saw Alexander Kuykendal, his left leg pinned beneath a tree.

The night was lit by cannon fire. All around, men screamed and moaned. "Easy, Alex," Jason grunted, using his bayonet to lift the limb.

"I think the damn thing's broken." Alex's voice was hoarse with pain. "A grenade . . ."

The tree came up. Jason stared in horror. Below the knee there was no leg. "Medic," he yelled. "Medic, over here!"

Then he was moving up again, looking for his brother in the night-dark madness all around. He slid into a ditch, four feet deep with water, then with an abrupt hurt look touched his fingers to his head.

231

For an instant he stared at the blood flowing down his hand, then slowly he moved on, up the pitted slope of the parapet.

Howitzers screamed. Grenades blasted men back into the ditch. Jason did not see Clay among the men around him, scrambling, clawing for a foothold further into hell.

Then he saw Clay on the ramparts, silhouetted in the flash of cannon. Perhaps fifty of their men were there. Colonel Shaw was at the center. They were fighting the Confederates hand to hand.

Jason saw the color sergeant plant their flag, and die. He saw Will Carney grab the flag, hold it boldly. Then a grenade exploded and Jason saw no more.

He was lying in the marsh when he came to, a blinding pain about his eyes, a bloody bandage on his head. Someone was shaking him. "Jason?" It was Carney.

"Yes, Will?"

"Clay's hurt real bad. A grenade blew him in the ditch. He's 'bout a quarter mile from here. You think you can make it?"

Jason stumbled behind Carney through the stink and carnage, the mangled bodies, the screaming, dying men.

"The supporting regiments got pinned down," Carney said. "More'n half our men wounded or dead. Colonel Shaw was killed on the ramparts. They sent word they buried him in the ditch with his niggers."

"How bad is Clay?"

"He's dying."

Jason held his brother in his arms, trying not to see the tangled intestines below the bloody bandage. The few medics attached to the colored corps saved their efforts for those who had a chance. He shuddered as Clay moaned. "More morphine," Jason shouted. "In the name of God . . ."

"Sorry." A medic shook his head as he looked up from a nearby body. "Sorry, we have no more."

"Jason." Blood bubbled on Clay's lips. "See those lights?"

"Charleston." Jason wiped the bloody froth.

"I did so want Bella to have my book of poems."

"Ssh. She'll have it."

Clay's soft brown eyes were clouding. Blood spouted from his wound, and each breath cost agony. Jason held his brother close and prayed death would be swift. "She'll have it. I promise you."

Clay's voice was barely a whisper. "I told you, Jason, we'd make it."

"Yes." Clay's eyes were closed now. Jason tasted his own tears. "We went through the gates of hell."

All night the cannon had been booming from Fort Wagner. Ben brought the whispered rumor that the 54th was fighting there. For hours, Isabella paced her bedroom, dispatching Ben to the roof, to the street, for further news. Now, as dawn broke pale and gray, she lay in alert exhaustion on her bed.

She heard the carriage stop before her door, the horses neighing with the sudden tightening of reins. Before she reached the window she heard the pounding on her door. Barefoot, her hands still fumbling with her robe, she rushed to the stairs.

Below her, at the door, she saw Monique, her hands clasped to her mouth. Then she saw her brother, his Union uniform, filthy, the bloody bandage on his head. "Oh, Jason!"

He saw her running down the winding staircase. He saw her outstretched arms, her smile. The bloodstained book was in his hand. Their brother's blood. "Clay wanted you to have this."

She faltered, a gull wounded in flight. "Clay . . ."

"His last words were of you."

"His last . . . ?"

"Clay is dead."

He saw the sudden whiteness in her face, her arm moving vainly for support. "Oh, Jason." Tears flooded her eyes, her voice was barely audible. "Oh, Jason, no."

"He was killed at Fort Wagner."

"No!" Her scream brought Monique to her side. Jason shoved the book into her hands. "Perhaps his blood will cleanse your soul."

Trembling, Isabella held the slim volume to her breast. Her tears splashed down on it. For a moment Jason stared at his sister, at home in southern opulence. Then, jaws clenched, he turned toward the door.

"Sir." Monique's soft voice. "Yo' grandma was too sick to move. She stayed to save our lives."

Jason turned, looked deep into his sister's eyes. "Is that true?"

"Oh, Jason." She fell against him, held him tightly. "Oh, Jason, I don't know."

Now it was evening and Jason was gone, taken by Monique to a shrimp fisherman whose small craft could slip by the ironclads in the

233

bay. The slim volume of Clay's poetry lay open on the nightstand, and Isabella, exhausted by Jason's words of her brother's and father's deaths, tossed in fitful sleep.

When she thought she heard someone call her name, she sought a deeper slumber. Then Ben's hand was on her shoulder. "Isabella, quick, wake up."

She turned and saw Ben's face, grim in the flickering lamp. "Ben, what is it?"

"It's Mr. Carleton. He's been shot." The stunned, vacant look on her face stopped his words momentarily. He reached for her hand. "Come on now. They brought him home."

Isabella followed Ben down to the foyer as the Confederate uniforms brought the stretcher through the door. She was shaking, she thought, with sobs, then peals of laughter rolled from her throat. She was dreaming it. None of it was real.

She clung to the banister, trembling, laughing, tears rolling down her cheeks. Ben touched her gently. "Easy now. Buck up."

She nodded mutely and wiped her tears as a private came toward her. "Mrs. Dulane, shall we take the captain upstairs?"

"Yes," Isabella whispered weakly. "Take the captain upstairs."

It was perhaps ten minutes before the soldiers came down. "He's conscious again, ma'am."

"Thank you," Isabella murmured, and walked slowly up the stairs.

Carleton was propped up on pillows. His face was flushed. A bandage already seeping blood covered the width of his chest. He touched her hair weakly as she sat on the bed. She could smell the fever.

"Isabella." His eyes caressed her face. "I had to see you and the baby. You should have named him Carleton." His lips, his tongue were parched.

She reached for the carafe and poured a glass of water. He drank it gratefully, then sank back against the pillow. "We got them, though . . . those nigger volunteers."

"Hush, Carleton."

He laughed, a harsh, choking sound. "Niggers playing soldier." His voice was a coarse whisper. "You should a seen them, eyes buckin' and rollin' . . ."

She got off the bed.

"Nigger soldiers. We put them against the wall and blew their brainless heads off."

She backed away, her heart pounding in her throat as she fought for self-control. He moaned and stretched his hand to her. "Don't leave me, Isabella."

Wetting her lips, she looked at the vials on the stand by the bed. "Did they give you anything for pain?"

"Morphine." He moved his finger. "That one, right there."

She felt him watching her as she picked up the vial. "But I should have been at Wagner." Blood came with his cough. "That's where they really had the fun."

Her hands trembled, spilling the contents of the vial.

He grinned as he looked at her. "Your old state, Massachusetts, sent those baboons down, a nigger regiment . . ."

"Damn you," she screamed. "Damn you, shut up."

He looked at her in surprise. "Isabella . . ."

She dropped the vial and faced him. "My brother, my brother Clay, was killed at Fort Wagner."

He looked at her, not comprehending, but feeling a cold shudder down his spine. "What are you trying to say?"

The burning tears rolled down her face. Her voice rose hysterically. "My brother, Clay, was killed at Fort Wagner."

His mouth hung open. "What's that nigger reg . . . ?"

"Carleton, your son, your heir, is a nigger."

"No!" he screamed it. "No!"

"Yes. Yes. Yes. A nigger like his . . ."

His hand shot out, twisting her arm. "Who was it? Who was it? Silas?"

"That happens in your family, not in mine."

"What the hell are you saying?" His fingers bit into her arm. His breath came in shallow pants.

Her words burst in choked spasms. "My brothers fought bravely at Fort Wagner. Their flag never touched the ground."

"Say it," he hissed. "Say it."

For a moment she caught her breath, then her words came slow and calm. "I am a Negro. A person of color." She remembered Clay's poem "Of Those Whom the Sun Has Loved . . ."

For a moment he stared at her disbelieving, his chest heaving, sweat pouring from his face. Then with a choked cry, he shoved her from him and seized the bedpost, trying to stand. "Silas," he screamed. "Silas."

"Silas is gone." Her voice was very low. "He was a spy for the Yankees."

His breath was coming hard now. "Lura," he moaned. "Lura . . ."

"Carleton . . ." She held her hand to him.

He crouched against the bedpost, tears on his fevered face. "Stay away from me, bitch."

They heard heavy footsteps coming on the run. Then Lura filled the doorway. "Mista Carleton . . ."

"Lura, be my witness . . ." Blood poured onto the bandage on Carleton's chest as he pointed, weakly, at Isabella. "This nigger bitch has deceived me."

Incredulity sharpened Lura's gasp. Isabella saw her eyes ricochet from Carleton's face to hers. Then Lura returned to ritual, purring, "Now, Mista Carleton, lemme help you back in bed."

"Goddammit, Lura." Carleton's voice was low and thick with pain as Lura bent over him. "You tell my father, hear me?" Tears ran down his face as he grabbed her attending hand. "Damn you, nigger, answer me!"

Lura looked down at him, her head cocked slightly to one side. "Carleton Dulane"—her hands were on her hips—"I ain't heard a word you said."

For an instant Carleton's eyes lost focus and blood flooded the bandage on his chest.

"Carleton," Isabella whispered, moving toward him.

"Stay away," he gasped. His eyes rolled back. His hands tore at his chest.

Isabella watched his convulsing form. "Carleton."

He looked at her from the side of his eyes. "Nigger," he hissed. Then he was still.

Carleton's body was taken to Four Winds for burial in the family cemetery. Joseph Dulane, delighted with his grandson, begged vainly that Isabella remain.

They stood together on the veranda waiting for Ben to bring her carriage. Holding his heir up to share the view, Joseph Dulane looked out over his lands. "Someday all this will be yours, Jacques Dulane. Even if the North should win the war, and I'm not sayin' they will, mind you, the South will win the peace. Everything will be the same. All the niggers running away now'll all be runnin' back. This is the only life they know. And the North shore don't want 'em. They pretty uppity right now, but one, two years from now, everything'll be exactly like it was."

Isabella's gaze went to the new grave on the hill. "No," she said softly. "It will never be the same."

Joe Dulane followed her gaze. "Well, not exactly. But I'm gonna build that boy a monument, the biggest in the state. I'm gonna put him into marble, him on his horse, that saber raised, them horse hoofs thrashin' the wind. Cap'n Carleton Dulane of Four Winds." Isabella saw Joe Dulane's nod of satisfaction. He thumped the baby's bottom as he turned to her again. "Just remember this, he left a fine son, Isabella, and one day Four Winds, as far as your eye can see, will belong to Jacques Dulane."

It will belong, she thought—but with no joy—to a Clavier.

For the next six months, the guns of Fort Wagner were turned on Charleston. In January, Monique ran into Isabella's room. "Miz Isabella, they say the whole harbor's full of whaleships."

"Whaleships?" Isabella wheeled to stare at Monique.

"Yes'm, from this place they call New Bedford. They say . . ." But before Monique could continue, Isabella had run from the room.

From her rooftop Isabella could see the sails of sixteen ships billowing in the bay. Then, as she watched, the line of ships began to sink.

She heard Monique come on the roof. "Monique." Her cry was shrill.

"They say they loaded with stone, Miz Isabella." Monique's voice was awed. "They say they sinking theyselves to blockade Charleston Harbor."

On February 17, Columbia, the capital of South Carolina, fell. In Charleston, the Confederates set fire to every building that could be used by Union forces and fled to join Beauregard's attempt to hold the advance of Sherman's troops.

On February 18, 1864, the 54th Massachusetts marched through the streets of Charleston. The soul of the Confederacy was broken.

Book Four

"RED SKY IN MORNING"
(Sailors take warning)

The question forced upon us at every moment of our generation has not been, as with other races of men, how shall we adorn, beautify, exalt and ennoble life, but how shall we claim life itself . . .

—Frederick Douglass, speech at the opening of Douglass Institute in Baltimore, Md., October 1, 1885

CHAPTER ONE

1865

"Damn it." Jason threw his pencil down on the hospital bed and swatted at the mosquito drawing blood from his arm. Gigantic green flies buzzed over his bandaged leg. "These damn blood-sucking insects . . ."

"Shit, nigger, you lucky you alive." In the bed next to Jason, Jim Harvey, best known as the Cat, or simply Cat, let a slow grin slide across his young, lean black face. "You got a hole in yo' head and somewhere in yo' brain a piece a shell roamin' round—an' that leg. Nigger, you lucky as hell that Dulane woman found that doctor with that carbolic stuff to operate on yo' leg. Fifteen men done died of infection in this broke-down, makeshift hellhole since you was brought in."

Jason followed Cat's thick-lashed eyes as he surveyed the dismal double rows of crowded cots in the ill-lit Charleston church basement. The stench was almost unbearable. Two nurses with blood-splattered uniforms moved wearily among the wounded men. A flour-streaked mouse stared hungrily from under Harvey's bed at the half ear of boiled corn and the fatty slab of salt pork, the remains of his dinner. "Damn it," Jason muttered, scratching his unshaven face with filthy nails, "I've got to finish this article . . ."

"When you get through with that one, you write about this here shit." Harvey groaned suddenly as the fierce pain in his arm warned him not to roll over. "And when we get outta here, I'm gonna take you down to the *South Carolina Leader,* the colored newspaper what I showed you, and make sure Reverend Cain print it. Remember that article I showed you last week what told that a hundred and seventy-nine thousand colored men had fought in the Union Army, and one outta every four men in the Union Navy was a nigger. And this is how they treat us now."

Jim Harvey started to sit up, then clenched his teeth in pain. "Lord, I could use some a that morphine now."

"That stuff's dangerous, Cat," Jason replied. "Make you dream your life away."

241

"Nice rosy dream's better'n this here nightmare." Perspiration rolled down Cat's face.

"Easy." Jason slid to the side of his bed and put his hand on Harvey's leg. "Easy." Cat had escaped from slavery when he was seventeen and had fought in the Union navy. He had been with Robert Smalls when the Negro pilot had stolen the Confederate steamer *Planter* out of Charleston Harbor and delivered it to the Union Navy.

"They fuckin' with us now." Cat used the pillow to wipe his face, then leaned back on the bed. "Every damn day they fuckin' with us now."

They were indeed, Jason thought, scowling. The stunning death of Lincoln; the succession of Andrew Johnson, a former indentured servant from Tennessee, to the White House. Now Johnson had allowed his provisional governors to reorganize the South along its old-time lines.

"Johnson's trying to undo the Civil War," Jason said grimly. "He's vetoing bill after bill sent to him by Congress to protect and strengthen the freedmen's rights." Jason shook his head. "He's moving with almost unrestrained power to eradicate the legacy of Lincoln, to blot out the single momentous achievement of the previous administration."

It was strange, Jason thought. In the 1850's Johnson more than Lincoln had been the champion of the Negro. "You know, Clavier," Cat turned to face him, "you oughta stay in Carolina. Like I told you before, this is where the black man's power's got to start. This is where we got our biggest weapon, our numbers. I bet niggers in this state outnumber white folks four to one."

"Probably." Jason nodded. "But it's going to take more than numbers." He eased himself back on the bed and picked up his pencil again.

Yes, Jason thought, it was going to take a hell of a lot more than numbers.

The Civil War had left the South in chaos. Plantations and smaller farms had been abandoned by the thousands. Land values had dropped almost 60 percent; Confederate notes were of no value. Millions in bank stocks, endowments, and investments had been lost.

But it was the Negro who, once again, was suffering hardest. Free —but in name only—without home, land, tools, or money, with no access to credit he was now at the mercy of men who would not, could not, allow him to be free.

Tens of thousands had already died of privation and disease. In some communities, the *South Carolina Leader* reported, one out of four had died of starvation. And while the Freedmen's Bureau was doing herculean work, feeding thousands, opening and operating schools and hospitals, and though courageous New England schoolmarms were rushing South to teach the newly freed, only two men, only two men of power, Thaddeus Stevens and Charles Sumner, stood between the Negro and disaster.

The South Carolina Constitutional Convention, dominated by ex-Confederates, had nullified the Ordinance of Secession. By a vote of ninety-eight to eight, it had deemed that the "slaves of South Carolina having been emancipated by the action of the United States authorities, neither slavery nor involuntary servitude shall ever be re-established in the State."

Then, having accepted the inevitable, the Convention had refused steadfastly to attend to the business of Negro suffrage. It moved instead to circumvent it. Negroes were being legislated into poverty, prohibited from all employment except farming or menial labor without a license which required both proof of fitness and a fee ranging from ten to one hundred dollars. Under the vagrancy laws, Negroes could not move to find jobs. It was a crime to walk off a job. Negroes could not preach without permission. There was even a law prohibiting Negroes and whites from looking out the same window.

But these were not the most horrendous aspects of the postwar period. One after another, Cat's frequent visitors had told of the bodies of murdered and mutilated Negroes found on highways, in the streets, the alleys, the fields. Riots, they reported, often organized by police and government officials, were staging grounds for the wholesale massacre of Negro men, women, and children, for the burning of their homes, schools, and churches. Bands of armed whites were roaming the countryside. Negroes were being held on plantations by brute force.

But, Jason frowned as he tapped his pencil on the paper, Cat was right. Despite all this, Negro leadership was beginning to emerge. Slowly at first, but gathering force with each new day. Mass meetings —to petition, to plan, to organize—were held and attended, sometimes to overflowing, by Negroes who risked their very lives to attend.

Last month, in November of 1865, the Colored People's Convention, the first concerted action by Negroes of South Carolina, had been held at the Zion Baptist Church to protest the all-white Constitutional Convention of Governor Perry and the Black Code it enacted. The protest was spreading across the state—across the South. And still the North was silent. It was only as the horror became untenable, as the South's intransigence unbearable, that the thunder of Stevens and the lightning of Sumner were beginning to have effect.

Oh, yes, Jason thought, there was work to be done. There was much that he must do before that bullet in his head moved further.

Jason's jaw tightened suddenly as he saw a tall, red-headed woman inching her way through the cots toward him. Mrs. Dulane. The wife of the Confederate officer who had known him so well when they were children, who had persuaded and paid a private doctor to operate on his leg. Goddamn her. Jason clenched his fist. Goddamn her for her lies.

The red-headed witch sat down beside him, a napkin-covered bowl in her lap. "I've brought you some soup." She smiled. "It's still hot."

"Go away."

"Jason . . ."

"Bella, go away."

"Jason." Her eyes pleaded. Her dress was dingy and work had roughened the hands that held the bowl. "I walked twenty blocks down here to bring you a hot meal." A sob caught her voice. "And this is the last of our tomatoes and our peas. For God's sake, stop being so damn self-righteous. Little Jacques and I have had only one meal today ourselves."

"Look, lady"—Cat touched her arm—"if he don't want it . . ."

"I brought enough for both of you." Isabella removed the napkin. "See, two spoons."

"Goddamn, Bella," Jason said softly. "You got more nerve than a brass-ass monkey."

A week later, Cat and Jason were released from the hospital. "Shit," Cat said as they walked past windowless and burned-out buildings, past one-armed and one-legged young men sitting with vacant eyes on benches in weed-filled parks, "this damn Reconstructing thing got everybody in a doozy." Cat slowed his long strides as he saw Jason puffing on his cane. "Look like folks 'round here got more

244

hankerin' for blood than a dry camel do for water. And Lord knows, I done already give two a my nine lives in the war. Only a fool be about these days without their blue steel, buddy." His long black fingers patted his side affectionately. Then abruptly Cat's expression changed. "Lord a mercy, Miss Suzanne Beecham."

Jason halted in mid-step. She wore a yellow dress and a crazy plumed hat pushed back on her head. Her lovely oval-shaped eyes sparkled as a young black soldier whistled at her saucy, unconcerned steps. She was no more than seventeen.

"How do, Miss Suzanne." Cat's hand made a motion that would have tipped his hat, had he worn one to tip.

Jason gasped as she smiled. Her eyes met his merrily. Twin dimples appeared at either side of her full, ripe mouth. Even white teeth flashed in cinnamon silk skin. My God, Jason thought, I've never seen such a woman.

"Miss Suzanne Beecham, this here is Mr. Jason Clavier," Cat introduced them with a flourish.

"How do you do," Jason said, annoyed to see the smile at the corner of Cat's mouth.

"Very well, thank you. And yourself?" The promise of a smile again.

"Well, I'm just out of the hospital, and I, uh . . ." With annoyance Jason heard himself stammering.

"Well, we'll be having a social Friday night at our church, Morris Street Baptist. Cat knows where it is if you'd care to come . . ."

"I would. Yes, I would indeed."

"Well." She turned mischievously to his companion. "Cat, you see Mr. Clavier gets there, now, you hear?"

"Yes ma'am," Cat said seriously, as though this command had not come from this lovely and self-confident sprite of a girl.

"And thank you." Jason could not take his eyes from her as she smiled her saucy smile again, then moved with quick, light steps away.

Cat touched Jason's arm. "Come on, man. The *Leader*'s office'll be closed."

Damn the *Leader*, Jason thought, but Cat's touch was persistent and he reluctantly followed his friend. "Cat, that's quite a young lady."

"Look, Jason," Cat replied with a sidelong look at his friend.

245

" 'Fore you get all carried away, there's something you ought to know."

"Yes?"

"Yes indeedy. She can afford to be right feisty. Her daddy's Bob Beecham. He gotta still outside of town. They say his father came from the Sea Islands. That's where the white folks sent a lotta them niggers that was impossible to break. Folks around here call 'em Geechies. And believe me, they don't take no shit off nobody, black or white.

"Them Sea Islanders talk this talk called Gullah, which they talk in that part of Africa where they came from which the Portuguese now call Angola. They got some funny ways, let me tell you. They put this blue paint on their windows and their doors to keep away the evil spirits.

"Bob Beecham." Cat shook his head. "Let me tell you, he's the baddest nigger in the State of South Carolina."

"I thought you were," Jason quipped with a grin.

"No, I'm only second."

And Jason saw Cat wasn't smiling.

Suzanne Beecham was still on Jason's mind when he and Cat arrived at 430 King Street and climbed to the second-floor office of the *Leader*. Jason was speaking with its editor, the Reverend Richard Cain, when Robert Brown Elliott, twenty-five, coal black, and already renowned for his brilliance, bounced up the stairs. Cain, and then Elliott, read Jason's article carefully. When Elliott finished, he looked at Jason and pulled back a chair. "Sit down, Mr. Clavier, and, in the name of humanity, let me entreat you to remain in South Carolina."

For nearly an hour they talked—Elliott fiery, eloquent, passionate; Cain shrewd, intelligent, dedicated. Their subject, their only subject, was politics. Elliott, like Jason, was from Massachusetts. Both had been educated abroad. Both had studied law. The Reverend Cain was from Brooklyn, New York, and had been sent South by the African Methodist Episcopal Church to proselytize among the freedmen and to reorganize and rebuild Emmanuel Church, closed since 1832, when it was discovered that Denmark Vessey had laid plans for insurrection within its sanctuary. By the hour's end, Jason had found his intellectual home.

"Whadda you wanna do now?" Cat asked as he and Jason left the *Leader* office. "Write another story, see Charleston, or . . . ?"

A wry smile touched Jason's lips. "I think I ought to pay my respects to Mrs. Dulane."

Cat frowned. "You know where she lives?"

"Yes," Jason replied thoughtfully. "I've been there once before."

"Jason," Isabella squealed as she answered her door chimes, pulling off the scarf that bound her hair. "You're out!"

"I'm out. Are you asking me in?"

"Oh." She pulled his arm. "Come in. I'm a mess. There's no one here but Jacques and me. Come on." She took his arm and started across the foyer. "I had to sell all the furniture in the living room and the study. We'll have to sit in the drawing room."

The drawing room was oval. The walls were Adams green. Magnificent woodwork surrounded each of the eight windows that reached nearly to the ceiling. An Aubusson rug of beige and rose covered most of the marble inlaid floor.

The furniture was Chippendale except for the piece on the far wall, where her portrait hung lighted by a chandelier over an exquisite table from the shop of Duncan Phyfe.

"I couldn't bear to sell these pieces," she said as they sat before the fireplace, "though the rest of the house is almost empty. But"— she shrugged—"I couldn't keep it up anyway. The day the war ended, they all left. They fled. Do you remember Monique? Well, she married that shrimp fisherman, and they got one of the plots of abandoned land the government gave to Negroes at Port Royal, to work and pay off on time."

"You and your son should come back to New Bedford, Bella. Mama and Aunt Jacqueline . . ."

"No, Jason." Her eyes were a sharp green in the thinness of her face, her mouth set in a tight, ugly line. "I have not gone through all this for nothing. One day my son will own Four Winds. Joe Dulane cannot live forever." She paused, her eyes fixed on his. "And one day a Clavier . . ."

Jason rented a room two blocks from the *Leader* office. Then, two days before Christmas, he received a telegram from his mother. He was needed, desperately she said, at home. He went again to see

Bella, but she steadfastly refused to leave. Reluctantly, Jason packed his bags and went home.

But there was no desperate need for Jason Clavier in New Bedford. Nor was it the same town he had left. The Civil War had virtually ended the whale fishery, and mills and factories in what was to Jason now a placid city were growing with each belch of smoke. Visiting his friend Alex Kuykendal, whose left leg had been amputated at the knee, he was astonished by the tremendous growth of his factory.

"We converted from shoes to boots during the war," Alexander said, rubbing the painful nub of his leg. "And though I can't wear both parts of a pair, the war made me a wealthy man."

But Jason saw no opportunity for himself in New Bedford. He saw instead the growing stranglehold of monopolies, the zooming power of the political bosses, the strength of ethnic voting, and realized more than ever that if the Negro did not make his bid for power now, it would be lost forever. Despite the fact that two black men, Edward G. Walker, son of David Walker, and Charles L. Mitchell were elected that spring to the Massachusetts House of Representatives, Jason believed it was in the South that real black power could be forged.

So, even as his cousin Isaac Woodson of "Woodson Carpenters and Masons: Signs Made to Order" carved the shingle that read "Jason Clavier, Attorney at Law" to hang outside the office he was negotiating to lease from Congressman Benjamin Oates, Jason made his decision. From time to time his head hurt fiercely, and he knew the shell fragment was on the move. It might be that he had but a little time to give. Packing his books in Grandpa Jacques's sea chest and leaving his mother, his aunt, and his house in Isaac's care, Jason Clavier returned to South Carolina.

CHAPTER TWO

1866–1868

Three black men sat in the sweltering second-floor office of the *South Carolina Leader* in Charleston: Jason Clavier, the Reverend Richard Cain, Robert Brown Elliott. They had been talking nearly an hour.

"I tell you, Jason, this is the hour, the moment." Robert Elliott's voice was barely a whisper, but his eyes glowed in his handsome black face. "Today, at last, the Congress has been heard from. They've overridden Johnson's veto and passed the Civil Rights Act. It's coming, Jason. Black men are going to have a real voice in government. And damn it, we are ready."

"Let's not delude ourselves that this new mood of the North is due to a sudden concern for the fate of the Negro," Jason said slowly, "though I'm certain there are a few to whom the Negro is the first consideration. But other factors are playing powerful roles. There are those who want the total subjugation of the South, a position I personally reject as dangerous. It could be a preamble to further violence. Others see a conflict between the interests of the industrialized North and those of the South and fear a coalition between South and West. Still others are trying to bolt the Negro to the Republican party and thereby insure its power."

"That's their divided agenda, Jason," Elliott said quickly. "Now is the time to forge our united one. The time is come when we must make our bid for power. We must seize it. We must use it. Or unborn generations of black children will scream curses on our names."

"You are coming tonight to hear Cardozo?" Reverend Cain asked Jason. "We're expecting more than five hundred."

"I'll be there." Jason pulled out his pocket watch and looked at it. "I have a stop I must make first."

"Where?" Robert Elliott asked. "Can I take you there?"

"No, I think not, Robert." Jason smiled suddenly. "From all I've heard it might not be safe . . ."

"Where, or should I say who . . . ?"

"Who." Jason's grin broadened. "I'm going to see the baddest nigger in the state and ask to court his daughter."

Jason walked slowly toward the Beecham house on the outskirts of the city. Perhaps it would be a mistake to ask Suzanne to marry him.

He loved her—God yes, more than he had dreamed he could love anyone. But she was so young, and that shell fragment, that damn shell fragment in his head . . .

Cat had guessed his dilemma. "Look, Jason, you can't just keep going to church socials and staring at that girl. Sooner or later folks gon' think you're batty. Shit, I know the tizzy you in, what with that bullet bouncing in yo' brain. But looka here, ain't no man born of a black woman ain't known the price a blackness could well be his life. The thing to do is give her what you can." Cat's hand had dropped on Jason's shoulder. "And I guarantee you, if it ain't but two years, it'll be the best two years in her life."

Jason saw the low white picket fence, then saw Bob Beecham, a man living his own legend, come out of his blue-painted door onto his low twilight-lit porch. Jason opened the gate and walked up the neat, azalea-bordered flagstone walk, keeping his eyes on Beecham's face. He was the rich, warm brown of well-aged Bourbon, with the unrevealing eyes of the master gambler. But there was another look in his eyes, one Jason had seen and not understood in the eyes of Papa Jacques. But Jason knew it now. It was the look of a man who has lived his whole life between the bullet fired and its impact in his brain.

"Mr. Beecham." Jason held out his hand. "My name is Jason Clavier."

Bob Beecham ignored Jason's hand and removed the cigarette from his lips, holding it between three fingers and his thumb. "I reckoned as much."

Jason dropped his hand, fastening his eyes to Beecham's. "I would like your permission to visit with your daughter, Suzanne."

Silently, Beecham kept his eyes on Jason's.

"I assure you, sir, my intentions are completely honorable."

Bob Beecham permitted himself a glimmer of amusement. "Mr. Clavier, I lived long 'nough to know that there ain't such thing as honable intentions between a man and a pretty young gal. It's only when intentions don't get nowhere he even starts thinkin' up the honable." He looked Jason over slowly. "An' beside, a filly need time to frolic. She don't need no racehorse out to stud."

Jason felt his stomach tightening. He let sarcasm touch his voice. "Mr. Beecham, I am a single man from excellent family . . ."

"Bob?" The voice, rich and sweet as maple syrup, flowed from the woman now in the doorway whose beauty was astonishing to behold.

250

Jason knew exactly how Suzanne would look in twenty years. "Now, why don't you show Mr. Clavier we're a good family too and invite him in for supper?"

Bob Beecham looked at his wife a moment, then turned back to Jason. "All right," he said curtly. "You can eat."

From then on, Jason went to the Beechams' often, courting his sweet, beautiful Suzanne. They sat on the porch swing in the evening, talking softly in the moonlight, watching her brothers and sisters peeking around the corner of the house, until Bob Beecham called, "All right, it's getting late. Enough is enough."

Often, however, they did not sit alone. Often evening brought others to Beecham's porch throne. They came singly and in twos and threes. Jason soon learned that curtness was Bob Beecham's way with everyone.

At first, Jason wondered at the deference and allegiance paid his future father-in-law. But as he grew to know the man, he gave credence to the legend: "White folks got they sheriff and they night riders. Niggers got Bob Beecham." There was hardly a Negro in Charleston who had not heard at least one Bob Beecham tale. And more than one was witness to their truth.

And so they came that spring to sit a spell on Bob Beecham's porch—freedmen on their first trip to a city, ex-slaves who had known the city all their lives, those who had sailed the seven seas on their master's ships, and those from the ten thousand Negroes who had been free in South Carolina long before the war. They were sharecroppers and small farmers, artisans and drifters. Some owned property, a few owned prosperous businesses. They were earth-toned men, from coal black to light as sand.

Sometimes as they gathered Suzanne would say good night and go inside. Then they talked "man" talk: of the drunken fool who drank a glass of pee thinking it was Bourbon, of the claps "a friend" had caught from the preacher's wife, of the widow in that shack who sold the best pussy in the world to support her seven young'uns. But always they settled into serious talk, their crucial talk, how, now that they were free in name, they could become free in fact.

And as they talked, as they planned, the powers of Reconstruction were stripped from Andrew Johnson. The Joint Congressional Committee of Fifteen, the new power of Reconstruction, put the South under military control and authorized new elections in which all males, regardless of color, could vote.

251

Emboldened by this support and pulled by the mighty wills of Sumner and Stevens, Congress sent the Fourteenth Amendment to the states for ratification. New Congressional Conventions were mandated for the southern states.

But even as Congress acted, Jason felt the countervailing winds.

In April, at the Maxwell House Hotel in Nashville, men from across the South met under the new generalship of the Civil War general Nathan B. Forrest, who had massacred black troops at Fort Pillow, and formed a new organization. Its name: the Ku Klux Klan.

The next months passed with the speed of moments. The *South Carolina Leader* carried the news to its readers: "At the earliest possible date, the district commander will convene Constitutional Conventions, delegates to which will be charged with the duty both of writing new state constitutions specifying political and civil rights for freedmen and of creating new state governments embodying the principles of the new constitutions. State legislatures, in turn, are required to ratify the Fourteenth Amendment as a condition for return of their state to the Union and representation in the Federal Congress."

On a June night lit by fireflies, sitting on Bob Beecham's porch, Jason made his decision to run as a delegate to the Constitutional Convention. For months he had sat quietly, listening, saying little to the increasing numbers of men who gathered in the Beecham yard. But ever more frequently they turned to him asking, "What you think 'bout that, eh, Jason?" "Jason, whadda *you* think we oughtta do?"

The men changed from night to night, from week to week, but they took from Bob Beecham's porch, to consider and repeat, the words and wisdom of Jason Clavier. And, as the time for the Convention approached, more and more they said, "You oughtta be runnin' fo' that thing, Jason. We need smart young niggas like yu'self to git this shit straight once and for all."

They were his sentiments, exactly.

"My God, no," Isabella exclaimed when he told her. "Jason, please, please don't. You don't know what these people are capable of doing. Jason, listen." She grabbed both of his hands. "Go back to New Bedford. You can have a fine law practice there."

"No." He withdrew his hands. "I have decided, Isabella. And you can no more win me to your view than I could you to mine."

"You are determined to throw away all of your training, to throw all of Aunt Jacqueline's hopes away."

252

"I am determined to put them to good use. Bella, more than at any time in our history our people need good leadership. I'm going to run for the Constitutional Convention, and if we win that, for the legislature."

"They will not let you win, Jason. In the end, they will not let you win."

"Then we'll give them one hell of a beginning. And if we lose, it won't be because we haven't tried. As Robert Elliott says, the hopes of unborn generations hang on our actions these next few months."

A soft, sad smile touched her lips. "All right, Papa," she said. She looked at her brother a moment more, then nodded. "All right, I know people you should meet."

"White people?"

"I know you may find this difficult to believe, Jason, but there are white people here who were against the war, and others who believe that now the law must be obeyed, that Negroes must have their full rights."

"I don't know." Jason scowled. "History must record that black men . . ."

"The only thing history will record, Jason, is, did you? Not, how."

Many of the men Jason had met with Elliott sought election. Late into the night they planned. Quickly now, a power base must be built and fortified. Negroes must be registered so that they could vote. No, the candidates explained as they spoke throughout the countryside, the vote was not something to put into bags or baskets. No, it was nothing to eat or wear. Yes, there was enough of it to go around.

Registration began in the state of South Carolina late in August of 1867. Not a Negro in the state was registered to vote. One month later, at the end of September, Elliott burst into the *Leader* office, his face glowing with excitement. "We've done it." He threw his arms around Jason and Cain. "Seventy-eight thousand nine hundred and eighty-two black males, ninety-four percent of those over twenty-one, have registered. In twenty-one of the state's thirty-one districts we hold the majority. A government based on equality is waiting to be born."

On November 19 and 20, Negroes went to the polls for the first time in South Carolina. Their choice: to vote for or against the Constitutional Convention and, if for, to vote simultaneously for the delegates to represent their district. Of the eighty-seven percent of the registered Negroes who voted, every single one of them, 68,687 voted for the Convention.

On January 14, 1868, 124 delegates to the Convention filed through the handsome grounds of Charleston's Club House on Meeting Street. Forty-eight were white. The seventy-six black delegates included Jason Clavier.

Inside the Club House, newsmen from across the nation were crowded around the president's desk on a specially built platform. The delegates, in armchairs in the middle of the room, were separated by railings from the throng of spectators on the benches along the walls.

Both hands on Jason's pocket watch rested exactly at the center of twelve when an attendant pushed an earthenware spittoon, weighing nearly a quarter of a ton, toward the front of the room. The spittoon was placed, the ancient tradition settled.

For the next fifty-three days, ex-slaves and former masters, the rich and the poor, the educated and the illiterate, pounded out the state's first democratic constitution. Maligned in the press as the "ring-streaked, the striped convention" and "the Congo convention," they defied a mythology two centuries old. Black men and white men worked as equals, and they did not fail.

Stunned, the old aristocracy was immobilized. Shocked, the sand-hill crackers realized the niggers meant business. They had helped write the state constitution and now, goddamn, they was talkin' a runnin' for the legislature. The foolishness had gone far enough. It was time for white folks to take over . . . again.

CHAPTER THREE

1868

"Let me say again, Mrs. Dulane, my offer will be more than fair."

"Oh, I'm certain." Isabella's work-roughened fingers caught in the torn lace of her sleeve as she tried to hide her hands. "I'm certain, Mr. Hardwick. It's just that I never dreamed of selling the portrait."

"I understand." Cornelius Hardwick's thin-lipped smile was placating. "Ingres himself described the Isabella Dulane as one of his finest works. And I wholeheartedly agree. It's remarkable. Quite remarkable."

Isabella's eyes followed Hardwick as he turned his attention to the painting again.

His letter had come eight weeks before. The finely drawn script on the heavy vellum paper had informed her that Cornelius Hardwick of New York was donating a gallery of his private collection of French painters to the National Gallery of Art. Hardwick, the letter said, had just learned of the existence of Ingres's Isabella Dulane. Now Ingres was dead, the painting more valuable. Mrs. Dulane could rest assured that Mr. Hardwick's offer would be more than fair.

Ingres was dead . . . the painting more valuable.

Quickly Isabella had learned that Cornelius Hardwick of New York was one of the wealthiest men in America: land, railroads, stock manipulation, oil speculation—a man who usually, one way or another, obtained exactly what he wanted.

Now, seated beside him in her drawing room, Isabella was certain he was all that she had heard. His voice was soft, but used to command. He seemed to see everything, but focused on detail. He respected intelligence and disdained frivolity.

He was, she thought, about fifty-five. His face strikingly fine-boned; his hair thick, curly, and completely white. His wide-set blue eyes were sharp, penetrating in fact, but his skin was pale and flaccid, with dark spots that spelled a liver condition. Although illness had twice forced him to postpone his visit, Isabella sensed the personal force that moved an empire.

She glanced at Monsieur Lesueur, the art dealer and Ingres expert who had accompanied Hardwick to Charleston, now peering at every

255

inch of her portrait through his magnifying glass. "This is excellent sherry," Hardwick interrupted her thoughts as he lifted his glass. "And so your grandfather gave you the medallion just before he died."

"Yes." Isabella moved her lips into a smile, hoping her crisp answer would end Hardwick's questions about the medallion. But he frowned as he looked at the painting again. "I know I have seen that design before. Not the boat and sail, that is unique. Nor, of course, the symbol worked in jewels. But that star and cross combination . . ." Hardwick tapped his fingers in concentration. "I'm not quite certain where, but . . . Was your grandfather a foreigner?"

"Not unless you consider Massachusetts foreign," Isabella laughed. "Which, of course, some people in these parts do."

Hardwick nodded absently. "I have an extensive collection of sculpture from many parts of the world, but it well may be that I have not seen the object itself, only a drawing or painting of it. Different, quite different. It strikes my fancy."

Isabella tried to control her growing discomfort. Perhaps it had been a mistake to let Hardwick see the painting. He had been so interested in every facet—how many sketches had been made, the designer of her gown, and especially in the medallion. She bit her lip and concentrated on her reason. Ingres was dead. The painting more valuable . . . she and her son would no longer be dependent on the meager handouts of Joe Dulane.

Not, she thought, that it would not mean a thing if Hardwick should discover the origin of the design. Had he not said he owned artifacts from around the world? But his perception was too keen. She had introduced her son Jacques to Hardwick when he had first arrived. After the boy had left the room, the millionaire had asked, "Do you, or did your husband, have Indian ancestry?"

"Why, no," she had answered quickly, too quickly, then remembered with a blush Jacques's olive skin.

"Oh?" An arching smile had accompanied his reply. "I would think that if one's family has lived in America for more than three generations, one would hardly answer 'no' to any blood."

"And does that make you uncomfortable?" She had struggled to regain her composure.

"No," he had replied with some amusement. "We have been here only two."

256

She had wanted to add, "And become so rich." But from all she had heard, one hardly bantered with Cornelius Hardwick.

"Monsieur Hardwick." Lesueur turned.

Isabella stood. "Perhaps you would like to be alone?"

"No, no." Hardwick stood quickly. "There is no need. We are both in enthusiastic agreement with Ingres that this is one of his finest paintings. His craftsmanship is at its highest level. And his subject matter"—a small smile touched the corners of Hardwick's mouth—"is almost without parallel. We will make an offer. Ten thousand dollars. And we would be honored, Isabella Dulane, if you would attend the dedication of the gallery."

Ten thousand . . . Doubt disappeared. Delight danced in Isabella's eyes. "Mr. Hardwick, you have just purchased the Isabella Dulane."

Isabella walked with Hardwick to the door, her assurance in the validity of her action mounting from the crispness of Hardwick's check in her still perspiring hand. She was waving goodbye when she saw a familiar figure trudging down the street. In one hand the woman grasped an enormous bundle tied in what seemed to be a bedspread. In her other arm she held a baby. Beside her a young boy similarly laden moved with reluctant steps.

For an instant Isabella stared in disbelief, then arms outstretched, ran down the steps. "Monique," she called, ignoring the sudden turn of Hardwick's head as his carriage pulled away. "Monique!"

The boy watched with sullen eyes as the tall red-haired lady threw her arms around his mother, then pulled back as with a cry of "Jimmy" she turned to embrace him too.

He sat in the corner of her kitchen as she culled her meager supplies to ease the crawling in his belly. He stuffed the food into his mouth, watching his mother as she did the same, while the red-headed lady cuddled his baby brother and brought the cup of warm milk to his lips. He saw his mother's suddenly tear-streaked face, heard her fervent whisper, "Thank the good Lord you was here, Miz Isabella."

In the drawing room, seated beside Monique, Isabella heard about her life these past five years. Monique and her husband, Gabriel Baker, had gotten a small farm at Port Royal. With the aid of other black farmers, he had built their home. She and Jimmy had worked beside him in the fields. With their first crop they had made their payment on the land and had enough left to buy a few things for their home.

They had brought in a second crop before the baby came. Then suddenly the government had repossessed the farm. Monique's husband had been killed fighting for his land. For weeks now, Monique and her sons had been on the road, sleeping in barns, in ditches, hiding from marauding murdering whites who swept through the countryside.

Monique halted her story abruptly, her practiced eye surveying Isabella and the room. "Looks like things been rough for you too, Miz Isabella," she said softly.

"Yes." Isabella took Monique's hand. "But it's over now. And, Monique, you and I and our sons survived."

CHAPTER FOUR

1868

Jason campaigned in the swamps and the farmland. He spoke in homes and in churches, in barbershops and brothels. At camp meetings and weddings, at picnics and socials, he preached and he reasoned. With the young and the old, the intelligent and the simple, the hearty and the lame, the bold and the fearful, he talked about freedom. He talked about voting. He talked about voting for black men.

Emotions and fears festered as election day grew closer. Bob Beecham and his deputy, Smoke, took turns on the back porch of the house Jason had rented in Edgefield County, their shotguns at the ready, while Cat, whose armaments were never seen, moved as naturally with Jason as his arms and legs.

A week before election, four of Jason's campaign lieutenants quit, assured by their employers that they would starve—or worse—that winter if they spoke another word in Clavier's behalf. Two days before the vote was to be cast, Isaiah Stone, a preacher whose church in Fayville Jason used frequently as a meeting place, was shot to death outside his home.

Early the next morning, despite Bob Beecham's glum predictions, Jason and Cat went to Fayville. It was a ride of twenty miles across open country. For mile after dusty mile Jason saw the backs of his people toiling in the heat-withered fields. His back ached from long weeks in the saddle. His butt burned from saddle sores. He grimaced as he watched Cat riding easily ahead. Damn, Jason grinned suddenly as he kicked his horse to a canter, this is a long way from the Sorbonne.

They rode fast and arrived in Fayville late in the afternoon. Jason tied his horse to the rail before Isaiah Stone's whitewashed church and walked up its sagging steps. The minister lay in his coffin inside, ready for the evening wake. For a long moment Jason looked down at the closed pine box, then went outside and stood on the church steps. His words soared over the fear in his gut—his eulogy to the bravery of the minister, his damnation on those who had committed the obscenity, his challenge that Isaiah Stone must not have died in vain.

A few Negroes shuffled by, averting their faces. Others, starting down the dusty road, turned to take another route home. For four full minutes Jason spoke, as Cat watched, with tensing muscles, the white folk gathering at the far end of the block. "We cannot, we must not let them reign by terror." Jason's voice rang clearly, "We must not let the bullet, the knife, and the rope become the supreme authority in our land. Justice demands our courage. God demands our trust . . ."

A young black woman, no more than eighteen, stopped and listened, her baby in her arms. An elderly black man joined her. Another woman. Two young men. Cat saw the whites move closer together. One flashed a pistol, and Cat felt for his own.

Jason was talking now about what the election could mean. Though still small, the crowd of Negroes was growing. Jason saw the whites starting toward them, saw Cat move up the steps and stand beside him as his listeners now punctuated his speech with solemn "Amens."

Cat knew Jason was aware of the whites, was choosing to ignore them. Cat's body went loose and ready. His hand moved to the butt of his Colt revolver and, in the group before him, he saw another black man's do the same. Shit, Cat thought, and grinned.

Cat's smile slowed the first white man who moved for his gun, but not the second. Jason felt the bullet graze his cheek, then Cat shoved him down with one hand and opened fire with the other.

Spraddled on his hands and knees, Jason heard the bullets, saw the stones coming like hellfire. His horse was struck in the head and lay thrashing on the ground. Behind the horse's twisting body two black men returned the fire while the other Negroes dove for whatever cover they could find.

The woman with the baby fell bleeding to the ground. As Jason moved toward her, he felt Cat's foot hard on his butt. "Goddammit," Cat hissed, "git inside that goddamn church."

Jason crawled inside the building. He saw blood flow from Cat's shoulder as Cat slid inside the door to reload.

"See the hell your bright idea has raised." Cat's face twisted in a scowl as he reached into his overalls and pulled out a stick of dynamite.

The fuse hissed, sputtered, caught. Jason stood behind Cat as he stepped through the door. Rooted in their tracks the white men stared as they beheld the smoking thing above Cat's head. With a wild shout Cat flung it into their midst. Jason saw him grin as the howling whites scattered like a breaking rack of billiard balls.

Then Jason heard the movement inside the church and, spinning, dove between the roughhewn pews. Four men crept past the pulpit. "Cat!" he screamed. "In here!"

A gun in each hand now, Cat crouched at Jason's side waiting for the whites to present a better target. Outside, the din grew fierce again.

"What's happening out there?" Jason whispered.

"Hell," Cat replied, shoving a gun in Jason's hand and reaching in his pocket for a third. "Now shoot as good as you talk. If them white bastards get to that door, be a slaughter run out there."

"Stand up, niggers, or we'll kill y'all on yo' knees." Looking around the end of the pew, Jason saw them using the casket, the pulpit, and the front pews as their cover.

"Yo' ass!" Cat squinted and put a bullet through the pulpit.

A half dozen shots rang through the church, but the pews, logs split by devout hands, were thick. For the moment, as the whites inched toward them, they were safe.

"You think you got any of them?" Jason whispered, handing Cat his handkerchief.

"Maybe one." Cat stuffed the cloth beneath his shirt to stanch the bleeding from his shoulder.

The firing resumed, heavier this time, and closer. Bullets bore into their pew, splintering it as Jason and Cat pumped their triggers. Jason felt perspiration rolling down his face.

"Easy," Cat whispered. "I'm dividin' up my nine lives with you."

Blood still oozed from the wound in Cat's shoulder, though part of the red circle on his shirt was crusting. The bullet that had grazed Jason's cheek had left only a burning sensation of which he was almost unaware. Crouching next to Cat, Jason prayed silently, "Let me live, oh, Lord of Moses. Let me live to lead my people."

Another hail of bullets sent them sprawling on their bellies. "Keep firing, keep firing," Jason panted.

"Damn," Cat hissed, both of his triggers working, "what the hell you think I'm doing?"

They heard a scream—a howl it was really—piercing and unreal, then the sound of mayhem.

"Shit!!!" It was Cat's most reverent sound. Crawling next to him, Jason peeked through a new hole in the pew.

"Oh, my God," he whispered.

In the exchange of fire, bullets had hit the coffin and the chest strap inside that held the dead in place. The lid popped open, and Isaiah Stone, no longer bound, sat upright in death.

The white man, whose gun rested on the foot of the coffin, fainted as Isaiah rose, eyes closed, face and hands composed for heaven. And another, near the altar, dove through the open window.

"God," Jason whispered again, and the hand that held his gun trembled.

"Amen." Cat grinned, and fired on the men now scrambling in retreat.

News of these events spread like wildfire in the night. The next day Jason Clavier was elected to the First Reconstruction Legislature of the State of South Carolina by a majority of three to one.

CHAPTER FIVE

It was that great getting-up morning when the last became the first. It was the day of crossing over Jordan, of singing the Lord's song in a strange land. The children who had walked in darkness saw a great light.

They had passed over into camp ground.

Jason Clavier, seated beside Suzanne, his bride of two days, felt the elation of his soul as his surrey moved through the scorched July streets of Columbia, capital of South Carolina. Down the street the State Capitol Building was still without a roof, but the Capitol was not necessary for the swearing in of the First General Assembly of the South Carolina Reconstruction government today.

"We've done it." Jason smiled at his father-in-law, who sat across from him in the surrey.

Bob Beecham, feeling conspicuous and ill at ease in tie and jacket, scowled. "But they moving to undo it. They moving to undo it even now."

Jason saw the old white man on the sidewalk mop his face with a red-checkered handkerchief, then spit a long arch of tobacco toward the black woman strutting by, holding her young son by the hand. But even as Jason stood to halt the carriage, the boy turned, waving his small hand at him. "Lookit, Mama, lookit." The boy pulled his mother's arm in excitement. "It's one a our colored congressmen."

The train was late arriving in Columbia. Isabella hurried from the depot and hailed a livery carriage. "Rainey Hall, on the University of South Carolina campus," she said as the wizened white driver moved to help her in.

The driver jerked back his arm. "I don't hold with no scalawag and nigger government," he said, glowering.

Isabella leaned toward him, her lips barely moving. "Do you hold with a dollar bill?" she asked. She leaned back in the seat as the driver pulled himself up and took the reins.

Inside Rainey Hall, Isabella saw that every seat was taken. Newsmen from around the world waited, pens and paper ready. Her eyes went to the Negroes on the floor of the Assembly: Robert Smalls, the Medal of Honor winner, sat beside Will Whipper, the lawyer, who sat by A. J. Ransier, the ex-slave. University of Glasgow-educated Francis Cardozo studied the crowd, while Robert Brown Elliott studied his papers. In the gallery fans fluttered and handkerchiefs found work on the foreheads of men.

Isabella pressed her hand to her mouth as one by one the members of the new legislature stood to be sworn to their duties according to the oath of office of the Constitution of 1868, Article II, Section 30.

"Cardozo . . ."

"Clavier."

Jason felt a tightness in his chest as he stood, his right hand raised, his left hand on the Bible. "I do solemnly swear that I am duly qualified, according to the Constitution of the United States and of this State . . ."

Oh, Papa, Isabella thought, if only you were here.

"I recognize the supremacy of the Constitution and the laws of the United States over the Constitution and laws of any State . . ."

But, Jason, oh, Jason, there is no law . . .

"I will support, protect, and defend the Constitution of the United States and the Constitution of South Carolina . . .

. . . there is only pain and death . . .

". . . as ratified by the people on the sixteenth day of April, 1868 . . ."

. . . Oh, Jason . .

" . . so help me God."

On the other side of the room Isabella saw Suzanne Beecham Clavier tuck her handkerchief inside her purse. Then, when the ceremony was over, Suzanne took her father's arm and moved with the crowd toward the door.

Outside, Jason was surrounded by handshaking, arm-grasping, backslapping well-wishers. For a long moment, Isabella watched her brother as photographers from two continents elbowed for his picture. Perhaps, she thought . . . Then, clutching the box in her hand, she whispered, "Oh, Lord, let it be."

She saw the smile break on Jason's face as she reached his side. "You came!"

"Nothing could have kept me away." She held out the box. "This belongs to you, Jason."

He opened the box and with a slow intake of breath lifted the wooden medallion. She saw his question forming. "I have what I should have," she said softly, "the imitation." She stood on tiptoe and kissed his cheek. "Wear it. Wear it, always, Jason. It will keep you safe." Then, lifting her skirts, Isabella left to take the train to Washington.

Jason watched her go. Then, for the second time that day, a thin gray shadow moved to block his vision.

Her gown was peacock-blue velvet. Her medallion was her only jewelry. Entering the gallery on the arm of Cornelius Hardwick, she saw the looks of admiration, heard the murmurs, "Isabella Dulane."

The gallery was crowded with rich and gracious people, speaking in rich and gracious voices before the work, the souls, of David and Degas, of Cézanne, Brascassat, Bouton, Monet, and Ingres, now, on canvas, immortal. Standing by Hardwick's smiling, gracious wife, Isabella had never been more in accord with her conception of herself. This, she thought, with a small, tight smile, is where I belong. Her hand clenched at her side. This is where I will belong. Her eyes roved the crowd, assessing its wealth. So rich, so secure in their richness. Oh, why had she married Carleton Dulane? Why was she a widow, with a child, at thirty?

She saw Mrs. Hardwick's quiet gaze. "It's splendid," Isabella exclaimed.

"Quite." Mrs. Hardwick smiled, her gray eyes sparkling.

Isabella saw a smiling young man approaching with rapid steps. He was Hardwick's son, no doubt of that, his youthful features a recast of the old. Tall, robust, ruddy-complexioned, he was impeccably attired in the height of fashion.

"Mama." He bent and kissed his mother's cheek, then turned with eyes as merry as that lady's own and smiled at Isabella. "So it is true. Ingres did not dream. The masterpiece is a living one."

"Mrs. Dulane"—Mrs. Hardwick smiled—"may I present my son, Robert Hardwick."

"The moment I set eyes upon your portrait . . ." embodied wealth began, taking Isabella's arm.

"But," she laughed, "it is a decade old."

"It cannot be." He was astonished. "Unless you have outwitted time itself."

He had finished Yale Law School and spent the last year managing his father's affairs in Britain, Isabella learned as they drove to the "small" dinner party for one hundred following the opening. No, he had never been to Charleston, the heir of the house of Hardwick said. "I was still in school during the war," he confided as he lifted his knife above the pheasant shot by the gamekeeper at the Hardwick place and shipped in ice to Washington.

"Are you his only son?"

"Yes. I have two sisters. One is a widow, like yourself. Her husband was killed in the war."

"And the other?"

"She's married to a doctor. They live in Ohio now."

"Then he has no interest in your father's business?"

"No, one day the entire burden will fall upon me."

She laughed. "It is a burden many would love to have."

"I suppose." His blue eyes clouded, and she felt his hand moving nervously on the napkin in his lap. "But it is such a responsibility, and father has such plans."

Her smile was a careful mixture of loyalty and concern as she squeezed his hand beneath the table. "And you will accomplish them all . . ."

She saw the sudden hunger in his eyes as he whispered, "Do you think so . . . ?"

Before she could reply, Isabella saw the senior Hardwick frown in their direction. So, he was not happy with his son's attention. Her hand lingered comfortingly in that of the successor to the nation's tenth-largest fortune, as, to ease the old man's concern, she turned to the glittering woman on her other side.

"You are the most remarkable, the most beautiful woman I have ever known," the scion of railroads, land, stock, and oil whispered in her ear.

Isabella laughed softly as he stood, taking her arm.

"I must return to New York the first thing in the morning," Cornelius Hardwick's heir explained. A full moon lit his carriage as he escorted Isabella back to the Willard Hotel. "I have an appointment there—business—which simply cannot wait.

"I don't think I have been in love before," he confessed as she hesitated a moment outside her suite.

"You are a tonic that should be bottled for those who need it most," Isabella demurred.

"I shall allow you to drink deeply when I visit Charleston next month." Millions of dollars lifted her hand and kissed it with devotion.

"And I will be ready," she giggled alone in her suite. Her eyes were shining as she undressed. She felt exactly as she had the day she had sailed for Paris. And now, there was so much more, so much more money, so much more power. And there was no doubt in her mind that Robert Hardwick would come.

Delighted and determined, Isabella returned to Charleston. She invested the proceeds from the sale of her portrait in re-establishing her old life style. With a good eye and tight purse strings she now bought furniture from other impoverished mansions: a brass, ebony, and tortoise-shell cabinet made by André Boulle, a Le Brun tapestry, Directoire chairs with sphinx and laurel leaves—the influence of Napoleon's expedition to Egypt. She purchased Wistar and Stiegel glassware to adorn Regency tables. From great house to great house, Isabella scavenged, heedless of the gossip that attended her buying spree.

She hired servants who, under Monique's direction, attended her acquisitions, a coachman came for her new carriage, a gardener. Dressmakers arriving with bolts of voguish fabrics found themselves directed, inspired, and worked to the bone until Isabella's closets could contain no more. Her bureau was lined with sachets. "Oh, Miz Isabella," Monique whispered. "It look even richer than before."

"And we're going to be richer," Isabella answered passionately. "So rich we'll never be poor again."

She spent hours before mirrors in all shades of light, studying, creaming imaginary lines. Each morning brought a new obsession: A gray hair? An ounce of fat? Was he twenty-five, or twenty-four, or twenty-three?

Her looks obsessed her; she was no longer the girl of twenty who had married Carleton Dulane. A decade had passed, a decade of war, death, and poverty. She was thirty—oh, the wretched sound of that word—thirty, a widow and a mother, and he was still in the bloom of youth. And there was no longer just herself but her son Jacques to consider.

And so she had hesitated at the drawing-room door the day Robert arrived, and he turned and saw her in that instant of wonder and caught her in the sunshine of his smile.

They were soaring, exhilarating days, days shared with Jacques, with nature and history. And nights, nights with only each other in the jasmine softness of her garden or walking hand in hand along the wharves, watching the fishing boats come in, or in violin-sweet restaurants spared the ruin of war.

It was a time out of time, with all unjoyous things forbidden, with laughter made from little things, when the possible assumes the guise of promise and singing comes naturally to the heart.

It was on the fourth evening when Robert, arriving from his room at the Mills Hotel, turned to Isabella with a gesture of his hand she had come to recognize as prelude to serious talk. "I hear you have quite a friendship with a Negro named Jason Clavier."

Though forthrightness was a quality Isabella did not possess, it was one that she admired. She met his eyes. "Yes. Yes, I have."

She saw he was waiting for her to continue, and admiration compromised. "I've known Jason all my life. I was one of his supporters when he ran for the legislature."

"You, the widow of a Confederate cavalryman?"

"Only among fools does a war go on forever. Jason Clavier is the kind of man South Carolina needs desperately. He's brilliant and well educated. He understood the reforms necessary to bring this state into the nineteenth century."

Robert frowned. "Then . . ."

Her laugh surprised him. "I assure you that there has never been anything illicit or illegal about my relationship with Jason Clavier."

"Then you've heard the stories?"

"Yes, I've heard them. And I also know people who believe the moon is made of blue cheese."

He took her hand. "I'm sorry, Isabella. I had to ask."

She drew her hand away. "Oh, Robert, don't be ridiculous. Whites and Negroes have been sleeping together for generations. It's just when they begin talking together . . ." The thought came impulsively. "Would you like to meet him?"

"Who?"

"Why, Jason Clavier, of course."

"I suppose, if he means so much to you."

"Then you will." She smiled. "Thursday night you'll meet Jason."

It was their first outing in social Charleston. For one bleak moment Robert Hardwick feared his mind had failed. On a candlelit veranda, before open French doors, Negroes and whites were talking, laughing, debating in the magnolia-scented night. This was no raucous barroom, no bawdy house. These were people of quality, their voices genteel, their conversation urgent, perceptive, wise.

270

Isabella moved gaily through the gathering, introducing Robert first to the young, handsome, full-blooded African, reported to be the most gifted orator, the most brilliant Negro, the most "dangerous" man in the South Carolina legislature: Robert Brown Elliott. The stunning octoroon beauty beside him was his wife, Grace Lee. Then Isabella turned to the Secretary of State, Francis Cardozo, a mixed-blooded man, extraordinarily cultured, who was deep in conversation with Supreme Court Justice Wright, the first colored man admitted to the bar of Pennsylvania. In vain Robert searched for the buffoonery, the idiocy, he had read of so often that "the Sambo of the Congo" "the darkness of Egypt and Ethiopia had laid over the state of South Carolina."

"There's Jason's wife." Isabella touched his arm, then called softly, "Suzanne." The young woman turned, smiling, and Robert felt his heart leap in his throat. No, he thought. No man would leave a woman like that—not even for Isabella Dulane.

Isabella's lips brushed Suzanne's cheek. "Suzanne Clavier, may I present Mr. Robert Hardwick." Robert bowed as he took Suzanne's hand, knowing he could not look into those eyes again. Then Isabella turned with a gay wave of her hand. "And here comes Jason."

There was an instant during the introduction when Jason's hand touched lightly at Isabella's side, when they smiled at the same time, that something vaguely disquieting slipped through Robert's mind. But there was no time to recapture it as he looked into the level, piercing eyes of the man before him. Within moments the razor-sharp mind of Jason Clavier dominated his attention, and it was forgotten.

Before the week was over, Robert Hardwick proposed marriage. Remembering his father's disapproval of his son's attentions to her, Isabella demurred, overriding Robert's certainty that he could not endure time without her. She urged waiting, keeping love secret to see if love endured.

Two weeks later she read of Cornelius Hardwick's death. She wrote to Robert, expressing sorrow at his loss, suggesting that after affairs were settled he might find Charleston restful.

Her letter was not answered. For nearly six weeks Isabella studied her nearly exhausted accounts and debated a second, more urgent note.

Early on a Sunday morning he appeared, pale and haggard, without notice at her door. She threw her arms around him. "Oh, Robert."

He moved awkwardly from her embrace, flushing as he saw her eyes.

"I must go to California," he began, feeling, even as he spoke, his heart, his nature, playing Judas to his will. "The transcontinental railroad will be completed in six months. We have a great deal of money invested in that and in other deals out West. I'll be gone at least a year.

"This then is goodbye, Robert?" Her voice halted his motion. Her eyes immobilized his will. For an interminable moment Isabella saw Robert's indecision. Then his hands took hers. "I love you, Isabella." His voice faltered. "I cannot deny that. Marry me. Marry me and come to California."

"Robert . . . ?"

"It will be a long trip, a hard trip, around the Horn, eighty days at sea. Life in San Francisco will be different." He touched her hair. "But California, California is still new."

Something in his tone made her own words catch in her throat. But he loved her. She could see that in his eyes. And she could stay young. She would stay young. "How long will I have to get ready?"

"The ship leaves in two hours."

She caught her breath, then raised her eyes to his. "You're certain, Robert? You are certain this is what you want to do?"

"Yes." He looked down into green, endless fathoms deep. "This is what I want to do."

CHAPTER EIGHT

1876

They came out of the State Capitol Building into the brilliant sunlit Columbia afternoon. Across the tree-shaded street the Trinity Episcopal Church guarded the graves of rulers of the old South.

"What do you think, Robert?" Jason asked.

"I believe that you must use power to insure power, or, damn it, you don't have it long." Some of the buoyancy had gone from Robert Elliott's step, but, Jason thought, he had lost none of his grace and vigor. "Come on"—Robert took Jason's arm as they approached his surrey—"ride with me as far as my house and let's talk some more. We've both been so busy since I came back from Washington."

Jason winced as he got into the carriage. Sometimes now, even the smallest exertion caused fearful pain in his head. He wet his lips as he eased himself into the surrey seat and turned to his companion. "I read the transcript of your speech for the civil rights bill in the New York *Times*." Jason smiled. "I wish I could have been in Washington to hear it. They tell me the Capitol was jammed with spectators, senators leaving their chamber to hear a black man answer the former vice-president of the Confederacy. Even some of our enemies are admitting that it was one of the most brilliant speeches ever delivered before the United States Congress. I've often wondered, Robert, why you decided to come back to the state legislature."

"Because here at the state level there is power to be used." Robert scowled as he slapped the reins against the horse. "We should have controlled the governorship and the lieutenant-governorship from the start. We had the votes. But no, too many Negroes listened to the white man's pleas to go slow, not to overstir the waters."

Elliott faced his friend. "Damn it, there're some things I'll never understand. Why? Why couldn't we coalesce, unify when we had the power? Why did so many of our people let the whites convince them not to put our men in the top office?"

"Ransier was lieutenant governor in '70 and Gleaves in '72, and both you and Lee were Speakers of the House," Jason said softly. "But the lynch rope, the burnings . . ."

"A rope that slides around a black man's neck will slide around a white man's too," Robert growled. "No, too many Negroes were too hesitant, too willing to believe the same white man who'd been cheating them for generations. For instance, look at Pinchback—a brilliant man—he could have been governor, not acting governor, but governor of Mississippi."

"Pinchback was nominated at that first convention and withdrew of his own free will," Jason said. "No, I think the real tragedy in Mississippi was Dumas, the other black man nominated. He wanted to be governor, and he stood his ground."

"Yes," Robert replied, "but don't forget Dumas was a slave owner. And even though he freed his slaves and led them into battle in the Union Army, his opponent, Warmouth . . ."

"a white Northerner . . ."

"Warmouth never let the freedmen forget that Dumas had held slaves." The frown on Elliott's face deepened. "I don't know. These are bitter times. In Georgia we have two most able men, Jefferson Long and H. M. Turner, but their bills get almost no support from their white colleagues. Jonathan Gibbs is waging a heroic fight as Superintendent of Schools in Florida. . . . There's Hood in North Carolina. But everywhere, everywhere we're fighting almost overwhelming odds."

They rode in silence for a moment, then Robert turned to Jason again. "What do you think Father Healey will do?"

"You mean the Negro who's just been appointed president of Georgetown University?"

"Yes."

"Well, Georgetown's influential," Jason said slowly. "It's the oldest Catholic university in America. I haven't heard much about his stand yet, but after the Colfax Massacre last Easter Sunday in Grant Parish and the Coushatta Massacre in Louisiana, he'd better make the words of mortal sin stick when he lifts that chalice."

For a moment or two the two men listened to the carriage on the cobblestones, feeling the sweetness of the soft scented air. "We won't resolve it in our lifetime," Elliott said quietly. "How I wish I had a son to carry on." He looked at Jason. "I was in Charleston the other week. I saw Suzanne and your tribe. They're still staying at the Beecham place?"

Jason nodded. "I think it's safer there."

"I heard they tossed dynamite through your kitchen window here."

Robert frowned. "They're playing rougher every day. Say, where's Bob Beecham now? I've heard so many tales."

"He's gone to Kansas. You heard how he rode down to Edgefield County after that mass lynching? He shot the sheriff and his deputy, then made for the state line on that big black horse of his, King Jesus. Smoke was with him when he crossed the state line." Jason smiled. "Smoke said old Bob wheeled his horse, dropped his handkerchief and yelled, 'Watch that handkerchief. Tell everyone you know, when it turns to banana peel, Bob Beecham'll be back in Carolina.'"

"Bob Beecham." Elliott smiled. "He's quite a man." He looked at Jason. "From what I hear, your son Clay's quite a bit like him."

"Yes." For a moment a private thought halted Jason's speech. "And I'm worried about Clay, Robert. Maybe it's just by comparison with my daughter Daisy, who talks all the time, but he seems unusually quiet. There is a toughness about him, I suppose from things he's seen and heard. He's smart as a whip, though." Jason paused again briefly, then continued. "His temper's quick. And though he's just a child, that's a dangerous quality in times like these. He's Bob Beecham's grandchild, no doubt of that. And"—Jason shook his head with a small smile—"like my grandpa Jacques, he's something of a pirate."

They had turned onto Taylor Street. Jason saw the mansard roof of Elliott's home ahead.

"Dangerous, but necessary," Elliott said as he drew in the reins. "What's that line you quote from your grandfather? Clay understands 'the weapons of freedom.'" Elliott jumped down from the surrey. "Come on, let's have a glass of lemonade."

Grace Lee, Robert's wife, brought the tall cold drinks into the library. Jason sipped his gratefully, then looked around the room. How often he had thought that he could stay here forever. Robert had one of the finest private libraries in the state. Outside the window, through the bushes, Jason could see in the soft falling dusk the long row of Elliott's stables. Jason sighed inaudibly. If only he had had the strength for his law practice in addition to . . .

"As I see it, Jason, the worst are these divide-and-conquer tactics." Elliott had drained his glass and was holding it for a refill. "I told you that when I was in Washington the light-skinned Negro congressmen met at one place, the dark-skinned at another, and none of us, octoroon, quadroon, mulatto, or black, could get inside the National Republican Club." For a moment Elliott pondered this, then turned to Jason again. "I'm worried now, Jason. Cardozo still has hope and, though I disagree with his politics, I can't deny he's one of our most brilliant men."

"Cardozo's too damn conciliatory. I agree with what you've always said: 'When you have the power, strike.'"

Elliott let his breath out in a low, rushing sound. "If only they had listened during those first crucial years when I was attorney general, or when I was Speaker of the House."

"Or when you were Assistant General of the Militia."

Elliott did not miss the tinge of jealousy in Jason's voice. How often his friend had bid for those same positions. Jason had even stood once for the federal Congress. Elliott rubbed his mustache, remembering. It was the year he had been elected to his second term.

Covertly, Robert studied his long-time comrade-in-arms. Jason Clavier was a brilliant man, no doubt of that. But Elliott knew the arguments that had been used against him. Clavier, some said, did not know, did not understand the common man. His goals were beyond their needs or expectations. He was, others said, too dogmatic, too aristocratic, too uncompromising. True, life was not as clear-cut as Jason Clavier would have it, nor did he possess the patience to win men to his will. But damn, Robert's black eyes flashed, what black and white people would have had had Jason Clavier had sat in the governor's chair!

"These are cataclysmic times," Robert Elliott went on more softly. "The Klan, the Knights of the White Camellias, Mother's Little Helpers, the Rifle Clubs, all deal in death. Our people are afraid. That lynching last week, those four teen-age boys the Kluxers burned to death . . . And the horror at Jake Cox's place two nights ago after he brought those people in to register. His wife was pregnant, again, with their fourth child. They grabbed her in the kitchen and slit her belly open. The baby fell out on the floor. Then the bastards cut off her head, cut it off and held it up, her eyes still open, still weeping, staring from death at her three children. That kind of thing makes an impression. It's too damn insane to deal with sanely."

"But we cannot stop," Jason said tensely. "Though they burn us, though they maim us, though they kill us. We know what we have done. When we took office, this state lay in ruins. Land, railroads, shipping destroyed. The state debt over eight million dollars. Slavery, the foundation of the economic and social life, gone forever.

276

"This state started a war in which they were defeated. On one day nearly half a million black souls in this state were freed, freed after two hundred years of the worst, the most degrading slavery in the history of man.

"They helped form a new government in which Negroes, two thirds of the population of this state, were, for the first time, able to play a role. That government has put this state on the road to recovery, and you and I both know it was in a position to destroy it completely."

Jason stood, pacing the floor. "They want to talk of graft in an era notorious for scandal and graft. By innuendo and suggestion they cast shadows on men's names. But what black hand have they proven to have touched the public till? And if there had been one, how could his deeds compare to Crédit Mobilier or the Tweed scandals or any of the dozen others which have rocked this nation? They will try to discredit us because they must to vindicate their ruthless persecution. What was it they called us, the members of the legislature? 'African slaves and gibbering louse-eating, devil-worshipping barbarians from the jungles of Dahomey, and peripatetic buccaneers from Cape Cod, Memphremagog, Hell, and Boston.'"

"Yes." Robert Elliott stretched in his chair. "Those are the undeniable facts. We've been in power eight years. We gave this state its first public school system, for white as well as Negro children. We increased the rights of women. The state has its first divorce law. We abolished imprisonment for debt . . ."

Abruptly Robert leaned forward in his chair. "Will you stay, Jason"—his voice was low, intense—"after . . . ?"

Jason ceased his pacing and turned to his companion. "Reconstruction will not end, Robert. Oh, there'll be years, many years perhaps, terrible years of great travail, but we are on our way to freedom."

"You've seen the depths to which they plunge, the filth, the obscenities they commit . . ."

"We are on our way, Robert."

"Our people are still poor, Jason. And even with a craving for education, so many are still illiterate. I know Suzanne would like to leave. And back in Massachusetts, your children . . ."

"They must learn to stand and fight. No, Robert, I cannot leave. Even if Reconstruction ends and the terror begins, our people will see us and remember. They will remember that once they held power and that it is possible again."

Jason declined Robert's offer to drive him home. He shook Robert's hand in the doorway, then walked out into the night. He had gone but a few feet when he stopped in panic. He could see nothing. Nothing. Above him there were neither stars nor moon, and all around was darkness.

He stumbled on a yard or two, then bumped into a tree. He felt it with his hands, its size. No night was like this. He stood there for a moment trembling, then turned back toward the house. There were no lights. "Oh, my God," Jason whispered. "Oh, my God!" he screamed. He felt his body shaking. "Robert," he yelled. "Robert, come here!"

He heard the running footsteps. "Jason, what the deuce is wrong?"

Jason stretched his arms before him until he felt Robert's grasp. "Robert," he whispered hoarsely, "tell me. Is there a moon—or stars?"

"Yes, Jason. Jason? Jason?"

"My God, Robert, my vision's gone."

"Let me help you to the house. Careful, Jason, hold my arm. Perhaps it will pass. You have been working hard."

Inside the hallway, Jason blinked. The forms were coming back. "Jason, are you all right?" Robert's face seemed crisscrossed by a net.

"Robert, please take me to my office."

"Your . . . ?"

"I must work quickly. Soon now the night will come inside."

CHAPTER NINE

1878

"Jacques, so this is how you're wasting time?"

Jacques Dulane looked up from his writing pad at the sharpness of his mother's tone.

"You know, they're going to put you out of Exeter if your grades don't improve this fall." Isabella sighed as she sat beside her lanky, handsome son. Above them under the clear blue New York State sky, the high limbs of the elm trees bowed in the breeze with a soothing sshhing sound. Ten feet away, a low waterfall gushed into a fish-filled stream. Isabella leaned her head against the tree trunk as she looked about her. The Hardwick Place, she thought. And her son. He was so much like Clay. Always writing something.

Jacques ran his thumb over the soft hairs that were beginning to darken his upper lip. "Why're you smiling, Mother?"

"You're just so much like my brother Clay."

Jacques nodded. She had spoken often—but vaguely—of this brother whom he resembled with his penchant for writing. He looked at her quizzically. She was given to telling odd tidbits about her family when they were alone, to never finishing her thoughts, to getting up suddenly, leaving the questions her information aroused unanswered. He kept silent. At least she was not fussing at him; at least now she was calm.

Jacques had learned to understand the signals that caused alternately his mother's depressions or her ire. They came from two sources: his stepfather's increasing obsession with politics and with power, and her fear that although Robert treated him well and would certainly see him to a position of prestige, he would not inherit "a Hardwick dime." Robert's money would be left to the control of one of his nephews. "Amalgamate, consolidate, and merge" were, it seemed, Robert Hardwick's favorite words.

Well, he didn't want a Hardwick dime. Once he fulfilled his obligations to them, once he finished Exeter and Yale, he would be off to see the world, to write books like Mark Twain or Melville or Hawthorne or Balzac or Dostoevski or . . . He saw his mother looking at him and smiled. Life had been fun at the Hardwick Place.

The Hardwicks were, Jacques thought, an energetic tribe of happy Hyperboreans, buoyant and resilient. Egalitarians who understood that few were truly their equal, they lived comfortably with their wealth, internalizing it as inherent and consistently functional to their being as a liver or a gall bladder.

Their headquarters was a magnificent forty-room Georgian stone mansion overlooking the Hudson. It stood on seventy-five acres, surrounded by deep ravines and tall oak trees, approachable only by a narrow road that curved across several streams.

Jacques had immediately felt at home after that year in California. "Grandmama" Hardwick, a sparkling waterfall of love, drenched him in affection, while five noisy, gregarious, running, swimming, horseback-riding playmates—Robert's sister's children—had taken him completely into their lively private world. . . .

Isabella watched the thoughts crossing her son's face through partially closed eyes. Somehow, some way, she must make certain that Joe Dulane left Four Winds to Jacques. She had written to Dulane telling of her marriage when she had first arrived in California. The old man had sent a blustering reply. "Jacques is a Dulane, and a Dulane he will remain, no matter what goddamn Yankee you married." But, Isabella frowned, her recent letters had not met reply.

And Jason's last letter had come years ago, telling of the birth of his son Clay.

She had written of her concerns to Monique, who now had a thriving business as a midwife in Charleston. Her long, painstakingly written reply had been full of news. Joe Dulane, Monique had learned, had had a stroke and was almost paralyzed. But Four Winds was doing well. Gossip had it that Old Joe had not put all of his money in Confederate notes but had plenty tucked away in English banks.

"The Reconstruction," Monique's letter told, "is comin' apart. Things is gettin' real bad for the colored again. They stealin' the colored land right and left. Jimmy is run away to New York. Gabriel, my baby, is studyin' at your brother's school . . ."

"Come on, Jacques." Isabella got slowly to her feet. "Let's finish packing your bags. I'll go with you to New York and put you on the train for school."

It was not until Isabella had seen her son onto the train, not until she was on her way to the suite Robert maintained in the Astor

House Hotel, that she realized that for the first time in nearly two decades she had absolutely nothing to do.

There was no need to hurry home. Robert, hoping to get the party's backing for his still undeclared gubernatorial candidacy, was in Washington for the week. She had no luncheon appointment to keep, no dinner, no play, no opera, no opening of a charity drive that she had to attend. She had, on her last trip into New York, seen the selections of the shops, and all that she desired was already in her closet. There were, of course, people she could visit, but there was no one she wanted to see. She was free. For the first time in seventeen years, she was free to do exactly as she pleased.

Thirty minutes later she boarded the train. That evening, at five o'clock, she was in New Bedford.

There was something familiar about the pretty little girl playing in the yard of the house on Arnold Street, although Isabella knew she could not have seen her before. As she came up the walk beneath the elm trees, the girl looked up with a smile. "Hello. Have you come to see my mother?"

For a moment Isabella hesitated. She had no idea who her mother was. "I've come to see all of you. I'm Isabella Clavier."

"Aunt Isabella!" the girl gasped.

"What?" came from inside the house. A woman appeared in the doorway. "Isabella Clavier. My God in heaven, it is you!"

The woman hastily wiped the remnants of dough from her hands onto her apron. "You don't remember me? Mary Dawson. I married your cousin Isaac."

Before she could answer, Isabella heard the footsteps, firm and rapid, coming from inside. Eyes dancing, Isabella ran into the house. "Aunt Jacqueline."

"Lord, if you're not your grandpa's child," the white-haired lady cried, holding Isabella in a tight embrace. "Goin' and comin' at the strangest times." She drew back, still holding Isabella's hand, scrutinizing her with eyes bright with tears. "And I know you have a tale to tell."

"Jacqueline?" The frail voice came from upstairs. "Jacqueline, who's there?"

"Mama, it's me, Bella." And Isabella laughed and ran up the stairs as though she were still a girl.

They sat in the second parlor, talking all at once, Thomasina and

281

Jacqueline telling of Jason's activities in the South Carolina legislature. Isaac Key Woodson, Jacqueline's grandson, blubbery and prosperous, sat at Isabella's side, trying to impress her with the clientele of his tailoring "emporium," which, he said four times, he owned in addition to the carpentry business.

"Senator Oates, whose great-grandfather sailed with Papa Jacques, has all of his suits made in my establishment." Isaac crossed his fat legs and leaned back in his chair. "And you know it was on the front page of the *Morning Mercury* when Alexander Kuykendal—the Kuykendals all live in Boston now—came to me for his suit for Grant's second inauguration."

Isabella saw the look crossing Aunt Jacqueline's face. What would she say if she knew she had on a pair of Kuykendal shoes? Isabella frowned as she remembered that she'd heard last week that the Kuykendals were opening a block-long store with a full line of women's fashions on Fifth Avenue in New York.

The little girl Isabella had first seen, Melinda, Isaac's daughter, now bathed and dressed for bed, moved to Isabella's side. Isabella smiled at her. "Has anyone told you yet that you are beautiful?"

"Yes," the child answered. "Has anyone told you that you are too?"

Isabella saw the questions in her mother's eyes as Thomasina leaned toward her. Quickly she turned to Isaac's son, Andy. "And how old are you?"

"I'm seven and I'm going to be a lawyer like your brother Jason." He was stocky like his father, like all the Woodsons, Isabella thought, his brown face as serious as his sister's was mischievous.

"Now, Isabella," Thomasina said finally, "tell us about you."

"There's nothing much to tell," she replied softly, grateful that the children's eager faces would forestall the more probing questions. "I'm married to a rich man," she paused. "And I have a son."

"That's all?" Thomasina gasped in dismay. "That's all you have to say after . . ."

"Yes." Jacqueline gave Thomasina a peremptory look. "That's all. The Claviers are still together, and that is all that counts."

Isabella had planned to leave early the next morning but stayed to visit her father's grave. With Aunt Jacqueline she roamed the garden behind the house cutting flowers, and together they carried them to the stone-fenced plot that was the final resting place of the Claviers and the Keys.

As was her custom, Jacqueline retold the family story as they paused before the sinking headstones that marked the graves of Alanya Clavier and her son Jacques. Behind these stood the granite slab of Jacques and Noni Clavier. Here Isabella and Jacqueline stood awhile in the soft breeze of early-fall sun while Jacqueline, with soft remembrances, turned life into legend.

"I'll go there." Jacqueline pointed past Alexander's grave and the place reserved for Thomasina. "Beside Andrew and my son."

There was a grave set apart, alone. "Who's over there?" Isabella asked.

"Clay. Jason sent him back to us. Claviers should be buried on Clavier land."

Slowly Isabella walked over and looked down at the headstone. "Clay Clavier, 1833–1863. Poet, Soldier, Brother, Son."

"I'll go there," Isabella said softly. "I'll go there, by Clay."

Jacqueline nodded. She did not ask how Isabella would arrange it. But if Bella said it, Jacqueline knew it would be done. She was like Papa Jacques that way.

"I ain't signin' nothin'. Nope, nary another thing." Jason saw the perspiration glistening on the farmer's brawny brown shoulders. Even the shoots of rice seemed to cringe before the blistering Carolina sun.

"Mr. Johnson . . ."

"I'm plain ol' Al, Mr. Clavier, and I ain't signin'."

"Al, this petition asking for federal troops is critical . . ."

"What ain't critical nowadays? I'm workin' sunup to sunset to hang on to these few acres I worked all my life to buy. And they watchin' us right now."

"Forget them for a minute . . ."

"Forget 'em! How the hell can I forget 'em? They watchin' us every minute, every minute, night and day. You know how many been lynched in this here county . . . ?"

"That's exactly why . . ."

". . . Standin' here talkin' makes both a us marked men. So, if you please . . ."

"Fear is their greatest weapon . . ."

"And death's they biggest bullet. Looka here, Mr. Clavier, you don't stay out here. You don't feel what happen out here in the night. Yo' wife twitchin', skeert to sleep. Yo' young'uns right beside you in the dark so the minute, the second you hear . . . They poisoned my dog so he can't give no warnin'. No dog, no gun . . ."

"I know it's rough, Al, but we've got to stay together . . ."

"We done been together and what good come a that? We 'bout worse off now than 'fore we elected colored. The troops is gone. They ain't comin' back. The white man . . ."

"Hayes sold us out to become President. Sold us down the river. He agreed to end Reconstruction and withdraw the federal troops in return for the South's electoral votes. He won by one damn vote."

"That what it was, eh? Well, by one vote he in the White House, and we in the Death House, and let me tell you, ain't a damn thing you or no other nigger can do 'bout it. You all should a jumped when you had the power. When Robert Elliott was Assistant Gen'ral of the Militia, or when he was attorney gen'ral . . ."

How often, Jason thought, he and Robert had fought for that same point. "We never had that kind of power," he said softly.

". . . No, first off you all go increasin' votin' rights . . . not just for Negroes, who put you all in office, but for that po' trash even white folks didn't want to have no vote. Buildin' bridges, cleanin' harbors. The cotton crop is higher than before. . . . Yep, I'll give you cred-ick." The farmer flicked a fly from his arm. "You all really recon-structed this state. And all the while you was givin' this state public education, for *white* and colored children, while you was buildin' poorhouses and crazy houses, you know what white folks was doin'? They was formin' clubs and takin' names. The Klan, Mother's Little Helpers, all them Rifle Clubs for shootin' niggers. Civil War gen'rals, gen'rals again in the same ol' war to keep niggers in slavery. And them old plantation owners, them Dulanes, them Sykeses, them Laurys, got them clay-eatin' crackers all riled up to do they dirty work. Sure our people skeert. Skeert to talk. Skeert to vote. Skeert to sign petitions. Where in this state can a nigger buy a gun? Where's you all's gun-for-niggers law?"

"What I'm trying to do . . ."

"Let me say this, an' I'm through. Niggers get a little education and start thinkin' like white folks 'steada like smart niggers. Get to forgettin', get to trustin' like a hound with a belly too full to wanna hunt. Get too used to crawlin' by the fire with the masta and forget about the foxes prowlin' in the night."

"We never forgot. What we . . ."

"What you gon' do when this Reconstruction over? Go back to Massachusetts?"

"No. I'll stay. I'll stay in Carolina."

"Well"—the farmer bent over his hoe—"they up there. Some red-neck cracker, po' as a weevil's turd, who ain't never gonna have shit neither, 'cept them words, 'At least you ain't a nigger.'"

"That's exactly what this petition is about. They're keeping black and white . . ."

"They takin' names, Mr. Clavier. Yo' name, my name, any black man who fights's name. They out there and they takin' names."

Jason walked slowly back to his horse. There were only ten names on his petition. Perhaps, he thought, to keep the death count low, the only name should be his own. He mounted his horse and headed for Columbia.

Cat was waiting for Jason near the State House. He shook his head as he saw the look on Jason's face. "You ain't gonna feel no better when you see inside."

"It's that bad?"

"Ain't never seen it worse." Cat laid a gentle hand on Jason's shoulder. "You know you don't have to go through with it, Jason."

Jason smiled sadly. "You know as well as I, Cat, that I do."

"It'll be the end of your career."

"Better my career, Jim Harvey, than my soul."

The last rays of the sun glinted through the smoky hearing room as Jason found his seat. He looked at the crowd, assessing its mood. His head hurt fiercely. As the committee chairman called his name, he saw Cat standing by the door. He stood, girding his will to try one more time.

"Gentlemen, there is but one question before us here today, one issue to which we must address ourselves, and that is the central question of democracy: whether there will be freedom, or whether there will not. Whether the interests of the people will be served, or the interests of a small but powerful elite—a small but powerful elite who manipulate, prejudice, and, in the end, destroy."

Jason clutched the seat before him as his vision fogged, eradicating behind a dense gray wall the faces on his right. "Gentlemen . . ." He heard his voice waver and paused, drinking in deep breaths the power to control. ". . . Gentlemen, the destiny of man is controlled as much by those who do not act as by those who do. Those who in self-interest, fear, bigotry, and that greatest evil, lethargy, watch this earth's most vital resource—man—erode, decay, crumple. We blind our eyes"—for a moment his voice faltered—"we hush our ears, we mute our tongues, we still our hands . . ." Jason's voice rang clearly now. ". . . we fear, we tremble to speak out . . . And we call ourselves the leaders of men. The law that does not protect all, in the end protects none . . ."

Jason looked around the silent room. Only Cat's eyes met his.

Then the fog encroaching on his sight moved suddenly. Except in the very center, the lights went out. And in the center, behind Cat, were three white men.

And they were taking names.

He stumbled as he came up the aisle. He heard the hooting, then felt Cat's firm grasp. "Leave your hoss," Cat whispered. "I got a carriage."

"Cat." Jason clutched his friend blindly. "Cat, what's that noise?"

He felt Cat's look. "What's . . . ?" Then Cat's grip tightened. "Hold on," Cat said. "Hold on, Jason. We're almost there."

Jason felt the fresh breeze on his face. "Watch out!" He heard the shout. He felt Cat's arms around him tightly, then the shots rang out. Jason felt a warm, oozing wetness. He heard the pain in Cat's deep breath. Cat's grasp loosened and slowly slid away.

"Cat?" Jason screamed. "Cat!" He felt blindly with his hands.

"Just step up. You at the carriage, Jason." Cat's voice came weakly from the ground. "Hurry. Hurry, Jason. We done used up all a our nine lives."

CHAPTER ELEVEN

1883

Isabella leaned against the woodwork of her bedroom window, looking out at the yellowing leaves of the Hardwick Place. Behind her on the bed, clothes still lay beside her half-packed suitcases. The numbness of exhaustion prohibited her from completing the task. Tomorrow she would leave for Switzerland. Robert had said last night that the château was ready.

She looked up at the ceiling, letting her head drop back until she felt the arching of her spine and then a soft movement inside her body. Her hand clutched her stomach. Yes, it was the baby kicking. "Oh, God," she whispered fiercely, "oh, God, why now?"—with Robert hoping, hoping desperately, to be the nominee for President.

She sat down on the chaise beside the window. How had she been so careless? Had she let menopause turn her into a fool, afraid to deny Robert's rare requests, afraid that he would become enamored of a younger woman? She knew there was but one love for Robert: politics. There was but one passion: power.

How ordained her life had become, how ritualistic. Outside the sanctuary of power, she had performed the obeisance of the faithful, while the high priest, Robert, drank deep from the chalice of ambition.

He was forever at meetings. He was forever gone on trips. Forever talking of deals and mergers. Newspapers with his morning coffee—stock sheets, balance sheets his partners in the bed. She had often thought how Aunt Jacqueline would have loved it!

And then last winter the party had refused to support Robert's second bid for governor. That had not been, they said, the time for the endorsement of such wealth, not the time to advocate such liberal views. State aid to the poor? Medical relief? Legislation preventing discrimination in employment of Catholics, Jews, Negroes? "Radical!" the party power brokers had blustered. "Dangerous!" "Not at all for the greater good!"

In disgust, Robert had withdrawn his financial support. In haste, he laid plans for a vacation in Europe, the first he and Isabella had taken in nearly five years.

In Nice, there were no urgent meetings. In their villa, high above the Mediterranean, there were no papers, no phone. Slowly Isabella and Robert had found each other again.

The child had been conceived in Nice. Of that she was now certain. She and Robert had gone on to Sweden. She had become suspicious of her pregnancy there. She had been a fool to excuse the absence of her menses on her menopausal cycle and her dizziness on the mountain air.

True, she had not known a doctor she could see in secret. Nor could she find one the next month, in Germany, where Robert's time was spent on business. She had waited, taking large doses of quinine and ergot, boiling herself in baths that left her faint, waiting until they would arrive in Geneva. The Swiss were so practical. They understood the vicissitudes of life. They could deal in any language.

It was too late. She was nearly three months pregnant, and at her age, to abort the child was much too risky.

She had taken strenuous hikes, had skated daily, had even tried the ski slopes. Then had come the telegram from the party's national committee. "Perhaps," they said, just "perhaps." She had told Robert three days later in their stateroom as they sailed from Calais home.

Isabella shuddered, remembering the look that had ravaged Robert's face when he heard the news. "No." He had wheeled and faced her, his blue eyes smoldering. "Oh, my God, not now." She had clung to the desk to keep from shriveling before his stare. "Damn you, why the hell didn't you tell me before we sailed for home?"

For awful moments, she had suspected that he knew. Meeting his eyes, it had seemed the truth could shatter the impregnable wall between them. But she had slunk from it, fearful of confrontation . . . thinking that maybe he had absolved himself of the burden of her lie, realizing that perhaps for him, knowing was not knowing until those words were said.

He had rarely mentioned the child since then. Disconcerted, speaking seldom, he had barricaded himself behind new reams of campaign strategies in their stateroom or gone alone for long strolls on the deck.

The voyage had been a waking nightmare that followed her from lonely deck chairs, wondering, to where her trembling hands held her cards for bridge. Evening after evening she had sat with newfound companions, dreading that inevitable moment when the ship's or-

289

chestra would play its final piece and she would say good night and go below.

On their return to the Hardwick Place, Robert had circulated the myth—or was it a myth?—that she was ill, not seriously, but would be returning to a specialist's care in Geneva. Quickly he had made arrangements for her to return to Switzerland, where, he told her, pregnancy would be more peaceful, saying that he would join her before the baby came.

"And Jacques . . . ?"

"He will of course remain at school."

And what, she had longed to ask, if your child is born a normal, healthy Negro . . . ? What will happen to Jacques, to me, to the baby then . . . ?

Isabella heard the knock on her door and her maid's low voice. "Mrs. Hardwick?"

"Come in," she answered, then paled as she saw the telegram on the silver tray. Her hands trembled as she picked it up. What dreadful thing had happened now?

She waited until the maid had left the room before she opened the yellow envelope. For a moment she stared at the words, then, in uncontrollable spasms, laughed aloud. She was saved. Jacques was saved. The baby saved! Tears splashed on her cheeks as she rocked back and forth, holding her side in laughter's pain. Saved! And by— of all people—Joe Dulane.

She picked up the telegram from her lap and reread its message swiftly: "Joseph Dulane died last night. His will leaves Four Winds to Jacques Dulane. Isabella Dulane Hardwick is executor of the estate."

Still shaking, Isabella reached for the phone. It seemed an eternity before Jacques was on the line. "Four Winds is yours. Is yours." She laughed and cried.

"Mother . . . ?"

"It's yours. Oh, Jacques, it is yours."

"Mother, please, I don't . . . ?"

"Meet me in New York tomorrow morning. There's an afternoon train to Charleston."

"Mother, I have an exam in the afternoon."

"Then leave tomorrow night. Meet me at the Mills Hotel at

Charleston. I'm leaving now. Nothing, nothing, nothing must happen to Four Winds."

"Mother . . ."

"Do you have money?"

"Yes."

"Then meet me in Charleston, and Four Winds will be yours."

Isabella moved quickly around the room tossing dresses, gowns, toiletries helter-skelter into suitcases. She closed them and picked up the phone again. For an instant she hesitated. She must not risk too much with Robert, but now at last . . .

His female secretary connected her to the inner sanctum. "This is Mrs. Hardwick," she said to the male secretary who answered there.

"Yes, Isabella?" Robert's voice was wary in her ear.

"Please make arrangements for me to leave for Europe from Charleston."

"Charleston . . . ?"

"Joe Dulane is dead. Jacques has inherited Four Winds."

She checked into the Mills Hotel in Charleston and sent for Joe Dulane's lawyer. He arrived, puffing pompously, within the hour, his briefcase bulging with Joe Dulane's affairs.

The house in Charleston was, of course, Mrs. Hardwick's. Mr. Dulane had kept it up during her long absence. Four Winds belonged to her son. They must wait for his arrival.

It was late afternoon when the attorney departed. Isabella dressed slowly to go to Jason's house. Suppose her brother would not see her? Suppose Suzanne slammed the door in her face—with all the neighbors watching? Suppose . . .

Her hands continued to dress her body, and as dusk fell she found a colored livery carriage two blocks from the Mills Hotel.

He was sitting alone in his yard in a ragged wicker chair, his hands folded in his lap. His open shirt was starched and spotless, but she could see the frayed cuffs of his sleeve. Behind the lace curtains in the windows overlooking the bare wooden porch, she could feel before she saw the child's eyes watching her approach. She had nearly reached her brother before she realized . . . Her breath caught in her throat. He did not see her. He did not see her at all.

"Jason," she whispered. He looked toward her, confused. She knelt beside him and took him in her arms. "Oh, Jason, it's me."

"Bella?" His hand reached up to touch her face. "Bella, is it you?"

She grabbed his hand and brought it to her lips. "Yes, Jason. Oh, yes, it's me."

She saw Suzanne standing in the doorway, her dress faded. Her face, still beautiful, was plump. Small lines marred the smoothness of her forehead. "Isabella?" Her voice was soft, the same. "Isabella Dulane?"

"Yes." Still holding her brother's hand, Isabella stood. "Yes, Suzanne."

Slowly, in the living room, Isabella learned the story. The end of Reconstruction had come with brutal force. Suzanne had feared for Jason's life.

He had been defeated in his fifth bid for the legislature and had returned to Charleston. Unable to find a job, he tutored students. His fee: a chicken, eggs, a side of beef. Very few had money. But this and their small garden met their needs.

The number of Jason's students had increased steadily. With the help of neighbors, he had turned their old carriage house into a school. Gabriel Baker, Monique's son, was one of the best students. For him, Jason held the highest hopes.

They talked for nearly three hours—over the kitchen table, where a single chicken was deftly carved to feed the six of them, beside the fireplace where sticks and lumps of coal were used sparingly to hold off the chill. Isabella bit her lip as she looked at her brother's children. The baby, Alexander, almost two, played with his top. The girl, Daisy, now nine, was as pretty and efficient as her mother. And the boy, who looked so much like his namesake Clay, whose dark steady eyes never ceased their study of her face, was just past ten. Then her roving gaze was arrested by the paper stuffed in the children's shoes.

Jason spoke only of the future, of the new black men he was preparing to, one day . . . As he spoke, Isabella realized that any mention of his return to New Bedford was forbidden, that his commitment, his claim to the future, was far greater than hers had been to the past.

It was past nine when Clay went out to find Isabella a carriage. But she did not go straight to the Mills Hotel. She had made a decision while seated before Jason's fire. She had less than fifty dollars in her purse. Her other funds had already been converted to French francs. But she had something of value, something that could buy food, coal, and shoes for her brother's family.

She knew the door. She had been there before, in those awful years during the war, before she had sold the portrait. The jeweler opened the door himself. He adjusted his glasses and looked at Isabella cagily.

"You do remember me," she said brusquely. "I'm Isabella Dulane."

"Ah, yes." He bowed slightly and admitted her to his foyer. "The widow of the Confederate cavalryman."

"I am once again in need of money." Her right hand slipped the great blue sparkling diamond, Carleton's engagement present, from her finger. "How much will you give me for this?"

The old man's eyes narrowed when he saw the ring. His mouth parted greedily as he took it to the room that was his office. He frowned as he inspected it. Why had she come to him and at this hour? Her dress indicated no need, no need at all, for cash. Why would she part with a piece like this? What kind of desperation . . . ? "Three hundred dollars," he said, turning back to her.

"Ridiculous. It's worth at least two thousand."

He held out the ring. "Then take it where it will bring that much. I have boxes of diamonds."

"But none like this."

He looked at her shrewdly. Perhaps he had overestimated her need. "One thousand. It's my final offer."

"I'll take it in cash."

Jason's house was almost dark when she returned. Only a single lamp still burned upstairs. She opened the door and let herself in, walking quickly to the kitchen. Her brother's pride would insist upon refusal. She left the money beneath a saucer on the table and went then to see Monique.

Monique's home was a small white frame two-bedroom house. Isabella had given Monique the two hundred dollars it had cost before she had left Charleston for California. There were no gaslights on the street in this part of town, but even in the moonlight Isabella saw the neatness of the yard.

Monique stared when she saw the figure in her doorway. "Lord a mercy, Miz Isabella," she exclaimed. Then, with a furtive look down the street, "Come in, come on in, quick."

"Joe Dulane is dead." Isabella's eyes sparkled as she sat on Monique's sofa. "I've come to arrange things for Jacques."

"Then he got Four Winds?" Monique's hands poured coffee.

"Isn't it marvelous, Monique? And"—Isabella leaned toward her friend—"Jason tells me Gabriel is one of his best students." Isabella saw the proud nod of Monique's head. "How's Jimmy?"

Monique's eyes darkened. "He got himself killed in a knife fight in New York." Her lips tightened. "He was a mean one, that boy. Too much Dulane blood . . ." Monique stopped abruptly, seeing the look on Isabella's face. "Come on, I'll let you see Gabe. He's sleep, but . . ."

Monique shadowed the oil lamp as Isabella followed her into the boy's bedroom. "Oh, Monique," she whispered as she saw his face, the black skin like mahogany on the white pillowcase. "What a handsome boy."

"Looks just like his daddy." Monique nodded. Then, as she led Isabella back into the living room, "I shore do wish I could see little Jacques again."

"Little Jacques?" Isabella laughed. "He's a whole head taller than I am. Wait, I have his photograph."

"A picture?" Monique sat eagerly on the edge of her chair as Isabella reached inside her purse and brought out the leather folder.

"Lord, them eyes, he shore do look like you." Monique laughed. Then her eyes narrowed suddenly. " 'Cept that mouth. That's shore nuff a Dulane mouth. Just think." Monique leaned back in her pillowed rocking chair, studying the photograph. "He was the first young 'un I ever brought into this world."

"Would you like to keep it?" Isabella asked impetuously.

"Oh, yes." Monique smiled.

It was nearly midnight when Isabella returned to her rooms in the Mills Hotel. She was exhausted, but as she stretched between the sheets she smiled. She had seen family and a friend.

Jacques Dulane arrived at his mother's door early the next morning buoyant with anticipation of pleasure which his twenty years on earth had taught him to expect. With the lawyer, they went to inspect Four Winds. As the horses turned up the pink gravel path that wound beneath the matched pines, Isabella realized with a soft melancholy sigh that nearly a quarter of a century had passed since she'd first traveled this path with Carleton Dulane.

"It's being sharecropped now," the lawyer explained briskly. "Twenty-seven croppers, all niggers. You'll see that the stables are in good order, though the blacksmith shed and animal pens have been closed down. Mr. Dulane had a staff of seven servants—two gardeners, a couple of stable boys, a cook, two maids. I didn't let them go because they know the place and I had no idea of what you . . ."

"My son is still in school," Isabella said crisply. "We would appreciate it if you would continue management of the estate until he finishes."

Isabella heard her son gasp as the Greek Revival palace came fully to their view. "No, Mother," Jacques Dulane said softly. "I'm ready to manage it all, right now."

All afternoon, while Isabella slept, Jacques walked over the land known as Four Winds. He stood a long time before the grave of the father he had never known. Climbing through high grass to a wind-blown knoll, he felt his blood's kinship with the soil.

He loved the language he heard all around him: "the safe" where the cakes and pies were kept; "mulatto stew," the rice and tomatoes bubbling together in a kitchen pot; and the idea that everybody was going to do everything "toreckly."

In the bedroom she had once shared with Carleton, Isabella twisted in troubled sleep. Something eluded her, a face she could not see. Frantically she searched for it, one arm pushing the pillow from beneath her head, the other pulling the sheet tight across the slight swelling of her stomach. On and on down a dark valley of sleep she rushed, looking, calling . . . Then the tall African appeared and turned with Carleton's smile and gave the black baby to Jacques. "It's your child," he said.

She woke trembling and got quickly off the bed. She must tell Jacques. She must. For a moment she shivered in the sudden chill of the room. Jason had been right, long years ago. She should have told Jacques then.

The moon was filtering a soft light onto the veranda. Isabella found Jacques sitting there. For a long while she sat in silence by his side. When she spoke, her voice was barely a whisper. "When I married your father, Jacques, my name was not Clay, but Clavier."

He turned to her, bewildered. "But . . ."

"I named you for my Grandpa Jacques and the brother I have spoken of so often, Clay. I saw my other brother last night, here in Charleston. His name is Jason Clavier."

She saw her son's puzzled look. "Maybe you remember Jason. He

295

came to our home in Charleston several times when you were a boy."

"No." He shook his head slowly.

"Perhaps I should begin at the beginning." For a moment she met his eyes, then she fastened her gaze on her hands. "My Grandpa Jacques, Jacques Clavier, was born in Surinam. His mother's father was a pirate, a Maroon—a bush Negro pirate."

"Negro?"

She heard incredulity in his voice. "Yes." She spoke quickly to forestall his questions. "Papa Jacques came to this country when he was about eighteen. He married Noni, my grandmother, who was from Africa."

He got up and looked down at her. "What are you trying to say?"

She caught her breath.

"What are you trying to say, Mother?"

She reached up to take her son's hand, but he backed away. "Oh, Jacques"—her voice was tremulous, low—"you must understand. In this country, in America, a person's race is the overriding value. Intellect is not honored, brains have little value, education has little value, beauty . . . if you are not white. Race is the final factor in determining what you will be, how you will live, what you will dream, if you dare dream . . ." She felt the tears hot on her cheek and turned to hide them from him.

"What the hell are you trying to say?" She looked up frightened as he bent over her, a stranger with blazing eyes and hissing voice.

"Jacques . . ." She cowered before the fury in her son's eyes. "Jacques, please, you must . . ."

He saw the truth in her eyes. "Oh, my God." He recoiled in shock. "My God, you're a nigger."

"Jacques . . ." Biting her lip to stay her tears, Isabella held out her hand to her son.

He turned his back. She heard the sob catch his voice. "I don't believe it. I can't believe that you . . ."

"And you." Her voice was soft. "You are my son, you know."

"No." He wheeled to face her. "Not me." He spat his words at her. "I'm a Dulane. I am master of Four Winds . . ."

"Because I made it so."

She saw his world collapsing in his eyes and stood brushing her tears with her hand. "Listen to me, Jacques. There's no difference inside of you between being black and being white. It exists only in the minds of those who try to twist the truth, to make others, black and white, believe . . .

"Jacques, you won't suddenly become stupid, inept, or lazy or any of the other idiotic things you may have heard. You won't want to settle for anything just to stay alive." She smiled tenuously. "Nor will you suddenly have rhythm, and be able to dance and sing. You'll still be the same, the same Jacques Dulane—what you are because of the way you have lived and because of what the world has allowed you to expect." She held out her hands to him again. "Jacques, my son, no race is better than any other. Mankind is simply and frailly man. Believe me. I am in a position to know."

Jacques saw exhaustion in her moonlit face, small lines that he had never seen before. Her eyes were a flat, dull gray, and her shoulders sagged as she studied her impeccably groomed hands. He stared at her, a middle-aged woman who once, just the truth ago, had been almost divine. "Then why did you do it?"

"Because," she whispered, hesitating, remembering, then once again he saw the whirlpool in her eyes. "Because . . . why not?"

Robert had arranged for the doctor. He had arranged for the nurse. He had arranged for the baby to be born at home. He arrived in Geneva three weeks before that event was scheduled to occur.

"Sherry, my dear?" Across the beam-ceilinged room of the château that had been her prison, Isabella saw Robert lift the decanter. Nodding, she sat at the chessboard before the fireplace for their evening ritual. Robert kissed her cheek as he handed her the drink. The amber liquid shimmered in the crystal glass. She forced a smile as she looked up at him. The blue of his smoking jacket complemented his coloring, the deep blue of his eyes; his skin bronzed the color of his hair by a weekend on the slopes.

"I came across a new book of poems by Alfred, Lord Tennyson. Some are quite superior. Would you like me to read to you?"

"Thank you, Robert. That would be nice."

She watched as he thumbed through the book, then closed her eyes as he began to read. The aroma from his pipe mellowed her, and his voice was soft and gentle with the verse. Thank God, she thought, they were not in New York.

The pain gripped her like talons, and on her clutched fist her knuckles rose hard and white. The pain passed, and she fixed her gaze on Robert.

She felt it coming again, shooting agony through her swollen body. Perspiration broke on her forehead.

She waited until the pain had passed, then stood on trembling legs. "Excuse me, Robert. I must go upstairs. Will you call the nurse?"

He looked up at her, noticing for the first time the gray in the titian mass that framed her pale, damp face. "Oh, Isabella." He stood and pulled her to him. "Isabella." He buried his face in the damp strands of her hair. "I love you. No matter what, I love you."

She sat on layers of rubber sheeting on the bed, watching as the nurse first rolled the Persian throw rugs against the wall, then turned to chase a speck of dust that cowered in a corner. The silver mirrors and brushes on her dresser had been replaced by steel canisters containing sterile instruments.

"Ich komme schon zurück," the nurse said, then continued in guttural English. "I go send da carriage to Herr Doktor. I bring good dry wood for this fire. It in da carriage house."

The carriage house! With a slow chill Isabella remembered. The letters. The letters from Suzanne and Aunt Jacqueline. Letters telling of her mother's death. The letters and that slim volume, Clay's poetry. She had put them under the log bin in the carriage house the day Robert arrived.

"No, wait . . ."

The nurse turned with those all-seeing eyes. Isabella could almost hear her: "Herr Hardwick, I found da letter and da book . . ." Damn! Why hadn't she burned them as she had started to a hundred times? "I'd like a cup of tea . . ." She saw protest coming to the nurse's lips. "Right now, if you don't mind." Isabella heard the nurse's quick steps as she moved down the hall, then bit her lip until she tasted blood as another pain ripped through her.

She heard Robert moving in the adjoining room, the room where the coats were kept. Cursing this outrageous ill fortune, Isabella slipped into a woolen robe.

The night cold outside was stunning. The ice on the sloping, curving walk cut her thin slippers. The pain in her back, her abdomen, her anus, slowed her movement, made her clumsy, and though the distance was short, her breath was coming in painful rasps when she passed beneath the great blue spruce and pushed open the carriage-house door.

It took but a moment to find the letters, a moment more to shove them through the grating in the potbellied iron stove that kept the horses warm. All but that slim, bloodstained volume, Clay's poems. Somehow it remained in her hand.

She had almost reached the house again when her water broke. Then agony forced her to her knees. Perspiration from her forehead trickled down onto the moonlit snow.

She felt her child present itself for birth and willed herself to her feet. But her strength was waning, and crumpling with the next pain, she could only crawl, searching the glistening slippery whiteness for a root, a branch to clutch.

Robert found her in the snow, holding the leather-bound book, and carried her to the house. Ashen, he stood inside the bedroom door, ignoring the doctor's orders to leave. Isabella's feverish eyes were on his face as the child gave its final push to life. From somewhere, far beyond her pain-torn body, she heard, "It's a girl." Then unconsciousness claimed her.

Sunshine and a soft cry from the bassinet woke her. Robert was holding her hand. "I'll get the nurse," he said.

The quick touch of her fingers stayed him. "Robert, the baby . . . ?"

He smiled. "A new Isabella."

Her eyes went to the bassinet. "Would you bring her to me?"

Robert saw the quick frown on her face and laughed. "She looks like you and me."

"What . . . ?"

"She looks white," he said.

As she held their child, he told her that he had known before they married. After his father's death, a packet Cornelius Hardwick had requested arrived from the Louvre, answering his inquiry about the origin of the design of the jeweled medallion. A curator's report said that it was a variation of a design popular among the Maroons, the bush Negroes of Surinam. The packet also contained copies of the sketches Ingres had made in achieving the "Isabella Dulane." Ingres had written on some of these sketches. On the bottom of one were the words "She too comes from a river, Isabella Clavier Dulane."

"I remembered your relationship with Jason Clavier, the uncanny feeling I had when I saw the two of you together. I hired a Pinkerton's man to find out what he could about the Claviers. I was crazy with the thought of losing you. I pretended to be a reporter and interviewed your Aunt Jacqueline." Robert smiled. "She told me all about the Claviers.

"When I came to Charleston, it was to say goodbye. But then . . ." His hand squeezed hers. "I saw your face again . . ."

Speechless, Isabella stared at her husband. He had known. All these fear-filled years—he had known. Her face turned on her pillow, a hundred questions—suppositions—rushing through her mind. She bit back her tears and turned her face back to her husband. At last, at last she was safe. No more lies were needed. At last, she was free to really live. "Robert . . ." she began, then felt the blood gushing between her thighs.

300

He saw her flinch, saw the sudden paleness of her face. "Isabella, what is it? Stay still, I'll get the nurse."

"Wait." She gripped his hand. Her eyes were wide, translucent, blue. "Robert . . ." For the first time he saw a plea in her face. "Promise, promise me that you will help Jason, Jason and his children."

He kissed her lips. "I promise. Now let me get . . ."

"No, not yet." The fire in her eyes was burning low. "Please, Robert, read to me." She saw his hesitation. "Please."

"Your brother's poems?" He picked up the book from the table by the bed. "Here's a page that's quite worn."

"Thank you, Robert."

He began to read, holding her hand as their child slept in her arms. "This is our time, my brothers—oh, rally those whom the sun has loved . . ."

Her hand went to her throat, for the medallion, felt the emptiness there. "Oh, Robert." He heard the thick whisper, felt the fierce grip of her hand. "Never desert the Claviers." Then her hand was limp.

A guttural sound burst from Robert's belly, erupted from his throat. "Isabella!"

He knew before he bent over her, before he screamed for the nurse. He knew as he moved their child from her arms, his tears falling on the newborn face. And even as he rocked her in his arms, kissing those still half-smiling lips, Robert knew that Isabella was dead.

There were seven persons present at the interment of Isabella Hardwick. But then, Jacques Dulane thought as he stood in the softly falling snow next to the grave of Clay Clavier, his mother would be pleased. Despite all that had surrounded her, at the end, her only cares, her only concerns had been herself and her family. For this moment, at least, she had brought them all together.

He had received Hardwick's cable and met his ship in New York yesterday. With the nurse and the squalling infant that was his half sister, he and Robert had journeyed to New Bedford. Mr. Oxley, caretaker of the Negro dead, had met them at the hotel, expressing shock and disapproval at the haste. "The family . . ." Hardwick had explained that he was carrying out his wife's wishes.

After a supper no one ate, his stepfather had given him the velvet

301

box. "Your mother wanted you to have this." Jacques had caught his breath as he lifted the diamond and emerald necklace to shimmer in the light. Then he had felt Hardwick's eyes cold on him. "Her will said it belonged to the master of Four Winds."

"She told you?" Jacques stared at the older man. "She told you that she was . . ."

"I always knew," Robert Hardwick said softly. "I loved her."

Now the casket was lowered into the ground and the unknown. The minister was completing the last ritual for the dead. Jacques, not wishing to think again of the sorrows and joys he had brought to her whom the earth now claimed, looked at the Negro beyond the open grave. The man saw his look and came around.

"I'm Isaac Woodson," he said, extending his hand, "Isabella's cousin. I received Jason's telegram only this morning. He regretted deeply that he could not come."

Hardwick moved quickly and took Isaac's hand. "I'm Robert Hardwick, your cousin's husband, and this . . ."

"Excuse me, sir." Oxley approached Hardwick's side. "Is there anything else . . . ?"

"Yes." Jacques saw that Robert's face was gray in the snow-filtered light. "A headstone. Mr. Woodson can give you the date of birth." Oxley bowed, the quiet, hand-clasped manner of those whose business is with the dead. "The inscription will read: 'Isabella Clavier Dulane Hardwick . . .'" Jacques saw the vow in Robert's eyes as he looked down into the open grave. " 'Rest in peace.' "

CHAPTER THIRTEEN

1887

The brown-skinned boys were playing baseball in the weed-grown Charleston field that was their playground. Alex, with other boys too young to play, perched on a tree stump watching as his brother Clay, in center field, moved back almost to the woods. Bo Harris was at bat. Bo was a good hitter. With men on first and third, Clay could not let this one get by.

The pitcher dipped into his windup. Clay, squinting in the dusk-dim light, groaned at the crack of bat on ball. The white sphere came hurtling through the air. As he chased it, Clay saw Fats Jackson puffing over from left field. The ball was going into the woods. It would be a home run anyway, but they had to find that ball. It was the only one they had.

He was on his hands and knees in the thicket when he heard the horses. Leaping to his feet, Clay choked in horror. Faceless, white-hooded riders galloped across the playground, whooping demons leaning from their horses, shooting, slashing at the running, screaming boys trying in vain to find cover in the open field.

"Alex! Alex!" Clay started toward them on the run, shrieking at the top of his voice. Then strong hands grabbed him from behind and he was thrown to the ground.

"Clay, for God's sake, stay down. They'll get us if they see you," Fats whispered. His haunches pressed squarely on Clay's shoulders, his hands locked across Clay's mouth. Flailing, twisting, biting, tasting blood from his mouth, from Fats's hand, Clay struggled to get up. But Fats's weight was too much for his fourteen-year-old strength.

Clay saw the roan horse move to a gallop as the rider dug in his spurs. He saw the lassoed black boy bounce in the dust behind. Forty yards from Clay the rider dismounted. His eyes shone in the holes of his hood as he walked with a limp to the screaming, kicking boy. He dropped a noose over the child's head. Then, as Clay watched, three other riders came on to hoist the six-year-old boy on the horse. One end of the rope was tossed over a tree limb. The child slipped from the roan, his scream wild, clear in the dusk-dark field. "Clay, Clay, help! Clay . . . please!!!"

Blood drenched the hand Fats Jackson held over Clay's mouth. He floundered on Clay's shoulders from the viciousness of his friend's kicking.

Clay heard the men laughing, saw them as they shoved the child back. The rope was secured to the tree, and the man with the limp slapped the roan.

For a moment the boy kicked in the air. Then the rope was cut and he fell to the ground. While the other men watched, the man with the limp slit the boy's throat. Then he called his horse, "Diamond," mounted, and rode away.

The field was empty, except for the bodies. Still Fats clung to the tense body beneath him. Darkness had fallen before Fats stood. He followed Clay to his brother.

Alex's eyes were open. His mouth was open. His throat was open. He lay in a pool of blood.

"Clay," Fats was sobbing. "I'm sorry. But they'd a killed you, too."

Clay did not answer. Nor did he cry. He bent and picked up his brother and carried him home in his arms.

Book Five

CLAY

The problem of the twentieth century is the problem of the color line; the relation of the darker to the lighter races of men in Asia and Africa, in America and the islands of the sea.

—W. E. B. DU BOIS,
"The Dawn of Freedom"
The Souls of Black Folks

CHAPTER ONE

1887

He knelt in the bushes at the side of the road, holding a rope in his hand. It was getting dark now, and he shivered in his thin jacket. Soon the man would be coming on his roan horse. The boy patted his knife and made ready.

He heard the horse coming and brought the rope taut, chest high across the road. Quickly he tied it to an iron ring in a tree. Then, knife in hand, he crouched, waiting.

The horse reared, neighing in terror as the rope slashed its chest. One foot caught in the stirrup, the rider spraddled the road, swearing in pain. Then the boy leapt upon him. For an instant the man struggled to gain the advantage of weight. For an instant. No more. He saw the boy clearly as the knife flashed down. Saw—and recognized him. "Clay Clavier," he screamed. Then the knife slit his throat.

Clay came the long way home, circling the city, keeping to the woods and fields as long as possible, then moving, a stealthy shadow, through gardens behind widely set homes until he reached his own. He saw the lights in the front room, the few silhouetted figures. He sat on his haunches and waited.

Inside the front room, Jason Clavier sat in a corner, his hands limp on the arms of the chair. Words moved around him, words of condolence and shared sorrow, but he could no longer speak. Alexander, his son, his six-year-old son, had been buried that afternoon.

Many things had crossed Jason Clavier's mind these past two days. The aborted hope of Reconstruction. Suzanne's pleadings to move North. Revenge against his son's murderers, the responsibility of the law. "What law?" Suzanne had asked. Jason's hands trembled on his chair, but he did not have the strength even to wipe away his tears. He felt Smoke's hand on his shoulder, heard Smoke's voice close to his ear, "I know. I know it's hell."

Smoke saw Suzanne across the room, still surrounded by the bonneted sisters from the church. Her eyes, and her mouth were puffy. Her face had a grayish tinge.

He crossed the room and took her aside. "Lemme get rid a these folks. You look exhausted, and Jason's beat."

"Thanks, Smoke."

"I tucked a swig a rye under one a them cake covers when the sisters wasn't lookin'. Now I know Jason's not a drinkin' man, but it'd do both a you a lot a good . . ."

"Thank you."

He frowned, seeing the torture in her eyes. "Is there anything else . . . ?"

"There's nothing, Smoke. There's nothing . . ."

Suzanne crossed to where her husband sat and touched his soft gray hair.

"Oh, Suzanne," he whispered, "I was wrong."

"No, Jason." Her voice was low and fierce. "No, the wrong was not with you." She held his hand, willing her strength into his body. He was a great man, her Jason, and though they had, with ruthless barbarism, stripped naked the fibers of his being, they had not, till Alex, touched his soul.

With calm and culture, he had faced their ridicule and disdain. With determination he had fought for power for his people despite the threats, the burning crosses, despite the face of ugly death. It was only when whites refused to hire black Republicans, when in the dead of night the Red Shirts concealed polling places in the woods and the swamps, it was only when the exercise of franchise meant starvation or death that black men had not returned his faith. And though, systematically, the new power structure had moved to starve them out, he was not bitter, he had not broken, her Jason, until Alex.

"Oh, Suzanne," he said again and she trembled at the strange sound of his voice.

"Yes, Jason." He felt her quiet strength, and his tears rushed anew. He slammed the chair with the flat of his hand. "Oh, my God, my God, what must we do?"

"We must stay, Jason," she said softly. "We must stay in Carolina." From across the room, Smoke saw the new look in her eyes. Not the smoldering coals of the girl he had known, but steel on fire as she took her husband's hand.

Outside, Clay watched the last of the guests leaving. He saw Smoke stand a moment on the porch, then go slowly down the walk. Clay went behind the house and came in the back door.

"Why, Clay," his mother began as she came into the kitchen. "I thought you said you were going to bed." Then she saw the bloodstain on his shirt. "Oh, my God, Clay! Clay?"

"What is it?" Suzanne turned to see Jason in the door. "What is it, Suzanne?"

"Papa." Clay walked over and touched his father's arm. "It was Mr. Brown who killed Alex."

"Brown? But why? Why? I don't even know a . . ."

"He killed Alex." Clay looked up at his father's blind eyes, knowing a deeper sight lay within and handed him the bloody knife. "I killed him."

Clay saw his father's sightless eyes on him. Then Jason put his arm around his shoulder. "All right. All right, son." Jason's voice was soft and steady. "Now we have to get you out of here."

They sat in the darkened parlor, talking in low voices, trying to form a plan, a plan that had a chance.

The stillness outside was broken by a carriage. Jason stumbled to his feet as a knock came at the door. "Quickly." Clay felt his father's hand on his shoulder. "In the kitchen. If I raise my voice, run to Smoke's. Stay out of sight."

The knock came again. Suzanne, hands clasped to her mouth, followed Jason to answer it.

The brim of his hat shadowed the face of the man outside the door, but through the glass pane Suzanne saw that he was young and white. He was smoking a long, slender cigar. He raised a gold-knobbed cane as Jason opened the door. "Are you Jason Clavier?" he asked.

"Yes."

Suzanne's eyes sped to the window. He was alone. No one was waiting in the surrey.

"May I come in? My name is Jacques Dulane."

"Jacques . . . ?"

The young man saw astonishment on Jason's face. "Please, it's urgent."

Inside the room Jacques began to speak at once. "Just moments ago, I overheard my valet say the Kluxers were looking for your son in connection with the murder of a man who had"—for an instant Jacques's eyes dropped—"killed his younger brother."

Jason's face was impassive. Jacques, meeting neither accordance nor denial, went on. "According to my valet, who had just come in,

309

they found a boy they thought was your son. They shot him. He fell near the place where John, my valet, was hiding. The Klansmen, satisfied it was your son, hung the dead boy and . . ."

"Why have you come to tell me this?" Jason snapped, trying to control mounting revulsion and fear.

"Because, according to my man, that boy was not your son. I heard John say he knows your son, whose name, I believe, is Clay. The dead boy was a drifter who had been in a tavern where my man was imbibing, trying to solicit work.

"Now, if that's true," Jacques went on quickly, "Clay is still in danger. He must be gotten to safety immediately, and you must claim the dead boy as your own."

Jason waited, sensing his nephew was not through.

"There's a train for Washington." Jacques checked his pocket watch. "In forty minutes. If we can find a way to smuggle your son into a compartment, I will see him safely to New York. From there he can take a train to your family in New Bedford."

"She told you, then?" His whisper conveyed Jason's astonishment.

"Yes." Jacques's voice was soft. "She did."

His eyes were used to the dark now. Jacques looked around the room. "The trick will be to get Clay through the station. That trunk . . ." Jacques pointed with his cane to the seaman's chest before the fireplace. "Could he fit in that?"

"He would suffocate!" Suzanne exclaimed.

"Grandpa Jacques's chest," Jason said thoughtfully. "If there were small holes beside the handles . . ."

"We must be quick," Jacques said. "Here, I'll give you a hand with it."

In minutes Suzanne and Jacques had readied the chest. Suzanne wrote a note to Jason's cousin, Isaac Woodson in New Bedford. Jason signed it and called Clay from the kitchen. Lifting the wooden medallion from his neck, Jason placed it around his son's. For an instant Clay knew his mother's teary kiss, then he stepped inside the chest.

With Suzanne's aid, Jason helped Jacques carry the chest to the surrey. When it was in place, Jason turned to his nephew again. "I am deeply grateful, Jacques Dulane."

Jacques bowed smartly. "It is a debt I owe my mother. She would approve of this return." Then he leapt into the surrey and snapped the reins. Twenty minutes later, after a hasty stop to pick up John to help with the trunk and return the surrey, they were on the train.

Inside the trunk, Clay felt the train begin to move. He heard the conductor ask for the ticket and, certain that either he would be betrayed or his lungs would burst, heard the door of the compartment slam.

Jacques Dulane opened the sea chest, then turned to light his cigar from the lamp beside the bed. He caught his breath as the boy climbed from the chest. "My God," he whispered to himself. "It's mother's face, in brown."

"Why are you helping me?"

Jacques looked at the tense young body beside the chest, saw the sharp wariness in the boy's eyes. He diverted his attention to the ash on his cigar, then tipped it gently into the receptacle beneath the window and looked at the boy again. "Because, Clay Clavier, whether you—or I—like it or not, we are cousins. First cousins. Now, lie back and get some sleep. We shall have to change in Washington quite early in the morning. And from all that I have heard, you've had a most eventful day."

CHAPTER TWO

1887–1892

It was dusk when Clay arrived in New Bedford. As he walked through the snowdrifts on the deserted platform beside the train tracks, he was grateful for the coat Jacques Dulane had bought him in New York.

One carriage waited outside the station. It was driven by a white man. Shivering from the cold, Clay politely asked directions to the address on the envelope his father had given him.

The man pulled down the muffler that warmed his cheeks and nose and explained in few words, then as Clay started to walk away, called after him. "You're not gonna walk, are you?"

It had seemed some distance, but Clay had never seen colored riding in carriages driven by whites. "Why, ah . . ." Jacques Dulane had given him twenty dollars in case he ran into difficulty.

The driver, who seemed to Clay to be at least one hundred years old, inched his horse forward a foot or two. "That's the Clavier place. You a Clavier or a Woodson?"

"I'm a Clavier."

"Well, hop on in. I'll take you there. It's too far to walk. And things are bad around here these days. All these dang-blasted foreigners coming in.

"I knew your grandpa, guess it was your great-grandpa, Jacques Clavier," the old man continued as Clay got in and the carriage moved along the waterfront. "I was just a boy, of course, but I can remember when his ships put in, right down there." Clay followed his gloved finger to the ships anchored in the ice-capped river. "Came from across world, they did. He was old then," the driver continued, "but I can still see him standing on his quarterdeck. He was a fine-looking man, your . . . grandpa . . . No." The driver turned to look at Clay again. "You couldn't be Alexander's son. I knew Alex well. He was on the board of the YMCA with my brother. I knew all his children. Clay, that was the oldest one, was killed in the rebellion. And Isabella, that was her name, oh, she was a beauty, she left here one day and nobody ever heard of her since. Now, you must be Jason's boy." He turned and looked again at Clay. "Am I right?"

For an instant Clay hesitated, then he nodded and returned the man's smile. "Right."

"Your papa was a congressman down in South Carolina. He still livin'?"

"Yes. Yes, he is."

"Smart man. Course, all the Claviers were smart folk." The horse turned onto a narrow street of gracious homes, and the carriage bumped more slowly over the icy uneven bricks. "But why any colored man would want to stay down there the way those crackers act, is beyond me. My boy was down there in the 2nd Massachusetts. Lot a fellas from this town went South to put down the rebellion. Well, here we are."

Clay felt a sudden apprehension as he stared at the large white house set back beneath snow-covered trees, its windows sparkling from the lights within. Suppose they did not want him here. Suppose . . .

He got down slowly. "How much . . . ?"

"Nothing. Wasn't much business noway, an' it's good to talk of the old times."

"Well, thank you."

"No thanks needed. I was on my way home."

The carriage rumbled off, and Clay stood for a minute outside the gate, hoping to catch a glimpse of someone inside. But no one came near the windows, and the air was sharp. He opened the gate and went quickly up the walk.

For a moment or two his knock went unanswered, and he was raising his hand to knock again when the door was opened by a girl a little younger than himself. "Hello." Her eyes were dark, lovely, like his mother's.

"How do you do," he stammered.

She opened the door wide, and he came into the foyer. Behind her, in the parlor, he could see the fire in the fireplace. She held out her hand. "I'm Melinda Woodson." Her smile was full of fun.

"Well, how do you do . . . again." He shook her hand. "I'm Clay Clavier."

It was as though he had sounded a firebell. People of all ages rushed to stare, to hug, to kiss. He was settled by the fireplace, served a heaping tray, answering their questions as well as he could, not telling, not yet admitting why he had come, without even a bag.

After nearly an hour the ancient lady who had sat next to Clay

313

from the start, Great-grandmama Jacqueline, began to speak in a voice shriveled by time. "We are mighty, mighty glad to have you, Clay. That's why Grandpa Jacques built this house, for his family. He was born in Surinam, South America, you know." His cousins smiled and lolled on the rug before the hearth as Aunt Jacqueline began her saga. But long before Great-grandpa Jacques got off the pirate ship, Clay Clavier was asleep.

Clay lived with his family in New Bedford for four years. In the winter he went to school and worked in the Woodsons' tailoring emporium. In the summers the family migrated to Martha's Vineyard, where Jacqueline had, years before, built a summer house not far from the lighthouse. Clay worked on the small boats that took visitors around the island.

His "Uncle" Isaac was a round man, formed of concentric circles. His head was round, his face was round, his shoulders were round, and his belly . . . Only his fingers, surprisingly slender and agile, deviated from this pattern of his being. He was a pleasant man, quite inoffensive if rather bland, who tended to be officious at church and on the occasions when they entertained guests for dinner.

Andy, Isaac's son, stocky, light-brown-skinned, was two years older than Clay. Andy was above all things dependable. He was, Clay thought, persnickety, and when he talked his *a*'s sounded like a sheep bleating.

His Aunt Mary laughed a lot. She was very "color struck" and talked about her Indian blood all the time. Irritably, Clay wondered to Melinda which Squanto had bequeathed her kinky hair. It was the only time Clay saw annoyance in his lovely cousin's eyes. "For goodness' sake, Clay. If a person with one drop of Negro blood is colored, why can't a three-fourths Indian be Indian?"

Mary Dawson Woodson's family had received the land on which Grandpa Jacques's lighthouse stood when part of the reservation had been divided among the Indian families who still lived there, after the Civil War. They owned the lighthouse and the legend.

The Woodsons were a pleasantly aggressive, high-spirited collection of individuals who took pleasure in doing things as a family—attending church, where Uncle Isaac was a deacon, or the affairs of the literary guild, of which Aunt Jacqueline had been president (so said his cousin Melinda) "for over a hundred years." They were not rich, nor were they, as Isaac Woodson claimed, "respectably poor."

314

Clay knew poverty, knew it did not put roasts and hams on the table, buy shoes from Kuykendal's, keep a summer home, plan for children's college or—and the greatest wonders of all—put toilets *inside* the house and a *telephone* in the parlor.

By and large, Clay's days were happy, filled with what Uncle Isaac called "forward-going activities." He studied hard, got excellent grades, and in hours with Aunt Jacqueline learned the family wisdom, tradition, and the dream.

But it was with his cousin Melinda that Clay (at first reluctantly) spent his most delightful hours. She always had plans for them to be together, skating in winter, watching the roustabouts haul up the circus tents in spring, sailing in the summer. She was always at Clay's side, lovely eyes laughing. "Clay, I've absolutely the most fun thing to do."

But there were times that Clay felt uneasy. His cousin Andy could be so damn condescending. It had begun—Clay still flushed when he remembered—his first night in New Bedford. He had excused himself and gone outside looking for the outhouse. Andy had followed him, had found him: "What in the world are you doing, standing in the bushes?"

Clay had seen the astonishment on his cousin's face as he shoved his freezing private parts inside his pants. "Clay, up here we have toilets inside our homes."

But it was not just with Andy—Clay felt uncomfortable with the Woodsons' complacency, with their emphasis on tradition. Many of the things they valued had no meaning in his life. There must be more, Clay thought, much more, to life . . .

His history teacher sensed his growing restlessness. "There's a new university opening next fall in Chicago. You know what they say, Clay. 'Go West, young man, go West.'"

And so when Clay was ready to graduate from high school and mentioned among his college preferences the University of Chicago, his Uncle Isaac urged him strongly in that direction. Andy was at Harvard. But Clay's relationship with Melinda was deepening, and though he had never mentioned it, Jason's brief message explaining his son's arrival had never left Isaac's mind. It was a shame to send the boy on to yet another city where he knew not a soul, but, Isaac thought with finality, Chicago would be the best choice in this instance.

The Woodsons had refused all money that Clay had offered them.

315

The money he had sent home had brought a strong reprimand from his father and a stern insistence that Clay save every dime for college. As he packed his bags, Clay calculated that with careful restraint, a part-time job, a cheap room, and by keeping his summer job on the Vineyard, he could hang on until his junior year. With pounding heart and high anticipation, Clay Clavier boarded the train for Chicago.

There, he went immediately to the department of student housing. Although the university did not allow Negroes in its dormitories, student housing would provide him with a list of families with whom its colored students could stay.

Several places on that list had already been crossed out. After stowing his bags in the James Hotel, a referral from a railroad porter, Clay began to look for the others.

During the next three days Clay walked for miles, seeing more of Chicago than he would for the rest of his student career. Three places on his list had burned down. Two already had students, and others had taken in relatives fleeing the South. One place he rejected out of hand because the structure could not boast to last the winter.

On the fourth day, still at the hotel, Clay registered for classes, then set out to see some places recommended by the hotel desk clerk. School was in its second week when Clay went again to the division of student housing. The exasperated young man with whom he spoke turned to his contact in the Negro community. "Jim," he asked the Negro sweeping the floor. "Do you have any idea where Mr. Clavier here can find housing suitable for him?"

"Naw, suh." The janitor rubbed his brow in concentration, then Clay saw the shrewd light in his eyes. "The onliest place I kin think of where Mr. Clavier kin find housing suitable for him is with Mr. Parker."

"And where does this Mr. Parker live?" the clerk asked impatiently.

"Mr. Parker, he live at 709 Axton Street. Jes' west a downtown. Now, he would have a lovely place for Mr. Clavier there."

Clay thought the janitor's smile looked malicious, but he was clutching at straws. In three weeks at the hotel he had already spent more than his letter from the housing department had estimated it would cost to live three months.

The clouds were low, ominous, when Clay got on the trolley. By the time he got off, the rain was slashing down in torrents. The address the janitor had given him existed, and only one block from the cars. It was a handsome building, three stories high. Clay ran up the stairs as the trees bent in the howling wind. He pulled the rope and heard chimes inside.

The girl who answered the door was not much older than he, twenty at the most. She was tiny, not quite five feet tall, a rosy brown with twinkly eyes and a wide, impish mouth. But it was not beauty that caused Clay to gasp, nor the fact that both her mouth and her cheeks were rouged (he had seen that before, in Boston), but what she wore—or did not wear. A what? A tiny yoke covered the minimum of the top part of her body. A slinky red-and-gold—skirt?—began its exotic job below her navel, clinging to every curve except along one side, where a slit revealed a full length of thigh. She wore perfume—real perfume, not sachets as did the ladies Clay knew—and the scent was both delightful and demanding.

"Excuse me," Clay stammered. "Are you Mrs. Parker?"

"Mrs. who?" Peals of laughter rolled from her pretty throat.

Clay stared in astonishment. "Mrs. Parker," he repeated politely, pressing close to the door to be out of the rain.

"No," she said finally. "No, I'm not. Have you come to see Mr. Parker on business?"

"Yes," Clay replied, he hoped firmly.

"May I ask what?" Laughter lingered in her eyes.

"Why, certainly. I was given his name . . ."

A frown. "His name for what?"

"I'm a student at the University of Chicago. I received his name from the student housing division . . ."

"Pete's!" Laughter's new explosion was greater than its first. "They sent you to live with Pete Parker?"

Perplexity was changing to anger when Clay heard the voice inside the hall—low, tense, tinged with a patois Clay had heard from time to time on the wharves of New Bedford. "Angelique? What the hell is going on?"

"Oh, Pete." She turned, still laughing, and Clay saw the slim, elegant man coming up behind her in the hall. He was tall, maybe thirty, dark, no—swarthy was the term—good-looking with pomaded sideburns (Madame Walker, Clay could detect the scent) and eyes so blue they seemed almost black. The smoke from a slender aromatic cigar curled around his diamond-studded pinkie.

Angelique touched his arm. "Pete, you won't believe this. The university sent this boy"—Angelique could not contain this news—"to you for housing."

An incredulous smile crossed Parker's face. He looked at Clay. "You sure they sent you to me?"

"Well, sir . . ." Clay began his story. By the time he reached his second desperate trip to the housing authority, he was sitting on a needlepoint settee in Pete Parker's parlor, a glass of sherry, the second of his lifetime, in his hand.

"So." Parker's lips twisted wtih cynicism. "This nigger janitor gave you my name and address and sent you here on a night like this."

"That's the way it was, sir." Clay put down his glass and moved to the edge of his chair. It was obvious Pete Parker had no need of boarders. "I'm sorry to have disturbed you. And I appreciate your hospitality." As he started to stand Parker held up his hand.

"Hold on. Hold on a minute." The diamond flashed impressively as Parker studied his cigar, then he looked into the dark, steady eyes of the young man across from him. He had seen eyes like that before. Eyes that had seen life come up snake eyes, that didn't flinch when they knew they had crapped out. Pete flipped the ash into a lacquered ashtray and turned again to Clay. "What're you going to do now?"

"Well, for a start, I'll get back to the hotel."

"Yeah, and then what?"

"I don't know yet, sir." Clay glanced at the hailstones pelting the windows.

Parker looked at Clay for yet another minute, then stood. "I live here by myself," he said with a shrugging gesture. "There's a room, a garret, really, on the third floor. It's not so bad. I stayed there myself before I bought the place. Take the room and use it till you find what you want. It'll be no bother to me and you won't be far from school."

"Why . . ." Clay began, but Parker went on.

"There's a bed, a desk, and a lamp. You'll be comfortable." He twisted the diamond on his manicured hand. "You eaten?"

Clay shook his head.

"Okay, we'll eat."

Pete seemed suddenly to remember the girl, who now, to Clay's amazement, was filling her glass from a bottle—his eyes blinked as he double-checked—yes, he was certain, it was marked "gin." "Angelique, tell Lovey to set another place. And that Clay . . . what did you say your last name was . . . ?"

"Clavier," Clay said quickly.

"Clay Clavier will be staying with me a few days."

Parker turned back to Clay. "Come on, I'll get you a dry shirt and you can see the room."

Clay, impressed by Parker's living room, was awestricken by his bedroom. A mammoth canopied bed with a coverlet of wolf fur dominated the room. Crossing to the armoire where his benefactor now looked for a shirt, Clay could see the outlines of a painting on the ceiling of the bed. As Parker tossed a choice of silk shirts on the bed, Clay peeked at the painting. The man and woman were both naked and they were . . . Clay jerked his head and looked at the rest of the room.

There were no lamps. Large urns filled with burning oil gave a shadowy light and filled the room with an exotic scent. The rugs were small, handmade, most with designs of mermaids and naked maidens in the clutches of cavorting minotaurs and centaurs. However, in the middle of the room was a large circular rug, also handmade, with naked, voluptuous Negro girls, ranging in hue from black to *café-au-lait*. Their legs were wide-spread to circle the rug's edge, their hands reaching to touch the erotic parts of the man woven at the center. Clay, now doubting his earlier conviction of luck at last, tried not to imagine what transpired in these environs.

"Where you from?" Parker asked as they mounted the steps to the third floor.

"New Bedford, Massachusetts." It was what he had put on his school application.

"Never heard of it." Parker shrugged.

"It used to be the whaling capital of the world."

"Yeah?" Parker replied with little interest. "Here's your room."

"Gee." It escaped Clay's lips slowly and despite the doubts of a moment ago, he smiled. The room was not fancy, as he had begun to fear, but comfortable. The floor was bare. The furniture was simple, the curtains and bedspread done in shades of brown and rust.

"You think you can make it here?" Parker's smile for the first time was genuine. "Go on, look around. You got a few minutes before dinner. I'll see you downstairs." Parker turned toward the door, then paused, his hand on the doorknob. "What was it you said you were studying?"

"Economics."

Parker nodded. "Good. Lord knows we need more of us in that. If we ever get a nigger who can figure out how to multiply nothing opportunities times nothing paychecks and come up with a damn thing besides nothing, including hope . . . be a mothafucka." With that observation Pete Parker closed the door.

After dinner that night Clay saw nothing of Pete Parker for nearly a week. He took his meals with Mrs. Lovey, a big, comfortable woman, full of smiles, little pats on the shoulder, and clever homilies. She had a way of making him feel wanted and important. "Now don't be no lazybones in the morning," she said on Clay's second evening there when his stomach finally overruled her insistence that he was still a growing boy. "Git down in time for breakfast. I ain't cooking for my own amusement."

"Doesn't Mr. Parker eat?"

"Course he does. But by that time it's well to night."

She saw the question in his eyes and said quickly, "He works hard and keeps long hours. He's a fine man, Mr. Parker is. I been with him nigh on five years."

Clay, understanding she would not appreciate questioning about her employer's strange habits, agreed with Mrs. Lovey that Parker was indeed—a phrase he'd recently learned—"a real good guy."

He was down in time for breakfast and, taking the lunch Mrs. Lovey had packed, headed for the Midway with a confidence he had not felt since he arrived at the university. This euphoria continued for a week despite the fact that he had not yet found a job.

On Saturday Clay had no classes. He spent the morning looking for a job. Luckless again, he hurried home at noon so as not to miss Parker. He had no idea whether his host's schedule included weekends. Parker must be seen, his own unchanged situation explained, and payment made for the week.

He met Parker on the stairway. The first look in his host's eyes led Clay to believe the man had forgotten his existence completely.

"Not at all, Schoolboy," Parker protested minutes later, over grits and sausage. "I just been busy as hell."

"I should be able to find a place this week," Clay proceeded earnestly. "I have appointments with the ministers of both Quinn Chapel and Olivet Baptist Church. I understand they're trying to help students. In the meantime, I would like to know how much I owe you for your generosity?"

320

"Ain't that sort of a contradiction, Schoolboy?" Parker looked up from the grits he was moving toward his mouth. "How much you owe for generosity?"

Clay flushed. "I didn't mean it that way. What I meant . . ."

"He knows what you meant," Mrs. Lovey said, moving toward the table, her oven-hot biscuits finding a place next to Parker's hand.

Parker grinned at her. "Oh, go on, Lovey." Then he turned back to Clay. "You like it up there?"

"The room? Why . . . a . . . yes."

Parker wiped his mouth with his linen napkin and dropped it in his plate. "You found a job yet?"

"No." Clay fiddled with his fork.

"Well," Parker said slowly. "In my business, we got books to keep. Not much to it. I can show you how I want it done. And, seeing as how you say you're good with figures, we can call it square for room and board." Parker looked pleased with his idea. Before Clay could respond, he went on. "I know that place you're at needs studying, but if you need a little cash I gotta friend who owns a shoe store. I'm sure he'll be glad to let you work a coupla hours after school and Saturdays for, say, four dollars a week."

Two hours later the job was Clay's at exactly four dollars a week. With that, and room and board provided for, Clay zinged into his studies with a vengeance. He rarely saw Pete except on Sunday afternoons when they did the books together.

It was a weird job. Clay was certain Pete bought none of the items he recorded. His landlord kept the register tapes and receipts, and read the figures aloud for Clay to balance.

Pete did not talk much and neither did Mrs. Lovey. Three months later, though he supposed a lot, Clay knew little more about his benefactor than he had the day he entered his home.

CHAPTER THREE

1892–1893

It was on Christmas Eve that Clay had his first glimpse of the larger world of Pretty Pete Parker. With school out for the holidays and the shoe store a chaos of fidgeting children, Clay had been able to work twelve hours a day. Now, even the indefatigable store owner was at home. Clay lay on his bed in Pete Parker's garret, staring at the ceiling, thinking of his family in Charleston and the Woodsons in New Bedford. He closed his eyes, envisioning the Woodson house, its wreaths of pine and holly, the staircase swags entwined with juniper and bayberry, the strings of popcorn, dried apple rings, cranberries and currants, and the tree, the full, candlelit tree, its shining star almost brushing the ceiling. And Melinda . . . Melinda, a sprig of mistletoe in her hair; Melinda caroling in her hooded cape.

Flopping over onto his stomach, Clay wished for the hundredth time that he had not decided to come so far from home.

But that was it. He had no home. The Woodsons had given him shelter, given him love in his exile. But he could not remain an appendage to that family. And he could not return to his own. This university was right. Chicago was right. They were new. A new place for a new start. And in a few days Christmas would be past.

There had been little time or opportunity for developing friendships in Chicago. There was no central Negro community, and only by chance did Negro students meet one another. However, study and work both demanded time, and there had been little time, until tonight, for the luxury of loneliness.

But now, alone, in this empty house . . . Clay thought of the two fellows he knew slightly, and resolved that come the New Year he would find time to make these friendships firmer.

He knew Nathaniel Moore better. Nat was a senior, an intense, earnest creature behind enormous bifocals who had already won the reputation of being one of the brightest students in his class.

Last week the dean had called Nat in. "The old crust asked what I would study in grad school," Nat related to Clay. " 'Biochemistry,' I said. He stared at me. 'Biochemistry? You mean medicine?' "

" 'No!' I told him. 'Biochemistry.' "

"He looked at me like as though I were demented and asked what

I hoped to do with it. 'Research,' said I. Well, his mouth fell open. Golly Clay, I'm not jesting, you'd have thought he'd never heard the word before."

Clay's other friend, Ken Jones, was an ambitious student who had come from Cincinnati to become one of the first Negroes to run track at the university under its famous coach, Amos Alonzo Stagg.

But both Ken and Nat were home for the holiday—Ken gone to Ohio and Nat to Michigan. And though the Reverend Jeniffer of Quinn Chapel, the historic Negro church that had served as a station on the underground railroad, had extended invitations for the Christmas service and social to all the Negro students, Clay felt that he would be awkward—a stranger and alone. And when they sang the carols . . . his homesickness would become unbearable.

Adjusting his pillow, Clay reached on top of his stack of books, and picked up *Principles of Business Management*. "It is a smart man," as his Uncle Isaac would say, "who makes the best of the worst of things."

Pete was standing in his door before Clay realized anyone else was in the house. He looked up with a start and saw Pete grinning. "I saw your light. What's that you're reading? Must be hot stuff, got you so involved on Christmas Eve."

"Principles of Business Management." Clay's voice was more rueful than he realized.

But his tone did not escape Pete. *"Principles . . . ?"* said he in mock amazement. "Hey, come on, Schoolboy, lemme show you management in action."

Armour Street was deserted, snow drifting across the crooked sign that said: "Pete Parker's Place." But even as his friend reached for the door, Clay could feel the pulse of the life inside.

It was the gathering place for the "sporting crowd," who now packed it to the rafters. Clay stared at the men in derby hats and peg-top pants flashing diamond-studded pinkies as they raised long cigars, while their ladies, clad in variations of the decrees of Marshall Field and Mandel Brothers, tossed ornamented heads with each bell-toned "Merry Christmas"—gay, subtle reminders that every star has many points.

But it was, Clay thought, the music from the upright piano that framed the scene, that captured it, that gave it truth, urgency, and an immortality of its own.

It was the strange combination of rhythm and tone that Clay had heard standing in the street outside the Ark and the other bawdy houses of New Bedford; close, insistent, knowing, demanding. It was the juice of life in sound; moving naturally with the body's flow, with the smiles, the laughter, with the aching of the room. White folks called it ragtime. Its real name was jazz.

Strutting through the narrow entranceway, Pete was hailed, it seemed, by every voice. He raised his hand in the smiling, nodding response Clay had seen used by war heroes and city officials. Arriving through the backslaps at the bar, Pete summoned one of its keepers and, with him, disappeared into a small room in the corner of the saloon.

The cash register had a rhythm of its own. Clay, boggling at the stash, was oblivious to the stares in his direction. As a barkeeper hoisted a sack bulging with coins toward the rear door, Pete waved Clay into his sanctum.

"Schoolboy, this is Rip. Rip, this here's Clay Clavier. Goes out to the University of Chicago. He's keeping my books."

"Glad to meetcha, Clay." Rip's handshake was firm but his eyes made Clay uneasy.

"You see"—Pete's cigar smoke formed an O or, Clay wondered, was it a zero?—"we doing things professional now. Real professional. Keep that in mind now, Rip, and make damn sure them tapes and receipts are right."

Pete, turning to flip his ash, did not see the look that crossed Rip's face. But Clay did. And he knew it was often followed by a knife.

Clay's concern about Rip's look was eased when, on their way to the second floor, Pete whispered, "Don't never tell that nigger nothing. He hates my fucking guts."

"Then why . . . ?"

"'Cause I need him and he ain't gon' do nothing. Neither steal, nor squeal. He ain't got the guts. You see, Schoolboy, I'm a hurricane and most of these jokers, shit"—Pete blew an impressive O—"they ain't even a breeze."

The door on the second floor was solid oak. Pete knocked sharply, and Clay heard the sound of sliding metal. The door was opened by Blue, a man Clay had glimpsed, from time to time, at Pete's home. Blue looked down from well over six feet, his muscles showing impressively under his tailored coat. His complexion had given him his name.

This upstairs room was crowded too, but here no one was laughing. Solemn, tight-jawed men studied their cards or followed the rolling dice with greedy eyes.

Pete held another of his brief conferences while Clay watched the flow of the "fins" and "sawbucks" across the tables. Then, with a nod here and a wave there, Pete led Clay down the back stairs to the alley. The shivering men shuffling patiently toward the back door of the saloon greeted Pete in muted semi-reverence while, in the doorway, a barkeeper gave each a cash blessing from the sack of Peter Claus.

Pete was buoyant, Clay silent as they drove to their next stop: Angelique's, a place of tapestries, oriental rugs, and Louis Seize furniture, an opulent, "By Appointment Only" bordello on Dearborn Street. There, fourteen girls, ebony through all the shades of brown, bestowed their favors on white men from the Gold Coast and Lake Forest to make Pete Parker rich.

Clay sat near the door, feeling a shadow of himself, unreal in the harsh reality of these rooms. He heard the crying in the laughter, felt the shudder in the swift embrace, saw the lie sealed quickly with the kiss.

Pete moved quickly, smiling—taking—amid fleeting forms and closing doors. A tray of hors d'oeuvres, a platter of fried chicken, buckets with champagne, bottles of scotch and Bourbon came across the dimly lighted room while a flicker of Angelique's jeweled finger directed Brooks Brothers to a room.

A piano player, Storyville, rolled notes, bass, bass, bass, and nipples and navel and golden brown moved before Clay until Angelique's quiet "No, Melissa, he's with Pete."

Melissa, Melinda, Clay felt the worm in the apple turning in his gut.

Then they were outside in the air again, Clay's eyes averted until, in the carriage, Pete touched his arm. "Look here, Schoolboy, this ain't no town for men with queasy bellies. This is the butcherin' capital of America. Bacon barons and cattle counts . . . and the dudes that run the Levee, down in the First Ward . . .

"Every one of those girls you saw in there is there of her own free will. And let me tell you, I turn 'em away in droves. Down on the Levee now, in them river wards—them Bohunks, Micks, Wops, Kikes? Shit, a good-looking girl go outa her own house for a minute and end up with a knockout drop and sold, for a coupla hundred dollars, to any whorehouse from here to St. Louie.

"I don't keep my gals drugged on cocaine and I don't work 'em till they wore-out wenches. Say what you want, my gals got class. And shit, Chicago runs on vice. Just take a peep at them society columns and see whose elbow rubs with whose."

Pete flicked the reins and glanced at Clay. "Chicago is still the way the rest of America used to be. It's all here for the strong to take." Pete nodded. "There's one thing you gotta remember, Schoolboy. If there ain't no money, there ain't no business, and all the principles just go down the drain."

Clay drew a deep breath, watching the softly falling snow.

"Now"—Pete patted his young companion's arm—"what you're doing is fine, learning all those white-folk theories. You can use it, if you remember how that shit applies to us. Like I told you, niggers got one constant factor, zero. And the interest on zero is zero." Pete gave a twisted smile. "One thing I know for sure, Schoolboy. Absolute power corrupts, but absolute poverty corrupts absolutely."

Pete was silent then until he stopped the horse before a small, well-kept frame house. Wondering what he would behold next this Christmas Eve, Clay followed Pete inside.

The older woman, with quick doe-soft eyes under a black mantilla, had once been pretty. She was Pete's mother. The frail, nervous girl was his sister. They were waiting with their coats on and, as soon as introductions were complete, silently followed Pete and Clay to the carriage.

Pete held his hat as they filed into the church. "Hodie Christus Natus Est," the ancient Gregorian chant, soared from the organ, rolled down to the creche, to the statue of the Sacred Heart. Pine boughs surrounded the fourteen plaques, the Stations of the Cross.

Clay watched as the Parkers began their communion with God, the ladies' hands entwined in their rosaries. A shiver touched Clay's spine as he glanced at Pete kneeling beside him. For he wondered whether his friend was Mephistopheles—or Faust.

However, when school began again, Pete Parker occupied little of Clay's attention, though more and more he questioned the wisdom of keeping that man's books. His hesitation was negated, however, by basic accounting which certified that a break with Parker necessitated a real financial risk. School, study, and work took most of Clay's time, though in the spring, through his attendance at Quinn Chapel, he was drawn into the growing concern of the Negro community with the Columbian Exposition.

The World's Fair, as the Exposition was commonly called, occupied a site adjacent to the university. Despite the attention given the achievements of other ethnic groups, the many requests for Negro exhibits at the Fair had been turned down. The only important Negro in attendance was Frederick Douglass, who had charge of the Haitian exhibit.

A meeting held at Quinn Chapel organized a protest. Among its leaders were Ida B. Wells, who had just returned from abroad, where European audiences had heard her vivid accounts of lynching in the United States, and Attorney Ferdinand Barnett, editor of the Chicago *Conservator*. With Ken and Nat, Clay carried petitions throughout the community where numbers of Negroes lived. And though he failed to share their exuberance fully when a Negro Day was finally proclaimed at the Fair, he did see fully and personally the conditions that had placed a hero's crown on the head of Peter Adolphus Parker.

Another event that spring gave Chicago's Negro community cause for celebration. A man, injured in a street fight with a knife wound near his heart, was taken to Provident Hospital, which had opened two years before, the only interracial hospital in America. There, the young Negro doctor who had helped found the hospital, Dr. Daniel Hale Williams, did what no surgeon in the history of medicine had ever done. He performed a successful operation on the human heart.

The word flashed round the world. By the score, doctors rushed to Chicago, to Provident, to watch Williams's technique.

Nat Moore was ecstatic. For a time he leaned toward medicine. But his work in the laboratory was dumbfounding his instructors. "I'd enjoy being a doctor," he told Clay again and again during days of exhilaration over Williams's achievement. "But research is the foundation of medicine, and I have some theories I have been examining with my professors. Clay, you won't believe this, but I believe, I just believe that I am onto a way of controlling the multiplication of certain malignant cells. Even the head of the department has come twice to see me."

And there were other enthusiasms Clay was feeling in the city. A young Negro named Oscar DePriest, who sounded much like his own father, was making speeches at Ed Wright's Second Ward Club. More and more, Chicago seemed to be the place to be. It was new. It was wide open. Things were happening.

CHAPTER FOUR

1893

In June, Clay returned to New Bedford for the summer. Isaac Woodson met him at the station. Melinda, more beautiful than ever, waited in the door as he came up the walk. But Clay sensed that night and the next day, as they made ready for their summer pilgrimage to the Vineyard, that there were things on his Uncle Isaac's mind that concerned him. And that first night on the Vineyard with Melinda near, he had seen doubt, even anger, in his uncle's eyes. Later, standing by a scrub pine on the beach, Melinda so close he could smell the sweetness of her breath, he broached the matter to her. "I think your father is angry with me for some reason."

"No." Her whisper was like the soft rush of the ocean to the shore. "He just doesn't want me to marry you . . ."

"Marry?"

Melinda's eyes were dark luminous moons. "You do intend to marry me, don't you, Clay?"

"Why . . ." He had thought of it a hundred times, that when he finished school, when he had a job, when his folks were taken care of . . . "Did he say why he doesn't want you to marry me?"

"No. He just said he was glad we were friends, but he'd be damned if it would go further."

A crooked smile touched the corner of Clay's mouth. "And what did you say to that, Melinda?"

"I told him I was going to marry you no matter what he said."

He touched her soft black hair, then looked for a long time at the sea. "Melinda," he said finally, "your father loves you very much." She drew back and he saw fear creep into her eyes. "Melinda." His hands found hers, his face was grave. "I came here because I killed a man. He killed my brother, and I killed him."

The moon slid under a cloud and he saw only her silhouette. Her small breasts were accentuated by the wide band at the waist of her muslin skirt. "So that was it," she said with hushed wonder. "Andy always wondered why you came so suddenly. Aunt Jacqueline said it didn't matter, what counted was you were here." Her arms went around his waist, her head against his chest. "I love you, Clay." Her

voice broke. "I love you. I don't care if you killed a hundred men."
Then she was running away from him, down the beach.

Isaac pursed his thick lips as he watched the two figures standing on the beach. He frowned as he saw his daughter turn and run. Yes, he thought, I must talk to Clay.

Not, Isaac mused as his long fingers scratched his balding pate, that he was not deeply fond of his cousin. Clay was bright and mannerly, but there was much in his nature that was alien, and frightening, to Isaac. There were too many subtle shades, too much beneath the surface, and even in his cousin's quiet half smile, Issac could perceive something volatile.

Clay was too good-looking, too intense. There was about him too strong a sense of urgency. The questioning, the hoping that brightened the eyes of other young men his age had all been resolved and settled in Clay's eyes as wisdom.

It was not the murder that bothered Isaac as much as that his cousin had experienced that which leads to murder, a murder by one whose primary trait was control. The control of one who has looked deep into the eye of life, seen the damage to the brain, and chosen, quite clinically, how he could deal with it.

He had looked too deep and seen too much and paid too high a price, his cousin, to marry the beautiful, sheltered, impetuous girl who was his daughter and the apple of his eye.

However, Isaac's plans for his talk with Clay were dispelled early the next morning. A hastily dispatched boat from the mainland brought the news that Jacqueline, who, in May, had celebrated her one hundred and sixth birthday, had fallen from her bed and been rushed to St. Luke's Hospital. Isaac and his wife, Mary, left immediately. Clay and Melinda waited for her brother Andy and his bride, Elaine, due that day from Boston.

Jacqueline Clavier Woodson had a deep and tenacious hold on life. Though she remained hospitalized all summer and her mind slipped back to the days of her youth, death walked easily toward her door. Isaac remained in New Bedford most of the summer to care for his grandmother, and Mary stayed to care for him. Melinda and Clay, supposedly under the supervision of Andy and Elaine, who had finished Vassar in June, were left largely to their own devices.

They grew closer that summer than they had ever been. Though their time together was often shared with friends from New York, Philadelphia, or Washington whose families also had summer places nearby, they felt no real need of any one save themselves. Melinda was the prettiest girl on the Vineyard, Clay the strongest swimmer. Often, after his duties to the Woodsons were done, Clay was able to make additional money taking the sightseers and the newcomers sailing. Melinda pouted on these evenings, saying that the women chose him because they loved to look at him: his well-made face, his dark wide-set eyes, his brown body, showing lean and hard when his shirt was dampened by an unexpected spray. But Clay laughed at her distress, knowing full well it was the men who chose him because of his skill with the sea.

Picnicking at Fort Phoenix, sailing down to the Bluffs, baking clams on the beach, or hiking alone to find arrowheads and other artifacts left by Indians long gone, Clay found it increasingly difficult not to touch the forbidden parts of his lovely cousin's body. But he knew Andy had placed him on his honor, and honor deserved respect.

Andy and Elaine entertained a great deal that summer. In addition to the Woodsons' Bedford friends, members of the Omar Khayyam Circle, the exclusive Boston literary group for women of color, arrived for a weekend, with what Melinda called "their elitist militancy."

James Trotter, a fierce race fighter, now the Recorder of Deeds in Washington, came with his wife, Virginia, and their son, William Monroe, who at the end of his junior year had become the first Negro Phi Beta Kappa at Harvard.

The attention Andy's Harvard friends paid to Melinda underscored the tension Clay had felt with her father. Bill Lewis, who had played All-American football there and was now in the Law School, and George Ruffin, Andy's roommate, were Isaac Woodson's ideals of a husband for his daughter.

Another Harvard friend of Andy's, who lived out in the Berkshires in Great Barrington, was also a frequent visitor that summer. He spoke often and eloquently of the urgent need for education, for uncompromising Negro leadership. His aristocratic intellectualism, his keen knowledge of Negro history and race fervor intrigued Clay. His name was William Edward Burghardt Du Bois.

It was on a Sunday in late August, only minutes after Clay had left the hospital, when Jacqueline Clavier Woodson gave herself to eternity. Seeing the New Bedford *Morning Mercury*, Clay realized fully what it meant to be a Clavier.

330

For two full days the lines of people moved slowly through the front parlor, where Jacqueline lay in state before the wheel of the *Leah-Alanya* and Papa Jacques's emblem from the *Jacqueline:* the black star, cross, and furled sailboat on the still green-and-red field. For two days, over coffee and tea and glasses of lemonade, the lives of Claviers and Woodsons were relived by descendants of those who had shared them, mixed occasionally with a question about how Isabella had been returned and who were the Dulanes and the Hardwicks inscribed on a Clavier tombstone.

The morning of the funeral, a carriage of extraordinary worth stopped before the door. Even in the kitchen, where he was helping Melinda scour coffeepots, Clay heard the rising murmur of excitement.

He had no need to leave the sink to learn the cause. Within the moment a cousin burst through the door to issue the awed proclamation: "Alexander Kuykendal is here!"

Alexander Kuykendal. Hands flew to heads to ascertain that every hair was in place. Eyes flew over silver platters and coffee urns to double-check their shine. In amazement, Clay watched the flurry in the kitchen, as aprons snatched off by hasty hands failed their aim and, ignored by the usually fastidious, slid to the floor.

Even Melinda, who generally cared little for circumstance, was caught in the stampede toward a glimpse of—a handshake with—Alexander Kuykendal. Within a moment after her mother left the kitchen, she too found urgent business in the parlor. The Woodsons had triumphed over death. Alexander Kuykendal was there.

Clay picked up the aprons and threw them on the chair, remembering Aunt Jacqueline's stories of Nils Kuykendal, the first mate who had been Papa Jacques's friend, of Carl Kuykendal, who had been a captain of one of Papa Jacques's ships, of Alexander Kuykendal, industrialist, Alexander Kuykendal, merchant prince.

They were sharp businessmen, no doubt of that, making smart clothes for rich people. The Kuykendals owned stores in Boston, New York, and Philadelphia, even as far as Charleston and Chicago. They didn't serve Negroes in Charleston and Chicago.

"Clay." Andy was waving from the door. "Mr. Kuykendal wants to meet you."

"For what?"

Andy read the look in his cousin's eyes. He came in and closed the door. "He asked if any of the Claviers were here. I told him you."

331

"So now he knows. The Claviers still live." Clay wiped a platter viciously.

"And you can't say hello to him?"

"It's not that I can't, Andy. I won't."

"Clay, I don't understand. The Kuykendals have been friends . . ."

"Friends?" Clay turned back to the coffeepot and shrugged. "It doesn't mean a thing, Andy. It doesn't mean a goddamn thing." He checked the pot and looked at his cousin again.

"Andy, for two days I've been in and out of that parlor, listening to folks whose families have been here in this town since back before the Revolutionary War, before this was even a country, listening to their glorious remembrances of Papa Jacques and Alexander and Jacqueline and all the rest."

"Clay, for Pete's sake!"

"The same white patronizing . . . We came to show how much we love our darkies . . . And when you get some education, some culture, some ambition . . . It's what you lack that holds you back. And colored folks with brains and ambition rush off by the thousands to buy that shit . . ."

"Make your point, Clay."

"Papa Jacques had ambition. And Alexander. And who in this town had more education, more ambition than my father? The same holds true on your side of the family. The Woodsons are now in their third generation at B.U. Two Woodson attorneys, poor as Job's turkeys, and one doctor, whose wife washes his sheets before he operates on his kitchen table. We eat with knives and forks and know the difference between Mendelssohn and Mozart and can conjugate French or Latin verbs. What I'm asking you, cousin, is how many corporations offered you a job when you finished Harvard Law last June? Or were you just kidding when you said the reason you're still sweating in the tailoring shop is 'cause you haven't had a client yet?"

Clay pushed a silver tray across the kitchen table. "The hell with Alexander Kuykendal and all the rest of them who show up so piously to bury our dead and just as piously turn their faces from our living."

"You have made a very strong point." Clay and Andy whirled to stare at the elegant man standing in the doorway behind the open-mouthed Melinda. "I'm glad of my determination not to leave until

332

I'd met Jason Clavier's son." The man smiled. "And you are his son." He held out his hand. "I'm Alexander Kuykendal."

Andy's face twisted toward explanation, but Clay's eyes met Kuykendal's as he shook his hand. "I'm Clay Clavier."

Kuykendal's eyes smiled. "And I see you wear the medallion." Kuykendal turned now to Andy. "I had heard that you had finished law school, but I did not know your situation. I need good lawyers." He handed Andy his card. "If you'll be in my office in Boston Monday, I promise you I won't piously turn my face from the living."

Kuykendal faced Clay again. "On a table in my office there's a model of a ship: your great-grandfather's ship, *The Voyager,* which my father captained. On the hull of that model, my grandfather carved with a penknife, 'No Clavier ship sails in time of stress without a Kuykendal.' We honor the pledges of our dead."

"Alexander! So this is where you're hiding. I've been looking all over for you."

"Ben . . ." Alexander turned, revealing the benign being now behind him. "Come in. I'd like you to meet Andrew Woodson, who'll be joining my firm on Monday as an attorney . . ." The two men shook hands. ". . . And Clay Clavier, who is at the University of Chicago. Gentlemen, this is Benjamin Oates, governor of Massachusetts."

Jacques Dulane sat facing the open window of his study, his brandy snifter cradled in both hands. On the green rolling lawn of Four Winds, his blond, blue-eyed daughter, Sue Ellen, now four, tapped her croquet mallet expertly against the wooden ball to win the game against her twin brother, Seth.

"It's not fair . . ."

Jacques turned, grinning, knowing Seth's protest, and raised his glass to his lips again.

On the shelves to his right were leather-bound copies of his novels. Jacques smiled. They had become quite the rage. In the still unopened package on the desk in front of him were the galley sheets of *The Shining Swan,* delivered three hours ago from New York. Beside it was the half-emptied bottle of Bourbon with which he had begun the afternoon.

Jacques's attention lingered on his children. No, he thought, no one would take them for anything but white. But taking that nose from Sue Ellen and those lips from Seth, damn, the nigger blood was still hiding there.

His hands shook as he put his snifter on the desk. For years he'd been so careful. Hell, he hardly slept with his wife, Rebecca, at all.

Jacques glared at the ceiling, thinking of her, lying above him, great with child again. No. He gritted his teeth. She would not fail him. She had not failed him yet.

His fingers drummed on the desk as he thought of his wife Rebecca Durham. He had been well into the eighth chapter of *The Gallant Years,* his first published novel, when he married her. Creditors and tax collectors had been hounding him. His lawyer had called to say he would lose Four Winds within a month. In the aftermath of war, women were desperate and fathers anxious. And her father was one of the few rich men left in Charleston. He had talked to his lawyer, completed the scene he was writing, dropped by the Durhams', and asked Rebecca to marry him.

When he heard of her first pregnancy, they had sailed at once for France. Rebecca had hated it, had bitched and cried until her eyes were nearly as swollen as her belly. But he had kept her there until the twins were born. The whole experience had put a strain on the vows of marriage. Rebecca stated flatly that she had performed the wifely chore. And he, delighted with such white children, let her keep her title of "Mrs." without fulfilling fully her marital obligations.

The knock at the study door startled Jacques. "Mr. Dulane," the maid's anxious voice came through the door. "You'd better call the doctor, quick."

Damn! Jacques's fist hit the desk, sending the brandy snifter and its contents to the floor. Damn last Christmas Eve. Last month he should have insisted Rebecca go to, damn it, anywhere. "But why?" she had persisted. "The children," she'd insisted. Damn her. Jacques got up and poured himself another drink.

Maybe he would call that midwife who had once been his mother's maid. The way she and his mother used to correspond . . . That would be the thing to do. Jacques took a deep swallow from the Bourbon bottle, feeling the liquor burn along his throat. He had located her house last month and started to knock on her door. But certainly, after three generations, or was it two? Or none? Jacques took another swallow. Damn that nigger blood was strong.

He heard the scream from upstairs, then, after a minute, the maid's running feet. "Mr. Dulane, please," she pleaded through the door. "It's time, and the doctor ain't here yet."

Jacques stumbled as he crossed the room and unlocked the door. "I'll go up and see her." He hiccuped.

"Oh, m'God," the maid breathed as he staggered toward the stairway. "Oh, m'God, he's drunk."

She looked inside the study and saw the bottles. What if he hadn't called? "Lordy me," the woman whispered as she picked up the phone. "Operator, get me Dr. Mason quick."

Upstairs in her bedroom, Rebecca Dulane twisted in pain. "Where is he? Where's Dr. Mason?" she moaned as Jacques came through the door.

"Take it easy, Rebecca," he said, weaving over her. "He'll be here in a while."

She screamed again and Jacques saw blood coming through the covers. "The baby's coming now. Right now," she cried.

"Mr. Dulane." Turning, Jacques saw the maid standing in the doorway. "The doctor will . . ."

"Get some boiling water and a clean, sharp knife."

"But . . ." the maid protested. Then as Rebecca screamed again, her legs were forced apart. Eyes wild, the maid left on the run.

Jacques sat down beside his wife. He had written this scene a dozen times. He knew exactly how it should be done. He moved the pillow from beneath his wife's head and, as she groaned in protest, turned her legs to the side of the bed.

Perspiration flowed from Rebecca like water from a fountain. She screamed and grabbed the bedpost, holding it with all her strength.

Jacques fumbled in the chest beside him, pulled out a Bourbon bottle and held it to her lips. "Drink it." She turned her head, but he forced the bottle on her. "Drink, damn it," he said.

The maid returned with a steaming kettle and a knife, averting her eyes from Rebecca's nakedness. "All right, get out," Jacques said, starting to the bathroom with her instruments. "I can handle it alone."

He saw the baby's head as Rebecca howled, then her scream choked her and she fainted as the shoulders twisted through. Jacques's hands trembled as he reached to take the baby. "My God," he whispered, "the goddamn thing is black."

He heard the horses coming up the drive and, seizing the knife, cut and tied the cord which bound the baby to its mother.

For still another moment Jacques Dulane's hand sweated on the knife. The boy baby whimpered, not a full cry, and turned his blue-brown eyes toward his father.

"Damn you." Jacques swore as he dropped the knife.

Lifting the baby, he turned him upside down, slapping his bottom until the cry came full. "Goddamn." Jacques clutched the child as he looked in grim confusion at Rebecca, still unconscious. "What the hell should I do now?"

The door chimes pealed. Seizing his wife's silk robe, Jacques tucked it around the still-bloody, howling infant in his arm and sprinted from the room.

"Shut up. Shut up, damn you." He pushed the robe over the infant's face as he ran toward the back steps, hearing the doctor's voice coming from the foyer in the front. He was on his horse with the baby in his his arms before his destination focused in his mind.

"Monique," he shouted as he reached her door.

"Yes?" She frowned as she opened the door and saw the disheveled white man standing there.

"I'm Jacques Dulane. Isabella Dulane's son." He was breathing hard as he pushed past her into the room.

She recognized him from the picture she still kept on her bureau. Her eyes narrowed. "And who's that you got with you, Jacques Dulane?"

He saw her eyes, knew that she knew. "My son." He held the child to her, the robe that covered him dragging on the floor. "Keep him, Monique. For God's sake, keep him."

Monique looked into the tiny face. "Oh, Lord, I'm too old now."

"Please!"

Monique saw tears on the face of Isabella's son. She took the child and held it to her breast. "All right. I'll do what I can. But you . . ."

"I'll send you money."

"Money ain't all."

"What? Anything. Just keep him, and for God's sake, Monique, don't tell a soul."

A week after Jacqueline's funeral, Clay received a letter from Nat Moore. His landlady, Nat wrote, had an opening for a student in the house where he lived. Clay left the next day for Chicago. Two days after his arrival, with the help of the Reverend Jeniffer of Quinn Chapel, he found a part-time job as a porter in the Palace of Fine Arts at the Fair.

Housing and a job provided, Clay went to see Pete Parker to explain his new situation.

Parker shrugged as Clay explained. "So long's you're happy." But Clay thought Pete looked hurt. During the first few weeks of school Clay found time to stop by the three-story house on Axton Street several times for an afternoon hand of poker or a trip by cable car to watch the thoroughbreds at Garfield or the trotters at Washington Park. Then his work began to pile up. Clay determined to make the Dean's list for the second year in a row and, happy in firm friendships with Nat and Ken, had little time to spend with Pete.

The year was generally uneventful, except in the spring, when Ken won national recognition in the 100-yard dash, Clay made the Dean's list, and Nat received his Master's degree, second in his class.

That summer Clay did not return to New Bedford. He could not bear to be with Melinda in such close quarters. He made the resolution in early May and began looking for work to supplement his salary from the part-time job at the Fair.

Clay had experience looking for work in Chicago, but had supposed much of his difficulty sprang from the fact he wanted only part-time work. Not so. Nor even from the new circumstances of only summer work, for he soon concealed that fact from prospective employers.

No, the fact to be faced was that the black man's plight in Chicago differed but little from his plight in Charleston.

Most unions were closed to Negro workers, many of whom had gained skills as carpenters, plasterers, masons, and plumbers building the residences and business places of the old South. Even the steel mills, the slaughter and packing houses, plants with the dirty, stinking jobs, refused work to Negroes, and the new wave of immigrants, using the twin battle sticks of race and religion were moving to take the few jobs left as waiters and butlers, maids, cooks, and laundresses.

It was the middle of July before Clay found a job in a foundry. It was hot, heavy work. He came home so filthy that Mrs. Hunter, his landlady, forbade him entry to her house until he visited the public bathhouse three blocks away.

However, Ken was also working in the foundry. They rode the traction to and from work together, discussing everything—William Stead's *If Christ Came to Chicago;* the Civil Federation's pious, genteel reforms—for whites only; Jane Addams and Hull-House; Clarence Darrow, the people's lawyer; the new philosophy of education advocated by the university's John Dewey; the new economic theories being taught by one of Clay's professors, Thorstein Veblen.

They spent hours discussing the changes in the conditions of their people. Negroes from the upper South, many of whom had held positions of responsibility during Reconstruction, were now fleeing North in what was being called the Migration of the Talented Tenth. Segregation patterns were hardening. A Negro ghetto was being born.

But the one subject that concerned Clay and Ken most, the subject they discussed with increasing urgency, was the problem of Nat Moore.

In the last three months, Nat had been ignored or turned down by all of the forty-seven companies, from New York to St. Louis, to which he had applied for a job.

"If only he hadn't married Oriole," Clay said to Ken one night as they walked slowly toward Nat's apartment carrying groceries. "All of her highfalutin ideas haven't helped him a bit."

"I told him last spring to apply for medical school or doctoral work," Ken answered sharply. "You know they'll let niggers study forever, even though they know they'll never get a job worth shit."

"He could have gotten a job teaching." Clay pushed the sagging wooden door of Nat's apartment building open, then hesitated a moment as he heard the quick scuttling of mice.

"By the time he realized that was his only alternative, all the teaching jobs were filled."

Oriole Beatty Moore, a graduate of Spelman College, where her father, the late Dr. Benjamin Beatty, author and lecturer, had taught history, answered their knock in a silk kimono. Her slender arms embraced the groceries Clay offered with the passion of the starved.

"Now, you all have a seat." She gestured to the wooden crates covered with pillows. "Dinner'll be ready in a second."

Clay glanced uneasily at the silver trays and crystal bowls, wedding gifts, placed haphazardly on the vile green table, the only piece of furniture in the room. "Where's Nat?" he called to Oriole in the kitchen.

"Oh, Clay." Her face was streaked with tears as she reappeared. "I looked again all day yesterday for a job . . ." Her sobbing increased.

"And what happened?" Clay asked gently.

"I'm not going to take a job cleaning toilets in a traction station." Her voice rose and fell hysterically. "I'm not going to let them do that to me." She held out her hands, her fingers spread apart. "You see these hands?" Her slim figure trembled. "They can play a piano professionally. And I have a degree in math. I'd rather starve to death"—her voice rose to a shriek—"than . . ."

"Where's Nat?" Clay asked, getting to his feet.

"He pawned one of the wedding gifts." Her voice was low, a whisper. "He's in the bedroom drunk again."

"Come on." Clay turned to Ken. "Feed him when he wakes up, Oriole. Feed him good."

Outside, Clay walked quickly. "Where're we going?" Ken asked.

"We've got to do something," Clay whispered. "His brain'll be embalmed."

Pete answered the door himself. His eyes frosted when he saw that Clay had brought a friend. "What's up, Schoolboy?" he asked in the foyer, his eyes still covertly watching Ken. Clay, relieved to see none of the semi-nude females or poker-playing males often present at that hour, introduced Pete to his friend. Hearing Ken's now famous name, Pete was most pleased to make his acquaintance. He showed them into his front room and summoned Mrs. Lovey to set the table for guests. As Clay began to explain their mission, Pete lit his cigar and settled into his role of adviser and—the one Clay had noticed developing—that of Clay's older, wiser brother.

Nat's problem, however, lay in provinces where Pete had no power. After a sumptuous supper, accompanied by a continuous stream of Pete Parker's wisdom and followed by a trip to the saloon —during which Clay saw he had taken on new importance in Ken's eyes—they returned home not having helped Nat's situation one whit.

There was nothing they could do. Not that winter. Not that summer. Not the next fall. Nat's drinking sprees became a constant stupor. And finally, he no longer applied for jobs at all.

It was the twenty-third of December. Clay walked slowly home from work, listening to the crunch of snow beneath his feet. Ken had already left for home. Clay cursed softly, dreading the emptiness of the approaching holidays, regretting that friendship demanded he spend Christmas with Nat Moore.

He was halfway up the steps when she burst through the door, her face shadowed by her hooded cape. "Melinda!"

Quickly, breathlessly, she explained that she had come to marry him. It was all quite rational, quite ordered in Melinda's mind. The distance between them, and her father, were their problems. Now Isaac Woodson was urging her toward marriage with a young lawyer who pursued a nightly courtship. "I know you haven't finished school, Clay." Her arms were around his neck. "But you are so close now. What could it hurt if we get married six months early . . . ?"

Visions of Nat popped like firecrackers in Clay's head.

"So you know this girl?"

The plump form of his landlady filled the doorway.

"Yes, ma'am, I do."

"Well, both of you get in out the cold and tell me what's going on. She says she's going to be your wife."

No, she could not stay, not even overnight, Mrs. Hunter declared in outrage. "What kind of decent girl would even think such a thing?"

Well, if they were married, maybe a day or two. After all, her place was for students, not for young folks carrying on.

Clay and Melinda were married the next day, with Pete Parker, Nat, and Oriole in attendance. Two days later, using Pete's most practical wedding gift, Clay found a small apartment with a brick fireplace in the kitchen.

Melinda found a job and, despite the rantings of her father which were delivered weekly by the postal service, the winter passed delightfully.

It was in April, when the rains were coming hard, that Clay came home to find Melinda gasping on the kitchen floor. With the aid of a neighbor who owned a fruit wagon, Clay took her to Provident Hospital. "An asthma attack, a serious one," the doctor said. And, what was more, she was three months pregnant.

For eight days Melinda lay in the hospital while Clay, with no regard for his empty bank account, insisted on the best specialists the prestige of Dr. Daniel Hale Williams could secure. On the ninth day, when he took Melinda home, Clay was more than one hundred dollars in debt.

Their landlord was unhappy when he learned that their rent would be late. The second time Clay signed for the groceries at the store next door, the grocer asked when to expect his money. One way out was apparent—Isaac Woodson—but neither Clay nor Melinda mentioned it.

Rushing from classes to care for Melinda and then to work, Clay told himself that it would be just a short time more—eight, seven, six weeks—until graduation; then, with the three years on the Dean's list, he would find a position that would allow them to pay their mounting bills. By the time the baby was born . . .

A list of positions for prospective graduates was posted on the bulletin board. Nightly, Clay wrote letters, detailing his course work, stressing his high grades, asking for appointments to discuss a position.

The replies at first were enthusiastic. Clay, in a new suit, bought on time from a friend of his first employer at the shoe store, left for his first interview.

The office was on the second floor of a downtown LaSalle Street building. Clay hesitated before the door to still the pounding of his heart. Sixteen dollars a week, and bookkeeping had been his best subject. His reflection in the window satisfied him that he looked the part, and he opened the door with a smile of anticipation at the jolly tinkling of the bell.

The receptionist looked up at him with a gesture of annoyance. "Deliveries are made in the rear."

He looked at her in amazement. Any fool could see that he wasn't making deliveries. Not in his ten-dollar suit. "Excuse me, I believe I have an appointment . . ."

"An appointment?"

"Yes, to see Mr. Anderson. My name is Clay Clavier." He could see his name clearly on the sheet before her.

"You must have made a mistake."
"That position is already filled."
"Mr. Roberts has been called out of town."

". . . no openings . . ."

". . . janitor . . ."

"You're overqualified. It would make trouble with the other men."

"We just don't hire niggers."

For six weeks Clay, careful to keep his job-seeking attire in shipshape order, dashed home between and after classes to clean his celluloid collar with an eraser, to dress, to take yet two more precious "jits" for the traction, to make the rounds of every business whose name appeared on the prospective-employer list.

From white classmates, some quite mediocre students, Clay heard of glowing job offers, often as not from places he had already visited only to be told that the position was already taken.

Melinda, begging to take a job, heard Clay's harsh response: "What are you trying to do to me now, kill yourself?"

Clay Clavier was graduated *magna cum laude* from the University of Chicago. The next day he went to work as a porter in the Palmer House Hotel. There was also, of course, the post office, which traditionally saved the bellies of Negro college graduates. Lawyers and Ph.D.'s found degrees were not discriminated against for letter sorters and mail carriers. But the waiting list there was long and Clay's need urgent.

Clay had written to his father and enclosed a copy of the graduation program, circling his name among the honor students. To his father's congratulatory letter, he replied that he had secured a position of merit and promise.

A week later he received a letter from his sister, Daisy. She had been admitted to Provident School of Nursing. Could she, her letter asked, stay with them her first semester?

"Oh, damn it," Clay shouted as he threw the letter on the table. "There's hardly room in these two rooms for you and me, and God only knows what we'll do when the baby comes."

Melinda placed a defensive hand on her protruding tummy. "Clay, I'm sorry."

"Why the hell should you be sorry?" He was pacing the floor now, the fire in his eyes accentuating the new gauntness of his face. "Or are you saying, how dare we have that kind of hope?" He snatched his tie from the chair and headed for the door.

"Clay?" The veins standing at his temple frightened her. "Where're you going?"

"To work. To say, 'Thank you, suh, for lettin' me tote yo' bag and draw yo' drapes and bring yo' supper. Thank you, suh, for lettin' me graduate *magna cum laude* from yo' university and givin' me this glorious job reflective of my ability and promise. Thank you, suh, for letting my daddy try to reconstruct the mess you made bringing my folks over here to work two hundred years for free to make you rich. Thank you, suh, for breakin' his back because he fought to make the laws you made for real. Thank you, suh, fo' yo' Declaration of Independence and yo' Thirteenth, Fourteenth, and Fifteenth Amendments, which make you feel it's all nicely wrapped and packaged and now you can cast yo' eye around to see how you can fuck up all the other colored people of the world . . .'"

Melinda stood wide-eyed through this tirade. Her Clay, her gentle Clay . . .

"So now, my beautiful, dear wife, I will go and do my thank-you's and you sit here and knit a bunting for our child, and plan the furniture for our place on Grand Boulevard and be certain the maid cleans up the dishes." He turned in the door and looked at her. "Don't be sorry, Melinda. Don't ever be sorry. Just be mad as hell."

The hotel lobby bustled with new arrivals. For nearly an hour Clay, wearing more braid than an admiral, rushed back and forth, carrying bags, pocketing tips. He had four bags beneath his arms when he saw Ken signal from just inside the hotel door. His expression warned he bore no good news.

"Clay," Ken began as Clay approached, then: "We'd better go outside."

Involuntarily, Clay stepped back a pace. "Not today. No more shit today."

"Man, I've got to tell you." Ken's face gave a curious twitch as he touched Clay's arm. "Nat Moore just hung himself."

"Boy, get me a cigar."

Clay watched the dime spin through the air, fall at his feet. Slowly he bent to pick it up, feeling the sharp jab of his wooden medallion against his chest. He rubbed the coin an instant, then sent it spinning back. The man grabbed it automatically, staring as the nigger said quite clearly, "Get it your fucking self."

He was on the street and moving fast, easing it, not forcing it, to his consciousness, until he saw the sign: "Pete Parker's Place."

"Is Pete in yet?" he asked the solitary barkeeper.

The ever-present Blue opened the door. Without a word of greeting he turned his head inside. "Clavier," he said.

"Let him in," Pete decreed with a wave of his long cigar.

There were twenty or so men already at the tables as Clay crossed to Pete. "I'd like to talk with you."

"Private?"

"Yes."

"Okay, Schoolboy."

They went down to the stale-smelling office on the first floor. Pete closed the door behind them. "What's up, Schoolboy?"

"You still want a bookkeeper?"

Pete's eyes narrowed. "You?"

"Yes."

A frown crossed Parker's face. "You sure? I know I've been after you a long time, but . . ."

"I'm certain."

The frown deepened on Pete Parker's brow. "Look, you could end up in jail and . . ."

"I could end up rich. I've been hearing things, and I've been thinking, Pete. There's big money to be made in this town."

"Yeah?" Pete replied, watching Clay's face as he tipped his ash into the butt-filled tray. "And just what you been hearing and thinking about, Clay Clavier?"

Clay leaned across the table, twisting his medallion. "The numbers racket. Policy," he said.

CHAPTER SEVEN

1911

Jacques Dulane, on the veranda of Four Winds, smiled over the top of his brandy snifter at the young people moving beneath the gay umbrellas on the lawn. "It's a lovely party," his wife, Rebecca, murmured at his side.

"Quite." Jacques nodded. "Quite." He raised the snifter to his vein-thickened nose for a whiff of its aromatic liquid. Yes, he thought, he had done quite well for his children.

As Jacques watched his children with their guests, his son, Seth, now in the United States Congress, and his wife, the former Georgia Barret, whose family had produced two governors of the state for which she was named, joined his daughter, Sue Ellen, and the young man who, next week, would be her husband: Jeb Stuart Sykes. Jacques beamed with pride. What matches he had made for his children! Jeb's grandfather, Cary Sykes, had once owned the largest plantation in the state, the Towers. And though the Sykes family had lost most of their land following the Civil War, young Jeb Stuart Sykes was rapidly becoming a power broker in South Carolina politics.

Yes, Jacques thought, he had done well in organizing the marriages of his children. No French, no Spanish, no Italians, no Greeks, no Jews. God only knew what blood flowed discreetly in those veins. But now . . .

In sudden gratitude, Jacques slipped his arm around the waist of his wife. "Why, Jacques," Rebecca gurgled. It was the first time in years he had demonstrated affection. Not since . . .

Rebecca's hands clutched her pearls as she remembered. That awful night so many years ago. Jacques, the doctor by his side when she awoke, saying quietly that the child had been born dead.

"But, Jacques, I heard it crying."

Rebecca's hands trembled at the awful memory of the weeks, the months she had protested until she realized that Jacques would never tell the truth. Until she realized that she feared to know. That she feared her husband, feared his rages, feared his power, feared her

346

lack of recourse as a woman, her disgrace if he discarded her. And that most of all, she feared the truth.

What deformity had been so awful? What idiocy could he detect? Or could . . . ? No. Rebecca forced her mind against that thought. But could he . . . ? Or she . . . ? No—she trembled. No, she must never think that thought again.

But it was not she, she knew that. Rebecca glanced sidelong at Jacques again. No, she clenched her fists, she must not think it. He was her children's father. And the only husband she would ever have.

Rebecca turned as Jacques held her tighter. "My dear, you have done well," he said. He saw the question lurking in her eyes and moved away as an uninvited thought pounded on his conscience. The other boy, Lincoln Grant, Monique had named him . . . Jacques scowled as thoughts of that misbegotten being came to his mind.

He saw Rebecca's quizzical look and, picking up his glass, moved from her side. There was one blessing. Monique had been faithful to her promise not to tell. She had never demanded money, though he sent her some each year. He saw the boy—his son—he glanced back at Rebecca, whose eyes still followed him—*their* son —their tall, thin yellow son—only at a distance. He had never, Jacques now reflected, said a word to him.

Monique had sent him, of all places, to Jason Clavier's little school, where her other boy had gone. Now Lincoln was at Morehouse College. Monique's second son, Gabriel, who had a Ph.D. in history, was a professor there.

Jacques frowned as he pulled a cigar from the breast pocket of his coat. He'd better pay Monique a visit. He hadn't seen her in nearly three years. Damn, Jacques Clay Dulane thought as he bit the end off his cigar, this family was a mess.

Jacques took a sip of his brandy, then, as the thought struck him, turned his head so that Rebecca could not see the liquor splatter back into his glass.

He had never thought of it before. He had never dreamed of giving it to Rebecca. Placing the brandy snifter on the veranda rail, Jacques clasped his hands in glee. It was a splendid idea. "Sue Ellen," he called. "You and Jeb, come here. All of you." He waved impatiently as his offspring, and their guests looked at him expectantly. "I have a wedding gift for Sue Ellen."

"Oh, Jacques. You didn't tell me," Rebecca cooed, hoping the closeness she had experienced a moment ago might continue.

Jacques grinned and took her arm. "Come on in and see."

He seated them formally in the drawing room and, smiling at his inspiration, went upstairs to the bedroom safe. He returned to the assemblage in the drawing room with a velvet box in hand.

It was an occasion, and he made the most of it, having Sue Ellen stand by him and close her eyes. He heard the soft "ahs" as he lifted the pendant from its case.

"Oh, Papa," Sue Ellen squealed as she saw it glittering on her breast. "It's Isabella Dulane's medallion."

Jacques did not see the sudden brightness of his wife's eyes or the sudden firming of her mouth. Nor did he notice as Rebecca turned and left the room.

CHAPTER EIGHT

1914

"I don't know." Monique scratched her gray head slowly as she looked at her son Gabriel's children playing beside her Christmas tree. "I don't know that it's such a good idea."

"But I tell you, Mama, we need a black college here in Charleston." Gabriel pulled off his thick black-rimmed glasses and leaned toward his mother. "Too many of our young men and women can't afford to go away. Tell her, Linc, about the . . ."

"Where you gonna get the money?" Monique asked before Lincoln could speak. "The one thing we all learned these past dozen years is colleges cost money."

"I'm willing to teach for no money," Lincoln said quickly. "And so is my friend Willie Smith, who . . ."

"And just how you all plan to eat?" Monique frowned as she looked at the two faces, one light and thin, one black and broad, looking earnestly at her. "Gabriel, you got three young'uns . . ."

"And a wife willing to help." Monique turned as Gabriel's tall dark-brown-skinned wife, Anna, came from the kitchen to kneel at her side.

"Look, Mama." Anna caught Monique's thin wrinkled hand. "It's his dream. It's all Gabriel ever talked about, a colored college here in Charleston. Just think," Anna smiled at Monique winningly, "your son the founder and the president of a college."

"Well, that's a mighty big dream." Monique's lips made a tight line.

"We don't have to start big, Mama." Gabriel's voice was soft. "I have a commitment of more than three thousand dollars from Negroes here in Charleston already, and I have more than a dozen very able men who are anxious to teach."

"Where you are going to put this school?" Monique asked. "In this house?"

"No. We haven't found a place, and that's a big problem. We'll need space so as we grow . . ."

"You're serious about this thing?" Monique looked incredulously at her son.

"Linc and I intend to do it," Gabe said as he took her other hand.

349

"Jason Clavier has given us the names of two other men who might help. His son, Clay, who might know people in Chicago, and a Mr. Robert Hardwick in New York."

Hmmm, Monique thought, lowering her eyes. And don't neither one a those men owe you a blessed thing.

She stopped as she saw the pink winding road of Four Winds before her. It had been more than fifty years . . . For a long time she stood there, following in her mind's eye the curving path to the big house. She adjusted her shawl and with aching feet started slowly up between the frost-touched pines.

At his typewriter in the study, Jacques Dulane heard the door chimes. He paid no attention, though, until he heard the knock and his wife's voice through the door. Cursing this interruption of the scene he was completing, he yelled for her to come in.

"Jacques?"

"What is it? Damn it, say what you have to say."

"There's a nigger woman at the front door."

"So, tell her . . ."

"She says she's come to see you on business."

"On business?" Looking up, Jacques saw the paleness of his wife.

"That's what I asked. She said to tell you Monique was here, on business."

Jacques's eyes narrowed as he stood. How dare she . . . ? How dare she come . . . ? He saw Monique behind Rebecca in the foyer. "All right," he whispered. "Show her in."

As she closed the door carefully behind her, Monique saw the furious wariness in Jacques Dulane's eyes.

"All right"—his voice a feline hiss. "What do you want?"

Her eyes looked steadily into those of this Dulane. "I want yo' son to have his share of Four Winds."

"What?" He moved like a stalking cat around the desk. "What the hell do you mean?"

"You know well enough what I mean, Jacques Dulane. I done kept my promise to you. I ain't never said nothin' 'bout you or Linc." Monique saw his grandfather in his eyes as he moved toward her. Her hands trembled and she clenched her fists. "But I done wrote a note . . ."

He stopped, looking at her. "Are you threatening me, Monique?"

"No." She kept her eyes, her voice steady. "I just want things set

350

somewhat to right. I done what you asked, and he raised and got his education. Now it's time for you to . . ."

He turned his back. "I want no part of Lincoln Grant."

"And he don't want none a you. Now, I was thinking that plot of land where the quarters used to be . . ."

He turned and stared at her again.

"That's where that Johnson family's croppin' now." She nodded. "It's way outta sight of this house. Where I lived when I was yo' granddaddy's slave. Where my son, Jimmy"—there were tears suddenly on her wrinkled face—"*your* uncle . . ." She heard his sharp intake of breath, saw the sudden new pallor in his face. ". . . was born. Four Winds owes us, Jacques Dulane. Four Winds owes us for your granddaddy's son and yours."

She saw the sudden sagging of his shoulders. "What does he want with it?" His voice came from a hollow soul. "Does he want . . . to live there?"

"Why, no." Monique's laugh gurgled like a spring. "They gonna build a college."

She saw disbelief flood his eyes, then laughter, wild, angry, painful, jerked in spasms from his throat.

"Jesus, Monique." He wiped the tears from his eyes. "You have just delivered the Dulanes the coup de grâce. Four Winds now gives birth to a nigger college."

CHAPTER NINE

1915

Robert Hardwick watched the fog closing about the ships in the silver-gray river as his chauffeur sped the Pierce Arrow up the narrow road along the Hudson. Well, he thought with a grimace, it would be Wilson's headache now.

He slumped back in the velvet seat. He never wanted to think again about the party's needs. The hell with them now, anyway. Twice they had refused him consideration for the highest office. Too rich, too liberal, and then, four years ago, too old.

Robert closed his eyes, then the wrinkles that surrounded them squeezed with his sudden smile. He'd almost had it once, though. Yes, he'd come damn close to the nomination in '08. What a convention! But Teddy had been impossible to beat.

No. The plain fact was, they didn't want him. Had never wanted him. Had stalled him, used him, and, in the end, ignored him. He who ruled a vast cartel, who won to his view Foreign Secretaries and Ministers of Finance; he who had dictated decisions of Presidents and Secretaries of State and who twice, through loans to the United States Treasury, had stabilized the value of the United States dollar . . . But they did not want him to be President.

Robert's gaze followed the young man cycling on the roadway. If only he had a son. But he could never marry again. Not after Isabella. And their daughter, and ambition, had crammed his hours, creating oblivion to the passage of years. His wealth guaranteed in perpetuity, he had begun his long, his futile climb to the pinnacle of power. Twelve years in the Senate, eight in the governor's mansion. Twenty years. How time—that naughty boy—stole life's fruit, youth, and fled.

And then she, his new Isabella, had brought him home: Forest Kuykendal, huge, Argus-eyed. Their marriage had solemnized the great, the colossal merger. Forest Kuykendal—oh, she was her mother's child—whose heart was a ledger book, whose arteries were railroad ties, whose blood was pure Grade A Oklahoma oil.

They were always gone then, the young Isabella and her Forest, in Dallas, Chicago, at their place in Buenos Aires, in Nice, Antigua, or

352

just outside Palm Springs. Robert frowned, remembering those lonely years until their boy was born. In the interest of stability—a child cannot call a ship or three continents home—the young Kuykendals had relinquished their heir, Stephen Hardwick Kuykendal, to Robert's care, to grow up in the security of the Hardwick Place.

Robert had taught the child to swim, to sail, to fish, to camp under the roof of God. He took him deep into the lairs of power, to know, to feel, to understand the men who, with a nod, a word, or with no nod, no word, authorized, denied, and, above all else, controlled.

But more, far more, Robert Hardwick inoculated young Stephen Kuykendal with his own philosophy, with a clear vision of what was right and what was wrong. He immunized him against fear and failure, and above all he transfused the creed of the Hardwicks: that there is a natural aristocracy among men that transcends nationality, religion, race.

Brilliant men, Robert taught his grandson, men of talent and true vision must seize leadership. Humanity across the globe must know a fuller, rich life or else the masses, crushed by an ever more sophisticated world, would bolt from their stupor and press forward the leadership of doom. The New York *Times* had described Robert, to his enormous delight, as the nation's Renaissance man.

The chauffeur turned onto the winding, leaf-canopied road of the Hardwick Place. Robert looked out at the scenes of his boyhood, the woods where once he had walked with Isabella. Once? It was only yesterday.

Too old, was he? Hell, no! Not while blood still surged through his heart. Not while it still flowed in the veins of his grandson. No, he wasn't through. Not yet. He had promised Isabella. He could not help her brother; Jason Clavier had refused all of his offers. He had refused to leave South Carolina, and Robert understood.

If only he had been there when that young man had come. Robert frowned, remembering. He had been in Europe, had not known of it for months. Grant Lincoln? Or Lincoln Grant? His damn secretary could not remember. The only thing he remembered was that a young Negro had been sent by the same Jason Clavier that Mr. Hardwick had tried to convince to come to New York.

He had wired Jason, had wired him right away. It was two days later, after he had called an associate in Charleston, that he learned that Jason Clavier had sold his home and left Charleston.

Robert's frown deepened. But one day he would do something. There were still Jason's children . . .

The lights of the Pierce Arrow swept the great stone front of his mansion. Robert saw the young boy, his grandson, Stephen Hardwick Kuykendal, dashing down the steps to meet him. Robert smiled as he opened the door and held out his arms to the boy. Yes, there were still the children. What else had it all been about?

CHAPTER TEN

1928

Clay Clavier swore as the shaving lotion splashed on the wooden medallion he wore about his neck. Everything was conspiring to make him late today. Jerking the medallion over his head, he rinsed and dried it carefully. Maybe it was lucky. The thought took him to the hall closet and the bottle of furniture polish. It wouldn't do to have it split on him. Not while that whore, Luck, was hiding.

He completed the rest of his toilet hastily, put on his shirt, and with his tie draped around his neck strapped on his shoulder holster. He checked the chamber of his Colt .45 automatic and slid it into the holster. His linen jacket was tailored to hide the gun. He pushed his comb through the thickening gray of his hair, his stetson adjusted low over one eye, he called, "Melinda, I'm gone," and hurried down the stairs.

Melinda . . . Clay smiled as he crossed to the curb. Pete Parker declared he was the only old man he knew still in love with his childhood sweetheart.

Melinda . . . "But policy king, Clay?" she had said. "It sounds so decadent."

"Which?" he had answered with a grin. "The policy or the king?"

But he had seen the questions in her eyes. Had she forced him to this? . . . And that bourgeois Negro notion . . . what would her family say?

Her family? Hell, he'd summoned Andy's Harvard-trained law skills to set up Clay, Inc.

"I don't know, Clay," that pompous ass had begun when he had laid out his plan. "Monies ungainfully derived . . ."

"Shit, nigger." Clay had leaned across his broad mahogany desk. "There is not, nor ever has been, any goddamn ungainful thing about a half million dollars. Now, if you can't handle it . . ."

"A half mil . . . ?"

Clay grinned as he unlocked his car. Ol' Andy. He'd damn near twitched with brilliance.

The Stutz purred to Clay's command, and in a minute he was moving swiftly with the traffic.

He turned off Thirty-sixth Street onto State, passing ex-slave, former lawyer, judge and cosmetics king Anthony Overton's Douglass National Bank. It was the largest Negro bank in the country. Clavier Real Estate kept its accounts there. Honking his way down "the Binga Block," Clay pulled to the curb before the Binga bank.

Jesse Binga himself, medium height, medium brown, stood with a smile as he entered. His greeting, "Mr. Clavier," came with a wave.

Clay returned the wave as he walked toward a teller. His eyes followed the quick dark fingers as they counted three thousand one hundred twenty dollars and fifty-five cents deposited to the account of his Friendship Mutual Burial Association. Next month, if the lawyers were on schedule, it would become the Friendship Life Insurance Company, capitalized at one point four million dollars. In the past fourteen months he had sold two hundred and fifty thousand dollars' worth of stock in the company without setting foot outside the ghetto.

"Thank you, Mr. Clavier." The bankbook slid back under the bars. Clay checked the entry and the total. It was all there. "Thank you, Mr. Jackson."

His pocket watch showed three-fifteen as Clay came out of the bank. The second drawing was over now. It had been at Stella's place this afternoon, just around the corner. Pete would still be there.

Stella's bar was crowded with plaid-shirted men and heavy with the smell of beer. Stella, six foot two of buxom darkness gussied up in orange and yellow, made a gold-toothed smile for Clay and nodded toward the back. That room was crowded, too. A different scene from twenty-five years ago when two runners had picked up the slips and nickels, dimes, and quarters from the shoe store, Pete's Place, and the Twenty-first Street traction station. All thirty-six runners were in there now, receiving their 25 percent cut from the mercury-fingered Pete, now known as "the czar of the Negro underworld." Clay watched as Blue, the czar's Rasputin, placed the three winning numbers back in their rubber tubes and returned them to the barrel.

"Hey, Clavier." It was Flint, who picked up the payoff for the cops and the necessaries in City Hall. "Big hit today, eh? Lady with four kids came in from Glencoe, a year's savings in her handkerchief. Hit the combination." Flint smiled his bag-man smile. "Well, she can kiss Miss Anne goodbye and buy a six-room house." Flint's eyes squinted nervously. "Uh, you got a little extra for the precinct captain? He got his eye on that new Packard."

356

With practiced eye, Clay approximated the day's take after all payments were appropriated. It was in the ball park. He and Pete usually split between eighteen and twenty-three grand each day. Every day. Six days a week.

He turned to Blue. "Drop five C notes on Flint, and . . ." He turned back to the man in the green-and-white flagstone suit. "Flint, tell your captain we'll be operating east of Wabash Street next week. I'll expect a return on the favor." Flint grinned, nodded, and took. That's the way things were, Clay thought, in "Hinky Dink" McKenna, "Bathhouse" John Coughlin, and "Big Bill" Thompson's town.

Pete had once said, "Any man who is willing to make money any way can make it in Chicago, if he's got the guts." It was not true, Clay thought, but there sure was truth in it. Hell, by the time his first child, Paul, had been born, he and Melinda and his sister, Daisy, who had been studying nursing at Provident, were living in a nine-room apartment.

Clay had not shared Pete's passion for flamboyant living, for the high-life circuit—Miami, New Orleans, New York. He had been careful with his money. Never again would his family want.

First had come the apartment buildings on Indiana and Cottage Grove. Then the mutual burial association. By the time that boy Lincoln Grant had come, with the letter from his father asking for a donation for that school—Christiana University it had become—he had been able to shell out fifty thou. It was a deal, a three-way deal. The money would go for the Jason Clavier Administration Building, and his father and mother would leave South Carolina and live with him in Chicago.

Two weeks later he had bought the fifteen-room stone mansion on Grand Boulevard. Jason had come to spend hours, gentle, wise hours with his grandsons, Paul (for Paul Laurence Danbar), William Edward (for Du Bois), and Jay (who was Jason's namesake). And at long last Clay had wiped those secret tears from Melinda's eyes. For despite Clay's posh real estate office and his small accounting firm, the whisper was abroad that he had linkage with the underworld, the "shadies." Many of the snotty society bitches whose friendship Melinda longed for did not think her "quite suitable."

No, Clay thought, he wasn't being fair. They weren't snooty. They were proud. Proud of their men who had won hard victories the right way.

357

Men like Theodore Lawless, one of the world's greatest dermatologists. Lawless had studied at many of the great medical centers of America and Europe. Now crowned heads of Europe with medieval titles, the rich, the famous, and the powerful sat side by side with everyday folk in his South Side office awaiting their turn for his skill.

And the colonel of the famed all-Negro 8th Infantry Regiment, Dr. Spencer Dickerson, a University of Chicago graduate. Dickerson, an eye, ear, nose, and throat specialist, was now on the staff of Rush medical school.

And Claude Barnett, founder of the Associated Negro Press, and his wife, the Broadway star Etta Moten Barnett.

And Frank Gillespie, who had founded the Liberty Life Insurance Company, and Robert Cole, born in a log cabin in Kentucky, who had founded Metropolitan Life.

And Walter Barnes, who played with the Chicago Civic Orchestra, and Maudelle Bousfield, the first Negro principal of a Chicago high school—Wendell Phillips.

And Ted Jones and Robert Jackson and so many, so many more . . . Oscar DePriest, who had just been elected to Congress—the first Negro congressman from a northern state. The first Negro congressman since Reconstruction.

Yes, Clay thought, Chicago was the place to be. And even if Negro society ignored him; he had power—in the bank.

Clay scowled suddenly, remembering the single event of Negro society he had longed to attend. One of their clubs had sponsored the great Negro tenor Roland Hayes in concert. He and Melinda had not received an invitation. Clay bit his lip as he remembered it. Who said you couldn't remember pain?

He had gone anyhow in his white tie and tails. Clay grimaced, remembering Melinda's face as he put his white silk scarf around his neck, her voice so soft, so anxious. "But, Clay, aren't you even going to tell me where . . . ?"

Yes, he'd gone to the concert. A sawbuck had gained him permission from a stagehand to stand in the wings. In the center of the stage Roland Hayes stood in the floodlights, his hands clasped before his slender body, as his song, born in pain, born in wisdom, rose in perfection from his dusky lips: "Little boy, how old are you? Little boy, how old are you . . . ? And Clay saw him then—saw him clearly on his roan horse . . . "Little boy, how old are you . . . ?" Clay closed his eyes. ". . . He said, 'I'm only twelve years old . . .'"

358

Clay had not heard the remainder of the concert. Silently he had stumbled to the door. Five minutes later he was in front of Royal Palm Gardens—the first, the only time in his life he had gone looking for a drink. From inside he could hear the hustle, he could hear the sweet sorrow of Satchmo's horn. He was heading toward the door when the scarfed woman stopped him.

"Mr. Clavier." She let her shopping bag fall heavily to the ground. "Mr. Clavier, I was going to have my preacher write you."

"Yes?"

"I'm Mrs. Lewis." Her face, her voice were sweet. "Don't you remember, with three little tykes?"

"Yes. Yes. I remember."

"I wanna thank you, Mr. Clavier. My landlord told me you'd paid my rent these last three months." She'd held out her hand. "I got a job now. We gonna make it from now on."

For a moment Clay had looked at her. Then, with an almost gasping sound, he'd pulled her to him in a fierce embrace.

"Why, Mr. Clavier!" She'd flushed. Then, "Why, Mr. Clavier, you're crying."

He had felt the tears then. "No, not really, Mrs. Lewis. It's just sometimes it hurts a little." He smiled and touched her hand. "But, goddammit," he had said hoarsely, "everybody's got to have some kind of dream."

But with Jason Clavier's arrival things had changed. His father had been in Chicago less than a week when Robert Abbott, publisher of the strong, militant Chicago *Defender* and himself from St. Simon Island off the coast of Georgia, had learned of his presence. Abbott himself called, seeking an interview with "one of the greatest, one of the most fearless leaders of our race." Surprisingly, Jason had agreed. A week later the *Defender* carried a full-page story telling of Jason's work in Reconstruction and of his father, Alexander Clavier's "monumental" efforts in the cause of abolition. Melinda had danced in glee as they received invitations to the Appomattox Club, the elegant Assembly Ball, the glittering Forty Club, the stupendous parties of Jesse Binga in the ballroom atop his bank. It was then that Pete Parker, instincts ever keen, had insisted that Clay have no more to do with the day-to-day administration of policy but turn his energy and training to making their loot legitimate.

That Clay had astutely done. Pete's holdings were at least diversified. Clay had added real estate to his partner's penchant for nightclubs, cleaners, a theater, and now, to Clay's chagrin, a baseball club, the Joplin Jazz, which had played the mighty Birmingham Black Barons in the American Giants' park on Thirty-fifth Street last week.

Clay had funneled his own wealth into the burial association and real estate. Clay grinned suddenly, remembering the biggest real estate deal of all. With three hundred thousand dollars ticking like a time bomb in his dresser, he had arranged the purchase of a luxurious fifteen-story apartment building on North Lake Shore Drive. He went there only twice a year, to check the state of repair, viewed by janitors and tenants alike as the maintenance man from the landlord. Not even the management company which monthly sent the check to Clay, Inc., in New Bedford dreamed who the owner was.

"That's all, boys. That's all." Clay's reverie ended as the czar in silk pin-striped suit dismissed his court. Pete, Clay, and Blue were alone. "You get my message, Clay?" Pete's hair was white, but his smooth, brown face was ageless.

"I got it."

"What do you say?"

"We gotta meet them, Pete."

"We could . . ."

Clay met his eyes. "We can't. The courts have decreed that Negroes won't rule crime. We know what cards we've got. We make the best deal we can. What time's the meeting?"

"Eight. My place."

"I'll be there."

Evening wore a light breeze off the lake. The summer streets were crowded. Clay knew the talk: politics and policy, baseball and bullshit, *their* musicians, their writers, their poets. The Duke and the Count, Noble Sissle, Fletcher Henderson, Countee Cullen, Claude McKay, James Weldon Johnson, and Langston—"Whadthathipmothafucka Hughs say today?"

A young boy pedaled his bike slowly through the crowd, looking up at the open windows above the stores. "Put your head out the winda, get yo' *Defenda*."

A lot of people had, Clay thought. Robert Abbott, probably more than any man, had been responsible for the "Great Northern Drive"

360

of 1915 that had spurred thousands of Negroes to leave the boll-weevil-stricken farmlands of the South for job opportunities in the North.

Under Abbott's ingenious direction, Negro Pullman porters had circulated the *Defender* throughout the South. Negroes had read and found hope. Agents from industries in the North, hard-pressed for manpower by the war, had arrived in southern cities with tickets in their pockets for Negroes to come North.

At first amenable to these proceedings because of its truculent economy, the South had soon recognized that the foundation of its economic life was fleeing. Job agents had been barred from many cities. In some the punishment for possession of the *Defender* had been imprisonment.

Clay wondered what the headlines were tonight. The NAACP's legal battles. The Urban League's employment battles. The Negroes' endless battles. The Chicago *Whip* was organizing a "Don't Spend Your Money Where You Can't Work" campaign. And Elijah Muhammad, "the Prophet of Allah," had come to Chicago.

The smell of barbecue and fried fish was on the air. The sound of music was everywhere. Louis "Satchmo" Armstrong and "King" Oliver were at the Royal Palm Gardens. Erskine Tate's orchestra, featuring Earl "Fatha" Hines, was at the Vendome Theater, and in front of the Grand Terrace, the Sunset Café, and the Pekin Theater, limousines from the North Shore were already easing to the curb. White folks had discovered the South Side with a vengeance.

Sound conspired with smell, and smell with sight, and sight then with the summer night, until longing, long-forgotten dreams, half formed, forsaken; life, half lived, forbidden—fused and became one central thought: his family and himself.

A summer gathering on Martha's Vineyard: the Woodsons and the Claviers celebrating the eighty-fifth birthday of Isaac Woodson and Jason Clavier's long-postponed trip back home.

"Never," Isaac had pronounced, "has there been such a time."

Clay had brought his family from Chicago. His mother and father and his sister Daisy with her six children and her doctor husband. Melinda, bubbling with happiness, was reunited with her family, thirty-five of whom still lived in New Bedford.

They came from New York that summer of 1914—Peter, Andy's oldest son, a doctor—and from Providence—Carl, Andy's second son, a merchant seaman. And both of them had children.

From Washington a Woodson cousin who played the sax and, so they whispered, "smoked 'rabbit tobacco'" came with his noisy progeny. And Andy and Elaine came from Boston with their third son, Clarence, still in law school, who too had begun the business of begetting.

It was the first time all had been together, and they performed the rituals of tribe, the younger testing their strength and heroism, swimming, diving, sailing, while the elders sat in council on the state of the family and the race.

They were all, the Woodsons and the Claviers, supporters of the ideas and strategies of W. E. B. Dubois's "talented tenth" and adamant critics of the "separate fingers" of Booker T. Washington. "Telling a race to lift itself by its bootstrap, when it hasn't even a boot," Andy, one of the founders of the Niagara movement, raged.

The work of the Urban League found its place on their discussion agenda, as did William Monroe Trotter's all-Negro and strongly militant National Equal Rights League.

They had much to talk about. In twenty years nearly three thousand Negroes had been lynched. Woodrow Wilson's administration had begun the segregation of government employees in the federal bureaus of Washington. A new shade of brown was advertised in New York stores as "nigger brown."

But despite Booker T. Washington's "Atlanta Compromise," Jack Johnson was fighting, Mat Henson had helped lead Peary to the North Pole, W. C. Handy had written the "Memphis Blues," and Carter G. Woodson had formed "The Association for the Study of Negro Life and History."

On the fiftieth anniversary of the Emancipation Proclamation a tally had been taken. Despite the stupendous odds, implacable foes, lynchings and burnings, despite rigid segregation in every area of endeavor, the Negro was fighting his way forward.

Seventy percent of the Negro population was literate. Negroes owned more than half a million homes, nearly a million farms, conducted more than forty thousand businesses, and had accumulated more than seven hundred million dollars.

Yes, there had been a great deal to discuss and a great, great deal to plan. They were a long way from equality, but the slow wheels of justice had, at least, begun to grind.

And with each setting of the sun, clams baked and the lamp from the lighthouse flickered over the beach, the old stories of Jacques,

Moses, and Anton, of Alexander and Jacqueline, were retold around the fire.

It had been, they all agreed as they stowed their bags on the ferry that would take them to the mainland, a most memorable event. They would, they promised as they kissed their goodbyes, meet again in two years. But life—and death—interceded. It would be many, many years before they gathered at the Vineyard again. For, from places never heard of on Thirty-fifth Street or Lenox Avenue came the march of booted feet. Answer, black men, hasten. The world must be made safe for democracy.

Clay gripped the steering wheel of the Stutz, remembering his oldest son, Paul . . .

The 370th U. S. Infantry, made up of Negroes from private to colonel, had received more combat citations than any other American regiment in France. Twenty-one Distinguished Service Crosses, sixty-eight Croix de Guerre, and one Medal of Honor.

They had sent Paul's body from the Marne River in France to be buried next to Jason and Suzanne in New Bedford.

And Dr. Peter Woodson, Andy's oldest son . . .

The 369th U. S. Infantry, the Harlem Regiment, bivouacked with the French, was the first Allied regiment to cross the Rhine. It fought for one hundred and ninety-one days under fire. It never gave up a foot of ground. It lost but one soldier through capture.

There was nothing left of Peter to bury.

Oh, yes, white folks had remembered that Negroes, denied almost every chance of living, were very good at dying.

Then had come the "red summer" of '19. Race riots had swept the country. The whites were afraid that blacks who had fought to keep the world safe for democracy might want to try a little for themselves at home.

But, Clay nodded to himself, there had been a difference in '19. Black men had grabbed their guns and clubs. And while their women prayed and cheered, black men had fought back.

Then had come the desperate early twenties. There was no need for the Negroes brought North by the tens of thousands to man the factories of defense. The white folks were back again.

The churches, the Urban League, the NAACP, had done heroic work, holding the Negro community together, keeping the children and the elderly fed, fighting for jobs, for a chance to enjoy the democracy so many dark young men had died to save.

Clay arched his back as he turned onto the Outer Drive, his gaze lingering on the soothing blue waters of Lake Michigan on his right. The meeting, in an hour now, would be a bitch. He wanted to be cool, collected, to keep his mind on his goal. Pete always said remembering was dangerous for niggers. A small smile touched Clay's lips. Not so. He had good memories, too. A lot of them.

William, his loquacious son, graduating from Morehouse with a desire to preach the gospel. William had done his graduate work at Boston Theological Seminary, then served as assistant minister in a small church in Evanston. William Clavier had won to his "practical religion of today" philosophies the admiration and devoted following of the younger members of the congregation. However, his eloquence and charisma, his biblical interpretations—"the gospel according to St. William," one of the pastors had said cryptically—had threatened the ruling men in black, and his tenure there was short-lived.

William had decided then to start his own church. But Clay, understanding that after prayers come payments and having detected in his handsome son a strong "Pete Parkerism"—a tendency to exploit the good sisters wheresoever they be found—promised to underwrite the "business," a nomenclature on which he insisted, to William's disgust, when his son demonstrated an ability to handle the practical side of religion in a manner commensurate with his eloquence as a preacher.

It took three years. Then Clay gave his son his blessing—in cash —and sent him on his way back to Boston to do the Lord's work.

And Jay . . . It had been Clay's hope that one day the Friendship Insurance Company would belong to Jay. But that was not Jay's decision, and Jay had never, since his decision to run track rather than play baseball at Harvard, doubted a decision he had "thought through." And Jay had thought through many decisions.

For Jay Clavier, life had a purpose, and its purpose was to make life better, and that was a serious business for serious men, in which category Jay graciously included his wife, Annette.

Life was a series of convoluting disciplines which must be dealt with both separately and jointly and always precipitously and exactly.

Jay Clavier was both brilliant and tenacious, but, Clay thought, "exactly" was the key to Jay's character. He had been the first man in the Ivy League to run the 100-yard dash in exactly twelve seconds, and he had represented the United States at the Olympic Games in Paris. His son, Clay smiled, had fallen from his hard standard of "exactly" only six times at Harvard, "A" being the measure by which one knew a subject exactly.

He liked such sports as golf—the second shot on the third hole—and drank each evening, before dinner, two shots of scotch with three cubes of ice, in his favorite glass, a Harvard glass with "Veritas" inside the crimson triangle.

While in Cambridge, Jay Clavier had been much impressed with William Monroe Trotter's militant Boston *Guardian* and had given that paragon of protest a year of service after his commencement in 1925. However, the *Guardian*'s financial position was precarious—had, in fact, been precarious for years. Indeed, the very appearance of the *Guardian* on the street—and Trotter had missed but one issue in twenty-four years—seemed due to an alchemy of its own. Trotter was old. He had no children, and it had been young Jay Clavier's conviction that the tradition of the *Guardian* must survive.

He had written his father asking him to invest in Trotter's troubled paper. But Clay knew of Trotter's lack of forceful diligence in collecting his bills. Sensing a stone wall in this matter, Jay had come home with talk of starting a newspaper of his own.

He had attended Northwestern's Medill School of Journalism while his wife, Annette, a Fisk graduate, worked on her Master's in sociology at the University of Chicago.

Medill accomplished, Jay worked first for the Chicago *Bee* and later for the *Defender*. The last year of his "apprenticeship" was spent with the new, militant Chicago *Whip,* whose readership was the working class of the West Side, getting an exact grip on the many facets of the Negro population.

William's return to Boston had signaled to Jay the time for his own. Six months after his brother, Jay Clavier made his departure with exactly the same cash blessing for his "Veritas" as his brother had received for his.

With both sons in Boston, Clay and Melinda went East twice a year. Melinda's mother had bequeathed the land where the lighthouse stood to her daughter. The house on Arnold Street had been left to Clay in Aunt Jacqueline's uncontested will. Little by little, Clay and Melinda had once again begun to call New Bedford home.

They had searched the old house together, finding in the attic the yellow, decaying logbooks of Jacques's voyages, Alexander's careful diaries, and Jacqueline's meticulous account books. They discovered letters and mementoes and scrapbooks and clothing and, carefully covered with old spreads and blankets, Noni's cracked and peeling spinning wheel, the wheel of the *Leah-Alanya,* and the splintering captain's chair of the *Jacqueline.* Neatly stacked beside the chimneys were chairs, desks, bed frames, and children's toys nearly two centuries old.

And, as they had as youngsters, Clay and Melinda investigated the dusty, cobweb-filled "secret passage" under the stairs, coming finally to the cornerstone, a stone quite different from the others. And, because electricity had never been introduced to that region of the house, they knelt and read the inscription by candlelight. "Fm my 1st house, pu'cd from J. Rotch by me Oct. '72; ds'td by British Oct. '78; set here by my hand May 14, 1784. J. Clavier."

They had never decided not to sell the house. They had just stopped talking about it . . .

Clay slowed his speed for the turn off the Drive. The Stutz rolled past the row of limestone Grecian women serving with spartan stoicism as part of the colonnade for a vast neo-Grecian structure. It had been built as the Palace of Fine Arts for the Columbian Exposition. He had worked there as a student.

More than three decades had passed since the art treasures from around the world had been packed and returned to their owners. The abandoned, empty Palace had stood amid the Exposition's decaying buildings, used again only for a few years to house the Field Museum. Now called, colloquially, the Rosenwald Industrial Museum, it was being rehabilitated along the lines of a German museum to become the Museum of Science and Industry.

Museums. The mementoes of man's passage. The few, collected accomplishments from the million-year struggle to climb out of the animal condition.

Well, Clay flipped the car's sun visor down as he came off the curve and headed west again, there would be no mementoes of his passage for museums. A life hard lived. The long war fought. A wife, three sons, a grandson.

For a moment Clay's mouth parted in his old half smile. His grandson. His namesake. A new Clay Clavier.

Clay had steadfastly refused Melinda's pleas to give one of their sons his name, insisting that they bear the names of great Negro men. But Jay, his stuffy son, had named his firstborn Clay.

Clay's jaw tightened as he gripped the steering wheel. No, he didn't have any mementoes of his passage for museums. He had a living one. And he would teach him, teach him the truths not found in books, the truth of Jacques Clavier: "Freedom is only a word until you have what you need to maintain it." And damn it, he would give this Clay Clavier, all these new Claviers, their shot.

Clay eased the Stutz under the gold-lettered canopy, "Pete Parker's Palace," then sat a moment fingering his medallion. What would old Jacques do now? He would have known that someday it would come to this. That one day the nickels, dimes, and quarters adding up to millions would decree that the syndicate intervene. Well, old Jacques, that day is now.

Clay got out of the car and went up the fake-grass steps and through the glass double doors. Pete's office was beyond the brass-studded door on the left.

The carpet was thick, deep blue, and wall to wall. Pete swiveled slowly in his black leather chair behind a vast mahogany desk at the far end of the room. Blue stood beside the window. "Come in, Clay." Pete waved his long cigar.

For a moment there was silence, Pete studying his ash, Blue, the drive beyond the silken draperies, Clay studying them both. Pete broke the silence. "We can't let them in, Clay."

"Shit, Pete, they're in. They are in. And it's nobody's damn fault but our own. We didn't have our shit together. We had the street. We had the money. But goddammit, we didn't organize."

"Clay, we can still . . ."

"Pete, we can't do shit. Those cats are hungry. Hungry like you were, like I was twenty years ago. Remember that pain that gnaws its way from the belly to the brain? The things it made us dare to do back at Pete Parker's Place, before we thought we were ready for a Palace? We thought we had it made, and we got careless."

"We weren't careless, Clay."

"We didn't get what we needed. We didn't dig down and solidify. We didn't build an organization."

"You gone organization crazy." Pete shifted his gaze from Clay to the ashes of his cigar, then looked at his partner again. "Look, they hit us, we do them. An eye for an eye. Right on down the line."

367

"Pete, this is no to the strong, to the brave game. This is a command decision, an official decree. No Negro will rule crime! If we stay alive, the cops'll bust us. The courts will sentence us till Resurrection Day."

"Living mean that much to you?"

"Not living. Winning."

Pete wet his lips. "Spell it, Schoolboy."

"Look, Pete, we're both millionaires, at the least. Fight them and we won't have a thing. This isn't the time for guts, Pete. This is the time for smarts." Clay leaned toward his aging partner. "Pete, they can make a dozen charges stick. Gambling, bootlegging . . . hell, you just beat that prostitution beef last year. It's over, Pete. Over. We've got to gather up our marbles and get in a new game."

"I don't like it, Clay."

"Hell, I never liked it. But I did it. And as of now, we've done what we started out to do. We got rich. Now we've got to make rich work."

Blue turned from the drapes. "They're here."

They came into the room, three men: Italian, Chinese, Jew. Pete offered drinks. They accepted. "Gentlemen," the one called Valenesco said softly, "you understand that this is purely business."

"That's why we're here, gentlemen." Clay's hard half smile. "To carry on the American tradition. To do business."

Book Six

THE HURRICANE
HOUSE

I returned, and saw under the sun, that the race is
not to the swift nor the battle to the strong . . .
nor riches to the men of understanding . . . but
time and chance happen to them all.

Ecclesiastes 9:11

CHAPTER ONE

1978

"Clay! It's political suicide." Clay heard the concern in Dave's voice and turned from the rain-spattered window of his office in the Rayburn Building to look at his friend.

"Listen to me, man." Dave's wiry brown arm shoved a clearing in the week's accumulation of *Congressional Records,* legal reference books, notes on bills that would soon come before Congress, then he sat down on Clay's broad walnut desk. On Dave's right in front of the floor to ceiling bookcase stood the flag of the United States. On his left, in the blue shield on the gold-framed white field, the Indian, arrow down in the symbol of peace: the flag of Massachusetts.

"Look, we've been friends nearly thirty years, and you know I'm going to give it to you straight." Dave pushed his horn-rimmed glasses up the broad slope of his nose. Behind the thick lenses his eyes seemed enormous, all-knowing. "We've been in Washington now sixteen years. Sixteen goddamn grueling years, building a tiny niche in the political power structure. Clay, don't blow it. You've got a hell of a fight on your hands just to blast that education bill out of committee. Look, stick with fighting for that . . ."

"Education, health care, housing, and South Africa have got to be our priorities, Chief," a second voice ticked somberly in the large gray room.

Clay rubbed his jaw as he turned from Dave Edwards, his administrative assistant, to the third, younger man in the room. Pepper Dee, in stocking feet on the edge of the cowhide-bound couch, had the title of legislative assistant.

"All right, South Africa too," Dave said curtly. "But damn it, Clay, leave big oil alone. Forget that speech you're planning for this afternoon. Let Sykes get that damn offshore drilling bill through, even if it fucks up environment from here to kingdom come. He's the one who's holding up your education bill now. Look, you've got to try to work out some sort of compromise."

Clay turned back to the window, leaving Dave's words to the unrecording edge of consciousness. Below him on Independence Avenue a group of school children armed with umbrellas and rain caps

371

against the Washington spring rain stared as their teacher pointed out the House Office Building, then moved on in the drizzle, a solemn double line toward the Capitol. They'd been told, Clay knew, that in these buildings were the men who made democracy work, who protected their rights and their freedoms.

He closed his eyes, letting his mind escape this time, this space, to travel to another where it could relax and gather strength. A day, a day just before World War II on Buzzards Bay. A day in those days when he was known as Skipper with his grandfather, Clay.

"Port, hard on the tiller, Skipper. We're heeling over."

The sloop sprang to the command of the tiller, and Skipper had seen his grandfather's grin as they threw their weight to the lee side of the boat, ducking as the mainsail swung over their heads.

"All right, Skipper," the old man had called. "Now loosen them all the way. We'll need to catch all the wind we can. We don't want to try to run through Quick's Hole on the riptide."

The old man, Clay Clavier, watched as the boy made his way forward, nodding approval of his handling of the ropes. "Another five or six years," Clay said, "and you'll be able to sail with the best of them."

A motor launch careened across the bay, and the boy's lip curled in disdain. "That requires no skill."

"It requires skill, Skipper, but not as much as sailing." Clay's voice was gentle, but firm.

The boy shook his head. "It's taking the easy way out, letting the machinery do the work instead of using your own mind." His dark brown eyes squinting, he looked at the flag atop the mast of their boat. The black cross and star on the red-and-green flag billowed above the sails. "Now, that's a sight to see."

Clay reached for his pipe to hide his amusement. He was being quoted, but he knew his namesake well enough to know that thought had preceded repetition.

They came out of Buzzards Bay into the smoother waters of Vineyard Sound, sailing easy with the other's silence, in the way of those who know each other well. Not that Skip didn't have a flair for words, Clay had thought. No, indeed. Clay had heard him read his class paper last spring in Boston entitled "On Looking Toward War." The subject was of no surprise to Clay. The boy was inundated with history and politics at home. But his style! He had sounded so much like his uncle the Reverend William Clavier that Clay had nudged Melinda, whispering, "Whose child is that? William's or Jay's?"

"Jay's," she had whispered back. "Only Jay would pay that much attention to detail."

But the boy had his uncle's flair for oratory, no doubt of that. And as manliness began to replace boyishness in his face, Clay had seen the pattern of William's lean and sensual handsomeness. However, the intellectual stamp was Jay's. The boy had his father's passion for scholarship, for getting things exactly right. There were times, Clay had confided to his wife, when it was enough to drive you nuts.

For it was Clay who had answered most of his grandson's first probing questions into the shades and meanings of life, holding him by the hand those glorious summer days as they meandered around New Bedford, spending time in playgrounds, libraries, barbershops, poolrooms, and Henry Woodson's sailmaking place.

As their boat moved across the Sound, Clay leaned against the stern, easing his hat forward to give shade to his eyes. Yes, he thought. He'd been right, he had long ago decided, not to discuss his holdings with his sons. Let the money lie, getting old and legal. Both William and Jay knew he had an interest in the Friendship Life Insurance Company and that he owned several buildings, but neither minister nor newspaper publisher realized the extent of their father's wealth.

And all of it was legal now. Clay smiled his old half smile . . . the documents in the sea chest in that room beneath the stairs. The dummy corporations and holding companies Andy had set up so that, by the time the tax-free dollars trickled back into Clay, Inc., in New Bedford, they were as clean as Ivory Flakes.

Clay clicked his pipe against his teeth. Yes, it was best, to wait until his money could be turned over to someone who could, and would, maximize its power.

He looked again at his grandson, busy with the ropes. "Skipper, have you ever thought what you'd like to be when you grow up? A newspaper editor? A minister?"

The boy had turned and, as he leaned toward him, Clay had seen on that young face an intensity he had once known years ago, talking to a man named Pete Parker. "You've thought about it, Clay?"

373

On that brown face, the Clavier half smile. "I think I'd like being President," Clay had said.

"Clay?" Dave hopped off the desk. "Are you listening to me?"

Clay opened his eyes. The children were gone. In their place demonstrators against apartheid in South Africa. Youth's dreams. Maturity's realities.

"Look, Chief"—Pepper's voice was soft, appealing—"avoid the oil issue. Everybody knows . . ."

"Damn it, you know as well as I do that I can't." Clay scratched his hand through the gray hair at his temple. "It's not just oil, Pepper. It's the total scope of what's happening in this country. Every minute of every day, power moves further from the people. More and more it's squeezed into the hands of a few. Oil is just our symptomatic target . . ."

"For a symptom, you've been hitting it damn hard," Dave snapped.

Clay shrugged. "Okay, Dave, you suggest another approach."

"I'm suggesting that you know they're out to get you. I'm suggesting that speech you're planning is the kiss of death. I'm suggesting that you stop and think, if you want to come back to Washington next year. Frankly, I've begun to like it here. Damn it, think, Clay. It'll be a long, long time before another black man gets the power you have. There's a hell of a lot you can do with it. A hell of a lot that needs to be done. Let this one go, Clay. They want it and they'll get it. Damn it, everybody already knows where you stand."

"Look, both of you." Clay's voice was low, intense. "If Sykes's bill passes, the Atlantic coast from Massachusetts to Georgia will become an oil coast. Rigs, refineries, petrochemical plants lining our shoreline, red-brown filthy oil slicks ruining our beaches. Offshore fishing, most marine life, will be gone forever. Millions of acres of resources leased with no assurance of protection for the public interest. We'll ruin and devastate our entire eastern coast for fuel resources the Academy of Science assures us will be completely depleted in twenty years—before the turn of the century."

"Great, Chief." Pepper moved to the edge of the couch. "Use it when you speak for Fleming in the Connecticut primary next month. Use it in Delaware. Use it in Maine. But not on the floor of the United States Congress. You know what the response of Louisiana, of Texas, of the other oil- and gas-producing states who've already

374

suffered environmental damage will be . . . the East must share that burden or let their asses freeze . . ."

"If I can say it in Connecticut, I can say it in Congress. Hell, I'm equally opposed to the provisions of that bill for oil-shale extraction and strip mining in Wyoming and Montana. Over a time that may be even more damaging to the environment than drilling on the outer continental shelf . . ."

"Look, Clay." Dave put his hand on his friend's shoulder. "Big business is on your ass. On your ass hard. You fought to strip away the depletion allowance, to extend oil price control until 1984. You muscled through that low that industries with government contracts can't move their plant from industrial inner city sites without a show-cause hearing." Or, Clay thought, without a minimum of eighteen months' notice to its employees, and mandatory rehiring of all employees willing to relocate.

"And," Pepper said quickly, "that addendum to the Howard Act." The Howard Act allowed the elderly to apply for emergency funds of up to eighteen hundred dollars and lowered their property tax to two percent of their yearly earnings.

"Quiet as it's kept," Dave interrupted, "you were the one who got Spence Tucker's student tax bill out of committee." The Tucker Act mandated a maximum of 8 percent taxes for students whose salaries went to finance education.

"And, Chief," Pepper continued, "you were the brawn behind Cathy Campbell's so-called housewife bill when it went before the House." The Campbell bill stated that corporations must hire 20 percent of their working mothers at three-fourths time so they could be home when their children returned from school.

"And who picks up all those tabs? Who?" Dave removed his glasses and wiped his face like a Baptist preacher at a revival. "I'll tell you who. Big business."

"Dave . . ."

"No, damn it. Now, you look, Clay," Dave stormed. "Most of the world's oil is found, produced, and sold by twenty-seven mammoth, vertically integrated American companies. Big oil is big, big, big. Their portfolios are highly diversified. They control not only energy-related enterprises—fifty-five percent of U.S. uranium, twenty percent of the nation's coal production, the low-sulphur western lignite coal in the Dakotas and Texas, a quarter of a million acres of shale-oil lands in Colorado and Utah—they are everywhere. Hell, Gulf even owns Ringling Brothers. And you want to keep fighting them? Jesus Christ, Clay, face reality."

"Not fighting them, Dave," Clay said softly. "I'm fighting the laws that allow big business to get bigger and at the same time make it increasingly impossible for the little man to have anything—his own business, even his own home. Dave, if things continue as they are, we'll see the day when the corner pool room is part of a multinational conglomerate.

"Look around this country. What do you see? What do you hear? What do you read? Our society is falling apart. And big business, big big business, is in a position to stop it, if they only would. The problem with our kids, the only long-range resource of any nation, is that they've peeped it. They see the lies and limitations. Look around you at the zooming expensive cheapness of our quality of life. Plastic, neon-lit, computerized, violence-ridden greed-motivated . . . I have to stop that bill if I can, Dave. I've got to."

The lights around the outer circle of the clock on the wall above Pepper's head lit up as a buzzer sounded. "Damn." Clay reached for his file. "It's quarter to twelve already. Let me get back to the committee before they leave for the Hill." He grinned as he saw the grim look on Dave's face. "Hey, don't worry. I promise nobody's going to shaft that education bill."

Dave watched silently as Pepper put on his shoes and followed Clay from the room; then, closing the door behind them, he sat down on the couch. He reached for the brown bag he brought each morning—to Pepper's chagrin—and fumbled in it for the yogurt and cheese. He needed that quick energy. He'd really slowed down this last year. Tired, exhausted most of the time. For the third time in a week Dave reluctantly admitted to himself that he was getting old.

But hell. Forty seven wasn't old. Not really. Not with the expected span of life these days. No, Dave thought, it was the way he'd lived these past seventeen years. Dave frowned. It seemed impossible. But it had been seventeen years since he'd gotten that damn phone call from Clay.

CHAPTER TWO

1958–1962

Dave Edwards had cursed as his new Chevy convertible bounced through the gully. "Slow down, Dave," he'd mumbled. "You know these Cape roads are a bitch." But in a moment his speed, like his excitement during those last twelve hours on the road, had been on the rise again.

Twelve hours, all night long, just because of one question on the telephone. "Hey, Dave, can you make it up to the Vineyard tomorrow morning?"

Yes or no. That was the way Clay Clavier saw life. Go or no go. The bottom line. And all that shit in the middle was just that, shit in the middle. And so there he had been, grimy and tired, driving down that defeated, sandy road at that ungodly hour of the morning.

The summer crowd was gone then. The brilliant flash of New England autumn had already brushed across Cape Cod, leaving its essential nature, bare, exposed. Gray clouds, gray sea, tall sparse spears of grass blowing against the gray Cape Cod sky. Gray clapboard houses, their white shutters like whitecaps on the gray Atlantic.

In many ways Clay was like the Cape, Dave had mused. Solid, secure in his tradition. Earthy, unassuming, whimsical Clay. But, Dave had grinned suddenly, Clay could be flamboyant too, as flamboyant as those Gay Head cliffs, the destination of this crazy midnight ride.

As he scratched his vicious night's growth of beard, Dave remembered that he hadn't even been shaving when he'd first met Clay. Jesus, what a yokel he'd been, sitting on the ledge above the steps of Widener Library trying desperately to feel as though he belonged at Harvard.

Two "colored guys" had passed by him, looking urgently Harvard. They hadn't even seen him. He'd never been one to attract attention. Oh, well, he had decided, mentally brushing off the hurt, he'd just have to wait, as he had in high school, till he blew their minds with his brains.

High school! Dave rubbed his eyes as he remembered. He had grown up, the youngest of six children, on his father's small farm eighty miles from Durham, North Carolina. When he was twelve, his mother's sister, who taught music in the city, impressed by his yearning for scholarship, had won his parents to her conviction that the city schools were the place for him. She was right. The entire Negro community, it had seemed, was mobilized to surround, protect, encourage, nourish its bright and promising youth, treating its young scholars with the deference and respect, yes, even the adulation paid to the athletic young in the Middle West. All the little speaking engagements in the Negro churches, all the little awards from the Negro businesses, all the proud looks and handshakes had built the confidence, the aspirations, of the Negro young. And when the word had come that Harvard had awarded him a scholarship, the church, the lodge had awarded scholarships of their own. And then, that last day before he left for school, his grandmother had broken open her piggy bank, started fifteen years before, and put three hundred dollars in his hand.

And so, Dave nodded slowly as he checked the route signs, he had been sitting on the steps of Widener library when he'd first seen Clay coming across the yard, book bag on his shoulder, that lopsided grin on his face. Dave had recognized him instantly from the pictures in the issues of the *Crimson* sent to him in Durham—Clay Clavier, football, writer for the *Crimson*. Clay Clavier, a man who did things at Harvard.

He was tall, lean, and agile like a good wide receiver ought to be, suggesting poundage rather than carrying it. "Hey, ace, what's happening?"

Dave had hesitated, wishing he could make the hip words sound right. Then he'd shrugged. "I don't know, man."

"I'm Clay Clavier." The handshake, like the grin, was genuine.

"You have any special reason for sitting there?"

"No. I'm just getting used to this place. Uh, my name's Dave, Dave Edwards."

"Come on, then, Dave. Let's walk over to the Square. You got time for a quick beer and to meet a few of my friends?"

"Why not?" For the first time Dave had felt secure enough to be cool. And crossing the Yard at Clay Clavier's side, he had felt for the first time as though he belonged at Harvard.

The attendant at the Woods Hole ferry had driven Dave's car onto the boat for the crossing to Martha's Vineyard. It was the last leg of the trip. Dave had stretched the muscles in his back as he walked up the stairplank. The twenty-minute boat ride would relax his exhausted body. The sea wind would be a tonic to his mind. He'd smiled as he leaned on the railing. What a fantastic place to call home!

As Martha's Vineyard had emerged from the horizon at Woods Hole, Dave recalled the first time he had taken this trip, ten years before. Clay had invited him down.

What a time that had been—he and Radiz, that skinny, haughty, handsome African kid from some colony Radiz had called Gambana but which had been listed as the Slave Coast in every book Dave had ever read. Intense, concerned, intellectual, Radiz Senatuma. He was Prime Minister of Gambana now.

And Harold Henderson, the Milledgeville wizard, a Georgia nigger who, rumor had had it, had received the highest college board exam marks in his freshman class. He was one of the six Negroes in Clay's class. Well, old Harold was at IBM, working his slide-rule magic to increase their profit picture.

Karim-al-Fatami, Clay's roommate, had been down that weekend too. The son of some Middle Eastern sheik, he was another econ major. But, Dave thought, in retrospect Karim had sho' nuff economics to think about! None of them knew then that a billion barrels of crude awaited Karim's return back home.

Clay had been definitely into charming them all, into being the centrifugal force that held all things together, making everything look easy with that special hubris all his own.

The boat had touched the wharf at Oak Bluff. As the few passengers descended the stair plank to await the cars emerging from the belly of the ferry, Dave yawned and stretched. The road now would wind through the center of the island, avoiding Edgartown, Menemsha, and Chappaquiddick, the tiny fishing villages, sloping gently, steadily up until it swept out along the magnificent cliffs of Gay Head and, a short distance from there, the summer home of the Claviers.

Dave had kept the car at a leisurely pace, sensing the New England complacence in the neatly harvested fields, letting his mind roam back to Harvard, to those years, those secure years with Clay and Harold. Preparing themselves for the demands of progress, certain, so certain that the force of their intellect, reason, and ability would snap the man-made chain of color and let them soar in the beautiful and spacious skies of their certain and inalienable rights.

They had been, above all, Harvard men, proud of that tradition and the right they had won by their intellectual prowess to be a part of it. They had been there, at the best school in the nation, because they were among the intellectual elite, because Harvard had recognized in them those values—and Harvard was high on values—ranked the most important among civilized men.

Their classmates had by and large, reinforced this belief. Much too civilized not to be liberal, scorning the crudity of prejudice, they could, then, afford the luxury of mocking the very myths that so many, years later, would perpetuate their power; myths that kept both blacks and whites in semi-slavery.

Harvard! The subtle lessons on the realities of life. Dave had shaken his head, remembering those not so few young aristocrats, heirs apparent to thrones of power beyond the dreams of Napoleon or Caesar. Dave, the perennial chronicler, had chronicled them all. His mind had gone beyond the dim, glass-bottomed labyrinths of Widener, through all the assumed rules of perception. He had seen the sons of the barons for exactly what they were—sons of the barons. And, being from the south, he had known that they could never be friends because they could never be equals, at least as America defined equals—by the blood and at the bank. The trick of being "in," though, had been to play equals, in itself another humiliating concession to the rich. It was, Dave had often thought, like when he was a boy—little white kids and black kids playing together in the South (although at Harvard the little black role was played by the poorer white boys too)—feeling good together until that day when, in the heat of dodge ball, Elliot Randolph Lee's mama called him home. "Now, Elliot Lee, don't play with the little niggers any more." Dave knew white folks. He avoided them.

But Clay somehow had the ability to normalize relationships with them. Clay, with his mischievous eyes and crooked grin, seeming to laugh at, rather than with. And through the insistence of his good friend and fellow writer for the *Crimson,* Keith Kuykendal, Clay became one of the few black members of those bastions of flinty snobbery, the Hasty Pudding Club and even the shadowy Porcelain Club. But he had his money and—much more important—class. The white boys had been safe with him, the rich slightly amused, the poor a little mystified.

Following graduation—and a long debate with his family—Clay had entered the law school. It was a compromise with his family. His father's dream had been that Clay would take over the *Gazette*. His Uncle William, whose only son had been killed in the war, had pleaded long and eloquently for the ministry. And his uncle, Clarence Woodson, then ambassador to Liberia, had insisted that Clay "think long and hard about the State Department."

His field was international law, though he had done intensive work in constitutional law as well. That last year in law school, as "important" law firms had picked and chosen among the cream of his class, Clay had spoken of himself often and bitterly as the "fly in the buttermilk" everyone was pretending was not there.

And then, suddenly, it had been over—the most privileged years of their lives—sheltered in the quiet peace of Harvard's Yard and Harvard's libraries, protected by the magnificence of the Pax Harvardiana, embraced by the illusion of good fellowship, of each man for his fellow man, immersed in that heady atmosphere where spirited issues and arguments were decided not by brute power but by debate and logic in which Mistress Veritas judged blindly victory or defeat. Suddenly it was over. Veritas turned her lovely head. Lady Randolph Lee called her sons home for grooming. And all of Harvard's little black bastards were thrust blindly out into the land of the megalasaurs.

"Fair Harvard, thy sons to thy jubilee throng."

Dave shook his head, remembering. They had been set up to be fucked.

He had picked up his M.A. in history and become a nigger again. For seven months he had been in psychic shock—who gave a fat rat's ass about values or brains or degrees in niggers' hands unless they were into education, social work, preaching, or burying? Then Howard University, the "capstone"—were not, in the end, the Negro universities the saviors of Negro brains—reached out, as Howard had so often, and plucked another of her black sons in to safety.

Strange . . . Dave had peered through the settling fog, trying to remember whether it was the right or left turn that led to the Clavier place—yep, it was the right—he had been thinking of Clay that first day he crossed Howard's campus. Clay had always called D.C. "fun city," said that the most beautiful girls were at Howard, the most elegant at Fisk.

But Clay had been five thousand miles away by then, stationed in

Casablanca, a navigator in the Strategic Air Command. Clay had used those years to visit African countries on furlough time. His Uncle Clarence Woodson's diplomatic connections and Clay's own friendship with the powerful Senatuma family became passports to interesting visits with the coming black men of power and to understanding at least some of the problems of the nations they would soon govern.

He had written to Dave of a weekend in Beirut when he had met Karim, then Prince Al-Fatami . . .

Clay, that lucky bastard. A wave of resentment had swept through Dave, followed abruptly by a series of more sobering thoughts. None of Clay's articles, those many articles concerning the problems of colonized people striving for independence, had appeared in a single leading American journal, despite their lucidity, their insight. Not a single magazine had been interested then in that young black man's enormous ability to dissect black men's problem and, discarding the extraneous and tangential, zero in on the crux of the matter, to understand which solutions would heal and which would merely patch.

It had seemed that—with what the brothers were into at home—Clay's best bet would be to line up a career in the State Department.

But then they had discovered oil in Gambana. Before any of the big American companies had known who was who in Gambanan oil, which village elders controlled what or whom, what was polite and what was Bogarting, Clay, with the aid of Radiz, (whose family had a finger in the big oil puddle), had struck a middleman's deal between a major oil company and the newly formed Gambanan National Petroleum Company. "Providing the American company with one hundred thousand barrels of crude a day for seven years," Clay had told Dave on an enthusiastic trip to Washington, his share of one cent a barrel would make his company $362,000 a year.

It had lasted less than a year. Less than four months. Then the steady pressure of the big oil companies started to take its toll. Oil meant money, and they had no intentions of having any maverick contender in the big white hunter's new lush African hunting grounds, especially not one who might have a long-range advantage.

Clay's black petroleum company had been ground under, despite the efforts of Radiz, while corporate scions at lavish banquets had repeated with the robot's sharp conviction, "We have to do something to help colored people. An affirmative action program to help Negroes help themselves."

382

Dave had been married to Christy by then. He had been married two years and at HEW one. Health, Education and Welfare, the Negroes' Pentagon, promised a decent future, and Dave was learning the nuances of political Washington. But excitement and vitality seemed to be seeping out of life, replaced by the authentic prestige of plastic cards, stereophonic sound, and full-color fantasy.

Clay had called him about two weeks after his last African trip. They had talked at length about a reunion, when and where and how good it would be. But for months it didn't happen. Clay, reluctantly in his Uncle Clarence's law firm, was starting to build his practice. His articles on Africa were now appearing in one or two scholarly magazines and he was going with a girl—it was the first time Dave had known Clay to admit a real attachment to any woman—whose name was Diana Patterson.

It was in October when they had met in New York—Dave and Christy, Clay and Di. Clay had been subdued, most un-Clay-like. It was only when they had bucked the crowd to Yankee Stadium, to watch the great Jim Brown play football better than any man had ever done, that Clay had shown any real enthusiasm, pounding one fist into the palm of his other hand. "It's those wind sprints, that discipline, baby."

Dave smiled, remembering. What a day that had been. One of those incredible balmy New York days, with just a hint of winter in the air—one of those days when you believe that you will stay young forever.

They had left Yankee stadium to go to Harlem's Seventh Avenue, to Jock's Place to eat. Next door to Jock's, in front of the Red Rooster, they had seen Adam Powell, "in all of the glory of his beauty and power—right before their eyes," surrounded by his entourage.

Then Di had wanted to see Dinah Washington at the Apollo and Christy had wanted to see Nat Cole and the Copa and he and Clay had wanted to oblige them both.

It had been after two oclock when they arrived back at the hotel and, hating to let it end, they sat around Clay's room saying the same old things about politics and some brand-new things about a brand-new thing called "the movement." Dave had read of it, isolated reports in the Washington *Post,* and the *Jet* and *Ebony* pieces. But Diana had been there, had spent the summer in Alabama. As she talked, her voice softening her incisive analysis, Dave had felt the

383

heady rush to become a part of what Di called "the war on the last frontier."

Dave had gone South, to Christy's horror—"What about the payments on the carpet?" she'd protested. "What about the payments on the car?"—anxious to participate in history. And he was pleasantly surprised months later, when the jails were full, to hear in a church basement headquarters a field marshal of the movement shouting, "Get Clavier on that phone!"

Then had come Clay's tough peer trials by the brave young SNCC freedom fighters. "Clavier?" What kind a name is that?" "I mean, where is your blackness?"

And Clay would flash that crazy grin against their skepticism toward his bourgeois mannerisms. "Hey, brother, you've done your part. How about letting me do mine?"

Dave's car had bumped to a stop before the Claviers' summer home. The door had flown open and, before Dave could get out, Diana, tall, slender, and brown-sugar brown, had run down the steps to meet him. "Dave, you made it."

"You knew I would."

"Clay's down at the beach. Come in." She'd tucked her arm in his. "I'll fix you something to eat, then run down and get him."

"And have me wait another hour to find out why I've been breaking the speed limit in four states all night? The food can wait. Unless you want to tell me what this is all about, Mrs. Clavier."

She'd blushed. The name had still been new. "No, I think Clay wants to tell you himself."

"You can't give me a gentle what is it?"

Smiling, she'd shaken her head. "Not even a gentle one. Except maybe, he's counting on you—a lot!"

A lot! That had been the story of their lives these past two years, Dave had thought as he walked back toward the road. And it had all seemed to happen so quickly. But no. Dave kicked a stone ahead of him, it hadn't happened quickly; not really. The new black consciousness had been like a flame smoldering in the brush, igniting here, catching there, burning for a long, long time before someone had finally shouted, "Fire!"

Maybe the founders of the NAACP had furnished the first cross-wind. Maybe it was the early political forays. Or just the very life breath of black men and women. But, by the Depression, you could smell the smoke. The house, divided, was on fire.

Had it been the Great Migration with its sudden concentration of blacks in the urban North and the new beginning of black political awareness that had begotten a change in the name of the political game?

Had it grown out of the dream and organizational genius of Marcus Garvey?

Was it the Negro press, ever watchful, ever militant?

Or the sudden surge of pride black men had felt as they huddled around their ghetto radios to hear Joe Louis preaching equality with his fists, or hear of Jesse Owens humbling Hitler with his feet?

Was it Asa Philip Randolph, in 1941, mobilizing one hundred thousand Negroes, ready to march on Washington, and FDR hurriedly signing Executive Order 8802 banning discrimination in war industries and apprenticeship programs?

Or the fact that a lady named Eleanor Roosevelt had been in the White House, too?

Was it the 99th Pursuit Squadron, trained in segregated units at Tuskeegee, flying their butts off in the death struggle high over Italy, or black soldiers storming up beaches called Anzio and Normandy?

Or William Dawson showing blacks how to build political power? And Adam Clayton Powell showing them how to use it!

Was it Rosa Parks, who said "no," she wouldn't move, and Daisy Bates, who said "yes," the children would go to Central High School?

Or those men of the Supreme Court—Earl Warren, Felix Frankfurter, Hugo Black, William O. Douglas—who read the Bill of Rights and believed?

Was it the arrival of black leaders of nations at the United Nations Building in New York and on Embassy Row in Washington—men like Kwame Nkrumah and Sékou Touré—who blew forever the myth of mumbo-jumbo king of the Congo?

Or the three men who had been the black man's embodiment of blitzkrieg—the most phenomenal legal brains ever combined in one century for the onslaught against injustice: Charles Houston, William Hastie, Thurgood Marshall?

Was it Martin Luther King, Jr., and Floyd McKissick and James Farmer and the brave cadres of SCLC and SNCC?

Or a group of students who'd said, "Shit! We've had a fucking 'nough. I mean, what's so sacred about a sandwich, Jack?"

But, whatever, it had been on—in the streets, at the lunch counters, on the buses. And though the North had tried hard to keep attention focused on the South, it was as plain as a ghetto that Messrs. Mason and Dixon had not defined the boundaries of ugliness.

So what new thing could Clay Clavier be into now? Whatever, Dave had thought, it had better be worth the hectic ride up here. Then, as he had rounded the curve and seen the lighthouse ahead, Dave had known for certain it would be.

CHAPTER THREE

Clay had been sitting on the rocks that formed the seawall for the lighthouse, watching the whitecaps dashing against the breakers below. His thoughts commanded his attention. Clay did not see Dave until he was almost upon him, moving cautiously, like a true landlubber, well inside the jagged edge of the promontory.

"Dave!" Clay had sprung to his feet, moving with the surefootedness of a cougar, then grinned as he saw the look on Dave's face.

Clay's smile had halted Dave's movement. It had still been open, still lopsided and wide, but there had been a tightness in Clay's lips and in his eyes. Dave had averted his own eyes and let his words come slowly. "I know I've said it before, Clay, but this is some view!"

"Want to go up top?" Clay had jerked his head toward the top of the lighthouse.

"That would be great. It's been years."

They had walked slowly, not talking at first, feeling the goodness of the place ease over them. Dave knew its history. Clay had brought him here on that first trip to the Vineyard. It must be good, Dave had thought, to walk on land that has been in your family from time immemorial. "As long," the Indians had said, "as grass shall grow and rivers run . . ."

They had shouted "hello" to John Woodson, the lighthouse keeper, Clay's cousin. Three generations on his side of the family had tended the lighthouse.

"The white folks are still ripping off even the little bit of land the Indians have left," Clay had said curtly as they entered the dank wooden building and started up the steeply winding stairs. "The government is allowing land to be sold off without permission of the members left of the tribe, in direct opposition to the non-intercourse act. The Free Lands, the land reserved to Indians for fishing and farming, are being grabbed up as summer residences for rich white folks."

"The Indians are fighting it . . ." Dave began.

387

"Hell, yes, they're fighting. I'm trying a case for them right now. But trying cases isn't enough, Dave. We've got to get to where the real power is, to where the laws are made." Clay slowed his steps as he heard Dave panting behind him. "I swear sometimes I don't believe it. The whites murdered most of the Wampanoag nation. Now they're saying there aren't enough of them left to make a decision as a tribe.

"And not only the Wampanoag on Gay Head, but over on Mashbee too. There the white folks in New Seabury even want to keep them off the beaches."

"A lot of them have intermarried," Dave had said quietly.

"Of course. What the hell do you expect when a nation has been all but exterminated? But damn, if you got a drop of black blood, you're black. But when that 'bad' blood entitles you to something white folks want, all that shit gets dropped fast. They ought to fight. And damn, if there is any justice, left, they'll win. It's their land."

They had come out into the sudden sharp blue of sky and water.

"My grandfather always liked this place," Clay had said, leaning against the rail.

"Yes, you can really think up here." Dave leaned next to Clay and waited. It would be an announcement, a special announcement. Clay had always prefaced them with a reference to his grandfather.

But Clay had not been announcing that day. His emotions rushed like water over rapids. "Just so far and then BOOM! The door slammed in your face by—goddamn, you don't know whom. Look at us, Dave. Look at us! What're we doing with our lives? Is this all— this nothing—that our forefathers worked two, three hundred years to get? I've tried to do something, something really worthwhile, something that will mean something. Something to vindicate the years of work, of training, my parents', my grandparents' dreams. But everything I've touched my black hand to . . . Boom, that door is slammed and, like in a circus mirror, every damn thing disappears."

Dave had listened, saying nothing, his eyes fixed on Clay. Yes, he had thought, they were essentially in the same boat, frustrated and full of potential. He nodded slowly as Clay went on.

"Hey, do you remember Bernie Frank? He lived in Kirkland House with me. Well, by the sweat of his brain he built up a gigantic leasing company. He was making big, big money. He wanted to take

388

over a WASP bank. You know what they did to him? Shit, they spanked his butt with so damn many legal hassles he ended up in bankruptcy."

It had been a raging, cold, gray desperation, like the pounding gray Atlantic a hundred feet below. Whitecaps of fury tossing mountainous swells of rage. To be resigned to this mediocrity. Well, they had underestimated Clay Clavier. He was still grinning, but the grin was eerie with terrible disappointment and a tidal wave of purpose.

Dave had never seen Clay like this before, Clay with a need—that was it—Clay with an unfulfilled need, with a gaping, bleeding battle wound that you could drive a tank through. A wound, Dave had thought, like his had been at Harvard before Clay had tucked him in. A need born of wanting, wanting so desperately to belong where you belonged.

It was the need felt by every educated, every ready black man, filled to the brim with tales of power and dreams of great deeds done, by every black man suddenly thrust, like a small rodent, into this terrifying world of the megalosaurs. Creeping, scurrying through the frozen waves of time, history, and destiny—other men's time, history, and destiny—to their little burrows. Boasting, bragging, bullying, like all oppressed and powerless people, with each other about some meaningless deed, some beetle smashed, some small nut or leaf scavenged from that terrifying world.

Suddenly Dave had seen it. They were equals. Clay, the world had decided, was just another nigger. A very special nigger maybe, a very lucky nigger, without a doubt, but just a frustrated, dreamless nigger, like himself or Christy or Harold . . . or Jack or Bubba or Deduck, or Jabo or Rap or Huey or Angela . . . Dave's mind had boggled. For the first time a profound sense of love for Clay engulfed him, a sense of love that could only come from true understanding, from a fellow seeker, from another nigger, from an equal.

Dave watched silently as Clay twisted the chain that held his wooden medallion. Then Clay's eyes met his.

"I'm going to run for Congress."

So that was it! A small smile touched Dave's lips as he met Clay's eyes. Yes, that would be Clay's best way to use his family's name, strength, and contacts. Dave knew that was why Clay had called.

For a moment Dave had struggled to find historical importance for this decision. He decided there was none. Organizational implications, his other framework of reference . . . Dave's eyes narrowed. That could be interesting.

But Dave found himself trying to talk Clay out of it.

"No, man, my mind is made. Look, Dave . . ."

Dave knew what was coming. Shit, Clay wanted him to run the rapids with him in his crazy dream. Down there in the house was a woman, Clay's wife. And back in D.C. was another woman, Christy, his wife. His woman, a little dizzy perhaps—a little screwed up by now—certainly. But wasn't that just her defense, wandering through this weird world of the megalosaurs? Wasn't it just her way not to see the huge heights of the cliffs, the jagged menacing rocks in the trail?

Dave had looked at Clay again, saw his need freezing into driving purpose, determination to go the course. "Those wind sprints," Clay would say. "That discipline." Or, Dave had thought, as his own grandmother would say, Clay had "the Calling."

Shit, why not? Together they had a chance. Stop fighting those lonely, futile battles in the burrows. Band together and crawl out. Crawling, clawing, scurrying together, they might find a territory and defend it from Tyrannosaurus Rex. The Irish had done it. And the Jews. And the Italians. There was still another frontier.

And Dave had known he was ready.

"You know, it'll take a miracle to get you elected," he began thoughtfully. "You know, better than I, how thoroughly Mayor Curley's regime screwed up any chance of a black man winning any office in Boston. Boston doesn't even have a Negro councilman. The City Council, the school committee are all elected at large, which gives the whites an overwhelming majority."

"But not the congressman."

"There's no real Negro organization to speak of . . ."

"That's why I need you, Dave."

Dave had looked at Clay for a long moment, assessing everything he knew about his friend, about the political arena Clay intended to enter.

"You'd be running in the Roxbury-Dorchester district, right?"

"Right?"

"You'll have to get past Kelly in the primary."

"Kelly has to go, Dave," Clay had said quietly. "His voting record stinks. He's pushing for further involvement in South Vietnam. He acts like a goddamn lobbyist, not for the textile or watch or shoe manufacturers who are a part of his constituency, but for the big oil interests.

"He was against the Peace Corps. He's made some very derogatory statements about the Latin-American Alliance for Progress. He voted against increased Social Security and medical aid to the elderly and the blind. The damn fool even said the Berlin Wall is a good idea because it'll keep Communists out of Europe."

Dave had listened silently as Clay lined up his ammunition. "Kelly's gone space crazy. He thinks the way to stand up to Khrushchev is to resume nuclear testing in the air. I mean, Jesus!

"He endorsed and pushed the McCarran bill. He tried to block Adam's appointment as head of the Health, Education and Welfare Committee . . ."

"Yes." Dave had nodded. "He's really trying to shaft Powell. But then a lot of them are. They don't want to see that much power in any black man's hands, especially a black man who'll use it." Dave scratched his cheek. "I don't know, Clay. Kelly was one of the early strong supporters of Kennedy, and they can't afford to forget it. Of course, Kelly's record is shaky, and it wouldn't be politically expedient for liberals to support him fully in a district that has that many blacks, against a black candidate. Not after the way blacks supported Kennedy. But they won't exactly be shouting, 'Go, Clay!' either. What they'll probably do is gently shake both trees and see which brings down the apples. That district's about thirty percent black, isn't it?"

"About thirty-five."

"How many registered?"

"Seventy-nine percent. The Kennedy election helped a lot."

Dave had pulled off his glasses and wiped them thoughtfully. "Unseating an incumbent in times like this is always tough. Kelly has a lot of chips to draw in. And, let's face it, a lot of your would-be constituency think they're doing fine. They don't want to start raising issues. They're as Boston as baked beans!"

Clay had listened quietly, knowing it was Dave's way to get rid of the negatives first.

"It takes a lot of money, Clay. You'd be starting from scratch. Well, maybe not quite scratch—your father and uncles are influential, and your appointment to the Human Relations Council could help. And, of course, your articles . . . I read that last one, by the way, in *The New Republic,* a very astute political analysis . . ."

Clay interrupted quietly, "Dave, I have to do it, after all these years, there is still the unfinished business of abolition."

For a moment the sounds from the outer office distracted Dave's remembrances. Then he closed his eyes and leaned back on the couch, thinking back on those first months in Washington. Walking into the White House was like crossing Harvard Yard. Clay had, it seemed, all the right connections. In all the flurry and movement, there seemed no limit to how far they could go.

Then had come that Friday in November. Stunned, the world had watched the riderless horse. "Kennedy," Clay had said, "may not have made America a better nation, but he made America believe that it could be."

Dave scratched his cheek as he remembered the years that followed, the turbulent Johnson years. War and some real victories in civil rights, war and real victories in Vietnam.

And then the years of hanging on. Moving, always moving to find a niche in which to build a power base.

For something had happened those years in America. Partly, it was due to a national lethargy, a cultural malaise—so much had happened so fast, so much of it beyond the control, the comprehension of the people. What was the use of anything anyway? There were too many problems, too many people, too much pollution, too many moral doubts. Voting against crime in the street, they had elected crime to power. It was too expensive to live and much, much too expensive to die. Was it better to be freaked out or fenced in? Was God dead or had He merely ceased to create man in His own image?

Love and food were both in short supply. Terror stalked the streets or dressed up and played, between commercials, in the family room.

Jet planes jetted and spokesmen spoke. Students dropped out to meditate and the meditators rushed in to grab a piece of the action.

The Holy Land still had its unholy wars. The rivers of blood ran on in Southeast Asia, and the jungles grew dense in the cities of America.

There were prophesies and promises and people wanted so much to believe. In what? What was real and what was false? Everything was everything and nothing was real. There was a crisis in the energy of the soul.

There had been times when Clay had seemed tired, exhausted

even, but he had the capability—"those wind sprints, that discipline, baby"—to reach down, deep in the fourth quarter. And with each new line that creased his forehead, with each new gray hair at his temple, damn it, he was getting better.

Increasingly what he did made news. Civil rights, the crises in the cities, the coming energy crisis, the growing power of big business, the demands of Third World nations for their cut of the pie, the slow, creeping stagnation of the American psyche. Over the years Clay had addressed himself to them all. And more and more during the Carter years he had become the man to see, to talk to, to invite. A man of thought who understood many of the baffling, complex problems of today. Clay Clavier, who had the guts to fight. Dave sighed. Who sometimes fought too hard.

Yes, Dave thought, getting slowly to his feet as the intercom sounded, Clay was right. They had to keep on fighting. For no matter by what new name you called it, there was still the unfinished business of abolition.

"Clay, please, just one minute." Millie, Clay's top legislative assistant, touched his arm. "Look, I know you're trying to get back to committee, but if we don't do something about getting some more partitions in the back rooms of this office, this place is going to be bedlam. Carl and I . . ."

Damn, Clay thought, turning from his quick scrutiny of his messages. "Pepper"—he kept his voice low, controlling exasperation—"find out who you have to call to get those partitions today. Millie, tell him exactly what you want and you two handle it, okay?" He shoved three or four of the message slips marked "urgent" into his pocket and headed for the door.

"I'll walk with you to the elevator," Pepper said as they came into the light green stretch of hall.

"They're too slow. I'll take the stairs."

"Chief." Pepper's dark, thin-featured face was anxious. "Look, listen to me and listen to Dave, but in the end, do what you think is right. You know better than either of us. Just deal. Deal from all the strength we've got."

Clay smiled as he touched his companion's arm. "I'm going to try, Pepper. I'm sure as hell going to try."

Pepper nodded as Clay ran down the broad staircase. He'd do it. Somehow, Clay always did.

An unaccustomed smile touched Pepper Dee's thin lips as he walked back down the hall, remembering the day he had called Clay from that jail. Not as a movement organizer, which he'd been when he first met Clay, but disillusioned years later, when he was twenty-three, from Boston's Blue Hill jail. He'd risked his one, his only phone call. Risked? Shit, Clay'd been the only soul he knew in Boston.

It had been a strange trip, Pepper mused, as his footsteps clicked against the cement floor of the House Office Building; the whole idea of it could only have happened to someone young and desperate. Setting off from Birmingham, Alabama, where he and his two brothers and his work-aged widowed mother had lived above a chicken shack—setting off almost penniless to find where freedom really lived in America.

He'd headed North, as so many of his family had, hitchhiking through Georgia, the Carolinas, Virginia. He'd spent a week in D.C. with an old movement friend, setting out daily to view the great monuments with their great words, to read on an empty stomach in the Library of Congress. So many books. So many words.

He'd gotten a ride from D.C. to Harlem, the black Mecca, and cooled it there a month, working part-time in a Chock Full o' Nuts. But even the Big Apple was full of worms and he'd been on his way again, north to Boston.

Now for sure when you're indigent, you can't stay at the Ritz, but who'd have believed that two-bit bitch who'd picked him up in Bean town would have tried to rip off his tape player and CB? They'd slammed that jail door on his trip. Locked it on him with a quarter and a token to his name. Told him he had one call out.

He'd sat there all night before he remembered Clavier.

"Hey, Pepper." Clay had come to the jail an hour later. "I got your message."

"Good to see you." What a fool he'd felt, funky and tired, calling a man he barely knew, on a tip like that. He'd stuffed his hands in his pockets. "How you been doin'?"

"Getting by." Pepper had seen the smile at the corner of Clay's mouth. "What's the beef, Pepper?"

"They say breaking and entering."

"They say, or . . . ?"

"Damn, I'd just hit town, man. The bitch invited me in."

Clay had posted his bail, had gotten him a room with a friend in Roxbury and a job. A week later he was free.

What was it—one, two weekends later?—Clay had been the speaker at the Masons' annual dinner. Pepper had counted twelve hundred and twenty-one in the hall. In the midst of the tumultuous applause that had greeted Clay's call for the expansion of Negro leadership, the Reverend Robinson, pastor of the largest Negro church in Boston, had stood, waving his black British-flanneled arm. "What we need," the Reverend Robinson's voice had rolled like the Commandments from Sinai, "is our *own* congressman."

It had taken the Reverend Clavier, who was presiding, a full minute to hush the applause so his colleague could continue. "And, my brother Masons, I haven't seen a man yet better able to handle that

395

job than our brother Clay Clavier, whose blood ties with our organization go back to our founder's day. Prince Hall, founder of African Lodge Number One, himself wrote of the contributions of Jacques Clavier, and the efforts of Clay Clavier's other progenitors, Woodsons and Keys, are inscribed in our proud history and in our hearts!

"I say"—Reverend Robinson had held up his hand to stop the cheering—"let the word go out. The black men of Boston, yes, the black men of Boston have decided this night that they will send one of their own to speak for them. And, gentlemen, gentlemen, gentlemen, Clay Clavier is our own."

The next week Dave had arrived and Pepper had begun doing again what he did best, molding an energetic, dedicated entourage into an effective political machine.

They had money to work with—a rare thing for a black political novice. It came, Clay had explained vaguely, from his grandfather.

From Dave, Pepper learned that though Clay would be the architect, Dave and Pepper would be the ones to execute the design, to lay the foundation, to do the nuts-and-bolts jobs, to make certain all the connections were secure.

And, starting in William Clavier's two-thousand-member New Hope Church, black-robed Negro ministers across Boston had pointed a righteous arm toward heaven and, in voices passionate with belief, had extolled their text from James Weldon Johnson:

"Up from the bed of the river, God scooped *the Clay . . .*"

"Yes, yes, he did!"

". . . And by the bank of the river, He kneeled him down. . . . This great God, like a mammy bending over her baby, kneeled down in the dust toiling over a lump of *Clay . . .*"

"Hallelujah! Bless His name!"

Volunteers from all walks of life had poured into Clay's storefront headquarters across from Dudley Station in Roxbury and on Warren Street in Dorchester. They had been quickly assigned to political-action classes by Christy, who was very good with people and who'd looked especially dedicated in her maternity dresses. No volunteer could receive a canvassing kit until he or she had attended at least five of the classes which Pepper conducted.

They were organized. They were efficient. The support of black civic and grass-roots organizations, of black fraternities and sororities zoomed. The efforts of the opposition to find a second Negro candidate to split the black vote failed. Mildred Moore from Michigan joined their staff as researcher and statistician and assembled a two-page handout of facts about Clay's opponent—the text of which appeared also on the front page of the *Gazette*—which no politician hoping for a black vote could defend!

Oh yes, Pepper thought, they'd been a great crew, with great style: William and Jay Clavier and Clarence Woodson—old hands with the ropes—who knew the storms through which they must sail; Dave and Millie, with their special skills, ready, eager to try to come about in the storm; the volunteers, men and women, who knew this was the day—the hour—and bent their minds and muscles to the task.

At the mass meetings Clay had been magnificent, driving home point after devastating point, mingling, as only he could, the erudite with the hip and making them love it!

Senior citizens and students canvassed the wards, passing out handbills, placards, bumper stickers, most with only the single word: "Clay." By early March the campaign had become a crusade. Walking through the black districts of Roxbury and Dorchester, Pepper could mark the distances from one Clay sign to the next. Gospel songs had new words: "Up on the mountain, our Clay spoke, Outta his mouth came fire and smoke. Every time I feel the spirit, moving in my heart, I will pray. Every time . . ."

Nor was it just with blacks. Whites too began to feel the Clavier magic. Not as strongly, not in such numbers, but more and more white students were turning up at campaign headquarters. The liberal guard had been spearheaded by old warriors named Kuykendal and Oates. Clay was invited into the white communities to speak. The party professionals did not want a split along the color line. That was in 1962. Bigotry, they had said, was in Birmingham, not in Boston.

It was a week before the primary when, provoked by a young liberal white reporter from WGBH-TV, Kelly had finally agreed to a televised debate with Clay. Pepper watched it from the hospital. He and Dave had just rushed Christy to the delivery room.

By the time the doctor came out to congratulate Dave on the birth of his son, Pepper had known that Kelly had made a terrible mistake.

The voters confirmed it!

They had gone to Gay Head after the primary victory to work out the strategy for the November election. Clay had been the party candidate then, and victory, as it so often does, had solidified his own organization.

E. J. Walker, a political science professor from Southern University and a speech writer of distinction, had joined their paid staff, and also Leon Crawford, a history professor from Howard and a highly thought of veteran of the Washington political scene. And Pepper, who knew better than most that black folk were more used to working than to writing checks, had wondered how far Clay's grandpa's money would stretch.

Clay had spent most of June on the Vineyard with Crawford, who primed him on the issues that would be crucial in the fall. And though Crawford showed a great fondness for premium Bourbons, Pepper had declared to Clay that he was "the only man in America capable of computing bloods."

Clay's opponent in November had been Dan Dawson, astute and experienced, but slow, aging, and lackluster, a fast fader in an age decreed by the Kennedys to be swift, young, and together.

By nine o'clock on election night, with only 65 percent of the vote counted, Pepper had driven to Jay Clavier's house, where the family was watching the election returns.

"What do you think?" Clay had asked as Pepper came into the den.

"Go pack your bags!" Pepper had grinned, reaching for the scotch. "We're joining the team to get America moving again!"

"Good afternoon, Congressman Clavier." The blond, tanned security guard at the entrance of the Cannon Building was southern, polite.

"Good afternoon." Clay checked his watch as he replied. Damn, he shouldn't have taken the underground connection. The committee would have adjourned by now.

"Clay!" Turning, Clay saw Baird Fredericks, the red-bearded young congressman from Vermont, hurrying toward him through the maze of congressional personnel. "Jesus, what took so long? I thought you were just going to answer a phone call."

"I knew you'd call if anything got to popping." Clay grinned as his colleague reached his side. "Anything else happen in the meeting?"

"Yes and no." Baird glanced around quickly and dropped his voice to a whisper. "I definitely get the feeling Dulane's open for a deal."

"No, dammit." Clay's face twisted in a scowl.

"Look, Clay." Baird touched his arm. "I was the Speaker this morning. We've got to get that education bill out of committee this week if we want to get it before the House this session. Clay." Baird saw Clay's interruption coming and spoke quickly. "Look, he feels strongly we can get it through the House this session. But this is an election year. Next year's crew could upset a lot of applecarts."

"What kind of deal?" Clay asked curtly.

"You know. Your vote on the offshore drilling for Sykes's on education."

"We need both Sykes's and White's to get that bill out of committee."

"You know, Sykes controls White, so yours and mine on the offshore. Clay, Sykes is about six votes short. His assistants were on the phone all morning calling congressmen, running in and out of the committee room with the count. The only reason Sykes stayed in committee was to block our vote."

They were walking slowly now, down the high-ceilinged lobby of the oldest, most traditional of the House buildings. Clay had often wished his office was here, in Cannon, rather than in that modern complex, Rayburn. The site of their office had long been Dave's chronic bitch. "Why the hell did we get stuck in the building farthest from the Library of Congress?"

But none of this was on Clay's mind now. He spoke absently to the congressmen and staff members who passed them in the hall, his attention fixed on Baird.

They came out of Cannon onto Independence Avenue. "Clay." Baird checked to make certain no one was within earshot. "There's another thing . . ."

"Yes?"

"It's top secret."

Clay nodded. There had to be a hundred top secrets a day in Washington. Everybody talked about them.

"No"—Baird saw Clay's look—"this is. Sykes's bill will never be law. The President is going to veto it."

Clay stopped and looked at Baird. "Who told . . . ?"

"I just found out this morning. And you know Sykes'll never get the three-fifths to override. Clay, believe me, that bill will never become law."

For a moment Clay stared at his companion. Of course, what Baird said could be true. The President had been vacillating on offshore drilling. But why was Sykes trying to force the bill through the House this week? Unless he hadn't heard about the veto. Or, Clay bit his lip, unless it was just a political gambit to make Sykes look good for re-election.

But then, Clay glanced at his companion, Baird could be wrong. His source could be all wet, or Baird could have misunderstood. The education bill was the first Baird had co-authored. In his eagerness to see it through he could have misinterpreted. Damn, Clay thought, I'd better check this out myself.

But if the President were to veto? And if Sykes would vote the education bill out of committee . . . ?

Clay clenched his jaw as they walked toward the Capitol. On the top of the dome stood the statue of an Indian, symbolizing what? . . . a nation built on false treaties?

He had to get that education bill out of committee. The schools had to have those funds in the winter-heating, the educationally handicapped, and the gifted-child provisions. The last three winters had devastated school budgets. Sykes was advocating local district autonomy either to shorten the school year by closing a month in the winter or to extend it into the summer. But Clay knew damn well Sykes's true agenda: the first step in the cutback of all federal aid.

The starting gun for the race to grab all funds from the under-privileged. The Bakke case had lined up the runners. What Sykes in effect was saying was let the rich communities, which could afford it, increase their local taxes to hire the needed teachers, buy the books, and send their kids to school all winter. Let the poor sit in over-crowded classrooms. Let them use, as in other times, the worn-out, outdated texts. Deny their bright children the enrichment programs that would expand their horizons. Let their mentally handicapped suffer. And let all of them stay home when it was cold. Stay home and lose the continuity of desperately needed skill building; stay in those homes where most often both parents worked; stay on their own, unsupervised; stay home and send up an individual heating bills by more than 30 percent; stay home in January and February, when there were few jobs for those teen-agers who needed them most.

Clay scowled. It was incredible. Now more than ever before, kids needed the best schooling they could get. And not just the children of the traditionally deprived—the children whose parents, grand-parents, and great-grandparents had been denied a chance for decent educations, educations with which they could understand the subtle-ties of the learning processes, educations with which they could help their children in their formative years. Educations with which they could get jobs above the frustrating, wearying, short-gap planning, subsistence level. Jobs which would allow them as they held their children in their arms to plan for their futures and to transfer these plans to their children, because they knew, they knew, they had a shot at making the money with which they could be carried out. The minorities must be guaranteed a stability in American society. Their futures could no longer be left to trendy circumstance.

Massive help was needed—at all levels. More minority college graduates translated directly into more minority children with better-educated parental backup. More minority college graduates with decent jobs would mean a more economically stable minority com-munity. More minority college graduates with decent jobs would provide the more positive role models for the young.

Black folks had done a hell of a job raising generation after gener-ation on the menial wages of back-breaking jobs. Mothers scrubbing floors and other people's toilets to send a son to medical school. Fa-thers working two, damn it sometimes three jobs, to get those kids through college.

And it could still be done. It would still be done! But how slowly and at what cost in human misery. And how many, through no fault of their own, would fall along the way. The thing most needed now was hope.

Every black, every Chicano, every Indian, damn it every white child needed to know he had a shot. The white kids were bombing out like crazy too. And Jesus Christ, their parents couldn't stand any more taxes either. And every parent wanted, deserved, the best the country could provide for their kids.

Clay's frown deepened. And if Sykes succeeded, aid to education would just be the first of the social programs strangled. Health would be next, then welfare, then the EDA and SBA programs. No more special provisions for the poor, for the aged, for the handicapped. End all opportunity to equalize ethnic opportunity in America. Assure a super race supported by powerless minorities. It would be the end of the American dream—the end of the greatest of all of the American promises: "equal justice under the law." And, finally, it would mean the destruction of America itself. Yes, Clay thought, the education bill must be his first priority.

Clay stood there a moment on the steps of the Capitol, looking up at the dome, at the Indian. Beneath this roof leaders of the land would debate the crises in pollution and energy. But the greatest energy crisis in America was not in oil but in minds. Young alcoholic minds on Indian reservations; young delinquent Chicano minds in East Los Angeles dropping out; young revolutionary blacks in Cleveland, Detroit, in ghettos around the nation, hollowed by dope, pimping, destroying; young white minds doped out, flipped out, fucked up . . . For despite all the interpretations, the college entrance tests, the SAT, the ACT proved white kids too were skidding, skidding in the energy of the mind.

Nor was it because of integration. Hell, no. Scores were no better in school districts that had never seen a nigger.

And pollution . . . which pollution? Noxious fumes that poisoned the environment or those pollutants, those subversive pollutants that poisoned the mind? Those forces that turned group against group, white against black, WASP against Jew, that had created a nation of little nations: Irish, Polish, Italian, Latino—a nation at war against itself. No, Clay thought, the greatest threat to America was not from without. It was from within.

"Clay," Baird touched Clay's arm. "What're you going to do?"
"I'll let you know in an hour, Baird."

402

CHAPTER SIX

The Secret Service man at the White House gate checked his list, nodded, and smiled with courtesy and efficiency. "You're expected, Congressman Clavier."

Inside the White House, the morning tours were over. The plush light blue carpet of the New England interior held mostly the tread of White House staff. Along the dark-wood-framed white walls was a treasury of American art, much of it Early American; Remington, Russell, and Catlin western and Indian scenes.

The bronze plaque on the door of Jack Burlin's tiny office said "Special Assistant." It was open. Jack came around his desk when he saw Clay.

"Clay, good to see you. My secretary told me you were on your way," he chirped as he extended his thin brown hand. With a quick look around the outer office, he shut the door. "What can I do for you?"

"I hear the President is going to veto Sykes's oil bill."

Jack's nose twitched like a rabbit's. "Who told you that?"

Clay knew the Washington paranoia. He hated the games. "Baird Frederick. Is it true?"

The twitching continued a moment more, then Jack nodded. "It's true."

"Does Sykes know it?"

Jack shifted uneasily. He liked being the source. "I don't know."

"Who would?"

"Ben Thomas." Jack shrugged, begrudging this admission. "Over in the Executive Building."

"Could I use your phone?"

"Sure, go ahead."

"Clay, what about your bill?" Jack hunched on his desk as Clay dialed Ben's number. "I've had calls all week from the N-Double-A, the Urban League, and a host of citizen committees."

"We're going to get it out this week."

"What about Sykes? Goddamn, you two sure have had it on for one thing or another for the past, what is it . . . ?"

"Sixteen years."

"Are you sure you can get it past him?"

"If the President is going to veto that bill and . . . Hey, Linda, Clay Clavier, could I . . . ? Thanks. . . . Ben, Clay Clavier. Can you spare me a minute right away? . . . Okay. I'm in the White House I'll be right over."

"If the President is vetoing the bill, what?" Jack persisted as Clay turned to the door.

"Let me call you tonight and I'll be able to tell you for sure."

Clay walked rapidly down the walk and through the parking area that separated the White House itself from the nineteenth-century French architectural monstrosity known as the Old Executive Office Building. Ben Thomas, ex-CIA agent, now executive assistant, had his office on the second floor. Austere, remote, Ben Thomas was without doubt one of the most politically knowledgeable blacks in Washington.

Ben's petite brown secretary smiled as Clay came in. "Clay Clavier, when are you going to buy me that drink you've been owing me a month?"

"Soon, Linda. Maybe next week. Can Ben see me now?"

She got up and opened the door to the inner office. "He's waiting."

Ben's voice was soft as he reached over his desk to shake Clay's hand. He indicated the chair across his desk, then slumped into his mammoth swivel chair again. Behind him, through the window Clay could see the White House grounds.

"Ben. I hear the President is going to veto Sykes's oil bill."

"True."

"Does Sykes know it?"

"I doubt it. He's been trying to get in to see the President for nearly two weeks. Two nights ago at Kennedy Center, the Secret Service gentled him back when he tried to get close to the President's seat. I'd say the old man is avoiding him."

"Thanks." Clay stood.

"So now you can vote for his oil bill"—Ben smiled thinly—"in return for his letting your education bill out of committee."

"That'll be the deal."

"It's a good one. In the end, you're not giving up a thing."

"I hope some other people see it that way. After all I've said, I'm going to look pretty damn silly."

"Which goes to show how deceiving looks are. One more thing."

404

Ben stood as Clay reached the door. "On this South Africa business . . ."

"I'm meeting them in New York tonight."

"Good. Let me tell you, Clay, it's the number one priority now."

Everything was, Clay thought as he walked down the stairs. Everything was number one priority—and now.

"I just got your message," Baird said as he joined Clay in the corridor of the Capitol just outside the Rayburn Room. "Jesus, Clay, the first bells have already rung for the vote." His voice dropped. "Sykes is desperate. He's still short five votes, I hear."

"We'll make the deal." Clay grimaced as a smile broke on Baird's face. "Don't look so damn happy. Here he comes."

Sykes's herringbone Abercrombie and Fitch jacket was molded to his athletic body. His face, framed by curly mixed-gray hair, was slightly tanned. His shirt was a soft beige, his tie, clipped with a silver replica of the state seal of South Carolina, a deeper brown. As always, he was the very embodiment of the aristocratic sportsman. He walked unhurriedly, but Clay felt the questioning behind the smoke-tinted glasses which, Clay knew, Sykes wore more to mask emotions than to improve vision. "You wanted to see me?" Sykes's voice was low, hard, polite.

"I hear you need just a few more votes to get your bill through today."

"Yes."

"I'll vote for it and so will Congressman Fredericks if you and White will vote the education bill out of committee tomorrow. And . . ." Clay saw hope mix with caution in Sykes's eyes. "I'll also send a note by the page to four or five other members of the black caucus asking them for an affirmative vote. Of course, I can only guarantee my vote and Fredericks's."

They heard the bell announcing the vote. Clay saw Sykes studying him and suppressed an inward grin. He didn't know about the veto. He still thought he had a shot. "Do we have a deal?"

The caucuses in the Rayburn room had ended. The room was emptying rapidly now. "I'd expected you to speak against the offshore drilling bill before the vote." Sykes's voice was even, well modulated.

"I didn't feel I needed to. You don't have enough votes now without mine and Fredericks's and the four or five I may influence to carry it."

Sykes nodded almost imperceptibly, but his mind was racing. Why was Clavier backing down now? True, he wanted that education bill out badly. But Sykes's thumb rubbed his slender silver wedding band. Where had Clavier been? He had seen him leave the floor more than an hour ago. To whom had he spoken? What did he know? Was he responding to pressure? Or did he just want that education bill out that badly?

Clay felt his heart pounding as he checked his watch. With an effort he forced emotion from his voice. "We have three minutes to get our cards in. The others may have already voted. Do you want the deal or not?"

"I'll vote your bill out of committee tomorrow," Sykes said, then turned and walked briskly down the hall.

The page waited as Clay hastily scribbled notes to four members of the black caucus. That done, Clay walked into the chamber, put in his card marked "aye," and left the floor.

His house was silent. Only the black Great Dane, Nefertiti, greeted Clay. "Di," he called, putting down his briefcase. "Hey, Di, I'm home." There was no answer. Clay frowned as he went to the kitchen. Where in the world could they all be?

He opened the refrigerator and stood a moment contemplating its contents. Then, deciding he was too hungry to wait for food to heat, he pulled out the ham and a bar of cheddar cheese. He sliced these generously, added two slices of rye bread, a chunk of lettuce, and poured on the Thousand Island dressing.

On the counter above the dishwasher, pushed back not to tempt the dog, was a still oven-warm pecan pie, his son Johnny's favorite. His son and—oh, damn it, Bill Johnson's—how could he have forgotten Bill? Bill's cousin, Tom, had been a mainstay in that first campaign and had done yeoman service in the constituency office ever since. And Bill had been one of the first friends Clay had made in Washington. His restaurant on Seventeenth and K made the best pecan pies in the world.

Now Bill's son was out of the service and wanted a job as a guard. Clay reached for the pie, cut what Di would call "a fat man's slice," poured a glass of milk, sat down at the breakfast bar, and reached for the phone.

"Congressman Clavier's office." Phoebe, his secretary, was crisp and efficient.

"Phoebe, is Pepper still there?"

"No, he's already left, making his rounds."

Clay heard sarcasm mixed with resignation. Phoebe and Pepper had never been friendly. Pepper's late-afternoon routine of visiting the bars around Washington, "gleaning information," which, if of consequence, he typed neatly each morning at her typewriter, was the bane of her existence.

"Is there anything I can do?" Phoebe's eagerness transmitted her agenda—a one-upmanship on Pepper.

"No." But give her strokes. "You're doing two people's work already. Just mark Bill Johnson in big red letters on my calendar for tomorrow."

Clay finished his sandwich and, pondering again the unusual silence of the house, picked up his briefcase from the hall and went upstairs to his study. In the top drawer were the papers he would need tonight in New York. They had been compiled largely from four sources: Fred Faragut at the State Department, Lennie Tucker at IRS, his own congressional tour of South Africa last month, and his South African associates. Putting on his glasses, Clay read the first two pages, a partial listing of laws that kept South African blacks in economic and social slavery.

The Pass Act, under which every African boy and girl at the age of sixteen must first be fingerprinted and then must apply for an identification number and reference book. The book, which had to be carried at all times, contained the identity number and personal details of its owner, the signature of all employers, and a record of tax receipts. And, all black South Africans over sixteen years of age had to pay taxes.

Clay frowned as he read down the page: the Influx Control Act; the dusk-to-dawn curfews; the Group Areas Act; the Job Reservation Act; the Riotous Assemblies Act—under which even prayer services and silent protests had been banned; the Unlawful Organization Act—which had banned the African National Congress and the African Congress, the black resistance movements; the Affected Organizations Act, which was structured to prevent help from overseas; the Departure from Union Regulations Act—an instrument of indimidation which also had the power to refuse or to withdraw passports; the Immorality Act, which made sexual intercourse between whites and blacks punishable by a seven-year prison sentence.

The Native Land and Bantu Trust Acts, which denied Africans the right to own land.

The Apprentice Act, which closed trade-union opportunities to Africans. The Bantu Labor Settlement of Disputes Act, which excluded all Africans from the definition of "employee." The Unemployment Act No. 28, which excluded Africans from unemployment benefits. The Terrorism Act, which outlawed, among other things, the writing of speeches which "embarrass the administration of the affairs of state"; the General Law Further Amendment Acts, which required permission to hold even funeral processions.

Clay groaned as he pulled off his glasses and stuffed the papers

409

into his briefcase. More than 350,000 Africans were convicted annually under the Pass Laws alone. The average court time for each conviction: less than two minutes. And South Africa was meting out more death sentences than any other country in the world.

In his bedroom Clay checked his watch as he pulled off his shirt. He had twenty minutes to shower and change.

He was pulling off his pants when he remembered. Damn, the Little League game. His son Johnny's first start at shortstop. He'd promised not to miss this one. Hell, he'd showered this morning. Deodorant and a clean shirt would have to suffice for tonight.

Johnny's thin, eleven-year-old face broke into a grin as Clay rounded the bleachers, but professionalism prohibited his waving from the field. Clay saw Di waving. Beside her, behind an enormous still-growing pink bubble was his daughter, Lorraine. She looked up when she saw her father. The bubble collapsed. Two fingers squeezed the gum into her mouth. "Hi, Daddy." She smiled as he moved through several handshakes to her side.

"Hey, sugar." He kissed her upturned sticky mouth.

"I'm so glad you got here, Clay. Johnny was so anxious." Di slid down the bleacher to make a space between herself and Lorraine. "Here, sit down."

"I can't. I've got to make a plane in fifty minutes." He saw the sudden tight set of her lips. "I'll explain to Johnny."

"How many times, Clay?" she whispered. "How many times will you explain to Johnny?"

"Di . . ." he began, then saw Lorraine's eyes on him and checked his watch. "Look, I may be home tonight. If not I'll see you in the morning." He raised his wife's chin and kissed her swiftly. "I love you."

The teams were changing sides. Clay walked to the bench.

"How's it going?" He laid his hand on his son's shoulder.

"Great. You should've been here two innings ago, Dad. We made a double play. But I'm up to bat in two more men."

"Look, Johnny." Clay felt a sudden gnawing in his gut. "I promised you I'd come, but I have to make a plane in less than an hour."

"But . . ."

"Hey, I'll stay till you get your turn at bat." He saw his son's eyes cloud with disappointment. "It's important, Johnny."

Johnny bowed his head and jerked his cap low over his eyes. "Sure, Dad."

"Johnny."

"Yeah, Dad."

"Look at me." The boy's eyes looked into Clay's, searching. Clay wanted to hug him, to kiss him as he could at home. But he knew the uniform, the ball and bat, the American machismo forbade it.

His son held out his hand. "It's okay, Dad. We're still friends."

Clay watched his son trot back to the bench. How do you explain to an eleven-year-old boy that you can't stay to watch him field a ground ball when eighteen million people are starving?

411

The main entrance to New York's Summit Hotel faces Lexington Avenue at Fifty-first Street. Clay got out of the cab around the corner at the entrance by the drugstore. It was closest to the elevator. Ben Kapalute always got jumpy when anyone was late.

Kapalute opened the door to Clay's knock. "Ah, Congressman Clavier. Good." The tall, well-built South African stood back to give Clay admittance to the book-and-suitcase-cluttered room. On the radio Earth, Wind & Fire stomped out the Serpentine Fire. On the thick-fibered couch were magazines from three continents.

"Clay!" The room divider opened and Fenie Akuiwe, the poet-revolutionary, came into the sitting room, a smile on his usually mournful face. "So you are still an abolitionist?" Fenie came barely to Clay's shoulder, but his hand beneath the frayed cuff of his shirt gripped like a vise. "It's been nearly a year, hasn't it?"

"Nearly. You look great, Fenie."

"Yes, but this year has been most difficult." Fenie's brown face resumed its usual dolefulness. "But things are looking up. How is your wife and your kids? Are they . . . ?"

"Excuse me for rushing matters," Kapalute's smooth British accent interrupted, "but I must leave for London at eleven. And"—he gestured with the soft deference of the trained civil servant—"these are not our rooms." Kapalute turned to Clay. "Our brother Kaifus Diatu is appearing here in New York. He is graciously sharing his accommodations with us."

Now, that could be a way to make up with Johnny, Clay thought quickly. Diatu's music was sweeping the folk circles and giving new impetus to American jazz. Johnny had at least two of his albums. Clay had heard them—sometimes till midnight. An autograph . . . "Is he here?" Clay could hear behind the room partition the melodious flow of South African voices.

"Not at present." Fenie saw Clay's glance at the room divider. "We have two of our students studying here. A warm room, a good meal . . ." Fenie moved the magazines and sat down on the couch.

"Congressman Clavier." Kapalute pulled off his threadbare jacket. "Our matters with you are of the utmost urgency."

"Is Wandiza coming?" Clay asked, sitting down by Fenie.

"Yes. His plane has landed. He is on his way here now."

As Kapalute arranged chairs around the couch, Clay recalled what he knew of the three men with whom he was meeting. He knew Fenie Akuiwe best. He had met him nearly fifteen years ago when Fenie had been a student at BU. He had heard of the poetry readings the South African was giving in the coffeehouses around Boston. One evening he and Di had gone.

From then on the intense, charmingly brilliant, and almost destitute Fenie had been a frequent visitor in their home, staying often, at Clay's insistence, entire weekends. From Fenie, Clay had received his first tutorial in the despicable, wretched results of apartheid, of the endless, senseless deprivation, humiliation, and brutal waste of human life.

Two years ago Fenie had introduced him to Kapalute.

Ben Kapalute, like Fenie, was a Xhosa. Both had been born of parents who had been removed from their native lush and beautiful highland country to a barren desolate Bantustan in the drought- and disease-devastated Kalahari Desert. Both had been sent by the almost superhuman efforts of their parents through costly separate black "public schools"—Fenie in Soweto near Johannesburg, Kapalute outside Pretoria. Both had left South Africa as fugitive revolutionaries.

At their first meeting Kapalute, who had just been graduated from the University of Edinburgh, had shown Clay picture after picture of black South African children from one year to eighteen months old who still weighed less than eighteen pounds, their skeletal limbs misshapen, their mouths with great bleeding sores, unable to stand or sit, the victims of programmed malnutrition.

Now, Kapalute had been in the United States four years. He was teaching economics and working on his doctorate at NYU and speaking across the United States and Europe against apartheid.

Since the Angolans had gained their independence, the gentle, intellectual Fenie spent most of his time in Luanda, writing revolutionary tracts based on the teachings of Frantz Fanon.

Clay had never met Cetewayo Wandiza, who had been named for the heroic Zulu-Kaffir (or, as they called themselves, Amazosas) warrior who had led the Zulus armed with assagais against the

413

machine-gun-armed army of England in 1879. But Clay had heard a great deal about him.

Wandiza had walked out of South Africa when he was nineteen. He had gone from his home near the Kimberley diamond mines to Pretoria as part of a funeral procession, circumventing the need for the pass demanded of every African traveling in his own land. From Pretoria he had moved by night 350 miles to the Mozambique border and then made his way to the Limpopo River. There he had met African freedom fighters who had helped him to Tanzania. After a year in Dar es Salaam, he had gone on to Kenya and a missionary school.

Wandiza was twenty-two when he finished high school. At twenty-six he had finished the London School of Economics. At thirty he had his Ph.D. from Michigan State.

He had taught a year at Yale, living in a room in the home of a New Haven black minister, saving every dime he could.

The next year he had returned to South Africa in secret to work with Albert Lithuli. After Lithuli was placed under house arrest for speaking against apartheid, Wandiza, seeing no hope that the South African government would soften its racial practices, had made his way out again and begun his arduous trip around the world.

In Malaysia, in Japan, in the Soviet Union, France, Denmark, Sweden, England, people heard the South African speak of his people's determination to be free.

The *Times* of London had described Wandiza's oratory as a delicate balance between the relentless rationality of William Wilberforce and the passion of Byron. But it was his father, Jay Clavier's comparison that had impressed Clay most. After hearing Wandiza in Boston, Clavier had written: "Wandiza combines the holy ethical persuasion of Frederick Douglass and Henry Highland Garnet with the fire of the great black orator from Chicago, Roscoe Conklin Simmons." Now, as the moment approached when he would meet the man, Clay felt his excitement heightening.

"Excuse me." The partition opened again and one of the young students came into the room. "Would anyone care for soup or coffee?"

"Ah, good!" Fenie looked up with appreciation. "I'll have a little of both."

"And me." Kapalute, too, seemed anxious. It was their dinner, Clay knew.

"And you, Congressman Clavier?" The young man turned, smiling, to Clay.

"Just coffee, please." Clay remembered the Summit's room refrigerators. Why the devil hadn't he stopped at Gristede's and brought up some food?

"Congressman Clavier." Kapalute sat down across from Clay. "As you know, these murders by fascist paramilitary groups, especially the murder of the American cultural attaché at Durban . . ."

"And the failure of the police to apprehend the killers," Fenie interrupted.

". . . have"—Kapalute nodded his approval of Fenie's addition—"made the American public more receptive of our position. I think now a resolution to boycott . . ."

"Getting a majority vote on a specifically worded resolution would still be difficult," Clay said slowly. "Resolutions are dramatic, but you must understand that Congress is not empowered to conduct foreign relations. Furthermore, as you know, the United States Congress is reluctant to pass restrictions of trade . . ."

"But now . . ." Kapalute persisted.

"Even now, parliamentary procedure could keep a resolution of specific measures from ever coming to a vote. True, a resolution would provide a barometer of the attitude of Congress, but it would still leave congressmen in a position of not voting for more than condemnation or the vague terminology of 'effective measures' because of the details that would be attached. The more gutsy way, I feel, would be an amendment to the Foreign Aid Appropriations Bill. An amendment that, one, reverses the tax credits now given for investment in South Africa; two, asks for a mandatory arms embargo; and three . . ."

"It would never work!" Fenie shook his head vehemently. "Your big corporations will shovel pressure against it, saying the same sanctions should then be applied against Paraguay, Argentina, the Soviet Union, and other African nations that have blatant human rights violations."

"Political polyglot." Kapalute waved in annoyance. "Of course, there should be condemnations of all countries that violate human rights, but none are as massive and degrading as the atrocities in South Africa, the International Red Cross has ruled that apartheid be considered a war crime, comparable with Nazism under Hitler's

Germany. Congressman Clavier, whether you realize it or not Zimbabwe, Namibia, and South Africa are a war zone."

Fenie touched Kapalute's arm and he turned, saying something Clay could not understand in his native Xhosa tongue to Fenie. For a moment they spoke softly, their voices almost musical, with the soft clicking sound of the Xhosa people coming at the end of each phrase.

Then Kapalute turned to Clay again. "We leave the means to you. We have no time to argue the politics of it." He checked his watch. "In just the twenty minutes you have been here, twenty South African babies have died of malnutrition—one dies every minute in South Africa. Twenty families have been thrown out of their homes. Twenty men have been arrested for not having proper passes, and the profit in gold in twenty minutes has exceeded thirteen thousand pounds, over seventy-eight thousand dollars profit every hour."

"We must have more than boycotts and arms embargoes," Fenie said softly. "There must be a total ban on United States investment."

Kapalute leaned forward in his seat, his knees almost touching Clay's. "Listen to me, Congressman Clavier. Listen to me well and repeat what I say to all who honor human dignity. In South Africa, while whites play golf and tennis and tend their polo ponies, one out of every two black children in many Bantustans will die of malnutrition and its attendant diseases before they are five. In the big, modern, luxury-lined Port Elizabeth, the center, if you will, of the foreign automotive industry, one out of three children dies before his first birthday. In most parts of South Africa one out of five blacks will have tuberculosis. In South Africa there is one doctor for every four hundred whites and one for every forty-four thousand blacks. Our women are old at twenty. I tell you, they are committing genocide."

"Or," Fenie said softly, "deliberately creating mutants by starvation. Our children face permanent physical and mental retardation because of malnutrition, because of lack of milk, lack of milk among a people who for centuries were famous for their cattle. The people from whom Diaz bought milk when he, the first white man to round the Cape of Good Hope, came in 1488. The white men came and destroyed the cattle. With machine guns they drove the Africans . . ."

"The history is too long to recount here," Kapalute said curtly. "There is enough evil, cruelty, and injustice today. They deliberately and maliciously break up families. Men must live in single-sex hovels hundreds of miles from the Bantustans, to which their uprooted families have been relocated—with no schools, no libraries, no recreational facilities." Kapalute's words were accentuated now with his tribal click.

"Not a single black apprentice in all of South Africa. Every managerial, every supervisory, every skilled job held by whites. No black trade union. Strikes by blacks held to be illegal.

"Blacks jailed for being absent from work, for trying to change jobs before the contract on the one they have expires.

"The average wage for whites is sixty pounds a week. The average wage for a black man is four pounds five a week, and the gap is widening every day.

"The Minimum Effective Level, or, as you say in your country, poverty level, amounts to, in your money, two hundred dollars a month for a family of five or six simply to survive. Ninety percent of the African people earn below the MEC.

"The average white farmer's income is nine thousand dollars a year. The average African laborer's wage is two hundred twenty dollars a year.

"The aim of the government is the mass removal of every black that can be moved to Bantustans—the so-called homelands—which cannot support the population they have now. More than seven million live there in areas not large enough to support two million. Four million more are slated to be moved.

"They legislate us into poverty and ignorance. We are completely disenfranchised. No African can vote. Schools are compulsory and free for white children. Blacks must pay for their education. More than forty-five percent of the black children can't afford to go to school." Kapalute had begun his native clicks again. "The government spends roughly one hundred and sixty-five pounds a year for the education of each white child and nine pounds for each black child. And, from their earliest childhood, our children are taught that equality with Europeans is not for them.

"In the country with the highest standard of living for white people in the world, in the country that has more cars, more telephones, more cameras, more household goods—except, of course, vacuum cleaners, not needed with so much cheap labor—it is illegal, in most areas, for blacks even to own their own homes."

"And an average of three Africans die on each shift in the mines," Fenie said harshly. "Nor are the Europeans in South Africa the only ones profiting from human misery. Lured by the promise of enormous profit, nearly forty percent of all industrial production in South Africa is underwritten by American and European firms who have also allowed themselves to become an integral part of South Africa's racist policies. More than half of the three thousand million dollars your corporations boast of as being invested in Africa south of the Sahara is in fact invested in the fascist, racist, imperialist Vorster regime of South Africa.

"And though in interview after interview these firms claim that their presence will lead to a betterment of conditions for blacks"— Fenie smiled sardonically—"despite the ominous warnings from Cape Town and Pretoria that the maintenance of the social situation is of graver importance to white South Africa than economic considerations—most foreign corporations pay *even lower* wages than South African ones. The barren, dust-blown, bookless, hopeless, corrugated-roofed shanty towns are proliferating."

"Black men must move up to three hundred miles from home to find work." Kapalute was speaking again. "Their families are forbidden to live with them in townships which are over thirty miles from the cities where they work. 'Black workers,' so says the South African government, 'must not be burdened with superfluous appendages like wives and families.' More than eighty-five percent of the male blacks in Cape Town are allowed to see their families only once a year."

Kapalute's eyes narrowed. "It is incredible, the obscenities which greed prompts men to promote. The murder of unarmed schoolchildren in Soweto. In fact, their whole new scheme for an independent Soweto is designed to isolate and dampen the soaring revolutionary mood of our people who are fighting for the total liberation of South Africa. And it is imperialist foreign investment, Congressman Clavier, that gives the Nationalist government the money and therefore the power to plan and maintain the vicious oppression of my people.

"American motor industries provide the army with police trucks to implement oppression, your computer companies provide the know-how for control, and the German and French companies provide the military hardware to put down our uprisings against their inhumanity."

A sudden wracking cough seized Kapalute. He doubled over, fumbling in his pocket for a wad of Kleenex. Then, as Kapalute straighted up, Clay saw the blood on the Kleenex. "You should see a doctor," Clay said, handing him a cup of tepid coffee.

"I have no time for doctors, Congressman . . ." Kapalute said hoarsely, wiping the tears that had accompanied his coughing spasm. "For they know what is coming. Every day labor unrest grows. The whites are preparing for the confrontation. The government has mandated that every white man, woman, and child be able to shoot. It is a compulsory school subject for both white boys and white girls. There is conscription for all white males."

"They claim they can put a quarter of a million men under arms," Fenie began. "And they can. With American weapons streaming into South Africa, through Israel."

"They know." Kapalute ignored Fenie's interruption. "They know. They know that despite their massive arsenal of weapons, much of which was purchased from the French in defiance of the United Nations resolution, despite their center for testing long-range nuclear missiles in the Kivu province in Zaïre—close to the borders of Zambia, Tanzania, and Angola—despite their submarine missile system, their air-to-ground missiles, their Italian planes with British Rolls-Royce engines, their French Mirage jets and British Buccaneers, despite their Sharpeville and Carletonville massacres, they know we are coming for what belongs to us."

"And white South Africa will learn the lesson of the French and the Americans in Vietnam, that there is no weapon greater than man's determination." Fenie stood, his hands jammed in his pockets. "Since the formation in 1912 of the African National Congress—the oldest liberation movement on the African continent—we have been fighting back.

"African women organized to fight the pass system. Hundreds were beaten and jailed.

"The African National Conference protested the handing over of Namibia as a territory to South Africa, mandated by the Treaty of Versailles.

"In 1943 our youth league was formed. They began boycotts, strikes, and civil disobedience campaigns—almost none of which were reported in the American press. On June 26, 1950, a one-day work stoppage was called in Transvaal. The police moved in brutally, killing, wounding. Since 1950 we celebrate June 26 as South African Freedom Day."

Fenie paused to sip his now cold coffee as Clay and Kapalute

419

watched silently. "Since that day"—Fenie put his cup back in the saucer—"our protests have met increasing violence. People have been shot in their homes and churches. More than eight thousand five hundred were jailed in our 'Defiance of Unjust Laws' campaign.

"In 1955 we adopted our Freedom Charter in a mass meeting near Johannesburg, copies of which are still today kept hidden in most African homes.

"In 1960 the Pan-African Congress began its passive resistance program. Hundreds were shot. More than twenty thousand jailed. The country was in chaos.

"Nelson Mandela, whom many call the Scarlet Pimpernel, went underground, touring the country, organizing a three-day strike. Hundreds of thousands responded to his call. The government retaliation was brutal. On the second day Mandela decided to call off the strike.

"It was then," Fenie said, sitting down again, "that it was decided to undertake armed struggle. Umkhonto We Sizwe, the Spear of the Nation, was launched. Hundreds of our young people marched in solidarity with Frelimo. Two years ago a half million workers in Transvaal came out on political strike. And though they do not recognize our trade unions we are organized in the factories to hit the enemy, to hit him where it hurts. We have formed a united front with the workers' unions of Zimbawe and Namibia. And to paraphrase the reasoning of Fanon, it is good. No people can be given power, they must seize it to know, to feel what power is."

"And we will," Kapalute began again. "At the convention in Lagos we . . . !"

The knock came quickly, three times, at the door. Kapalute sprang to his feet as Fenie rushed to open it. Clay saw the man in the doorway and came slowly to his feet.

He was tall, about six foot five, black and solid as a slab of anthracite coal; the image of the Zulu chieftain. The very center of his head was bald from his forehead to his neck. The thick hair covering the rest of his cranium was mixed with gray. His eyes, beneath thick lashes, shone like onyx. His voice was low, melodious, as he embraced Fenie. "Ah, brother. It is good to see you again."

Wandiza moved next into Kapalute's quick embrace. "Amandla! Matla! Power!" Kapalute said hoarsely.

"Amandla! Ngawethu! Matla Kea Rona. We shall win," came Wandiza's fierce reply.

420

Then Wandiza turned, his hands outstretched to Clay. "Congressman Clavier." Clay took his hands. "I recognized you immediately from Fenie's most apt description."

"I am honored to meet you, Mr. Wandiza."

"First," Wandiza said, settling himself in a chair, "let me thank you in behalf of my people, the nearly eighteen million blacks, the two and one third million colored, and yes, the three quarters of a million Asians, all the oppressed people of South Africa. You must know they appreciate the support that you and the black caucus, indeed the support which so many black and white people throughout the United States have given. The sale of the krugerrand, the symbol of racist oppression, has been almost stopped in most leading American cities and, where it has not stopped, it has become almost covert. But"—Wandiza leaned toward Clay—"that is not enough. The assassination of Steve Biko and the subsequent failure of the police to bring his murderer to justice became the starting gun of a new hunting season on blacks and those whites who speak against apartheid. As you know, three white professors, two ministers, and a journalist have been murdered in the past two months, in addition to your own cultural attaché, who was killed last week for entertaining a black student in his home. What you may not know is that the student and his wife are also dead."

"No . . ." Clay began slowly.

"Nor the fact that in the past six months more than one hundred South African blacks either have been killed or have mysteriously disappeared." Wandiza saw Clay's startled look and nodded. "The censorship is becoming increasingly severe. Last week a smallpox epidemic broke out in a Bantustan near the Mozambique border."

"Small . . . ?"

"Yes." Wandiza continued. "The white doctor who volunteered to come to the Bantustan declared that he believed the virus had been brought in in a contaminated blanket."

"Oh, God," Clay said softly.

"A tactic, as you know, that has been used in your own country."

Clay nodded. More than one Indian tribe had been decimated or wiped out entirely by contaminated blankets sold deliberately to them.

"The doctor was recalled to Durban. A week later, while his children were at school and his wife shopping, he accidentally fell from his bedroom window. He died an hour later."

"Is John Gugando . . . ?" Fenie began.

"John is also dead. Like Lithuli, he accidentally stepped in front of a train."

"Oh, goddamn." Fenie began to pace the room.

"Each day things grow worse. What we need, Congressman Clavier, what we must have, is a total cutoff of American investment in South Africa.

"You must understand, Congressman Clavier"—Wandiza waved off Clay's attempt to speak—"that South Africa, despite its boast of economic self-sufficiency, is vulnerable. It faces a severe balance-of-payments problem. Much of this has been created by their own apartheid policy. The wages of the blacks are so low they cannot afford to buy enough goods to promote expansion of the economy. And the natural market for South Africa's textile goods—the poorer African countries, which do not produce textiles—refuse to buy from South Africa and are willing to pay higher prices for these goods from other countries. Unemployment is rising. The growth rate is slowing down.

"Congressman Clavier, the economic stability of South Africa now depends on two things: one, the sale of gold, and, two, massive capital inflow. It is still highly dependent on foreign capital, particularly risk capital, to achieve a high rate of growth. Without these investments the government of South Africa cannot survive."

"I'm afraid what you ask is impossible, Mr. Wandiza," Clay said quietly. "As you know, Cardiss Collins's resolution of condemnation passed the House only because specific sanctions were left out, which of course she knew they must be for it to pass. However, what I can do . . ."

"Nothing else will be enough." Wandiza shook his head. His voice was soft. "We must have a total cutoff of American investments in South Africa, the restructuring of the now favorable tax credits for such investments, a boycott of South African goods, a total arms embargo."

"Those things, I'm afraid, Mr. Wandiza, the United States is not prepared to do."

"The United States, my friend, no longer has a choice. The United States, through its imperialistic and racial policies, is delivering the Third World into the Communist camp. Where else can we turn? Like Ho Chi Minh and Castro, we came to your country first. And like Ho Chi Minh and Castro, if your country does not hear us . . .

Congressman Clavier"—Wandiza's words were husky with emotion —"we are determined to be free."

For a moment silence hung heavily in the room, the only sound that of the radio playing softly behind the partition. Yes, Clay thought, there is still the unfinished business of abolition, now on the worldwide scale.

"Clay?"

Clay saw Fenie's anxious look and nodded. "I'll try, Fenie."

They all turned as a chair in the other room clattered to the floor. Then the student yanked the partition open. "The United States consul at Pretoria has been murdered." His eyes were wide. His voice was low.

"What?" Clay came to his feet.

"Some rightist group burst into his house and . . ."

Wandiza put his hand on the student's arm. "You have heard that on the radio?"

"Yes, just now. His wife saw . . ."

Wandiza turned, his eyes blazing, to Clay. "And now, Congressman Clavier?"

Clay stood. "Now, Mr. Wandiza, I think I can go a step further. I am prepared to ask that the United States sever, at long last, its diplomatic relations with South Africa."

Keith Kuykendal pulled off his coat as he came into his walnut-paneled office at the New York *Star*. In the corner the antiquated teletype machine sounded three bells, signaling a bulletin.

"Oh, Mr. Kuykendal." His trim, demurely dressed secretary turned from the letters she was putting on his desk. "Your father called."

"He did?" Keith ran his hand through his thick brown hair, still wet from the lunchtime shower at the Racquet Club.

"He'd like you to meet him at his office at your earliest convenience."

Keith's angular features broke into a grin. "And did he give you any idea what time my earliest convenience would be?"

"Yes." His secretary curtailed her smile. "Right away."

"Keith!" The door to the office opened following a single knock, and Bill McKay, the white-haired, leathery-skinned editor-in-chief of the *Star*, hobbled in, leaning heavily on his cane. "Jesus Christ." His eyes fell on the paper from the teletype now in a thick roll on the floor. "You haven't seen the story?"

"What story?" Keith asked, moving quickly toward the video scanner on his desk.

"Clavier just placed a resolution before the Congress calling for the severance of diplomatic relations with South Africa."

"Holy . . ." Keith pressed the code combination and as the story came on the screen read swiftly. "And, goddammit, Sykes is leading the opposition."

"Yeah," McKay replied. "It's our headline for the bulldog edition, unless of course . . ."

"Set it up to run. And unless the President has a stroke and dies, or somebody explodes a nuclear device on New York . . ." Suddenly Keith remembered. He turned to his secretary again. "No wonder my father . . ."

"That's just what was going through my mind." McKay's long nose twitched beneath his gray-green eyes. "Stephen Hardwick Kuykendal has a great deal of money, even for him, tied up in South Africa. What do you think our editorial policy should be?"

"Shit, you know damn well what it should be. We ought to get out. We should have been out."

"Granted." McKay's head bobbed quickly. "But given that, your father . . ."

"Damn it, Bill, my father doesn't own this newspaper. I do."

"All right, Keith." McKay made a shrugging gesture.

But Keith saw the look: don't bite the hand . . .

"Look, Bill," Keith said softly. "Get Stimson to handle the story. He believes in it."

The seventy-five-story, triangular glass-and-steel feat of engineering known as the National Heritage Building was less than twenty blocks from the *Star*. In the traffic the taxi took eighteen minutes. The time and the noise set Keith's nerves on edge. Why would his father insist on interrupting his day? Maybe he wanted to talk about the Clavier resolution and maybe even the *Star*'s position. But hell, he could do that on the phone. Keith frowned. Well, one thing was damn sure, he wasn't going to let the old man get into the habit of dictating editorial policy. His father didn't own the *Star*. Maybe a whole lot of the rest of the world, but not the *Star*. Keith's frown deepened as he thought about his father. You really couldn't tell about the old man. He might have even liked Clay's speech. "Tough" was his father's favorite expression. Or "positive leadership." And the craziest thing about the old man was "the teachings of my grandfather, Robert Hardwick," as he put it. He was rich as Croesus and yet, undoubtedly, one of the true liberals in the country.

Keith smiled suddenly remembering the cartoon the New York *Times* had run during the heyday of Vietnam protest: his father in the street with a group of student protestors, sweat shirt declaring: HELL NO, I AIN'T GONNA GO, while he staggered beneath the burden of oil rigs, refineries, petrochemical plants, pipelines, mines, and sawmills which he carried on his back. That sure was the old man. How the hell he lived with his positions . . . how he rationalized them, deep down, in his gut . . . But Keith knew he did. He knew all his father's speeches well.

But, Keith let his lower lip slide slowly between his teeth, if his father didn't like Clay's resolution . . . ? McKay was right. Stephen Hardwick Kuykendal had a hell of a lot of money tied up in South Africa. Well, Keith thought grimly, this would be one of the few times he would disagree with his father. The only other real argument be-

425

tween them had been when he'd announced that he was not going into politics. Keith let his breath out slowly. What a doozy that had been. And then, five hours later, his father had quietly written the check for eight million dollars that had allowed Keith to buy the *Star*.

Keith tapped his fingers on the ashtray on the taxi door, wondering how rich his father really was. *Fortune* had estimated five hundred million, but they hadn't included the TV stations in Atlanta, Denver, and San Francisco, or a word about those big oil refineries in the South, or his subsidiaries in South Africa.

Keith grinned suddenly. Clay was really giving it to them today. Oh, sure, Sykes was answering with a lot of bombast, but Clay was right. That old soon-and-someday bullshit wouldn't wash. People were dying now!

Yes, Keith nodded decisively as he got out of the cab before the marble archway of his father's skyscraper, he'd stand up to Stephen Kuykendal on South Africa.

As he pushed through the revolving door, glancing down at his great-grandfather's name on the ancient cornerstone, a sudden nauseous feeling roiled in Keith's gut. For he knew full well as he pushed the button of his father's private elevator, that despite his own convictions, he might not.

426

"It's good to see you, Keith." Stephen Kuykendal came around his desk, smiling, as his son came into the sun-brilliant office on the sixty-fifth floor. "You look good."

"That's a miracle." Keith forced a smile, hoping to keep explanation from sounding like apology as he shook his father's hand. He hadn't seen the old man in nearly a month. "I've been working ten hours a day seven days a week since I . . . we bought the *Star*."

"It's always that way at the top." Stephen Kuykendal permitted himself a small sigh as he took his son's arm. "But your mother misses you. Why don't you bring the family up this weekend?"

Low-key. Keep it very low-key, Keith thought as he took the maroon leather seat indicated by his father. "Sunday might be good."

"We'll expect you then. Perhaps we can get in a few holes of golf."

"That would be great." Keith kept his eyes on the older man's face, realizing suddenly that ever since he'd finished college his father had treated him in almost the same manner that he did his business associates. The amenities first. And then the demands. What had happened to those close, warm, fun-filled days they had known together when he was a boy? With a jolt Keith remembered the boyhood exhilaration of leaping down the bottom stairs of the Hardwick Place into his father's arms, the swimming excitement of his first electric train circling around the mountains and Indian tepees his father had built on the huge table in the recreation room. What had happened . . . ?

"I suppose you're planning to headline the Clavier resolution?" Stephen Kuykendal said as he sat behind his desk.

"Yes," Keith replied firmly.

Stephen Kuykendal nodded thoughtfully. "We're facing an entirely new concept in business, the shift of economic power from the manufacturing nations to the raw-material-producing nations of the world. Until now big business has operated on the now erroneous thesis that it would acquire its raw materials free, or almost free. We've never factored in the real cost of raw materials in our operating budgets.

427

"Nor unfortunately, have most large corporations considered seriously the social implications of business, the social contracts of business, or, if you will, the ethics of business."

"And"—Keith said quietly—"what about the ethics of your business? You have several large subsidiaries operating in South Africa."

"That's true. But just before you came into this room I gave the order to start pulling out."

For a moment Keith stared at his father as the older man crossed his legs and leaned back in his chair. "It's strange how power and ethics crisscross," the elder Kuykendal continued, slowly. "Strange but real. And we stand at the crossroads where we might lose all to the Communist world. The great corporations must realize that it is to their self-interest to run on the liberal tide.

"You know as well as I, Keith, the deepening economic recession has been caused by market saturation—at least in the Western nations—of our manufactured goods. What we must do if we're to reverse our rising unemployment is develop new markets in Third World nations—those very nations which, to a large degree, we have alienated by exploitation. But," Stephen Kuykendal said slowly, "it is the only hope we have. The old trading partners—Western Europe, the United States, Japan—have become trading rivals."

With effort Keith kept irony from his voice. "Is that how you feel the editorial should read?"

"I feel those are important factors that should be stressed. However"—Stephen waved aside his son's interruption—"I haven't asked you here to discuss the Clavier resolution but Clavier himself. You and he were friends in Cambridge. What is your assessment of him?"

Keith stared at his father. Surely he hadn't brought him here, at the busiest time of his day, to discuss Clay Clavier. He saw his father's sharp stare and said slowly, "Well, Dad, you've met Clay—the couple of times when he was at the house. He's bright, honest, aggressive, a real 'can do' guy. Do you mind if I ask what makes this so urgent at this moment?"

"He seems to me to have exceptional insights, a unique sense of balance! I would tend to believe that he is one of the best mentally equipped men on the Hill."

"Well, the Hill being no measure of mental giants, I would say Clay is far beyond most of them."

Stephen Hardwick nodded slowly. "I believe so too." He looked at his son. "I've been reading Clavier's articles and following his speeches. He makes a lot of sense." Stephen stood abruptly, holding out his hand, indicating the meeting was over. "Keep an eye on him, Keith. Watch him closely. Your friend Clay Clavier may be going a hell of a lot farther than most people think."

Dave stared out of the window, trying to ignore the subdued whine of the Concorde, then glanced at Clay, asleep in the seat beside him. Gradually, admiration replaced envy. Clay would step off the plane when they landed at Dulles looking as though he had just come from his shower, showing no effects of having flown damn near eighteen thousand miles in ten days, of having sat through nearly fifty hours of meetings on three continents, of having met with the presidents of two nations whose fading goodwill was crucial to the United States.

Leaning forward, Dave rubbed the throbbing ache in the small of his back, knowing it signaled his urge to give it up, to live like a sane man again. For once! For a little while! Dave glanced at the thickening gray of Clay's hair. For the little while they had left.

Resisting a sigh, Dave slid back in the seat. How the years had flashed by. His own son, born during Clay's first campaign, was practicing law now. His daughter would make him a grandfather for the second time any day.

Maybe Clay wouldn't run again this year. He had been talking of leaving the Congress. But, the sigh escaped this time, Clay had said those things before.

Maybe he meant it this time. Dave glanced at Clay again. The long, bitter fight for minority jobs during the depression that had gripped the nation during the early eighties was over. And, Dave thought, that resurgence of bitter prejudice had welded black Americans as nothing else could have done. They had closed ranks and faced a common threat. As Clay had said, it had "brought all the Josephs home."

And now, Dave thought with a smile, Zimbabwe, Namibia, and South Africa, now known as Azania, were free.

The old battlegrounds, housing and education, now stricken with rapidly declining enrollments, still had crucial problems, but younger men could address themselves to these now. Civil rights still needed champions. And Dan Fleming, Clay's enthusiastic choice, was facing stiff competition in the presidential primaries. Damn, Dave thought, I'm tired.

It would be nice to go home each night to Christy. A small smile touched Dave's lips. She wasn't the Christy of twenty years ago maybe, who, by turns, had excited, delighted him, and infuriated him with her rantings against his long absences, his long "apprenticeship" to Clay. She was the Christy who understood the harsh truth he had long before admitted to himself—that he did not have the drive, the confidence for leadership. "Would you ever have believed," she had asked, snuggling next to him a month ago, "that the bed would be the place where we would read?"

But Clay would always find a challenge. A man, a group, a nation needing help. And the way the country was polarizing, Clay would never, willingly, give up power. Dave's smile broadened. One thing was sure, Clay had it now. How had the caption under his picture on the cover of *Time* read last year . . . ? Dave frowned a moment, then remembered. "Clay Clavier, the most powerful black politician in the nation's history. Respected by the intellectual elite. Trusted by the man in the street."

The light over the cockpit door went on. Dave looked up as the stewardness leaned over him. "Fasten your seat belt, please."

Dave looked out at the snow flecks falling against the window. He checked his watch. Seven-oh-three. On time. He nudged Clay gently. "Hey, old man, we're getting ready to land."

"Where?" Clay, sleepily.

"Dulles. We're home."

Clay ran a hand over his eyes, stretched the length the seats allowed, then reached under his seat for his briefcase. "Look, Dave, when we get to the office, I want you to get on this right . . ."

"Tonight?" Dave gasped.

Clay looked at his companion for a minute, then grinned sheepishly. "Okay. First thing in the morning."

"Chief." Pepper met them as they cleared customs. "Thank God you're home."

"Why?" Clay began as Pepper reached for a suitcase. Then he saw the look on Pepper's face. "What . . . ?"

"Sykes has declared his candidacy for President. Endorsements are pouring in. Goddammit, Chief, Dan Fleming could be in serious trouble." Pepper laid one hand on Clay's arm. "And you may be in for a hell of a fight to get back to Congress."

431

Keith Kuykendal's Tahoe-tanned face scowled as his telephone at the *Star* rang and the indicator above his private line lit up. Who the hell was calling at this hour? He'd just talked to Susan, his wife. Damn it. He had to get this editorial done. He could feel the vibration of the presses rolling four flights below his office.

The phone insisted, and Keith jerked the receiver to his ear, growling, "Hello," a warning that no voice was welcome.

"Keith?"

"Dad?" Mellower, much mellower.

"Susan told me you were still at it. I'm sorry to have to interrupt you. I'd like you to come up tonight . . ."

"Tonight?" Keith checked his watch. It was already past ten. "Is anything wrong?"

"No, not immediately, but I think we ought to talk as soon as possible."

Keith bit his lip as he swiveled in his cowhide chair. Through the blowing snow he could hardly see the lights across the street. But it wasn't often that his father summoned him to the family place. "All right. I'm finishing an editorial about Sykes's candidacy. It'll take at least another hour to even get halfway down the list of why not Sykes." Keith paused to see if that subject and the indication of the lateness of his arrival would either elicit the reason for the urgency or buy delay until tomorrow. But Stephen Kuykendal was silent at the other end. "I'll be up as soon as I finish."

"Good. I'll see you then!"

There was a click inside the receiver. Keith stared at it a moment before replacing it. Something must be brewing. He didn't know his father still stayed up past ten o'clock.

It was almost midnight when Keith Kuykendal's Ferrari GTC swerved up the Seventy-second Street entrance onto the Henry Hudson Parkway. At least the traffic's eased up, he thought. He hadn't intended to spend that much time on that editorial; in fact, he rarely wrote his paper's editorials. But Sykes? Goddamn, the country was really going to the dogs.

432

The car skidded in a patch of snow and Keith swore eloquently. Why the hell, on a night like this . . . ?

The George Washington Bridge arched its double row of lights toward the shrouded palisades of Jersey. Silently Keith thanked God he didn't have to cross that bridge in this weather. He was having trouble with his blood pressure again, and it was increasing his acrophobia. The acrophobia was one of the major reasons he hadn't gone into politics. He could never take all that flying.

He had never told his father that was the reason. The old man would never have understood. He'd never had a sick day in his life. Keith frowned, remembering his father's answer to all Keith's boyhood hesitations and small fears. "You have to learn to tough it out. You can go against any odds if you've got the will."

You can go, but can you win? Keith frowned. Even his father knew that. Even Stephen Hardwick Kuykendal knew about losing— about losing the one thing he wanted most of all. For twenty years the old man had dreamed of being President. For twenty years he had devoted his money and his time. Oh, he'd been Secretary of the Treasury and ambassador to both England and the Soviet Union, but, as with his grandfather, Robert Hardwick . . . Damn, Keith, thought, it had been the country's loss.

Keith's foot eased down on the accelerator, and the Ferrari zoomed along the parkway. The road here was clear. To his left, the Hudson River was lost in darkness. "Where I walk to school each day, Indian children used to play." Keith shook his head, remembering the boyhood poem. What would this all be like in another century? If there was another century, which with Sykes . . .

It was one-fifteen when Keith drove through the great stone gates of the Hardwick Place. He had called Susan and told her he would be spending the night at his father's, and he knew his wife would be timing his arrival for her phone call. "Did you get there all right? I was worried about you driving after a long day."

Checking on him! Always checking on him! Well, if she had seen him flying in this snow, she'd have had another worry. What the devil could the old man want?

He saw the light reflecting in the stained-glass windows of the study and, even as he started up the stairs, Frederick, the butler, was opening the door. "Your father is waiting in the library, Mr. Keith."

"Thanks, Frederick." He shucked out of his coat and left it on that

433

man's arm, then sat down on the bench in the foyer to pull off his boots.

He was still in that twisted position when he heard his father's voice. "Sorry to have you travel in such weather, Keith, but something quite urgent has come up."

Behind his father, a fire blazed in the fireplace. A bottle of Harvey's Shooting Sherry sat between two glasses on the table. Keith shoved weariness from his mind. They were in for a night of it!

Keith followed his father across the hunting scene woven into the Persian rug. He eased himself back on the down-filled suede sofa, watching as Stephen Kuykendal opened the silver humidor on the table and took out a slender silver-gray tube. "It seems"—Keith contrived a convival tone—"that Sykes's candidacy could seriously impair Fleming's chances."

Carefully the old man broke the seal and extracted a cigar. Still standing, he reached for the lighter, then looked at his son. "Dan Fleming is out."

"Out?" Keith came to the edge of the sofa. "What do you mean, out? I just talked to him, what was it, two days ago."

"If you knew before New Hampshire, why did you drop so much money in Pennsylvania? Why didn't you . . . ?"

"Because I was waiting until I decided who would replace Fleming . . ."

"Until *you* decided . . . ?" Keith heard irony underscore incredulity and softened his voice. "And who have you decided?"

For a moment Stephen Kuykendal studied his son, then he uncorked the sherry, poured two glasses and handed one to Keith. "Do you remember several years ago I told you to keep your eye on Clay Clavier?"

"Clay?" Keith put his wineglass on the table and stared at his father.

"Would you say, Keith"—the elder Kuykendal's voice was calm—"that, all things considered, he's the best man for the job?"

"Probably. But what's that got to do with it? Clay can't win. You know as well as I do that racial intolerance. . . . Dad, no black man . . ."

"Keith the time for petty prejudice is over. The issue of today, of tomorrow, is survival. National survival." Stephen Kuykendal rubbed the palms of his hands together as he paced before the fireplace. "A

434

depression more devastating than any our people have ever known is closing on us *fast*.

"We're losing our former favorable trade agreements for both raw materials we need on which production depends and the markets for the goods that we produce."

Stephen Kuykendal lit his cigar and sat down beside his son. "The time is here when we will either have to share the wealth or give it up entirely. I say let's make that decision before one is forced on us. I agree with Clavier's position that a free enterprise system does not exist when control of the lives of two hundred million people rests on the wills of two, three hundred corporations. I agree that free enterprise does not exist when conglomerates gobble up small business. When the only choice a man has is which master he will serve. It deadens the nerve endings. It eradicates creativity. It stagnates . . ."

"I agree with Clavier," Stephen continued slowly, "that the giants of this nation can no longer continue to rout this country, to grow ever wealthier and more powerful, while the majority of our citizens exist in tacky absurdity, in overpriced daydreams, as human robots taking the eight-fifteen train to oblivion . . ."

"According to *Fortune*, you have more than eighty thousand human robots taking the ticky-tacky to oblivion. How many multinational corporations do you control, Dad? Four, five . . . ?"

"Seven." Stephen Kuykendal ignored the sarcasm in his son's voice. "And I intend to continue to control them. But I have always tried to remember my grandfather's teachings, that my workers are human beings with human needs . . ."

"I know that speech . . ."

"Then you know why Clavier."

"No, I don't know why Clavier."

"Keith, the multinationals must have continuing access to the developing nations. Not only for the raw materials they provide but also as markets to utilize our capital, our means of production, our goods and services. A lot of money is flowing and will continue to flow through those people's hands, with or without the United States. They want and are now able to buy the higher standard of living that machines and technology can produce. So, as you yourself have advocated, a brand-new relationship must be worked out with the darker people of the world. And I'm not speaking of the stickups and rip-offs to which your friend Clavier refers."

435

"So your idea is to stick Clay up there so the darker races will be a little more amenable to letting you stay in business."

"To letting America stay in business. Do you know how many millions of Americans are dependent on the resources of Third World nations for their daily bread? Can you imagine what unemployment figures would be if those resources dry up? Have you any idea what prices will be if we decide to try to go it ourselves completely? Damn it, Keith, look at how many American corporations are already doing most of their production abroad."

"Now"—Keith smiled—"you're quoting me. But"—the smile disappeared—"that doesn't explain why Clay. I know the Gallup Poll showed him to be the most respected American among the Third World nations and he's greatly admired in Europe too. But did you see the evening papers? If Sykes's candidacy really takes off Clay may not make it back to Congress. And you know as well as I they'd slaughter him in the primaries . . .

"Look, Dad, I agree we can't let Sykes get the nomination. Jesus Christ . . . ! But what about Jenson of Connecticut, or MacDonald at State?"

"Jenson is a good man but he's just not tough enough. No." Stephen's white head shook thoughtfully. "Jenson doesn't have the tenacity. He'd become the pawn of Congress in three weeks. And though MacDonald is a genius of foreign policy—it was pure jealousy that kept him from being Secretary—capable, so capable . . . but he has no idea at all of domestic issues . . . of whom to see and whom to leave alone . . ."

"Well, since both you and your grandfather wanted to be President, why don't you will it to someone in our family? We've got two cousins in governor's mansions. What about Polly's husband, Tom West? You admire his thinking and he doesn't share the onus of our wealth. And, let's face it, as governor he could slide into the Pennsylvania primary. Or Carl, there's a Kuykendal for you, and he's on the poorer side of the family. Carl's got the power to make himself or Tom look damn good in Massachusetts. And then, in those primaries where your money counts—a lot . . ."

"Tom's not ready yet," the senior Hardwick said crisply. "He can handle the State House but not the White House. Maybe in eight years, but . . ." Stephen ran his hand through his hair and said ruefully, "Who can guarantee I'll be around to help him then? No,

Tom will make a damn good Secretary of Defense. And I'd like to see you at Treasury." Stephen smiled. "My old job."

Keith shifted in his seat for a better look at his father as the older man continued. "Your point about the primaries is well taken. It is harder to control the vote. But I wasn't planning to have Clavier run in the primaries. Fleming would stay out there, getting those delegates pledged to his support, then in the convention . . ."

"Fleming has agreed to that?"

"Dan Fleming owes me everything he has. And he believes that, if Clavier can make it, he's undoubtedly the best man we have today. He wants to go on the first ballot—and I believe that's best—and pledge his delegates to Clavier on the second."

"You're really serious about this?" Keith frowned as he reached for the sherry.

"Absolutely."

"But why are you sold on Clay? Dad, Sykes will . . ."

"I can control Sykes." Ignoring the shocked look on his son's face, Stephen Kuykendal continued, "I am, as you say, sold on Clavier because he represents, in most areas, that for which we, as a family, have stood for over one hundred and fifty years.

"He's a humanitarian, but not a naive idealist. He understands power and the positive uses to which it can be put. He's aware of the issues with which this country must deal in this decade, and he's just and fair. I am sold on him, Keith, because he is the best!

"As for our cousins, Carl and Tom, neither of them knows much about foreign policy, which is crucial at this juncture. And, as far as cousinship goes, Clay Clavier is the same relation to you as Tom or Carl. No, Clay is your second cousin, once removed."

The stem of the wine glass cracked in Keith's hand. "Clay Clavier?" Keith gasped as he stared at his father. "Dad, are you sure?"

"Of course," the old man nodded, then seeing the wine spill close to the cuff of his son's pink Pierre Cardin shirt, "Get that off your hand. Frederick will bring another glass." Stephen stood and touched the bell on his desk. In a moment they heard the butler's deferential knock. "Come in, Frederick. Please bring another napkin and another glass."

Keith's eyes were fixed on his father during the silence that accompanied Frederick's task, then Stephen Kuykendal began again. "My grandmother was Clay Clavier's great-grandfather's sister. His grand-

437

father, of whom you said Clavier spoke so highly, was my first cousin."

"This sister and brother?" Keith asked curtly. "Were they white or black?"

"They were black."

It took a moment for the thought to find expression. "Your grandmother was black?"

"Racially speaking."

"Well." Keith could not keep the sarcasm from his voice. "We *are* our brother's keeper!" He looked at his father. "I suppose you've known this for some time?"

"My grandfather used to talk about it. As he grew older, he became obsessed with the fact that he had never been able to keep his deathbed promise to his wife, to help her brother's children. He asked that I carry out that promise. It was his last request."

For a moment Stephen Hardwick Kuykendal was lost in his own thoughts. "When I was a boy, he used to take me to Washington just to look at her portrait. I can remember, I guess I was about nine or ten, standing in the Hardwick Collection in the National Gallery of Art . . ."

"You mean Isabella?" Keith looked at his father incredulously, remembering his own boyhood visit to the portrait, and the pictures of Isabella Hardwick in decaying leather family albums. "Jesus, you'd never know it."

"My grandfather said her brother, Jason Clavier, was quite brown."

Keith let his breath out slowly as he studied his father. "Mother knows, of course . . ."

"I told her when we became engaged. But then"—a smile touched Stephen's lips—"she was marrying a Kuykendal, wasn't she?"

"Well, I must say, this is quite a shock!" Keith looked around the room. It was still the same. Nothing had changed.

"I can assure you, it has happened in many families," his father said with asperity. "Now can we get back to Clavier? It's nearly two o'clock."

"Ah, yes!" Keith wet his lips. "Clay. Cousin Clay. Jesus, I had dinner with him just last week. He doesn't know anything about this, does he?"

"I have no idea. I'd like for you to bring him up next week, after we get these details worked out!"

Keith stared at his father. "You're determined to do it your way?"

"A trait I understand I inherited from my grandmother." Kuykendal smiled.

For a moment Keith was silent. He had always thought he knew the old man so well. "Okay, Dad," he said softly. "But at least answer my question. Over and beyond the bullshit . . . why Clay Clavier?"

Stephen Kuykendal permitted himself a smile as he looked at his son. Over and beyond the bullshit. His sharp blue eyes narrowed . . . the years of service, the hundreds of thousands of dollars he and his grandfather had given to the party. His grandfather Robert Hardwick's lifelong dream to become President, deemed inexpeditious by the party. A good man, but too rich, too progressive to deserve the public trust.

His own years of service, his own aspirations for the presidency— but once again the party had been too fearful of his money, of his liberalism, and most of all, too fearful of the conservative South—of the Sykeses—of the Dulanes.

All of his, his grandfather's manipulations, money, influence. Half of their lives spent in pursuit of that office, the presidency of the United States . . . to be ignored. And now, his own son, with no interest in political office. No, Stephen Hardwick Kuykendal thought, he could not live another ten, twenty years to see a grandson grown. If he was to do it, he must do it now. Now or never. And damn them, he would have it. He had learned the lessons well. If not himself, if not his own body, then . . .

"You want Clay to be your surrogate." Keith said it softly, wondering that he had not thought of it before.

"Men of power control the presidency," his father replied. "And we are men of power."

The younger man of power sat motionless for a moment, then raised his eyes to meet his father's. "I think you'd better get Clay up here and see if he's interested. And, Dad, I think I ought to warn you, just for the record, Clay Clavier will be no man's surrogate. I wouldn't try to dictate terms of employment." Keith looked at his father a moment more, then, with a wry smile he leaned back on the sofa. "But damn, if Clay is interested, this could be one hell of a show."

439

Clay fastened this seat belt as the warning light went on and the Lear jet began its descent to Teterboro airport. Whatever Stephen Hardwick wanted, Clay mused, he had spared no expense making certain he arrived to hear of it. The press was probably already having a field day speculating about what was going on.

That was, Clay frowned, what he hated most . . . they wouldn't let you piss in peace. Well, the hell with them. Keith was an old friend and if you couldn't spend an evening with an old friend and his father—even if the father was one of the richest men in the world . . .

One thing was certain, Clay thought as he looked around the plane's cowhide interior. They really did live in style. A private jet to pick him up in Washington, pilot, copilot, steak dinner, even the telephone beside him. Clay grinned, remembering Diana's shocked voice when he had called and told her he was passing over New York City via private jet and would not be home for dinner; that Keith Kuykendal had called and asked him to his family place.

"It must be urgent." Di's voice had been appropriately awed. "What's it about?"

"Don't know. But Keith has been damn kind to me in the *Star*. I thought his invitation should be honored. I'll be home tonight."

"Congressman Clavier." The copilot opened the cockpit door. "The limousine is waiting. We'll be on the ground in two minutes. Button up. It's five degrees."

Five minutes later Clay was sprinting from Lear jet to Rolls-Royce, his breath frosting on the air as he shook Keith's hand. "Feels like fifty below."

"It's always cold as a witch's tit up here this time of year." Keith followed Clay into the back of the car. "Do you want a drink." A touch of a button brought a bar to view. "Scotch, Bourbon, cognac? There's ice and seltzer water."

"Ice we don't need. I suppose you know what this is all about?"

"Yes, but Dad wants to tell you himself. Did you see where we beat Princeton 98 to 67?"

"No. I can't get past the editorial pages. Thanks for your kind words, Keith."

"Not kind, true. And, Clay, let's stay off politics until we see Dad. I guarantee you'll hear enough about it then."

Stephen Kuykendal stood as they came into the study, his hair silvery in the firelight. "And so now it's Congressman Clavier. Come on, have a seat."

Clay sat down in the leather chair indicated by the senior Kuykendal. The older man settled himself across from him, studying Clay intently. "Congressman Clavier, I asked you up here because, as you yourself have so often said so eloquently, our nation is in crisis. Not only in terms of energy, ecology, spiraling inflation, crime, the devastation of our cities, wars and rumors of wars, but fundamentally—morally. It is crucial, if our ship of state is to ride out this storm, that we have the best man, the very best man we have, at the helm."

"I think we'll have that man, in Dan Fleming," Clay replied quietly.

"Dan is out." Stephen Hardwick saw the shocked question in Clay's eyes and said quickly, "I cannot divulge the reasons."

Clay glanced at Keith, saw he was following his father's words intently. "Dan Fleming will continue in the primaries, then when his delegates are committed . . ." Kuykendal leaned forward suddenly, his sharp, piercing eyes level with the dark, steady eyes across from him. "Clay Clavier, we want you to run for the presidency."

Kuykendal ignored the stunned look on Clay's face, saying, "I need not mince words with you. We are both men of the world. We know how the world is changing, has in fact already changed. There's no doubt in my mind that you are of presidential timber, and had you been white, our party would have looked to you for leadership as far back as the early seventies—a movement I would have heartily endorsed. But those years now belong to a different world."

Kuykendal scrutinized the man before him. He knew that Clavier understood what this offer, from a Kuykendal, meant. But the face opposite his was a mask. It was impossible to read the younger man's thoughts.

"Americans have long tried to P.R. the world that we represent the standard by which all values should be judged," Stephen Kuykendal continued. "That the height of our skyscrapers, the gleam of our chrome plating, the speed of our supersonics, our voracious consumption, and our stupendous technology are somehow the criteria of excellence to which the world aspires.

"But that P.R. job isn't selling any more. Its believability factor is zero. The so-called developing nations know we've grown rich on their riches. They're demanding a fair price and access to technology in exchange for their resources. They want an equal share of the world's good things. And much of Europe is ready to deal."

Kuykendal drew a deep breath. "What I'm saying, Clay, is that you are a man whose word is respected by the leaders of the world. You can offer America leadership in the light of the new reality. Together we can give the American people a chance to pass through the dangerous shoals ahead. And then, the choice will be theirs. But we will have done our part."

Clay was listening intently, mentally recording not only the issues Kuykendal articulated but those which he did not, analyzing the older man's persuasions and the depth of his commitment to them. Kuykendal's assessment of his worth did not flatter him. He knew his worth, well earned. He was concerned, however, that Kuykendal realized he had his own agenda and that not even the presidency, particularly a powerless presidency, was enough to sway him from it. Not that he was an idealist. He had been in politics too long for that.

Clay frowned. Kuykendal, of course, was interested in the Third World nations. His corporations did big business there. The rising cost of raw materials had to be hurting him. But did he really see beyond the broad spectrum to the ramifications of the redistribution of wealth?

Some crazy at Defense had published a new thesis on limited neutron warfare. No property annihilation, just a few selected million people here and there. It was, the author said, the simplest way to accomplish two much needed objectives: to assure access to raw materials and to hold the population in line. The strange thing was, they had never figured out that the making of those bombs was like the secret of a small-town schoolgirl's pregnancy. Sooner or later, everybody knew. And who had all the makings?

And the crucial question—who would feed the starving? Food and human reproduction, still the most elemental and crucial questions of this sophisticated time.

Hell, he didn't need it. Johnny and Lorraine were almost grown,

442

and he hardly knew them. He didn't want that to happen with his youngest two. And there were a hundred things that he and Di had planned and never done. Hell, no he didn't need it. He had his place on the Vineyard and more than one hundred fifty thousand dollars a year for the rest of his life, if he never lifted a finger. His grandfather had seen to that. And damn, there'd be a thousand bullets, all pointed at his brain.

Kuykendal saw the look crossing Clay's face and matched it with a reason. "There would, of course, be the element of danger, real danger to your life."

Clay nodded. Yes, Malcolm, King, a hundred black martyrs had proved that. But, could he let it go without a try? He had asked himself why he stayed in Washington before his last election. And now the range of power could be greater, far greater. And damn, he knew what to do with it.

Who needed it—the hours, the endless hours of mind-bending work? Why take the risk? Oh, what a risk. It wasn't feasible. It wasn't even probable. It was a ridiculous idea.

Who had done that "trust poll" last week? The CIA had squashed it, but the word had leaked anyway. Clay Clavier was the most trusted American—outside the United States.

No. Hell, no. Why put himself in that bind? The pressure . . . It was bad enough now.

Clay looked beyond Stephen Kuykendal at his gilt-framed progenitors on the wall, at the ship's model above the fireplace.

What would old Jacques have said? Hell, he'd say, "Go and get it." And so would his Grandpa Clay.

Suddenly, inexplicably, Clay wanted to laugh—to laugh for David Walker, for Nat Turner and Denmark Vesey, for Jacques and Alexander, for Jason and his Grandpa Clay, for his father and Sojourner Truth and Harriet Tubman and Mary Smith and Sally Jones and all the brothers and sisters who had walked through the back doors of life. To laugh for the mute bones of those who had left the motherland and never seen these shores—those seventy thousand, Du Bois had said, whose bleached bones floored the Atlantic from Boston to Benin.

He shook his head denying the tears that cried behind his eyes. Too much was at stake. Much too fucking much. Too many had died, and too many had cried. He could not refuse.

443

Clay looked into the fire, hearing Kuykendal again. Yes, they were all the right words, rightly intoned. Have a glass of sherry and, by the way, how would you like to be President of the United States—for real?

Another time, another face—"Have you ever thought about it, Skipper?"

"What do you think, Clay?" Stephen Kuykendal asked softly.

Damn. If not, why not! Under his shirt Clay felt the wooden medallion hard against his chest. "Let's talk about it," he said.

It was four hours later when Clay stood to leave. As he shook Kuykendal's hand, he said, "You've told me many things this evening, Mr. Kuykendal, but I'd like to ask again, your reason for choosing me."

Kuykendal crossed to the mantel and took down the ship's model and placed it in Clay's hand. "Two days ago, I had this sent from my cousin's office in Boston. It is the model of Jacques Clavier's ship the *Voyager*. My great-grandfather was the captain of that ship. The words you see were carved by a man named Nils Kuykendal almost two hundred years ago. 'No Clavier ship sails in time of stress without a Kuykendal.' This, Clay Clavier, will be by far our most difficult voyage."

It was dawn when Clay got out of the cab in his driveway. In the light from the upstairs hall he could see Di snuggled deep in sleep. For the first time the easy access to his home bothered him.

For a moment he considered this, then, as he always did, went to say a silent good-night to the kids. Johnny and Lorraine were now away at college. His son Clay, eleven, was sleeping beneath a collection of faces peering out from football helmets, his homework, Clay knew, still half done.

In Mary Lou's room the night light burned. She was snuggled with a giant stuffed turtle. He could hear her sucking her thumb clear across the room. Smiling, he pulled her thumb from her mouth and bent to kiss her.

A frown replaced Clay's smile as he closed the door. They slept so soundly now. Could he put them out there . . . into all of that?

"Clay?" Diana stood in the doorway of their bedroom. As he came toward her, he could smell Germaine perfume. "I thought I heard you. What did Mr. Kuykendal say?"

444

"He wants me to run for President."

The smile with which she favored her children's aspirations started on her lips, then wavered. "For President?"

"Yes." He sat down and started pulling off his shoes, then looked up at her and grinned. "Of the United States."

Within a month Clay's secret campaign was under way. Before the meeting with Kuykendal, he had agreed to a speaking engagement at Berkeley, and more than three thousand students jammed the auditorium. But Kuykendal made a difference. This time his speech was carried on TV.

In rapid succession, he was scheduled at Michigan, at Cornell, at Howard, at Antioch, at Arkansas A & M; at forums in Pittsburgh and Scarsdale, in Palm Springs and Newark, in Harlem and Winnetka, always, ostensibly, speaking on problems which his role in the Congress encompassed.

He was interviewed by the influential news weeklies. He did the intellectual talk shows, one of which, on the Middle East, created a national sensation. Both the Israeli and Arab panelists had been enthusiastic about Clay's proposals. At the hour's end, the sign-off had been given and, thinking they were off the air, the Arab had leaned across the table and said, "Congressman Clavier, it is too bad you are not the President." To which the Israeli had enjoined, "Yes, it could make quite a difference!"

It was carried into two million homes.

In May the Third World Congress of African-Asian-Latin American nations met in Ghambana. Clay addressed the Congress on its opening night. The major newspapers of the world carried the president of the Third World Congress, Radiz Senatuma's introduction: "A man who truly understands the problems of the formerly colonized as they move into their new place in the sun. A man who is just. A man we can trust. My friend and the friend of man—Clay Clavier!"

Now they were moving fast. Jeff Lawson, the young, bright, ambitious president of the Black Caucus, with whom Clay shared his "secret," garnered a task force to step up black voter registration. The president of Christiana University in Charleston invited Clay to address—from the steps of the Clavier Administration Building—the six thousand students of its seventy-fifth graduating class. Dave, Pepper, and Millie combined forces to write incisive speeches. Uncle

Clarence, in his wheelchair, opened up his wallet and pulled out the crumpled private numbers of heads of state who might invite Clay to address a major forum. The World Health Organization invited Clay to Geneva to open its Emergency World Food Convention and, from Paris, a citation "In Behalf of All Humanity." In his office in the Rayburn Building, Sykes commented to an aide, "I'm telling you, every time Clavier makes a speech for Fleming in a primary, or opens his mouth anywhere on this globe, you'd swear the nigger was running for the presidency."

Other people thought so too. Jeff Lawson had to fly up to New York to squash a write-in vote. In Pittsburgh and Chicago, in Atlanta, in Detroit and L.A., the word went out: Be cool. It's not time yet. But before the convention opened in Charleston, in Sykes's home state of South Carolina, the smart-money reporters were asking, "It's not yet time for what?"

"J.D., it's getting worse, I tell you. Goddammit, I don't like it at all."

Sykes adjusted his smoke-tinted glasses and looked up from his desk in the Rayburn Building at Randy Whitfield, his administrative assistant, blustering above him. "What specifically, Randy, don't you like?"

"The whole damn thing stinks like a Commie-nigger plot. Every time you open a paper who do you see grinning at you but that damn Clavier. Look, I've been keeping my eye on who's been rushing in and out of his office. And you know who they are? Everybody who hates your guts. I'm telling you, J.D., we gotta stop him." Randy's fingers, like thick pink sausages, pounded on the paper-cluttered desk. "He's talking against everything we're for. And a lotta folks are listening. If we don't shut that nigger up, he's gonna end up Vice-President, or Secretary of State. I'm telling you, J.D. . . ."

J. D. Sykes frowned, controlling his contempt for his thick-necked companion. That was what he hated most about politics, the people you had to rub elbows with. The ignorant, great unwashed of human society. With effort he controlled the disgust in his voice. Randy's father controlled two key counties in the state. "Do you *really* think Clavier is a Communist, Randy?"

"What else? What red-blooded American would be backing that . . ."

Sykes shifted the papers in front of him uneasily. Of all the pathetic, lost, outmoded, clutching at the flag . . . Then a slight shiver coursed Sykes's spine. He was the one who had taught Randy. He, and his forebears, were guilty, guilty of imbuing frustrated, fearful constituencies with hate, with ignorance—no worse—with lies. It had been their modus operandi. It had been their means to power.

Sykes twisted the silver wedding band on his finger. God, how his grandfather had hated niggers. Hated them more and more as he grew old. Even refused to have them work as maids. And that last book he had written—*The Achilles Heel*—had been so rabidly anti-black that even the libraries in Charleston had refused to buy it. His mother had given him the book to read when he was in high school.

And it was soon after that—to his mother's chagrin—that he had refused to be called by his given name—his grandfather's name—and begun to use formally his boyhood nickname—the initials J.D.

Sykes lifted his glasses and rubbed the inside corners of his eyes, irritably ignoring Randy's hovering presence. Goddammit, despite their long and bitter battles over civil rights, despite the fact that he had been one of the chief proponents of the Southern Manifesto and had taken a hard line against aid to Third World nations, privately he agreed with many of Clavier's positions. There were just too damn many niggers in the United States to make it economically feasible to keep them forever at the bottom of the ladder. And the United States had to deal equitably with the nations of the so-called Third World too, though God knew he wasn't certain they were ready for such equality, yet. From the jungle to the U.N. in one generation? Not that they didn't have some pretty sharp boys, but . . . ? And God, those Chinese. The Japanese were a little better. A little more amenable to Western ways. But those Chinese and all those East Indians. Sykes frowned as he rubbed his wedding ring. And who even knew about those South Americans? He'd heard that Brazil had more black people than any other country in the world. And all those browns, blacks, and yellows were the ones that had what white folks needed. God only knew why He had given them what He had. But He had. And he, J. D. Sykes, was certainly not one to question God's ordinance.

Sykes looked up as he heard Randy's anxious voice. "What do you think we ought to do about Clavier?"

"Nothing!" Sykes heard the sharpness in his tone and changed the subject. "Did we get any more endorsements this morning?"

"Did we?" Randy's broad face broke into a grin. "You should see the telegrams and the checks. Lobbyists for the oil companies, the utilities, even big steel."

"I know," Sykes said softly. "But Kuykendal's still silent, and he's the biggest of them all."

"Lemme tell you, J.D." Randy bent over the desk. "You'll be the nominee. And, you'll be President." Randy's sausage fingers pounded once more on the desk. "If we stop Clavier."

The bow-tied Negro waiter bent beneath the moosehead mounted on the walnut-paneled wall to wipe a speck from the sheen of the round dining table. With a small flourish he placed scotches and Bourbons before the four men seated there. "If you'd like, dinner can be served in ten minutes, gentlemen. I'll be glad to bring a menu. The specialty of the club tonight is lobster thermidor."

"No," Randy Whitfield said quickly. "Not tonight, John." The waiter bowed and moved away, and Randy pushed his thick neck toward his companions. "We've held off long enough," he said tersely to the three other men at the table. "Clavier hasn't got sense enough to give up." He drew a long breath and let it out slowly. "The good Lord knows I don't like to deal in such matters, but . . ." He looked at his associates, whose eyes found business elsewhere in the room. "Face it," Randy said hoarsely. "Clavier's hitting all of us where it hurts. Some of the biggest papers in the country are jumping all over J.D.'s ass. The Senate has started an investigation of your company, Tom." Randy glanced at the man beside him, then jutted his head toward the man across the table. "And, Ken, you know damn well you're gonna be next. Clavier isn't going to stop unless we stop him. We've talked about it and talked about it, but now, damn it, we gotta act." Randy's clenched fist came soundlessly to the table. "We can't let that nigger . . ."

"Does J.D. know about this, Randy?" Ken Johnson ran his thin fingers over his bald pate.

"No." Randy scratched his nose nervously. "No, he don't. But the only reason I didn't tell him is he's got too much on his mind already. All that Commie garbage Clavier's been spewing . . ."

"Spare us your rationale, Randy," Clyde Stewart, the immaculately groomed man across from Randy, said quickly. "Just tell us simply what you propose."

"We can't afford to . . . uh . . . have him . . . uh . . ." Ken Johnson began nervously.

"No, for God's sake. The one thing we don't need is another nigger martyr," the stubby, ruddy-faced Tom commented.

450

"We gotta discredit him." Randy hunched across the table. "Look, I got some letters made. Even a friend of mine over in the CIA said they looked authentic. I got it all set up. A faked-up stop and search by a cop friend of mine. And let me tell you, when he busts Clavier with them letters on him, that nigger won't be able to get a job shoveling dog shit. They say . . ."

"Spare us the details, Randy," Stewart snapped.

"I got the man." Randy's voice was eager. "He's good. He's ready."

"Then do it, for God's sake," Tom muttered. "Do whatever has to be done. I just don't want to know."

"Crap." Clyde Stewart's head turned sharply. "We all know. But" —he turned to Randy—"let's get it over with. Here's the thousand you asked for, in cash. And . . ." He put an envelope on the table. "Randy, let's not see each other again."

"Then it's agreed?" Randy looked around the table, at the bald-headed man dropping his envelope and gulping down his drink, at the ruddy man still opening his briefcase.

"Jesus, we don't need a frigging recount, Randy." Ken Johnson stood. "Just do it, now."

"No." Pepper kept the telephone to his ear as he reached to draw the draperies in Clay's office against the late-afternoon sun. "I have no idea what time he'll be back. As I said before, if you'll give me the message I'll tell the Congressman . . ."

The connection was broken abruptly, and Pepper cursed. "Hostile motha . . . That's the second time in twenty minutes."

Phoebe turned from straightening the pile of papers on Clay's desk. "That must be the same man who called this morning. Something about Christiana University." Her trim shoulders shrugged. "He says it's urgent."

"Every damn thing is urgent," Pepper snapped. "Have you any idea what time the Chief'll be back?"

"He called this morning. He decided to go straight to Boston from San Francisco."

"Damn . . ."

"The meeting with Amalgamated was important. They're big contributors to the campaigns. He had lunch with Governor Kuykendal, then made a stop at the Skate for Life the park district's having to raise funds for the research wing of Peter Brent Bingham Hospital. Diana drove Cathy up to participate. That kid is really good."

"The Chief's not driving back with them?"

"No." Phoebe smiled smugly at the alarm in Pepper's voice. "He's taking the plane. He should be back by eight or nine. Did you get . . . ?"

"I took care of everything." Pepper picked up the San Francisco paper from the couch. "How'd his speech go in Frisco?"

"Great. More than four thousand . . ."

"Jesus." Pepper dropped the paper back on the couch. "I hope he's back by nine. I assured President Senatuma that he'd be at the Ghambana embassy."

"He'll be back in time." Phoebe pulled a Kleenex from her pocket. "Pepper, could you turn up the air conditioner? It's awfully hot in here."

"Hot?" Pepper began, then saw the perspiration standing on her

452

forehead. Damn, he thought, Dave was right. She was going through the change. A slight frown crossed Pepper's face as he walked to the air conditioner. Had that many years gone by? Phoebe had been a girl, really, when they first came to Washington. Foxy Phoebe, they'd called her then. Pepper watched as Phoebe patted her cheeks daintily with the Kleenex, noticing the gray peeking through brown-tinted hair. For the first time he appreciated Clay's suggestion last year that he let Phoebe display more authority. "Let her be the big shot once in a while, Pepper," Clay had said. "She's one of the best members of the team. She's good, reliable, and durable, works ten, twelve hours a day."

She saw him looking at her and flushed. "Clay will probably stop here before he goes home. Will you be here?"

Pepper checked his watch. It was four-fifteen. "Yeah. I'll drop back while I'm making my rounds."

"Good. Tell him the urgent stuff is in the middle of his desk. The things that can wait until tomorrow are under the paperweight."

"Will do." Pepper stood in the door a minute, watching as Phoebe efficiently arranged Clay's desk. So that was what things broke down to in the end. "Foxy Phoebe" had become "good, reliable, and durable." Damn it, Pepper thought as he walked out the door, tomorrow I'm going to bring that girl some flowers.

The stale-smelling bar at Fourteenth and K was almost empty. The dark, Ultra-Sheen-pomaded bartender checked the bottle beneath the yellow, fading autographed photographs of Minnie Minoso, Larry Doby, Ollie Matson, and Dick (the Night Train) Lane. "Wannanother drink?" he aked the tall, light-skinned Negro watching the newscast on the TV above the bar.

"Naw, I'm fine."

The bartender picked up a glass and wiped it without interest. He didn't like this stranger. He had started coming in three nights ago, always ordering the same thing: one lousy glass of Almadén burgundy. He could afford better. That cashmere coat went with cognac. But every night he ran the same act. One lousy dollar's wortha wine.

The bartender's eyes narrowed as he looked covertly at his customer. The wine was just an excuse to stay till he got the call he did each night. He was high on something else. Coke, he guessed from the glitter in his eyes.

Yes, it was Coke. The bartender pressed his full lips together. He could always tell when niggers were fucked up on that shit. But, his eyes surveyed the stranger's hands, his tie, this was hardly the place for a big-time nigger with cocaine bread.

The bartender felt suddenly uneasy. He had thought for months about giving up this gig. Too damn many crazies. He kept his eyes on the stranger as he picked up another glass, remembering that night six months before when a dope-crazed pimp had tried to kill a fed one foot from where the stranger stood. The bartender twisted his mouth. Shit, he'd been lucky as hell, Pepper'd been around. He'd got Clavier to save his liquor license.

But now he and this coke freak were alone—except for them cash-and-carry lovers in the back.

Reluctantly the bartender capped the bottle of olives. Ten o'clock. No more martinis tonight. "You sure you don't wannanother drink?"

"No, thanks." The stranger got up as the pay phone rang. "In fact, you can pour mine back in the bottle." The phone rang again, and the stranger grinned salaciously as he hurried to answer it.

454

"Mike?" The white man's voice at the other end was low, cautious.

"Yep."

"Okay, we moved you again. You're registered under the name of B. Smith in room 1116 at the Queens Motel."

"Whadabout my . . . ?"

"The key to your room is on the dashboard of your car. There's an entrance to the room directly off the parking lot. You won't have to pass throught the lobby. You remember what you're supposed to say? The name is Baker. From Christiana Univer . . ."

"I know." Shit, he knew it cold. Them white mothafuckas always wanted to be teaching somebody something. Hell, he was the best switch man in the business. It was just this hanging around that was making him so fuckin' jumpy. That's how he'd got busted four years ago. Had to hang around too long to set up his mark. Well, the stranger flexed his long fingers, he had no intention, no intention at all of going back to the joint. He wanted no record of even being in the city, if they had to switch him to ten goddamn motels.

"He's in his office now. Call him. Get him down there. Everything's ready."

"Whadabout my bread?"

"Two thousand is in the trunk of your car now. The other two will be there when you leave the motel."

"It won't take an hour."

"Just do it. Do it now."

The stranger dropped the receiver back in place. He fished two coins from his pocket, then, feeling the coke-induced euphoria rising, quickly dialed a number.

Clay stood at his office window, looking at the faraway lights of the colonnaded buildings. Wearily he wondered of which they reminded him—ancient Greece and Rome, liberty and democracy at work—or of Babylon. He ran his hand over his eyes. Jesus, he was tired.

"Well, chief, I think that wraps it." Pepper, his shoes off as usual, leaned back on the couch rubbing his eyes with his fist. Above Clay's desk the clock said ten of nine. "I'll get on this stuff first thing in the morning. You going to the Ghambana embassy now?"

"In about an hour. I have to make a stop to see a couple of South Africans first. Do you want to go?"

"No, I'm beat. I'll finish my rounds and hit the sack." Pepper saw Clay's smile. "Look, you and Phoebe scoff if you want, but some very important information has . . ."

"I'm not scoffing, Pepper. But *every* night . . . ?"

"The night I'd miss would be the night I shouldn't. Anything really urgent in Phoebe's center pile?"

"Yes"—Clay yawned—"but it can wait till tomorrow." He scowled as the light on the phone lit up. "Who the devil . . ."

Pepper made a halfhearted move to get up, but Clay reached for the phone. "Yes?" His exhaustion was in his voice.

"Congressman Clavier?" In the phone booth the stranger heard the "yes" and felt exploding exultation. He had him. He had him at last.

"My name is Jimmy Baker." Cool it, cool it, he thought. Don't let that shit get ahead of you. "I'm sorry to disturb you at this hour, but it's urgent."

Shit, Clay thought, it always was. He glanced at the wall clock as the telephone voice went on.

"As you know, your grandfather stipulated that the building be preserved as a permanent landmark at Christiana."

No, Clay thought, he didn't know. But there was a lot he didn't know about his grandfather.

". . . need your permission to move the building to a new site on campus."

Pepper, his shoes tied, got up slowly. "I'm splitting," he whispered as he walked to the door.

"I'm sorry," Clay interrupted his caller. "I have to be somewhere right now."

The stranger broke into a sweat. "No, mothafucka," he whispered to himself, "no, you don't have to be nowhere but with me." His hand was wet on the receiver as he pulled open the phone booth door. Shit, the coke was fuckin' with him now. Controlling his voice, he said, "I could be there in ten minutes. I mean I could be there in five. It would only take . . ."

"I'm sorry," Clay said abruptly, "I have to . . ."

The stranger gulped and wiped his forehead. Goddamn this bourgie nigger. He felt his high plunging down. "Congressman Clavier." The coke eased him into cunning. "Your grandfather specifically stated that the Jason Clavier Memorial Building . . ."

Oh Jesus, Clay thought, why tonight? He saw the hands on the

456

wall clock move to nine and cursed silently. He should be meeting the Africans right now. "I'm sorry. I can't wait . . ."

"Tomorrow?" the voice whined from the phone.

"Tomorrow I have to go to New York." Clay grimaced. What kind of folks was Christiana hiring now?

The muscles under the stranger's eyes were twitching. This goddamn nigger could fuck him now. Goddamn he needed that money. "Could I meet you somewhere?"

"Look," Clay snapped. "I'm going straight out New York Avenue . . ."

"New York?" In the phone booth, the stranger's eyes shone. His head bobbed back and forth from excitement. "The Queens Motel is on New York. It would take two, one, one half a minute for you to settle your grandfather's bequest."

Shit, Clay thought. "Okay."

The Queens was a small motel not far from the Capitol. Clay had been there before. The Queens was a favorite spot for those with small expense accounts who had business in Washington that would span several days. It was also becoming known for its racquet and handball courts.

There was only one window on the parking-lot side with the draperies open. As Clay pulled into an empty parking space, he could see the tall colored man inside the room.

Inside the room the stranger stood, flexing his long fingers. Goddamn it, he had to control that coke. Then he grinned. Everything was humming. Humming like a well-oiled machine. Nobody, nobody on earth could make the switch as fast as he. Planting this letter would be child's play. In a minute Clavier would have those letters in his pocket. And as soon as he pulled out of the parking lot . . . The stranger put on his tinted glasses and a smile and walked to the patio door.

"Mr. Baker." Clay held out his hand as he stepped into the room.

"Congressman Clavier. Come in." The stranger's grip was strong. "This won't take a minute." He led Clay to the diagram on the table, standing close by Clay's side as he explained how the building would be moved. "There should be little damage either to the exterior or the interior. The new site, as you see, faces the meadow. The building will be as inspiring there as it . . ."

"I see no problem." Clay nodded curtly. "May I see the papers?"

"Here you are."

The envelope and the letterhead said "Christiana University." "Is there anything else?" Clay asked, opening the envelope and reaching for his glasses.

"No." The stranger smiled politely. "After you sign the letter, everything will be completely taken care of."

Pepper Dee stared in horror at the young man outside the bar at Fourteenth and K. "Man, are you sure?"

"Would I tell you if I wasn't, Pepper? Man, I been three places looking for you tonight. They're planning some kind of bust on some South Africans tonight. I don't know who. I don't know where . . ."

Jesus, Pepper thought. If Clay . . . maybe that was why that man had been trying to reach him . . . a brother who was in on the bust . . . ? No, that wasn't likely . . .

"Hey, thanks, man." He slapped his companion's shoulder, then ran inside the bar.

"Hey, Pepper," the bartender called as Pepper dashed into the phone booth.

"Jesus Christ," Pepper muttered as he slipped a coin in the slot. "If Clay's gone . . ."

Five rings, seven—no answer. Pepper hung up and dialed again. Slowly, he came out of the phone booth. Why the hell hadn't he gone with Clay? Or known the address? What the hell should he do now?

The bartender finished pouring two gin and tonics for the red-wigged whore and her dapper john at the end of the bar. Then, wiping the wet towel down the bar, he came to where Pepper stood. "The Congressman's back, eh?"

"Yes." Dejectedly. "I was just trying to reach him."

"Well, there's a coincidence for you. Fella was talking to him just a while ago on that very phone."

"A little . . . ?" Pepper frowned. "Who?"

"Never seen him before a coupla nights ago. Comes in, orders a dollar's wortha cheap wine, hangs around till he gets a phone call."

"Hey, Bennie." Pepper leaned over the bar. "Could he be a fed?"

"A fed?" For a moment the bartender stared at Pepper. Then with a shrug he said, "Not unless they really changed their style. He looked to me like a coke user. Kinda slick, you know, like a con man." The bartender nodded in response to Pepper's stare. "From what I gathered he's meeting Clavier right now at the Queens Motel."

Pepper looked at Bennie sharply. The Queens Motel. Maybe that was where the Africans . . . But what would a coke user . . . Unless he was a front . . .

"Goddamn." Pepper brought his fist down on the bar. "I knew I shoulda gone . . ." He thumped the bar with a clenched hand. "Damn it . . ."

"You think something's wrong?"

"Shit, I don't know. But I just got a tip . . ."

"Well, the hotel room number's . . . wait, I wrote it on a napkin. Thought I'd play it in the morning." Bennie abandoned his towel and

459

fumbled beneath the bar. "Yes, here it is, 1116. Sounded like a good number."

"Bennie," Pepper began hoarsely. "You got a piece?"

"You asking what I think you are?"

"Look, he could be in trouble."

"Yep." The bartender nodded. "He could."

"You got a piece or not?"

For a moment the bartender studied Pepper. Damn, he thought, Pepper had probably never shot a gun. His eyes drifted to the back of the bar. Nobody . . . Only that whore twiddling that long phony red braid and her john at the bar. Bennie frowned, the Congressman had been damn good to him. "All right, you two." Bennie waved his towel. "I'm closing up." He turned to Pepper. "I'm going with you. Just in case."

"Whachusay?" The whore looked up.

"I'm leavin'." Bennie called, then turned to Pepper again. "Get your car." He opened the register and stuffed the cash in his pocket. Then he reached beneath the bar for his gun. "Come on." He glared at the couple. "I'm closing up."

"I haven't finished my drink," the whore protested loudly.

"Here's your money." Bennie threw two dollars on the bar. "Come on." He slapped the towel loudly. "Come on, damn it, let's go."

"Wait, nigger." She flounced her wig. "Don't be in such a hurry. Hell, I ain't never coming here again." She bent over the bar, reaching with painted nails for the money, while the john took a free feel of her ass.

Bennie, standing impatiently in the doorway, slammed the iron gate closed as she came through.

"Bennie." Pepper shouted from his Grand Prix at the curb. "For God's sake, hurry, man."

"Hey," the whore shrieked suddenly. "My wig's caught in the gate. Hey, damn you," she screamed, twisting to free the length of red, as Bennie, his towel flapping, jumped into the car.

The letter was two pages long, its legal terminology correct. But a puzzled look crossed Clay's face as he read the first page the second time. Something was wrong. He frowned in concentration, rereading slowly.

"Anything the matter, Congressman Clavier?" The stranger's face was nervous. He felt his hands starting to sweat. The machinery was clanking now, like a piece was stuck.

"Something I can't figure out," Clay mused. Then he remembered. Halvestine. How could he forget a name like Halvestine. Halvestine Brook was the attorney for Christiana now. He reread the signature slowly. "Benjamin Tolbert, attorney for Christiana University . . ." Damn it, Ben had died last winter.

Clay reread the date on the letter and then turned and faced the stranger. "This letter says Ben Tolbert is the university lawyer."

The stranger felt his cool high skidding. Goddamn, if those white folks had fucked up their part . . . He took a deep breath, held it tightly. "Yes? Yes, so what?" he said.

"Ben Tolbert's been dead five months."

Shit! Aw shit. This bourgie nigger . . . Goddamn, he was gonna get his bread. "Well, I uh . . ."

Clay crossed to the telephone.

"What're you . . . ?" The stranger felt his body strangling.

"I'm going to check this with Frank Jackson, the president of . . ."

"He'll tell you . . ." The stranger felt the sweat on his back now. Goddamn him.

"I hope for your sake that he does. Do you know the area code?"

"No." You ass. You fuckin' ass. It could have been so easy. It could have been so cool.

Clay felt the tension. Even before he looked up he knew he had made a mistake. Then he saw the gun. The narrowed eyes glittering like ice. With a quick intake of breath, he put the phone down slowly.

"Just get over there and close those drapes . . ." the stranger whispered. "I've got to make a phone call now."

Pepper made the twelve-minute drive to the Queens Motel in eight. As he pulled into the parking lot he saw Clay's car. The drapes in the window in front of it were closing. Then he saw Clay in the corner and the stranger and his gun.

Pepper hit his brights and floored the accelerator.

"Pepper?" Bennie howled in horror. "Pepper, what you doing?"

"Hold on." Pepper gripped the steering wheel. "We're going in that room!"

The car skidded onto the patio outside of the glass door. Moan-

461

ing, Bennie held his towel on his face. The car crashed through the door with the sound of a bomb exploding. Pepper saw the stranger run from the room as the drapes slid from the windshield. The car splintered the bed as Pepper braked.

Clay sprang from the corner as the car stopped. "Jesus Christ," he shouted as Pepper twisted to open the back door.

"Come on." Pepper saw the deep cut on Clay's chin as the door opened. "We're going out like we came in."

"What about his car?" Bennie whispered as Pepper pushed the gear into reverse. "In a minute . . ."

"Oh shit," Pepper said.

"Slow down. Stop. Gimme your keys." Bennie turned to Clay as they backed through the window.

"What're you gonna do?" Pepper yelled as Bennie grabbed the keys and his towel and jumped out.

For a second Pepper watched as Bennie threw the towel over Clay's license plate. Then he saw the drapes, the doors opening in other rooms. He saw Bennie as he jumped in Clay's car. Then with tires squealing, Pepper pulled away, away from the Queens Motel.

The bells beneath the gilded wooden sphere atop the great white steeple of St. Michael's Church in Charleston chimed three o'clock. By city ordinance, no thermometer flashed the temperature. But, as his car inched its way in the two-lane traffic toward the corner of Broad and Meeting streets, Clay knew it was at least ninety-five degrees outside. Squeezed as he was on the back seat between the bulk of Bart Simmons and Pete Horton, guard and tackle, respectively, from Notre Dame and Syracuse, who had volunteered themselves to him as bodyguards, it was at least one hundred and five. The car had air conditioning, but energy waste and pollution control were two important issues and, to the disgust of the driver, Clay was determined not to use it.

Only two cars made it through the intersection on the green light. Pedestrians hurried from the four corners, between the post office, city hall, courthouse, and the momentary cool beneath the tall palm trees in front of the arched windows of St. Michael's Church.

Clay checked his watch. Damn it, he'd been out of touch almost half an hour.

"Piece of gum, Congressman?" Clay winced as the crane that passed for Simmons's arm jabbed him on its way toward the athlete's pocket.

"No, thanks. What I need is to get back to headquarters. There's the Mills Hyatt House down the street. We can get out here."

"And walk?" Simmons protested, then flushed, seeing the grin on Clay's face. "Look, Congressman Clavier, you'll be safer in the car. We got to protect you."

"Look"—Clay put his hand on Simmons's arm—"if anything should happen to me, your job is to live to finish mine."

Simmons smacked his gum as he and his two-hundred-eighty pound companion followed Clay to the curb. Down Meeting Street, in front of the hotel, they could see the signs bobbing above the crowd. "Hey, signs with your name." Bart's six-foot-seven frame moved excitedly on tiptoe.

Clay grinned and waved his way through the throng to the Mills

Hyatt House, then went quickly into the hotel, sensing the heightened excitement his presence brought in the crowded lobby. He was caught by television floodlights and immediately surrounded by reporters.

"Congressman Clavier"—the clipped enunciation of John Roberts of the New York *Times*. "I understand that Massachusetts governor Carl Kuykendal is placing your name in nomination tonight as a favorite-son candidate and that his nominating speech will be seconded by both Governor West of Pennsylvania and Jeffrey Lawson, the president of the Black Caucus."

"So I've heard."

"This is really more than the usual favorite-son routine. It makes you a legitimate candidate."

Before Clay could answer, a TV mike, accompanied by another voice, came under Clay's nose. "I understand there'll be a sizable demonstration for you. More than two thousand participants," said the evening-news face of Sean Casey.

"I don't know anything about that." Clay flashed the disarming Clavier smile.

"Congressman Clavier, you do know that black voter registration has zoomed all over the country. UPI estimates that eighty-nine percent of the eligible blacks are now registered. In fact, the Census Bureau is revising its figures of the black population upward by nearly nine percent."

"The registration drive has been a special project of the Black Caucus under the generalship of Jeff Lawson. I think you should ask him the statistics," Clay replied. "However, I can say that black people are determined to play their full role in American politics."

"Congressman Clavier." Glen Turner, another TV newsman, spoke. "Have you heard the statements issued by Congressman Sykes this afternoon? That if you should be the party choice for Vice-President, it would mean ruin for the party as well as mass violence . . . ?"

"I have no idea what Congressman Sykes is saying now. But, as we all know, he hasn't done too well in the prediction department."

"Congressman Clavier"—a British accent—"Congressman Sykes has said that there will be a bolt from the party as there was . . ."

"Again, I have no idea of what the Congressman is saying."

"Congressman." Clay's expression did not change as he turned to see Ace Smith, known as Sykes's top man in the Fourth Estate. "Is

464

there any truth in the rumor that Dan Fleming has cancer, that this is all a setup for him to throw his votes to you on the second ballot?"

It caught Clay off balance. Kuykendal had said nothing about Fleming being ill. Clay had assumed Fleming wanted out. "No. No, I know nothing about an illness. It's got to be only a rumor! Dan Fleming is one of the finest and most knowledgeable men in American politics."

The truth of his conviction showed in his eyes.

"Congressman"—Carter of the Boston *Globe*. "There are reports that Governor Kuykendal is placing his political career on the line by nominating you. I understand he's faced a lot of pressure since the word got out today, not to place your name in nomination."

"I've heard nothing about it." If Fleming was sick . . . If Kuykendal was under pressure . . . "Now, if you gentlemen will excuse me . . ." Clay began to move away.

"Congressman, is it true that Kuykendal's cousin, former Secretary of the Treasury Stephen Kuykendal, has masterminded this nomination . . . ?"

"Please, I have no more comments." Simmons and Horton folded themselves around Clay, using their enormous bulk to manipulate him to the elevator.

The press was in wait again outside his suite. Quickly Clay gave the same answers he had given below, then entered into bedlam.

Dave, E. J. Walker, and Millie saw him as he came in and signaled him simultaneously to three different phones. He went to Millie's. It was closest. "It's Jeff Lawson from the Black Caucus," Millie whispered, her hand over the mouthpiece. "He says . . ."

"Thanks, Millie." Clay took the phone. "Hey, Jeff!"

"Clay?" Jeff's usually buoyant voice was tense. "This Sykes business in getting very serious. A couple of heads of delegations Fleming had lined up to support you on that second ballot are ready to default . . ."

"I gathered that downstairs."

"Reporters?"

"Yes."

"They're all around here, too This race-baiting has reached new levels of insanity. If Sykes's flunkies keep this up, we could have a full-scale race riot by tonight."

"When I saw you a half hour ago . . ."

"That was a whole thirty minutes. Randy Whitfield, Sykes's top assistant, just announced that they have proof positive that the nomination and secondings are part of some Chinese Communist plot . . ."

"Ah, shit, nobody . . ."

"Oh, yes, somebody—a lot of somebodies, including a black jackass in our caucus who also believes niggers don't have enough sense to organize. Any nigger but himself, that is. We're going to have to repudiate Sykes, and quickly. There are reporters outside our door. I can handle it, if you want me to. Henry, Ed, and Louise are here now, too. They have clout, and they'll back my statement. Make a united black denial except for addle-ass, whom we can control"—Jeff sighed—"at least for a while."

"All right, Jeff. It would be best coming from the group."

"You know we're hanging in. What are you going to do?"

"I need a minute to think about it. Let me get back to you."

"Don't take too long. Minutes are precious. Hey, by the way, just so you won't feel the world's against you, my gal just told me you've received more than eight thousand telegrams here since the word got out this morning. Some pretty weighty folks, too. Black, Chicano, Jewish, Latino, and quite a few Wasp types in the batch. And I understand the president of Christiana University and his staff have already contacted more than one hundred thousand former students and their families for your support. Major demonstrations are being organized in Chicago, L.A., New York, and D.C. to go off simultaneously with the one in the Coliseum, if, of course, our ponies don't bolt the gate"—Clay heard the whistling sigh escaping Jeff's lips—"which I don't need to tell you would look pretty bad after all this talk, not only for you but also for the rest of the black congressmen. Think on it, Clay, we just may have to try to Bogart this thing ourselves. It would change the scope, but at least we won't fall flat on our asses. Call me." Jeff clicked off.

"Clay," Dave's hand waved frantically. "I've got to talk to you."

Clay moved through the crowd to Dave's side. "Sykes again?"

"Clay," Dave whispered, "this whole mothafucka is about to go down the drain. This Communist shit . . . The pressure on the governor is tremendous."

"Carl will hold. Any word from Stephen Kuykendal?"

"Not yet. He knows, of course. He's got an earphone in every pocket in this convention. But for some goddamn reason he's laying in the cut. Or maybe he's finally run out of rabbits, or of hats. Personally"—Dave looked around at the feverish activity in the room— "I never thought it would get this far. And Di just called from the Coliseum. She says there are about a thousand demonstrators with flags and all the rest over there already."

Clay frowned. "Maybe we were wrong to trust that bastard."

"Who, Kuykendal?"

"You're damn right. That son of a bitch swore he could control Sykes. Now Jeff says Sykes's talking riot talk."

"Goddammit. And Kuykendal's silent as the dead. But why would he . . . ?"

"Who knows?" Clay gritted his teeth. "I thought I'd peaked his game. I hope to God I wasn't mistaken."

"This would be a hell of a time to be wrong."

"Well, I've been wrong before. Look, call Jeff back and ask him to come down here. What's the racial mixture of those demonstrators?"

"Diana says thirty-five percent black, about forty-five percent white, the rest a good mixture of all the other people who make up America. Hey, you've done a lot for a lotta folks. And sometimes, people appreciate . . ."

"The problem is Sykes, damn it! And what the hell is Kuykendal's game?"

"Clay." Mildred waved frantically. "It's Diana. She says she has to talk to you."

Clay started toward Mildred's phone, then E.J.'s hand shot up. "Clay, Keith Kuykendal's on the phone."

"Keith!" The phone had the peculiar whine of ship-to-shore. Clay covered the mouthpiece. "Millie, tell Di I'll get back to her."

"Clay," Keith's voice crackled through the whine. "Dad wants to see you right away!"

"He's heard about Sykes?"

"Yes, he's heard. There'll be a light blue two-door Ford downstairs for you in two minutes. This will be a private meeting."

"How private?"

"Very. The driver will ditch the reporters. See you in a while."

The driver of the Ford nodded as Clay approached, followed by anxious reporters. Who was he meeting? Kuykendal? The Black Caucus? Was he prepared to answer Sykes?

As they pulled away, the driver said, "Mr. Kuykendal is on his yacht. I'll shake these reporters and go to the boat basin. A launch will take you out."

467

Of all times to be playing cops and robbers. Clay grimaced. And of all places, on his goddamn yacht.

The launch was waiting. As they moved down the Ashley River toward the harbor, Clay felt his confidence returning. Keith, in white ducks and T-shirt, was waiting on the deck.

"Thanks for the column yesterday," Clay said as they shook hands. "Pretty strong stuff."

"Wait till you see what awaits you next," Keith replied, leading the way forward.

"It'll take dynamite . . ." Clay began as they reached the saloon and Keith opened the door. Clay saw Stephen Kuykendal standing to greet him. Then he saw the second man in the room—J. D. Sykes.

For an instant all of Clay's sensations numbed. He felt nothing but the shudder of his heart. Then fury congealed in his gut. He held it, reaching back for the wisdom of his tribe. "Never jump"— Clarence Woodson—"until you know the ground on which you'll land."

"Anger"—his father—"is a muddling emotion. It gives value to words, not deeds."

"You can't control the wind, Skipper"—his grandfather—"but you do control your rope and sail. The skill is to take advantage of the wind."

Clay turned to Sykes, noticing shock on his adversary's face. "Good afternoon, Congressman."

"Have a seat, Congressman Clavier." Stephen Kuykendal indicated the leather chair at his side. "Brandy, gentlemen?"

J. D. Sykes's gaze flickered from Clavier to Kuykendal. Something was wrong, he thought. Terribly wrong. When Kuykendal had called, less than a half hour ago, he had thought that haughty bastard had gotten the word, that Kuykendal wanted to make a deal: his support in return for, say, a cabinet post for his cousin Tom West.

West, maybe, Sykes thought, as long as he was away from Defense. Agriculture. That could be a deal. West probably did not know the difference between a gelding and a stallion . . .

Sykes frowned . . . Maybe Kuykendal was working Clavier in on the deal. But why? And what? No, a deal wasn't likely. He had to give the devil his due. That nigger had integrity.

Kuykendal could have him by the balls, though. Sykes rubbed his wedding ring in concentration. Four days ago, when he'd first heard

468

the rumors of Clavier's nomination and that Kuykendal was behind it, he'd had his staff check the corporations Kuykendal owned or controlled in South Carolina. The report had come in yesterday. Four big ones. Almost thirty-five thousand employees. If he threatened to lay off in this recession . . .

The Kuykendals had started moving in—Sykes frowned as he put it in perspective—right after his uncle had stomped on Kuykendal's political career. They should have listened to old Seth C. Dulane. He'd warned them not to let Kuykendal in, to be careful in those mergers. But those mill owners had been so goddamn greedy, and Kuykendal knew how to make money look so good.

Clavier and Kuykendal were in cahoots. No doubt of it. But why? Damn it, why?

Kuykendal had filled four snifters. He placed one in front of each of his guests and handed the fourth to his son. "I know both of you gentlemen are quite busy but, before we proceed, I would like to propose a toast.

Keith saw wariness perch on Sykes's face.

Stephen Kuykendal lifted his glass. "To us . . . to our family!"

For a stunned moment Clay stared at Kuykendal. Then, suddenly, it all fit. He saw it—carved in stone—on that grave in the family cemetery which they had visited on Memorial Days when his grandfather was alive: Isabella Clavier Dulane Hardwick. Jesus! Keith Hardwick Kuykendal! And, Clay caught his breath, Jacques Dulane Sykes!

The glass in Sykes's hand trembled. "I presume you have some point to make, Mr. Kuykendal, and I would appreciate your making it."

"Maybe I should be more specific," Kuykendal said curtly. "To our mutual ancestors, Jacques Clavier, the black sea captain, and his wife, Noni, whom he bought off the slave block in the city, Charleston; to their son Alexander and his wife Thomasina, who named their firstborn Clay, for the earth . . ."

Sykes was rigid, his face ashen.

"And to the other children of Alexander and Thomasina Clavier, whose names were Jason and Isabella. Jason Clavier, a member of the Reconstruction Congress of South Carolina, and Isabella Clavier Dulane Hardwick. I believe I saw a picture of you, Jacques Dulane Sykes, in front of your great-grandmother's portrait, which hangs in my great-grandfather's gallery, on the cover of *Time* last year."

Perspiration rolled down Sykes's face. He tried to steady his trembling hands. "You're crazy!" he whispered, his voice husky with rage, with fear. "You're goddamn insane."

"I thought it odd at the time, Congressman, that you chose to stand with the Negro side of your family." Stephen Kuykendal's voice had all the danger of an iceberg. "But since you have, and we can prove it, I think you should go all the way."

John Dulane Sykes licked his lips, then glanced nervously at Clay. He had no doubt that Kuykendal was telling the truth—and that he had proof.

His eyes slid back to Kuykendal. "She was your great-grandmother, too!" His words were accusing, hoarse, uncertain.

"My grandmother. Clay Clavier's great-grandfather's sister." Kuykendal's voice was clipped and firm. "Now let me go on. First, of course, you will repudiate that ridiculous statement about Communist involvement in Congressman Clavier's campaign. That I want done within the hour, and, in the same statement, you will mention Clay's worthiness for the office of the President."

"This is blackmail!" Sykes leapt to his feet, his face blotched with anger.

"There is a kind of poetic truth in that." And for an instant Clay saw his own half smile on Kuykendal's face. Then lightning played in that old man's eyes. "Now sit down, Sykes, and let me tell you about tonight."

The business of that day was done. The Mazda lamps were dark. The vast cavern of the Coliseum empty. In the balcony, above the giant cardboard likenesses of the leaders of the land, men in gray pushed brooms through the rubbish, and the smell of smoke defied the exhaust pumps of the air conditioners.

Clay Clavier stood just inside the rear double doors, his hands in his pockets, his white linen shirt open at the neck, revealing the medallion against the soft hair of his chest. He squinted in the semidarkness down the long aisle toward the podium. From that spot, tomorrow night . . .

But it was not from that spot. No, not even from this place. This was but another lap, another lap in a journey begun years ago. Years and years ago . . .

His mind went back to the stories of his grandfather, the stories told those days on Buzzards Bay. And he knew, standing in the semidarkness, why old Jacques had had to build his ship so well. He had known who would be sailing, and how long the voyage took.

Alexander going down into Maryland. Going "down into Yammycraw to fetch old sister Caroline." And Jason below the parapet and Clay on the parapet . . . Joshua fit the Battle of Jericho . . . And then Cain slew Abel . . . again.

All in the by-and-by will understand why . . . When manhood becomes mankind.

Clay stood there feeling time collapse and that Coliseum fade into all coliseums. One man alone becoming all men alone and that moment was like all other moments when family, race dissolve. All issues dissolve, all causes, all fading one into the other, dissolving into the one momentous issue of man against time, destiny, and fate. They all are the same.

Pheidippides poised at the start of his race. Alexander approaching the shore of Asia Minor. Hannibal gazing down into the valley of the Po. Caesar at the Rubicon, his legions around him, awaiting his decision that would change the course of time. Beethoven deep into his Ninth Symphony—the Ode to Joy—Washington and his Delaware. Oh, those halcyon days when the sun burns like a brass disk in the sky. Crazy Horse dancing his pony across the Big Horn and Sally Jones lifting clothes from the washtubs and singing "Nearer My God to Thee."

Had Roosevelt felt the same when he faced the podium, knowing the torment of the nation, or Elijah when he said, "I am the Messenger"? Or Joe Louis under the lights against Schmeling, or Jesse Owens, running, running hard, against time and man and hate?

Or Acheson when he stood against McCarthy or Malcolm X mounting that podium in Harlem or Martin Luther King when he stood on the mountaintop and saw the promised land or Muhammad Ali, in that African dawn, when he proved again he was "the greatest"?

Had Bobby Kennedy thought in those last moments of his time that they had blown the dream asunder and that no man would lift his cross? Or did he smile and think like Henry that it must be liberty or death?

And then He broke the bread and said, "This is my body, which is broken for you . . ."

All down those labyrinths of time, Clay wandered to that hour when man and God and time stand like old generals and whisper their brief counsel to each other, telling their secret yearnings, and part each one to work his will . . . The triumph and the tragedy, man through all his strivings cannot become God. And in the end, the young warrior dies on foreign soil or, older, turns to Brutus' knife.

What was it then, this thing called Life, called Fame, called Glory? What power as man meanders toward oblivion? What fossil remains shall all our efforts be?

Or was there still a chance? Man's folly and his greatness was to dream, to dare. Could he even now overcome himself? Man's enemy was man. Oh, yes, Thy will be done!

"Clay?"

He had not heard her come in. "I thought you'd be here." Diana smiled, putting her arm through his. "Were you thinking of tomorrow night?"

"Yes. I was thinking of tomorrow night."

But he did not tell her that, after two hundred years, he knew *all* the shoals, and . . .